THE LORD'S

A Novel of Hawaii

ANOINTED

Ruth Eleanor McKee

THE SUN DIAL PRESS, INC.

GARDEN CITY   NEW YORK

PRINTED AT THE *Country Life Press*, GARDEN CITY, N. Y., U. S. A.

1938
THE SUN DIAL PRESS, INC.

TO KATHRYN AND MIRIAM

with my love

CONTENTS

THE LORD'S ANOINTED
A Novel of Hawaii

PART I

"THE FAMILY"

THE last female passenger had been pulled and boosted up the swaying rope ladder that hung against the side of the brig *Thaddeus;* the last barrel of provisions had been hoisted aboard; the last small boat was stowed away on deck. With a great clanking of chains and scraping of iron against the side of the vessel, the sailors weighed anchor, and the *Thaddeus,* done with teetering restlessly at the edge of the Boston harbor, plunged seaward, her sails bellying before the brisk wind.

Twenty soberly dressed men and women and five children leaned against the railing to look their last upon the small crowd of friends and relatives gathered on the shore and rapidly losing their individual identity as the brig gathered speed. On board the *Thaddeus* the men, with the exception of four tall, dark-skinned youths, were uniformly grave. Of the eight women, five were unobtrusively shedding tears, one looked solemnly elated, one was alternately rueful and serene, and one was watching the assembled voyagers with a faintly sardonic smile.

It was in the neighborhood of two o'clock on the afternoon of Saturday, October 23, 1819. The brig *Thaddeus* was on her way, bearing what the voyagers themselves were pleased to call an Embassy of Mercy to the benighted heathen of the far-away Sandwich Islands. The nineteen fully qualified members of this First Company, sent forth by the American Board for Foreign Missions to establish a church in the "pagan islands of the Pacific," were busily engaged in smothering such qualms as arose in their breasts at the thought that they might never again behold the shores of their native New England or the faces of their families or their friends; now came sober realization that they were actually on their way to a strange and in all probability hostile land, there to live and very possibly to die, unless the God Who commanded them to go forth to the ends of the earth to preach the gospel should take it into His awful and unfathomable mind to destroy His own anointed in mid-ocean.

The accounts they had heard of customs in the Sand-wich Islands were not reassuring: there had been distress-ing tales of heathen laws called *tabus*—one forbidding men and women to eat together, and the penalty for dis-obedience was death. Death was the portion of the woman who ate of pork or bananas, or coconuts, or any food deemed suitable for men alone. Death claimed the woman who crossed the threshold of her husband's eating house. Death was sure though not necessarily swift for the woman caught looking at an idol's temple. Uneasily the female missionaries wondered if foreigners were always exempt from these practices.

It is wrong to say that all nineteen members of the First Company were preoccupied in this particular fashion. Three of the number were young Hawaiians—Thomas Hopu, William Kanui, and John Honolii, who, since the sailing vessel that had brought them to the New England coast had cast them off, had been converted and then edu-cated in the mission school at Cornwall. Now, after a num-ber of years of exile, these converts, trained to teach their own race the ways of Christians and prepared to teach the innocent members of the missionary family something of the ways of the Hawaiian branch of the Polynesian race, to say nothing of teaching them the Hawaiian language, were able to see the shore of New England dimmed by distance without sorrow. Their brown faces were animated; they chattered together in their own tongue. Perhaps it was joy at the prospect of spreading the word of God among their benighted kinsmen; perhaps it was merely the awareness that they were at last going home. Besides the three converts was the fourth Hawaiian on the passenger list. He was the son of the king of Kauai; he had been sent abroad some years earlier lest a hostile stepmother injure him. Now grown to manhood, he was returning to his native land, hopeful that his stepmother's hatred might have abated with the passage of the years.

Most astonishing of all the astonishing features of this small group of determined human beings was the extreme youth of the company. Only one couple among the eight married pairs had been married longer than a few weeks. Daniel Chamberlain, called Captain because of his service in the War of 1812, and the only farmer in the company, was thirty-seven years old. His wife, Jerusha, was nearing her thirty-second birthday. They had been married thirteen years, and now with five children, under stress of the revival that had recently swept New England, uprooted themselves from their land and home for motives of simplest piety—to teach, to pray, to put to such use as circumstances would allow Captain Chamberlain's knowledge of farming.

Captain Chamberlain had a shrewd, kindly face, broad enough to look comfortable; it was surmounted with rather absurd sandy hair which began misleadingly with sparse sideburns and then unexpectedly mounted his skull in a luxurious topknot. His piety seemed to rest easily upon him: he had none of the look of intent absorption and harassing introspection that marked a number of others in the company. His wife was plump and rosy and matronly. She, too, had the untroubled eye of the person who does not feel constrained to probe too far beneath the surface of life. Her five children kept her busy. She was calmly just. She loved the five towheads, but not foolishly. She could chastise or comfort them as the need arose and lose nothing of her natural serenity in performing either obligation.

First in authority, not by vote but by reason of an irresistible forcefulness sprung from the fury of his passionate faith, was the Reverend Hiram Bingham, not quite thirty. He was a tall man with large sharp features and grim though full lips set in a face that tapered sharply from breadth at the cheekbones to narrowness in the pointed chin. His unhealthy pallor and the burning darkness of his eyes beneath their bushy black brows gave him a dramatic appearance; but the harsh determination folded into the set curves of his mouth and the fire smoldering perpetually in his deep-set eyes were alike of such a nature as to inspire awe and the fear which fosters hate in undedicated hearts. He frowned as he contemplated the receding coast line.

Beside him stood his bride of nine days. It was Sibyl Bingham whose face was strained with solemn elation. She was a tall, emaciated figure. Her face was colorless and so thin that her mouth pulled away from her teeth, and her skin seemed painfully stretched over the bony structure beneath. Her palely blazing, enormous eyes saw neither the crowd on the shore nor the austere man at her side. Her eyes pierced the October haze that hung above the sea, and she saw her own soul mounting the Judgment Seat. She saw her soul escorted by multitudes of humble brown souls, her brothers and sisters in Christ, and her neatly covered ears were hearing a Voice, mighty yet sweet, that said, "With each of these souls thou hast laid up for thyself a treasure in heaven." She was twenty-seven years old. She had been converted at the age of five.

The Reverend Asa Thurston whose age was thirty-two and whose wedding had taken place on the preceding Saturday, stood beside his round-faced bride of twenty-four. His broad brow was gathered into knots, and his fair eyebrows were drawn together over his bright blue eyes. He was realizing for the first time that he was leaving behind him all earthly things he had ever loved. The wife at his side was still a stranger. Three months ago he had never heard of her. Exactly one month before the date of sailing their meeting was arranged. There had been a suggestion from the board that he should take a wife with him into exile; then the board tactfully recommended Lucy as a neat housewife, as a sensible girl with a fair amount of schooling, and, above all, as a communicant of the church. Lucy had been approached by her cousin; after the conversation she lay awake in an agony of hesitation, fear, and dismay; then, harrowed by her vision of perishing heathen, she bowed to the will of God and agreed to meet Asa Thurston. Asa, on the deck of the *Thaddeus*, glanced down at Lucy's round, still babyish face with something of compassion. She seemed young to him, but, and he looked away again, she was a grown woman, fired with the desire to broaden the boundaries of Christ's kingdom on earth. In his unworldly modesty it did not occur to him that his remote kindliness, his fair hair with a definite wave in it, and the pleasant wrinkles that sprang suddenly from the corner of his eyes when he smiled had something to do with Lucy's calm acceptance of this trying moment.

Samuel Whitney, leaning over the rail to strain his eyes for a final glimpse of his mother, presented the brethren with the sort of profile more often seen on old Greek coins than in life. He was listed on the books of the American board as a teacher and mechanic. He looked more like a poet as he stood on the deck of the *Thaddeus,* his light rather long hair tossing in the wind, his gray eyes brooding beneath their shapely coal-black brows. His secret dream was to fit himself for the ministry, but the strong wind of the revival had caught him halfway through Yale, and he had seized the opportunity to make one of the company of missionaries. He knew more of the Scriptures by heart than any other member of the Family. He was impersonally, absent-mindedly, gentle with anyone he met. He was perhaps a shade gentler and a shade less absent-minded in his dealings with his wife of two weeks. Mercy was sniffing quietly at his side. She was frightened: she disliked the oily swirling water lapping up against the boatside. It appalled her to think of spending the rest of her life, provided she lived through this voyage, with this dreamy scholar who seemed to forget that he had a wife during the day when she would like some attention, and then remembered most disturbingly that he had one at night when she was entirely willing to forget that she had a husband. Mercy shut her small prim mouth tightly; she thought being married was horrid. Then she looked frightened and guilty: was she rebelling against the will of God in resenting the way of life that He had ordered? Meekly she dropped her round brown eyes and unbuttoned her mouth to pray, "Not my will but Thine be done, and please make me not mind so much!"

There were the Loomises. Elisha Loomis was not quite twenty-one years old, and his face was set very ferociously in a barely successful effort to keep back an unmanly sob.

His wife attempted to slip a sympathetic hand into his, but he brushed it aside—not in annoyance with her but in panic lest his hard-won self-control desert him at the slightest gesture of sympathy. Later he would explain to wide-eyed, sweet-tempered Maria. He was getting really fond of Maria. Although she was two years older than he, she seemed a good deal like his little sister. Elisha was a printer, and was taken along partly because he was a good lad and went to church piously and believed all the things he ought to believe, but principally because the missionaries were planning to translate the Scriptures into the Hawaiian language as soon as they knew enough of the language to manage, and to print special schoolbooks in the native tongue for the benefit of the pupils they expected to instruct.

There was Samuel Ruggles, a teacher, twenty-four years old. His face, youthful as it was, expressed a purposefulness that made it seem stern, but his hazel eyes were kind. His wife, Nancy, was four years older than he, a bustling, aggressively virtuous little woman with sparse eyebrows and faintly pouchy cheeks that suggested a squirrel rather than a woman.

The next man in line was conspicuous among these grave men by reason of the buoyant vigor that radiated from him. He was tall and straight, and his attraction lay not so much in the regularity of his features and the slight curl in his thick black hair as in the warmly human good will that animated his features, the impression he gave of enjoying the mere fact of being alive; these things set him apart from his fellows. At the moment he was bending his head with the tenderest concern over the golden brown curls of his wife, sister of Samuel Ruggles, and his arm was frankly about her very small waist. It was this woman, Lucia, who was alternately rueful and serene: rueful when she looked toward the shore and the ever dimmer figure of her brother who had always loved and spoiled her, but smilingly serene when she turned her eyes to her young husband. Dr. Thomas Holman and his wife were in a class by themselves: they had married a few weeks earlier in accordance with plans which had nothing whatever to do with the mission. They were deeply and unashamedly in love with each other.

Last of the New England group was the newly married Williams couple. Jonathan at twenty-six had snow-white hair, a memento of the prolonged siege of typhus he had suffered a few years before. His eyes were dark and burned with a flame as turbulent and even more restless than the flame that burned in the Reverend Hiram Bingham's eyes. His features were almost too delicate for a man—with the exception of his chin, which thrust forward slightly as if he were forever squaring his jaw for a tussle with Satan. His naturally full lips he forced into a narrow straight line—whenever he remembered to do so. Just now he wore what his wife privately called his consecrated look. It was Constancy who, having no family at the docks to see her off and having recovered from the earlier parting with her mother and father and little sister, was able to turn that faintly sardonic smile upon her fellow passengers. She scrutinized each one of her future associates with very long, uncompromisingly green eyes that tilted upward at their outer ends, eyes which she could veil effectively by dropping ever so slightly her unorthodox, curling black lashes. Her hair was done more plainly than that of any of her sisters. It was a day of elaborate hairdress, and the most sternly virtuous women were wont to conform to fashion almost without thought. Where even Mrs. Bingham had a flat curl on either cheek, Constancy Williams drew every honey-colored hair in her small head into a demure knot at the nape of her neck. If one did not look too sharply into the cryptic depths of her green eyes, or too clairvoyantly at the even waves in her shining crown of hair and suspect that this was the most becoming way Constancy could possibly have found to wear her beautiful hair, one might easily have seen in Constancy a potential saint. Constancy was nineteen, the youngest missionary of the Company; she had been married ten days; she had met the Reverend Jonathan Williams three months before her wedding; she had undergone the mysterious experience called conversion just two weeks after meeting Jonathan.

2

At eleven o'clock on the following day Constancy sat on deck, a writing board on her knees, her left hand steadying a small bottle of ink, her right guiding a long quill pen rapidly across the pages of a small cloth-bound book. Tied to the leg of her chair on a generously long rope was the three-year-old Chamberlain child nibbling at a green apple and nursing a misshapen rag doll.

A gust of wind picked up the letter Constancy had just written and carried it down the deck. Clasping the writing board to her and holding the ink bottle well out from her dress, Constancy darted after it and rescued it just as it caught against the railing. Sitting down again, she laid aside the cloth-bound book to reread this first entry in her journal letter to her family in Connecticut:

"My dear Mother, Father, Prue, and, if he is with you, Uncle Nate: We awoke after our first night at sea to a bright cool day and a stiff breeze which carries us southward at about eight knots an hour, so the good captain tells me. Save for the sadness of parting from my family, I am of good cheer, rejoiced to be a small part of so great an enterprise, and wondering at the Lord's mercy in sparing me the inconvenience and discomfort of the malady which keeps all the rest of our company in their beds save only the second youngest child of the Chamberlain family, who plays quietly at my side, tied to my chair on deck lest she come to harm. My dear family, excepting the three native boys of our Company and the other native boy, George, who is a chieftain's son and travels in the care of Captain Blanchard, all passengers are grievously indisposed with seasickness. Each rise and fall of the vessel seems to give them intolerable anguish. The captain tells me I am a good sailor and that it is most uncommon for anyone to escape illness during the first few days of a voyage. He and the native boys are kindness itself to the afflicted, the captain carrying broth and pickles to them with his own hands, and the native boys performing the most personal services with the greatest kindness and praying aloud for them.

"Our staterooms present an appearance of the utmost confusion, being small, no more than six feet square; and the beds which are called berths one above the other are far from comfortable. Two couples inhabit each stateroom with their trunks and personal provisions, so that it is hard to move about without stepping over boxes and obstacles of one kind or another. There is one large cabin some twenty feet long and a little less wide, which Dr. and Mrs. Holman and Mr. and Mrs. Loomis share with Captain Blanchard and his fellow officer, Mr. Conant. It is in this room that we have our meals around a large table, semicircular in form, at which twenty persons may seat themselves at one time. So far, however, the ship's officers, the native boys, the second youngest Chamberlain, and I have been the only ones capable of eating. Although it is the Sabbath we have had no regular service, our ministers all being too ill to raise their heads from their pillows. But Thomas Hopu prayed eloquently in the cabin that it might please God to restore our suffering members to health soon, and we who are in good health sang several hymns.

"I shall write at intervals during the long voyage such details of our experience as I think you may care to hear, and pray for an early opportunity to send you this word from your absent child."

She folded the long sheet covered with small, close writing and tucked it between the blank pages of the cloth-bound book in her hands. Then, taking up her pen, she continued the entry in her private journal under the date, Sabbath, October 24th, 1819:

"If I could free myself of the thought that the vengeance of God is but held in abeyance, I might sink myself in the beauty of the day, be glad of my youth, and the pleasant circumstance that I am not one of those who must retch their very inwards away in the oppressive warmth of the staterooms, but in this matter I am far from easy in my mind, for remembering how the Lord chasteneth those whom He loves, and is not this very health of mine a proof of my spiritual disease when the truly good are all stricken? And was I not inhuman to be obliged to turn my face to the corner as I sponged the holy Mr. Bingham's brow, for that my misguided mind saw fit to laugh at the sight of a mighty oak turned aspen so ingloriously? And when I quoted the Scriptures to him, mentioning Job who was likewise good and sorely tormented, he did but look the

greener and utter a most hollow groan before reaching
out for the slop jar. But it pleased me to observe how
young Doctor Holman, who is himself wretched, must
hold his wife's head whenever the nausea came upon
her and speak to her as gently as one would address a
sick babe.

"My dear Jonathan suffers silently, but in his weakness he leans upon me so that my heart yearns over him.
To have him rest his head against my shoulder and allow me to stroke his brow and wait upon him is sweet.
It is hard, other times, to remember always that I am a
minister's wife who must never falter in preserving a
modesty and the most dignified propriety in my behavior. Did God or His arch-enemy cause Jonathan to
appear so exceeding beautiful to my eyes the first time
ever I saw him? But there can be no doubt who tempted
me at that gathering where I did boldly swoon and then
stare fixedly into space as I had sinfully enacted the
scene before my looking-glass, and protest that Christ
was entering my soul, and that God had placed His seal
upon my spirit.

"I am in truth a very hardy sinner, for in my heart I
know there is no regret for so covenanting with Satan,
nor will there be for so long as I may be near to Jonathan and keep from giving offense to him. And Jonathan, so shining a spirit is he, that he would never believe how one so young would be capable of acting so
black a lie! Yet if I discipline my unruly tongue and
heart, and imitate virtue steadily, perhaps I may become virtuous, but I think that I can never learn to love
a God so fierce and so unpitying. Were any man in my
sight to treat cruelly the weak, I must pit my strength
against him whether or no it were to any avail, but
how dare one woman, who still so often feels herself to

be a child, pit her puniness against the omnipotence and awful omniscience of God?"

The little girl at her feet was beginning to fret. Constancy stared blankly down at her for a moment and then smiled. She set her writing board on the deck and put the stopper into the ink bottle. She lifted the child to her lap and planted a kiss on the round pink cheek.

"Have you heard the story about Goodie Two Shoes?" she questioned seriously. The child shook her pale yellow shock of hair, eyed Constancy a little doubtfully, and then lisped faintly, "If you tell it me, mutht I tell you the moral?"

Constancy's smile broadened. "No, child," she said dryly, "and I think I can leave the moral out altogether, if you like."

She told the story without the moral and to the satisfaction of her listener, and then looked up to see Mr. Conant standing beside her. His cloudy blue eyes were less remote than usual. He smiled down at her.

"It is well for the little one that you bear up like an old sailor," he said. "A little thing such as she could easily slip through the rails. But now"—and he shifted his eyes away from her face for an instant, only to bring them quickly back to her tilted green eyes—"dinner is in readiness for those of us who can eat. You will find a few of your company up now."

Constancy rose with an exclamation: "I have been neglecting my poor husband. I must go to him," but she first took a small key suspended from a ribbon about her neck and carefully locked the clasps on the cloth-bound book, slipped it in a hidden pocket in her voluminous skirt, and received the writing materials from Mr. Conant's hands. She disappeared down the companionway, the child clinging to her skirts, and Mr. Conant absently fingered the railing and stared blankly at the pale horizon, his mind groping for a line to follow the verses that had just taken form in his head:

> *Her eyes, green pools, are bottomless*
> *Wherein a soul may drown,*
> *Ta-da' ta-da' ta-da'-da-da'*
> *Ta-da' ta-da' ta-da'.*

He muttered and beat out the rhythm on the railing. His stare grew even more blank and he mouthed the words, "Brown . . . crown . . . drown . . . e-own— no, no such word . . . frown . . ." and lapsed into complete silence.

Constancy stopped before the door of the Chamberlain stateroom, knocked, and then entered. Two of the tow-heads were staggering uncertainly about the limited space of the room. Mrs. Chamberlain still lay with her face to the wall, abjectly miserable, but she turned her head slowly and opened one eye at Constancy.

"The Captain thought he could bear to get up, and he just went down to the cabin for dinner," she said hollowly. "I guess he can look after the children now. It was a charitable thing for you to tend Sister all this time. Maria here's well enough to help her father with the little ones now."

Constancy went over and smoothed the covers over Mrs. Chamberlain's plump shoulders. "Perhaps if you sleep, the nausea will leave you this afternoon—truly you look better now. Once you can get up, the air on deck should do you good." She glanced at the two prostrated little Chamberlains on the middle berth, perceived that they were asleep, and shooed the others from the crowded close room. "You take Sister and go to the cabin, Maria. Mr. Conant said dinner was ready—and mind you hold tight to the baby's hand lest she fall over board. I must see if there is aught I can do for Jo—Mr. Williams."

She sped down the passage to the room she and her husband shared with the Thurstons. The lower berth held a limp double burden. Neither the Reverend Asa Thurston nor his wife flickered an eyelash as Constancy came into the room, but Jonathan's shock of white hair appeared over the edge of the upper berth, and his brown eyes, their consuming flame for once extinguished by ignoble misery, sought hers imploringly. She crossed to his side with an inarticulate tender murmur and passed her cool hand over his forehead. She quickly squeezed the water from a sponge lying in a basin of water and, standing upon a stool, gently washed her husband's face.

"What have you been doing?" he asked in the querulous tone of a sufferer.

"Tending the little Chamberlain girl," she said quietly. "She is a little thing that might come to harm unwatched, and her mother is unable to tend her now."

Jonathan nodded slowly. "It is well that you should be useful." He suffered her to hold his hand, and in his weakness even clung to hers. "Must you be with the child for the afternoon?" he asked faintly.

Constancy smoothed his hair back from his forehead. "No, Jonathan, her father is about now and two of the older children. I shall stay with you, if you wish me, this afternoon."

He relaxed his grip on her hand. "It would be comfort to hear you read from the Scriptures," he said, "and it may be that from them I shall gather strength to overcome this trial which the Lord has in His wisdom seen fit to visit upon me."

Captain Blanchard appeared in the doorway. "Mrs. Williams, your dinner is waiting for you. You must not let your patients distract your mind from food or they will lose their kind nurse."

"Yes, go, Constancy," murmured her husband. "You must husband your strength."

Constancy's mouth curved childishly at its corners, for this was the first time her husband had addressed her by her given name before a third person. She tripped on light feet beside the captain to her dinner of boiled beef, boiled cabbage, and boiled potatoes.

3

In twenty-four days the *Thaddeus* had progressed only five and one half degrees toward the equator. Winds had sulked and refused to blow at all, winds had turned capricious and blown the brig back along its course, winds had lashed themselves into a gale and threatened the missionaries, shut in below while all hands fought to save the vessel from the fury of the storm. Then, tall and gaunter than ever from his prolonged illness, the Reverend Hiram Bingham had towered above his flock and prayed serenely, "Thou knowest, Lord, we are as grains of dust before Thy might, and naught availeth but Thy infinite mercy. Into Thy hands we commend our spirits, and if Thou smilest upon our mission and preserveth us for Thine own ends, we are well pleased, and if Thou art moved in Thy unfathomable wisdom to destroy us with this storm, still do we bow unto Thy just and awful will." And the storm abated. The missionaries praised God for His lovingkindness and devoted themselves more sedulously than ever to prayer and meditation and study of the Hawaiian language.

They devised and adopted Family regulations: each day they rose at six, sang and prayed together at seven, breakfasted at eight, studied, wrote, meditated or prayed from nine to twelve, ate dinner at one, studied or wrote again from two to six, ate supper at six, held evening prayers at eight, retired not later than ten. On Tuesday evenings the Family gathered for an hour of singing, and on Friday evenings the sisters united in social prayer.

By the sixteenth of November all members of the mission family were able to observe the regulations. It was true that some of them still showed a yellowish green cast of complexion and a tendency to look with loathing upon such food as was set before them in the cabin, but they managed to ignore their discomfort for the greater part of the time. Mr. Bingham, of all the sufferers, found the malady most tenacious. His cheeks were hollow, his clothes hung slackly on his tall body, and he scarcely touched his food at the table. Nevertheless he drove himself, scornful of his weak flesh, and preached more often than any other of the three ordained ministers aboard, prayed more passionately, and kept the most vigilant eye upon the activities of his fellow voyagers. On this sixteenth day of November he had just finished making note of the fact that they had approached the equator only by $5°$ $30'$; in the collective journal kept by the ministers of the company most of the entries were in the hand of Mr. Bingham. He brooded over the neat page before him, his heavy brows meeting as he pondered. Then dipping his pen in the ink, he wrote:

"We cannot but conclude that He who controls the winds and the waves, and conducts all the affairs of nations is either kindly withholding us from dangers and disasters at Cape Horn or operating changes in the

Sandwich Isles favorable to the introduction and success of our enterprise. He is kindly inuring us to a life of toil and hardship."

His pen poised in mid-air, he considered for a moment the information Captain Blanchard had begun issuing in small doses to prepare the missionaries for their life in a pagan land. First he had told them that polygamy was the custom; a little later he mentioned the fact that incest was not unusual among those of royal blood. He spoke disturb· ingly of the pagan priests, curious men with uncanny powers, skillful in bringing death to their enemies—to all appearances by prayers and incantations. *Kahuna* was the name given these men. The captain had added that they were known to be learned in the art of brewing viru- lent poisons. Pondering this mixture of information, Mr. Bingham closed his eyes and murmured resolutely, "The Lord is my Shepherd, I shall not want!"

He dipped his pen in the ink and tackled the next para· graph.

"The Sabbath was disturbed by catching a large turtle." He described painstakingly though disapprovingly the let- ting down of the boat, the shouts and unseemly clamor that had attended the catching of the turtle, paused, bit his pen, compressed his lips, and with a slight shake of his head wrote honestly, "But we enjoyed the meat."

He looked up to see Constancy Williams pass through the cabin with her writing board and bottle of ink and a small gray book.

"Ah, Mrs. Williams," he asked kindly, "and what book have you there?"

Constancy barely prevented herself from giving a guilty start.

"A book of verses by two English gentlemen, Mr. Bingham," she replied. "It was given me by my uncle just before I left home. It is called *The Lyrical Ballads,* and the verses have given me considerable food for reflection and pleasure on the voyage." She was studying him through the thick veil of her lashes, her eyes glinting through the black fringe.

Hiram Bingham's eyes shifted from her eyes to her mouth and rapidly away to the book in her hands. "Verses may be instructive no less than prose," he conceded, "but many poets are ungodly souls who write lightly of worldly matter. Avoid them."

Constancy just restrained herself from bobbing a little curtsey, as she had been taught to do at school when dismissed from the presence of a mistress. She turned to go on deck and was a little surprised when Mr. Bingham followed her: he was wont to cling more closely to the stuffy cabin than to the deck. She climbed the sloping ladder, conscious that he was immediately behind her. As she stepped on deck, she saw Mrs. Holman lying back in a low chair, her head thrown back, smiling up at the doctor. The young doctor bent suddenly and pressed his lips against the whiteness of his wife's throat. Oblivious of chance watchers, Lucia Holman with a little cry clasped her husband's head in her hands, holding his face against her throat, and rested her cheek against his hair. Constancy's hand flew to her heart, pushing against the pain that grew there, and quick tears rose to her eyes. "Jonathan—Jonathan," her love cried silently and bitterly within her. She heard a startled, choked exclamation behind her, and turning, saw the Reverend Hiram Bingham leap down the companionway, his hand over his forehead, as if the archfiend were after him.

She too returned down the companionway, but her fear was only that she might disturb the two who were unabashed at their love for each other. In the next few days she was to find herself involuntarily seeking the presence of the Holmans. When Mr. Bingham preached on the following Sunday a more than usually impassioned address from the text: "This I say then, Walk in the Spirit, and ye shall not fulfil the lust of the flesh. For the flesh lusteth against the Spirit, and the Spirit against the flesh; for these are contrary the one to the other," Constancy's heart went out to him in compassion. But later on that same day as she sat alone on deck with Mrs. Holman there was a scene with Mr. Bingham that quite removed the compassion from her heart and left in its stead a furious scorn.

Mr. Bingham came striding down the deck, his brows knitted in meditation. He looked upon the two women and frowned the more. While Constancy read once more "The Rime of the Ancyent Marinere" Mrs. Holman delicately peeled and ate an orange. Mr. Bingham angrily paced up and down for a moment and then, pouncing upon Constancy, demanded, "Is it fitting, Mrs. Williams, that you should read profane matter on the Lord's Day?"

Constancy blushed, but she regarded him levelly from slightly narrowed jade-green eyes. "It had not seemed improper to me," she said quietly, but he scarcely noticed her response, so eagerly did he turn upon Mrs. Holman.

"And you, Mrs. Holman, do you not know that it is suspected by the Family that you are taking to yourself property which was consecrated to the mission, property to which you have no individual right?"

Mrs. Holman's hazel eyes opened in amazement, and her broad dark eyebrows lifted a half-inch. "Why . . ." she said, startled, "no! . . . Why . . ."

The man leaned toward her, his eyes burning with intensity. "Do you not know that it is thought that the oranges and lemons which you make so liberal a use of are some that were put up by some friend for the use of the whole Family?"

Constancy felt her own jaw drop and saw Mrs. Holman jump to her feet, stamp one of those small feet imperiously, and then burst into tears of vexation. "You do me a great injustice, Mr. Bingham!" she sobbed wildly. "I do assure you that this orange—and whatever oranges or lemons you have witnessed me eating—are from a box my own brother purchased and put up for my individual use . . . together with raisins and peppermints." Her tears flowed freely, and she made small futile efforts to find her handkerchief until Constancy slipped her own into the trembling fingers.

Mr. Bingham surveyed her gloomily and unbelievingly. "It will be happy for you, Mrs. Holman, if you are able to prove it. It is truly unfortunate for you that the Family cannot help their suspicions."

Mrs. Holman gave a fierce dab at her eyes and raised her chin. Her voice was no longer trembling. "Mr. Bingham," she said haughtily, "allow me to refresh your memory so far as to mention that I distributed three fourths of my box among the brethren and their families, keeping only one fourth for myself, because my physician warned me that my health would be seriously impaired did I neglect doing so. I have at least been liberal with my possessions."

"Ah!" and Mr. Bingham leaned toward her exultingly. "The very circumstance of your distributing them so freely serves to strengthen the finger of suspicion against you."

Mrs. Holman regarded him stormily. "Perhaps it will satisfy your doubts if my brother, a most reputable merchant in Brookfield, sends you his statement regarding his gift." And she swept angrily from the deck.

Constancy scornfully gathered up her belongings and swept after her, her small nose tilted upward. There was no place for the outraged Mrs. Holman to go except the large cabin which served also as sleeping quarters for herself, her husband, and four others. Constancy followed close on her heels and perceived that Mrs. Holman might have the cabin to herself if Jonathan, writing at a table, were to remove himself. Without hesitation Constancy rushed to his side and seized him by the arm.

"Come!" she said imperiously. "Come out of here at once."

Jonathan, giving her a dazed look, rose and did her bidding. She pulled him along to their own stateroom, which, for once, was empty, and poured forth the tale of Mrs. Holman's woes to him. Her indignation caught her off guard.

"Truly, Jonathan," she said feelingly, "I do think that Mr. Bingham is unjust to Mrs. Holman for no better reason than that he is envious of Dr. Holman for having so beautiful a wife when he himself has only that pale shadow of a woman who scarce knows whether or no her gown is on hind side foremost!"

"Mrs. Williams!" and the minister's voice was terrifying to his wife. "Are you a prey of Satan's wiles that you set yourself in judgment against the holiest of our company? Never speak so of him again! Never dare to think so! Nor do you let me hear you speak slightingly of the pious Mrs. Bingham! The Holmans are a misguided pair, too wrapped round by a carnal mesh. The doctor has worthy qualities, but the woman is a frail, light-minded piece, weak and vain. It may be so that the fruit is rightfully hers, but I think it quite probable that she has made free with Family property."

Constancy, who had looked frightened at his first

words, and then rueful, merely looked withdrawn into herself by the time he had finished. "I should not have spoken so of Brother Bingham, Jonathan. I forgot myself, but I still feel," firmly, "that he is mistaken in the matter of the oranges. Jonathan!" and her voice pleaded with him. "Do not be angry with me, Jonathan. I cannot bear it when you look at me so unlovingly!" She raised his hand timidly to her cheek. His eye softened, although his voice remained stern.

"Constancy, you are yet a child, and need concern yourself less with my affection for you and more with the love of your heavenly Father. It is His forgiveness you need to entreat for belittling our worthy leader, not mine."

Constancy shyly moved his hand so that her lips rested upon it. Her husband rose to his feet, turned to go, and then awkwardly leaned down and kissed her forehead. Involuntarily her arms went around his neck, and her lips were clinging to his, and quite as involuntarily he was straining her body to his and crushing her mouth beneath his mouth. Constancy felt fierce joy surging upward through her veins and a certainty that Jonathan loved her, a certainty that had never been sealed by his joyless performance of his duty as a married man in the sight of God. But before the joy could reach her brain and so annihilate thinking in her, Jonathan's arms dropped away from her, and he tore her arms from about his neck and flung her violently away from him, so that she fell against a packing box. She lay there, aghast, while Jonathan stood covering his face with his hands, and agony wrenched haltingly from him, "Lord, Lord, the woman thou gavest me, tempted me. Give me strength of the spirit to subdue the unholy burning of the flesh, Lord! I fear myself!" He tore his hands away from his face and turned such horrified eyes upon his wife that she flinched, and then, the bitter-ness of the moment forcing itself upon her, she laid her face upon her arms and sobbed heartbrokenly.

Presently she heard a sigh from her husband and felt his hand gingerly placed upon her shoulder. "Do not cry so violently, Constancy," he said gently. "We have both sinned grievously in our hearts, but you are so young! I was at fault. Get down on your knees beside me, child, while I petition God in His infinite mercy to strengthen us against the lure of the vile flesh."

And Constancy, with the dull anguish of utter hope-lessness, dropped silently to her knees and meekly bowed her head to his prayer that the moment that had seemed to her so beautiful might never be repeated as long as they both should live.

4

December came, and with it brisk winds to urge the *Thaddeus* southward. The vessel bounded through the tropics, and in the heat the missionaries perspired freely; the men exchanged their woolen underwear for cotton, and, in the case of one or two daring souls, for none at all. The women left off their flannel petticoats, merely wear-ing two or three stiffly starched and beruffled garments of calico or cambric. On December 15th they passed a ship. Seeing the sails against the horizon early in the day, they hastily gathered together the letters they had written, pre-pared to send them across in a small boat should the vessel come near, and eagerly they stood at the rail, few making even a pretense of following the daily schedule of study and meditation. But at noon the sails of the passing ship glimmered no nearer to the course of the *Thaddeus*, and silently and regretfully the missionaries retrieved their letters—except for Mrs. Loomis, who frankly shed tears of disappointment and ran sobbing to her stateroom.

The boat sailed swiftly toward the Cape, the tropics left far behind, and the missionaries again donned, according to sex, their woolen underdrawers or flannel petticoats. Stimulated by the cold and the feeling that they were indeed approaching their goal, they applied themselves more diligently than ever to the study of the Hawaiian language. By Christmas every one of them could repeat the Lord's Prayer in the Hawaiian tongue, and they knew from a dozen to a hundred and fifty phrases of the language. Daily each one of them carried on a laborious and halting conversation with the natives, who smiled always and politely applauded all efforts. But the young Chamberlains, who had not been delegated to learn the peculiar language and spent no time in studying it, could have been heard at any odd moment chattering glibly and expressively with authentic gestures, in the tongue that seems to have more use for the letter "k" than any other language in the world.

Elisha Loomis in these days was often to be found regarding his wife with a blend of pride and anxiety, and was wont to help her up and down ladders with a suggestive solicitude. As for Maria, although protesting blushingly that she was no longer troubled with seasickness, she was frequently unable to finish her breakfast and on one or two occasions seemed loath to leave her bed before noon. When she was able to be on deck she preferred the company of Mrs. Chamberlain, placid mother of five children, to that of any other person on the boat, and the two were often seen engaged in whispered conversations. The other wives studied her discreetly with varying degrees of curiosity, respect, alarm, or envy, according to their natures.

There was a perceptible tendency on the part of the Holmans and the Binghams to avoid each other in the brief periods when the latter were not engaged in study, prayer, or meditation. Mr. Bingham, in these moments of relaxation, strode slowly up and down the small deck, his eyes fixed upon the horizon, or at times upon his own feet, and apparently did not see Mrs. Holman as she sat gazing absently across the water and eating a lemon with sugar or writing a journal letter home in which she made no allusion to the indignities she had suffered.

Jonathan Williams spent long hours poring over a makeshift Hawaiian vocabulary in a not altogether successful attempt to translate his favorite psalms into the new language. Constancy, except for a few moments of heaven-sent solitude which enabled her to write in the small locked journal, busied herself with mending, with washing and ironing in the cook's quarters, and with a fierce concentration upon the complexities of Hawaiian speech. Her face looked older than it had at the beginning of the voyage; her features had molded to an austerity which still seemed foreign to them, and she seldom spoke unless directly addressed by one of the other passengers.

Christmas arrived and was celebrated with plum pudding and rum sauce at dinner, an extra sermon in the afternoon, and the singing of a song composed for the occasion by young Mr. Conant, who, although he had never been entirely satisfied with the poem he had written about one of the female passengers, felt in his shy heart the glow of the creator as he stood and listened to the lusty singing of his Christmas hymn by the missionaries:

"All hail the bright star that the east once illumed
And blest with its radiance the shepherds and seers,

When religion the emblem of mercy assumed
And glory appeared in this valley of tears.
It rose o'er the gloom that enshrouded the earth,
And announced, as it burst from the portals of heaven,
That the Savior of sinners—divine in his birth,
The Conqueror of Death, to the world is now given."

So pleased was he with the reception of his work that, when the New Year dawned on the following Saturday, he was ready for the occasion with another hymn. This one bore more directly upon the mission; it had some eight or ten stanzas of praise for the venture, and ended triumphantly:

"Soon may the heathen bless the light
Which dawns to close the pagan night
And say with truth forever more,
'Owyhee's idols are no more!"

Thus they sailed ever nearer the Horn, and for the most part the brig plowed its way through a cold white mist that chilled the blood and penetrated to the bone. The sea sparkled icily and the missionaries, gathered on deck and wrapped to the ears, their noses bright pink in the frosty air, exclaimed at the small icebergs that bobbed and glistened on the choppy sea. Over the waste of indigo water and gleaming ice and beneath the rays of a distant reddish sun there flew one morning a bird with a snowy breast and black markings on its wings and head, and a majestic wing sweep. It came nearer, cleaving the air with its great wings, seemingly motionless, until it perched on the very rails of the *Thaddeus*. It sat, a guileless giant, balancing awkwardly with small flops of its wings and a great teetering on the deck rail, and with an air of mild surprise surveyed the missionaries.

Constancy and Mrs. Holman exclaimed with delight, and Constancy ran below to get it some sea bread. But when she came back and was running up the companion-way, the deafening explosion of a gun made her flesh shudder; she clapped her hands over her ears, supposing that a whale had approached near enough to be shot (it had happened once before in warmer waters). Coming on deck, her hands filled with the hard sea bread which she had broken into crumbs of a convenient size for a bird's mastication, she uttered a cry of horror at the sight that met her eyes. She ran to the limply fluttering creature lying with its ungainly bill knocking pathetically against the board floor. There was blood dripping from its breast, and close beside it stood Captain Chamberlain, gun in hand.

"Oh!" she mourned. "How *could* you kill so harmless a creature!"

She knelt beside the bird and took its limp neck and head into her lap, crooning to it and stroking the soft, sleek feathers.

Captain Chamberlain looked disturbed. "Now," he said uncomfortably, "Sister Williams, I didn't bear the creature any ill will, but we've been without fresh meat for long now, and albatross is as good to eat as anything you can find in these waters. . . . What's wrong with you?"

He paused to stare at Constancy, who sat back on her heels, her face deathly pale and her green eyes round as saucers. "You killed an *albatross?*" she articulated, slowly and painfully—incredulously.

"Aye," said the man simply, and then with pride, "And it's as big a bird as you'll find anywhere." He grasped its wings and spread them out on the deck. "Ten feet of wing spread I'll be bound! And you'll be glad enough I killed him when you have him nicely roasted for your dinner, Sister Williams."

But Constancy, with a smothered cry of "God have mercy on all of us!" was fleeing as if for her life down the companionway. She halted her mad flight only when she was mercifully alone in her small stateroom. She flung herself down upon her knees, addressing the Almighty for the first time since she had perjured her soul in New England. "O God!" she wailed. "Have mercy on these thy servants who know not what they do. He killed the albatross in ignorance—not knowing that albatrosses are dear to Thee. Visit not Thy wrath upon these, Thy anointed ones, and, especially, visit it not upon Jonathan!"

And so Jonathan found her, in tears and on her knees. "What ails you, Constancy?" he demanded, quite unprepared for the flood of words a sudden rising indignation loosed from her lips.

"Ails me indeed!" she sniffed. "What does that great monument of ignorance, Captain Chamberlain, do but shoot down an albatross! And albatrosses are sacred to God, and one who harms an albatross is inviting the direst misfortune. I tell you, Jonathan Williams, the *Thaddeus* is doomed!" Her voice rose excitedly. "We're doomed to lie, becalmed, as idle as a painted ship upon a painted ocean till the Lord's ire is assuaged. You see if we don't!" she ended, her voice quavering childishly.

Jonathan was bewildered but impressed. "But, Constancy, the good Captain did what he did only because we are short of provisions. He shot the bird for the good of the company, and you know the creatures of the earth were made subject to man."

"Here!" and almost viciously Constancy drew her well-thumbed copy of the *Lyrical Ballads* from a packing box under her berth. "You just read this!" And she handed it to him, opened at the beginning of "The Rime of the

Ancyent Marinere." "Then maybe you will understand
that the Captain did wrong to harm the poor bird!"

With some curiosity Jonathan took the book from her
and began to read. Within a moment or two he was deeply
sunk in the tale. Jonathan, in the days before his conversion, had been wooed by poetry. Indeed, he had read by
candlelight far into the morning hours the works of one
William Shakespeare, and had put away his first love only
when the adoration of God filled his heart. So he read
eagerly till he had finished the last word, drawing a long
sigh at the end.

"It appeals to the sensibilities, Constancy," he said. "It
is a noble poem, but do not disturb yourself because of
Captain Chamberlain's act." He thought of the number
of times he had eaten salt pork and dried peas or beans in
the last few weeks, and his gorge rose. "The Lord assuredly
sent the bird to nourish us," he concluded firmly. "After
all, Constancy, this rhyme is but a fancy of a poet who
may likely be an ungodly person, and it is not to be confused with the Scriptures."

Again Constancy sniffed. "The likelihood is greater
that He sent it to see how His favored children could endure temptation at a time when their stomachs rebelled
against dried beef and salt pork. Wait, Jonathan, and see
how the Lord regards this crime. I, for one, shall not eat a
mouthful of the poor thing. If it were not for my feeling
for you, Jonathan Williams, I could wish I were safe back
in Sedley teaching Latin grammar to the farmers' boys!"
And she flounced huffily from the stateroom, leaving her
husband thoughtfully stroking his chin.

True to her word, Constancy at dinner that day made
a scant meal from unappetizing gruel and sea bread while
her fellows ate heartily of the great bird. She was not at all
surprised, when she awoke the following morning and

went on deck, to realize that the *Thaddeus* rocked as peacefully and as unprogressively on the water as if it lay at anchor. The ship was in the strait near the Horn, and the crystal-clear morning air revealed on either side of the *Thaddeus* menacing dark mountains that offered no promise of a haven but only of destruction against their hideous black rocks that jutted far out into the sea.

Captain Blanchard joined Constancy on deck and cheerfully pointed out the danger of drifting against the rocks. "We'll lie here for a few days," he said comfortably. "It's likely enough in these parts, and, so long as the current grows no stronger, we shall be safe enough, though it is tiresome to be delayed."

Constancy made no response. Her eyes were closed, and her lips moved soundlessly in a prayer to the God she hated to spare the lives of His anointed lest the benighted heathen remain unregenerate. Wilily she elaborated upon the value of the mission to those unsuspecting natives of the Sandwich Islands, until she felt that in His own interests God could not afford to neglect her petition.

They were becalmed for seven days and seven nights, with the current pulling the vessel almost imperceptibly backwards until it drifted in a line with the entrance to the strait, and Constancy awaited, tense and hollow-eyed, the annihilation that she anticipated.

The eighth day found the brig leaping ahead through the waters, the strait behind them, and before noon Captain Blanchard was summoning them all on deck to see Cape Horn which in all his voyages he had never seen until this moment because of the heavy mists that hung above it.

Constancy, assured that the matter of the albatross had been overlooked in the light of the identity of the ship's passengers, relaxed and began to look forward to the islands. In March, with the ship becalmed for ten days in tropic waters, doubts again assailed her. She wondered uneasily if the Family had not overestimated the importance of their venture in the sight of God, and if a God capable of forbidding man the apple from the tree on pain of eternal punishment even while He knew that man must eat, a God capable of decreeing both the sin and its penalty, were not also capable of leading His anointed to destruction. To Constancy, God was an inexorable and capricious taskmaster, as given to visiting discomfort upon His faithful servants for some celestial whim as upon those sinners who had the hardihood to withstand Him. Constancy, believing horribly in the power of God, credited Him with no virtues, distrusted Him entirely.

In the long period of idle drifting on a glass-smooth sea, the nerves of the Family were severely tried. Mrs. Loomis, fretful in the early stages of her pregnancy and fearful of destruction, wept often and openly. Mrs. Bingham's pale lips moved ceaselessly in noiseless prayer as she washed clothes, mended, or sat brooding over the bright waste of ocean. Mr. Bingham exhorted the Family to repentance for lack of faith, for frivolity, for all the weaknesses of the flesh; and his eyes burned more disturbingly than ever in his parched face. As he preached to the small gathering, his eyes turned inevitably toward Mrs. Holman, who, for the most part, fixed her own eyes upon a point just beyond the minister and looked unmoved. Occasionally her will failed her and she flushed or paled or even gave way to tears.

They were all anxious, all restless, and more and more the refrain of prayers ran, "Lord, Lord, in what way have we offended Thee?" Yet, although prayer and meditation were the general order of these days, there were moments when childish perversity entered these consecrated spirits: Mrs. Ruggles and Mrs. Whitney exchanged a few sharp words over the question of which of them should be first to use the tub for washing on a certain morning when they arrived beside it simultaneously, their arms stacked with soiled clothes; Jonathan Williams nursed a secret and, as he himself acknowledged in agony, ignoble grievance because Mr. Bingham rose up one Sabbath morning and preached a fiery sermon from the text, "Strait is the gate, and narrow is the way, which leadeth unto life, and few there be that find it," which happened to be the text about which Jonathan had prepared, with the intention of delivering it that very evening, what he considered the most moving sermon of his brief career. Although he had been able to adapt much of his former sermon to the substitute text of, "Ye serpents, ye generation of vipers, how shall ye escape the damnation of hell?" he bore the holy Mr. Bingham a faint grudge for several days.

Undoubtedly the climax of this trying period occurred in the cabin one morning when the Family was breakfasting unenthusiastically upon tripe and bitter tea, and Mr. Bingham, helping himself to sugar, was forced to scrape the bottom of the bowl with his spoon. He looked severely up and down the table.

"The sugar," he said distinctly and ominously, "is being consumed *very* fast." His eye, after roving from face to face, settled permanently upon the pretty one belonging to Mrs. Holman, "*too* fast indeed," he finished significantly.

Mrs. Holman, looking up, caught his eye and colored angrily. "Having drunk neither tea nor coffee on the voyage, Mr. Bingham," she said a trifle sharply, "I presume I have not used even one fourth pound since coming on board."

Mr. Bingham's long forefinger thrust forward accusingly. "Stop!" he cried full-throatedly. "Mrs. Holman, stop and recollect where you got the sugar you eat upon your lemons so plentifully!"

Mrs. Holman disdained him with her eyes. "*Not* from the company's supplies, Mr. Bingham," she said coldly. "My brother Samuel has given it to me from some he had put up for his own consumption."

Dr. Holman and Samuel Ruggles were both on their feet, the one looking angry, the other pained.

"You go too far!" shouted the young doctor.

And "My sister speaks truly," more quietly from Samuel Ruggles. "She has ever been delicate, and I brought with me extra sugar especially for her comfort."

Mr. Bingham settled back in his chair. "It is fortunate for you, Mrs. Holman," he said grimly, "that you have your brother present to prove it, for it has been strongly suspected that that, too, belonged to the mission as well as the lemons."

Thomas brought down his fist upon the heavy table, and a fork flew into the air, somersaulted into a glass of water, and splashed water over Mrs. Bingham's slight bosom. The doctor turned in apology. "Forgive my clumsiness, Mrs. Bingham," and then to her husband, "This outrageous persecution of my wife must cease. I appeal to your sense of justice—nay to your wits! Is it fitting, is it dignified, to bicker about absurd childish trifles? Is it fitting that a man of Mr. Bingham's position should stoop to badgering a defenseless woman for a fault that she has not committed? Mr. Ruggles has proven to you that the sugar was her own, and in due time you will have a letter from Mr. Ruggles, the merchant, testifying to the truth of her assertion about the oranges and lemons, and let me say, now and for all time, that the demand for such proof on your part, Mr. Bingham, is insulting to both my wife and myself, and, were it not for the respect I bear your cloth, I should force you to rue your words."

He sat down and savagely gulped a cup of scalding tea. A scandalized murmur ran round the table, and Mr. Bingham's face was livid. Samuel Ruggles leaned forward, his gentle face rosy with the stress of his emotion. "Not only Brother Bingham," he said firmly, "but others in this company have been sadly lacking in that charity which thinketh no evil and which was enjoined upon all Christians by our Lord."

Mrs. Holman wept silently but bitterly, her face in her hands, and her husband, patting her convulsively on the shoulder, again leaped to his feet. "You have wronged my wife, and some redress ought to be made her. Her feelings have been wounded in the tenderest point, for she has ever been anxious to share with her friends whatever bounty she enjoyed, and kept out only so much of her personal gifts as the doctor had strictly ordered her to do."

Mr. Bingham rose to his feet, once more the master of his feelings. "May I respond for all?" he said slowly. There was a confused murmur which might have been assent. "Then, Dr. Holman, on behalf of the company, allow me to say that we cannot help our suspicions, but it is Mrs. Holman's misfortune. I shall pray for her guidance."

Mrs. Holman's sobs grew louder, and Dr. Holman looked as if he were ready to forget his respect for the cloth, when Constancy created a diversion by rising from her place at the table and going over to Mrs. Holman's chair.

"Do not cry," she said softly but distinctly. "Such suspicions against you are unworthy of any professing Christian, and the person whose soul is so warped that he can hold them is in far greater need of pity and prayers than you." And she bent to brush her lips lightly against Lucia Holman's tear-stained cheek, and would have left the room, but Thomas Holman sprang to his feet once more and grasped her hand in a painful grip.

"Thank you! Thank you!" he stammered.

Constancy gave him a quick shake of her head and a fleeting smile and turned to go out.

"Constancy!" Jonathan's voice, grim as the Reverend Hiram Bingham's, arrested her at the door.

She turned and raised inquiring eyebrows. "Yes?" calmly.

"Ask Brother Bingham's forgiveness for your thoughtless and rash behavior! I am shamed that my wife should be guilty of setting herself up in judgment against her superiors in the sight of God."

Constancy slanted her eyes from Jonathan to Mr. Bingham. "I regret the necessity for displeasing you, Jonathan," she said gently, "but indeed my words to Mrs. Holman were no more than my honest opinion. Have you forgot how St. Paul has written, 'Though I speak with the tongues of men and of angels, and have not charity, I am become as sounding brass, or a tinkling cymbal'? And again how he wrote, 'Love taketh not account of evil; rejoiceth not in unrighteousness, but rejoiceth with the truth'? And Jonathan, I cannot feel that Brother Bingham was rejoicing with the truth—truly it seemed to pique him. Let us all pray for his guidance."

Now she really left the room, decorously enough, but her mouth twitched irrepressibly once her back was toward the Family. She suspected that Jonathan would not be too hard on her, for she was aware of his grudge against Mr. Bingham on the score of the sermon.

No sooner had Constancy disappeared than Mr. Bingham, his face darkly flushed, pushed back his chair and strode from the room. His wife rose and followed him, her face more than usually colorless, her lips moving inaudibly. The rest of the Family sat for a moment stricken to utter silence, a cloud of discomfort settling upon their souls. Then, with a concerted movement, they scraped back the chairs and filed out of the cabin.

In the open air they regained the use of their tongues, and little groups of women whispered excitedly about the scene at the breakfast table, awed at the daring of Dr. Holman and at the daring of Constancy Williams, the youngest member of the company, in defying so stern a man as Brother Bingham. No one seemed quite easy in mind. Everything was strained and unnatural. The other members of the company rather pointedly avoided Holmans, Binghams, and Williamses, feeling unsure of the proper course to pursue. Mr. Bingham was their acknowledged leader; how could he do wrong? Yet his assailants had backed their arguments with the authority of the Scriptures.

The women were not much inclined to be lenient with Mrs. Holman: she was too unfeignedly feminine; they were prone to censure her for the fact that her husband waited upon her and consulted her wishes in all things. There was an air of delicacy, of remoteness in Lucia Holman that the other members of the Family, the women in particular, found hard to bear. Dr. Holman, they were disposed to believe, was a likely enough young man, but unfortunately enslaved by the wiles of his wife. Constancy Williams was another matter. Her conduct had astounded them. They had accepted Constancy, even felt a real affection for her, for, in the days when seasickness laid the Family low, she had been unfailingly kind and thoughtful in her dealings with them all, and she was still wont to perform small services for her fellow voyagers. Now they were disturbed. Was Constancy just a heedless and rebellious girl, or had God animated her to speak as she had?

No one was able to feel quite himself until an incident occurred which banished temporarily at least all personal grievances. John Honolii, unable to bear the sticky heat a moment longer and wooed by the limpid blue water, tore off his clothes and, naked except for a loincloth, poised for an instant, straight and brown, on the rail and curved swiftly and sharply into the inviting coolness of the sea. The missionaries, secretly glad of diversion, and the deck-hands, openly rejoicing in it, crowded to the rail to watch him sport in the water. Thomas and William were excitedly throwing off their shirts and preparing to join their countryman when they were arrested in their movements by a wild yell from the throat of the swimmer. He kicked mightily in the water, screaming frantically, his features twisting in terror. Through the water the peering men and women saw, dark and awful, the shape of a huge fish and caught the gleam of teeth.

"Shark!" roared Captain Blanchard and, shoving the now screaming women right and left, ran to a lifeboat, pulled a pole from it, and hurled it straight at the shark's head. The evil, shining black head leaped above the water, the mammoth mouth snapped on the pole and stayed shut, the teeth clamped tightly into the pole. Enraged, the shark threshed the water with his glistening tail, dove furiously, and was gone from sight, even before the exhausted John was hauled aboard at the end of a rope.

The women hovered anxiously over the prostrated gasping figure of the Hawaiian boy and the captain hurriedly poured him out a drink of whiskey, but Hiram Bingham raised his clenched hands in an exultation that annulled the bitterness of the morning and cried resonantly to the heavens, "Even so, Lord, didst Thou close the lions' mouths to preserve Thy servant Daniel. So shall it be with the enemies of this Thy mission to Owhyhee, Lord. They shall be confounded, their jaws closed tight before righteousness!"

But the Polynesian Daniel sat up grinning broadly and scratching his head to say, "*Too* close! Scared like anything! *Too* much thank you, Captain!"

The Family recognized the timely intervention of Jehovah through the agency of Captain Blanchard with his pole by a special prayer meeting in the afternoon, and in the evening they gathered again to sing their praises of the infinite mercy of God. Thus the matter of a nineteen-year-old girl reproving the spirit of their leader crept away into the hinterland of their minds, to be remembered only at idle moments, to be spoken of only when so much time should have passed that the occasion for remembering at all would be the imperiousness of a grandchild clamoring for a story of "when you were young, Grandma, and it took such a long time to come to Hawaii."

The morning of March 30, 1820, found the brig plowing steadily along before a good wind that ruffled the surface of the water, and the missionaries hung over the side of the boat, exclaiming at each flying fish that skimmed in low flight over a stretch of sea before vanishing beneath the surface. The joy of motion after ten days of aimless drifting wooed them away from serious study, and so when at precisely eleven o'clock in the morning the shifting of a long, straight cloud along the horizon disclosed the blue height of a mountain rising loftily above the paler blue of the sea, the hearts of the missionaries leaped as one,

and the Hawaiian boys embraced each other with laughter
and tears, crying, "Maunakea! Maunakea!"

5

All day the brig moved steadily toward the island of
Hawaii, and to the eyes of the voyagers the blue of
Maunakea became momently deeper. A streak of dim
green appeared along the edge of the sea, a streak that
grew to a wide band and then rose like a slow tide against
the mountain height till only two blue summits lifted
above it. Toward evening Hawaii lay on the left of the
Thaddeus, and to the right rose another island which the
Hawaiians told them was Maui. Before darkness obscured
the outline of the islands, the voyagers were able to note
with wonder the thin snowy ribbons that streamed down
the green velvet sides of Hawaii, ribbons that accented
the lush green of the cliffs.

"One . . . two . . . three . . . four, five, six, seven,
eight . . ." mumbled Constancy. "I can't *count* the
waterfalls!" she protested; and then, "Oh, Jonathan! I had
not dreamed it would be so beautiful!"

"Home!" sang the hearts of the native boys pridefully.

"Home!" echoed the Family faintly, a little questioningly, and blinked eyes, long accustomed to monotones,
to scant herbage, to rocky soil, at the richness that lay before them. Children of frugality, they hesitated, instinctively distrustful of a land that nature decked so prodi-
gally. A hundred waterfalls where a New England eye
expected one; rank herbage hiding the bare bones of the
earth with green that lay like a priceless carpet, soft and
seductive, where a New England eye expected a rocky,
barren land with here and there a trim field wrested from
hostile nature and forced to yield a living to its owner.

"Too much, Lord," protested the sensibilities of more than one of the anointed. "We come to try our souls with the hardships of a desert island, and lo, we find an opulent land that has in its bounty something of wantonness that offends decorum."

Captain Chamberlain looked upon Hawaii with the eyes of a farmer. His soul was not troubled with the exquisite points of casuistry. He beheld a green land with apparently infinite resources of water, and the farmer in him rejoiced. "Crops'll grow like mad here, heathen or no heathen," he whispered to his wife. She nodded. "It's a pretty place, too," she said wonderingly.

The Reverend Hiram Bingham drew closer to his wife, who stared doubtfully at the land before her. "It is possible," he said musingly, "that God in His unfathomable wisdom sees fit to try our souls with lavishness—to lay before us the temptation to an easeful life to test our resolve."

Lucia Holman rubbed her cheek against her husband's shoulder and spoke in a whisper. "It is a happy-looking land, Thomas. The people must be happy, too—like children. I can't bear to think that they have been, all unknowing, in the shadow of hell. How glad they will be that we have come to save them."

Constancy peered through the twilight and doubted that the God she had been taught to fear had anything to do with the creation of these islands. One of the other gods, kindlier, that people are warned not to put before Jehovah must have created Hawaii, she reasoned, and Jehovah, being the stronger, was besieging it with missionaries now.

Early morning found them lying off the northern shore of the island of Hawaii. Thomas Hopu, who had paced the

deck all night in the excitement of his homecoming, and
John Honolii were sent ashore with Mr. Hunnewell, one
of the ship's officers, to make inquiries, to learn the state
of affairs on the island and the present location of the
king. In their absence the missionaries walked restlessly up
and down the deck and hung over the rail trying to pierce
the green that had swallowed up their ambassadors. Three
weary and anxious hours passed, and at last they saw the
three men enter the little boat and make all haste to return to the vessel.

Mr. Hunnewell scurried up the side of the vessel.
"Kamehameha is dead!" he babbled breathlessly. "His son
Liholiho is king. The *kapus* are abolished—the images—
burned—the temples destroyed! There has been war—
now there is peace!"

Over the rail swung Hopu, his eyes shining. "God looks
with favor upon the mission," he began formally, and
then, excitement getting the better of his speech, "Kamehameha—*make*. Gods all *pau! Wahines* eat same time with
men—*can* eat bananas. Same kind all islands. King stop
at Kailua—some more *alii* at Kawaihae!"

As Hopu paused, out of breath, Mr. Bingham threw
back his head, his eyes smoldering. "O God, we thank Thee
for delivering these benighted heathen into our hands, and
for causing their chief to abolish their idols and their
kapus. Thou hast vanquished them by half, for now they
are as a field lying fallow, their old superstitions cast away,
and we have but to sow the true word amongst them!"

Verily the Lord was heaping blessings upon them. The
Family stood, bewildered but humbly grateful. They had
expected a rock-bound island where life was a struggle,
and had found a land that seemed to flow with milk and
honey. They had anticipated finding a people wedded to
idols and clinging to ancient pagan superstitions, and had

found a new king who pronounced unlawful the ancient practices. The people, temporarily without any religion, uneasy beneath the awareness of godlessness, were indeed as a field lying fallow and waiting to be sown.

Constancy, looking sharply at Jonathan, had a fleeting impression of disappointment in his face. Was it possible that Jonathan regretted the helpfulness of the Lord? Had Jonathan's soul craved conflict and impossible odds? She laid her hand upon his arm.

"What is it, Jonathan?" she asked gently.

Jonathan clenched his hands and uttered a stifled groan. "Constancy," he whispered, "I am indeed unworthy of the trust imposed upon me. I am full of vanity—the worst of sinners. Pray, child, that I may be sensible of the Lord's infinite mercy and wisdom!" And he rushed away to their stateroom. Constancy, staring thoughtfully after him, reflected compassionately, "He is a boy—in spite of his goodness and his learning, he is very like a little boy."

Almost at once her thoughts were diverted from her husband to the long canoes that were now skimming across the pale green water toward the *Thaddeus*. The nearer the canoes came the more startled grew her gaze, for she observed that the men wore only a loincloth and the women a tight wrapping of odd brown-and-white material which covered them from waist to knee and left their brown and overwhelming breasts bare to the embarrassed gaze of the missionaries.

The natives drew their canoes close to the ship and offered gifts of bananas and coconuts and taro, chattering and pointing excitedly at the female passengers, who were the first white women they had ever seen. They were eager, friendly, smiling children, these brown heathen. The cloud of doubt lifted from the minds of the missionaries: these guileless children of nature offered no menace.

They leaned from the vessel and called *"Aloha!"* self-consciously, and "Thank you," and the natives showed flashing teeth and waved their hands in departure.

Slowly the brig rounded the northern end of the island until it lay off Kawaihae. The missionaries were impatient to land, but Captain Blanchard, no less than the three native converts, raised his hands in horror at the thought. They must wait for the chief's permission. In the meantime Hopu should go ashore and invite some of the chiefs to come aboard. There was nothing to be done until royalty chose to call upon the Family. There was ceremony to be observed in dealing with kings, even though their skin might be brown. So the missionaries wandered about the deck, staring at the white sand beach where the coconut trees thrust up from the very sand and leaned toward the water, at the lush green of the valley and the mountainside beyond, at the grass huts that sprinkled the shore, and at the natives they saw moving about beneath the coconut trees.

They stayed on the boat and prayed, with varying degrees of irritation, for patience. At last they saw a canoe pushed into the water by half a dozen men who sprang into it and started paddling toward the *Thaddeus.*

"He comes!" squealed William Kanui with glee, and the Family rushed to the side of the vessel to watch the approach of royalty. The canoe darted over the water till it hovered at the edge of the brig, and one of the paddlers grabbed the rope ladder to pull the canoe beneath it. Then uprose the figure of Kalanimoku, virtual prime minister to young Liholiho and a chief in his own right, the most reassuring if spectacular sight that had yet met the eyes of the missionaries. He climbed briskly up the swinging ladder, swung his legs over the deck rail, and held out his hand to each of the men in turn.

"*Aloha!*" he said smiling amiably, and "How do?" and stood, tall and massive, before them, arrayed, in the words of the ship's journal, "in a neat dimity jacket, black silk vest, nankin pantaloons, white cotton stockings, black shoes, plaid cravat, and a neat English hat." Beside his attendants, who wore only the *tapa* loincloth, he was as Solomon in all his glory. When he had finished shaking hands with the men he made a low and respectful bow to the women and then shook hands with all of them. His attendants scrambled up the rope ladder bearing gifts of huge sweet potatoes and the great purplish tubers of taro, the food that was to constitute the staff of life to the missionaries for many years, and bananas. Falteringly the missionaries pronounced brief sentences in the Hawaiian tongue, delighting their royal visitor. He retorted in a torrent of Hawaiian which left his audience gaping until one of their converts translated.

Two more canoes drew up to the boat, and with puffing and wheezing two of the largest women the missionaries had ever seen climbed aboard the *Thaddeus*. After them swarmed a retinue of attendants. The larger of the two queens was Kalakua, mother of three of the young king's wives. She and her companion were both dowager queens of the late Kamehameha (he had possessed five wives). They wore loose, shapeless cotton dresses that covered them adequately but revealed bare brown feet. Presently two of Kalanimoku's colossal wives appeared over the boatside. They, too, were dressed adequately if unbeautifully. By the time one chief and four queens with several attendants apiece were gathered on the deck of the *Thaddeus*, there was little room left for the missionaries.

As he talked, Kalanimoku smoked a longish pipe. He strode up and down, his chest thrown out, uncomfortable but proud of the clothes he had donned at the humble request of Hopu, who had said that the missionaries were unaccustomed to nakedness and therefore distressed by it. At a sudden barked command, an attendant rushed up to him with a small polished round box made from a tiny gourd, into which the chief carefully spat. The attendant reverently covered the box and secreted it about his person until it should be wanted again. The *kapus* might be gone, but no dignitary was going to run any chances of his sputum or nail parings falling into the hands of an enemy.

The queens sat ill at ease on chairs. They groaned and muttered and kept their attendants busy fanning them with palm leaves. One setting the example, they all pulled their top dresses over their heads, revealing a single garment very like the outer one beneath. Kalakua pushed back her chair with a grunt and, waddling over to a bench, stretched herself full length upon it, her vast stomach rising mountainous, her plump feet and mammoth legs projecting from her disarranged skirt. Her sister queens, seeing no other benches, stretched themselves on the deck. The ship's officers hastened to bring mattresses for them, and the queens clucked and smiled their approval.

The Hawaiian women scrutinized every detail of the missionary women's persons and attire, fingering the texture of their dresses with loud approval, touching their faces, their hair, examining their hands finger by finger. The missionaries endured the inspection nervously but patiently, one or two of the more precocious linguists crimsoning at the frankness of some of their guests' comments on the figures and biological possibilities of their hostesses.

The hour for dinner approached. The visitors were invited to dine on board. Kalanimoku accepted, but the queens, after a brief parley, refused: they would eat on board, but they would have their own food brought on later. So, while Kalanimoku sat at the common table in the cabin, gravely imitating the behavior of the missionaries, the queens distributed themselves in the limited space remaining in the cabin to watch, laughing and chattering together while their attendants peered in at the door. When the meal was cleared away, the attendants of the queens brought forth large quantities of raw fish and huge bowls of the pasty white, gluey mass known as *poi,* which the queens ate noisily and greedily with their fingers.

A little later Kalanimoku announced, beaming, that he, the queens, and all of their attendants would be pleased to accompany the missionaries aboard the *Thaddeus* to Kailua to see the king. The announcement brought dismay to the stoutest of the missionaries. There were no vacant staterooms; every bed was taken. Politely they explained the difficulties to royalty. Royalty dismissed the difficulties with a wave of his hand. There was space for mattresses on deck, wasn't there? And wasn't it cooler and pleasanter on deck? Very well, as soon as a few pet dogs, gifts for the king, and other necessities could be sent for, they would be ready to start. Meekly the missionaries bowed their heads.

6

Constancy, alone in the cabin, unlocked the clasp on her private journal and, seating herself at the writing table, dipped her pen in ink and began to write:

"*Tuesday, April 4, 1820.* After 163 days of sailing, the *Thaddeus* anchored early this morning before Kailua, the dwelling place of the king, Liholiho, called formally Kamehameha II. We have enjoyed a novel experience in the few days of sailing from Kawaihae. Some thirty Hawaiians and five lap dogs joined us at Kawaihae and sailed with us to see the king. They slept upon hand-woven mats on deck and during the daytime lay or sat upon them. Each of the queens was surrounded by several attendants supplied with *kahilis*, which are fly chasers of feathers mounted on sticks and resembling elaborate feather dusters, palm leaves, spit boxes, and back scratchers to be used at the pleasure of the queens. Truly these women are monstrously large, as much as six feet in height and seeming to be nearly that broad. They have never done actual work in their lives, and are smiling, self-indulgent, heedless creatures like young children. It is the custom with them to put their own children out to nurse in order that the royal mothers need not be bothered with them.

"At first they wore unbecoming but decorous enough clothes, donned at the behest, or so we learned later, of Thomas Hopu, but before long they threw off both the outer dress and the single garment beneath that, and sprawled on deck or in the cabin with nothing on but the wrapping of native material made from bark and called tapa, which covers them only between the waist and the knee. The sisters and the brethren are disturbed at their lack of modesty. I examine my conscience and regret that I deplore not their nakedness but their extreme fat. If they were beautiful to look upon, being slender and well formed, I feel certain that their nakedness would not disturb me at all—which is very reprehensible of me.

"Sunday, the day after sailing, we found hard. The natives were disposed to play at their favorite game of cards, and though Brother Bingham and Jonathan ex-

plained with patience and much diplomacy, I thought,
why it was offensive to the Lord for man to indulge in
weekday pastimes on the Sabbath, they were marvel-
ously insensible to the arguments, saying they did not
know the white man's God yet. They went on playing
until the regular service was held. Thomas Hopu translated in brief the sermon Brother Thurston delivered to
the Family, and the Family with the captain and officers sang hymns, at which the Hawaiians showed great
pleasure.

"The prime minister seems a superior man. He re-
tains his clothes though all the rest cast theirs off, and
he speaks and conducts himself with dignity on all occasions. He is humble, too, in wanting to learn to read
and write; and as often as not, it is small Daniel Chamberlain, five years old, who sits at the chief's feet or on
his knee and gravely teaches him the alphabet. It is
curious how much more apt the Chamberlain children
are with the native language than are we older folk who
spend such painstaking effort upon it. They chatter in
most intimate fashion with our guests, who make a
great pother over the children and play with them.

"The queens and their attendants have been learning
to sew on this short voyage. All ladies gathered on deck
and formed the first sewing circle ever to be organized
in these waters, with Kalakua as directress. She it was
who, within a few hours of meeting us, produced a web
of white cambric and demanded that we make her a
gown similar to our own, and that we finish it so that
she might greet the king, her son-in-law, in it. When
she learned that we could not sew on the Sabbath Day,
she was considerably upset for fear the dress should not
be finished in time, but we assured her that, with so
many ladies working on it, it could easily be made in a

day. We sat on deck, brown and white, side by side, and while the rest of us sewed busily on Kalakua's mammoth dress, Mrs. Holman and Mrs. Ruggles cut out work and supervised the first struggles of the royal ladies with a needle. It was quaint to see them squatting in their barbarous attire, intent upon joining pieces of calico patchwork, muttering when they pricked themselves, but proud of themselves when they had accomplished a little.

"This morning the Hawaiians all went on shore immediately after we dropped anchor, Kalakua an imposing sight in her white dress, which fit as well as anything would fit a woman of her bulk, and wearing besides a lace cap and a lace neckerchief which were presented by our ladies to complete her costume. We observed that the natives on shore gathered about her in much excitement as soon as she stepped upon land. Apparently the gown was a triumph.

"At the moment, Jonathan, Brothers Bingham, Thurston, Hopu, and Captain Blanchard are ashore in parley with the king. We fear that it is vain to hope that the young king should be as personable and strong a man as his prime minister, but the brethren are determined to interview him and read to him the letter from Dr. Worcester of Boston and from the Prudential Committee of the American board, and explain with Hopu's help just what the mission hopes to accomplish.

"It seems, truly, a fair land, and I trust we may not be put off. It would be a sore disappointment—almost a killing one—to Jonathan if circumstances prevented him accomplishing his purpose.

"The brethren and sisters accept me as one of themselves and do not seem ever to suspect that I am as a whited sepulcher. Am I so hardened, then, although my

years are not great, that I can act so calm, take my turn
at prayer in the women's meetings, perform the every-
day duties, knowing that inevitably the fires of hell are
awaiting me? At first the thought was a constant horror
to me, yet already it needs the pricking of Brother
Bingham's eloquence, the exhortations of the other
brethren at prayer, to stab me to the more acute realization of my plight. In truth I am less than the least of
our company, and yet I am frequently guilty of vain
complacency that I have a pleasanter face to look upon
than another worthier sister. It is only when I think of
having a child, and having that child perhaps tainted by
its mother's sin and so brought to destruction, that I
realize the heinousness of my sin. Yet it is sweet that
Jonathan relies upon me and trusts me and feels affection for me, sweet enough so that I forget for spaces
that I am not what he thinks me."

Sounds from the deck told her that the men were returning from their interview with the king. Hastily lock-
ing her book and hiding it in her pocket, she ran to hear
the news. The returning missionaries shook their heads.
Their fate was in the hands of the Almighty. The letters
had been read to the king. The mission and its purpose had
been explained to him, but he had temporized and invited
them to return the following day to eat with him, bringing as many of the Family as could come. Hopu had discovered that British agents had told the king that the missionaries were coming to take the islands away from him
and give them to the United States. The earnest convert
had carefully explained that the missionaries were not
come to deliver the islands to the United States but to deliver the souls of an ignorant people to God, that they
came without money, without clothes or any provisions

save those that the Board of Missions saw fit to bestow upon them, that they shared alike, and that there was no gain for anyone. But Hopu reported regretfully, "Liho-liho think maybe I speak big lie. We speak some more to-morrow."

The Family dined thoughtfully on roast chicken and taro and bananas. Afterwards they held a long and earnest prayer meeting, perceiving that God in His wisdom was merely substituting unexpected obstacles for the ones they had anticipated.

7

Next morning Mrs. Loomis and Mrs. Whitney, who were reticently pregnant, chose to stay at home with the youngest Chamberlain children. The rest of the Family struggled down the swaying rope ladder into the small boats and were rowed to shore. A throng of natives awaited them on the beach and immediately pressed about them, feeling the strangers' clothes with their brown fingers and discussing the oddities of the newcomers in their native tongue. Royal soldiers shoved the common people back with irritated clucks and growls and escorted the visitors to the large grass house, euphemistically called the Palace. There the missionaries found their way blocked by the royal guard. Although it was eleven o'clock, the king was sleeping. The disgruntled visitors could see through the open doorway several monstrous forms reclining on piles of mats. The guards shrugged when Hopu asked when the king would waken. Sometimes he woke earlier, sometimes later—they could not say. He must not be disturbed.

The missionaries exchanged glances of disapproval at such sloth, and glances of helpless outrage for their own position. They shifted from one foot to the other, but be-

fore waiting had grown too tiresome, a bulk within the
house moved and sat up. It was the king. He stared
blankly for an instant at the delegation waiting before his
door; then he waved an affable hand. *"Aloha!"* he hailed
them genially, but before they could respond he leaped to
his feet with surprising agility and rushed out of the rear
door of the house, to return shortly, adjusting his malo.
The missionaries stood outside while a calabash of water
was brought in and set before the king. He washed his
face and hands somewhat sketchily, received a feather
headdress from one attendant and adjusted it with great
care, and allowed another attendant to place a *lei* of small
creamy flowers about his neck; it lay palely against his
powerful brown chest. He was prepared to receive his visitors.

"Aloha!" he said again and shook hands all around and
presented them to two of his lesser chiefs who had performed similar toilets and were now all interest and attention. Kalanimoku entered the doorway, and the missionaries turned to him as to an old friend. He had not failed
them: he wore a complete suit of clothes. Behind him
crowded a group of queens. Their four friends of the voyage, Kalakua still in the new dress, which was now in a
spotted and wrinkled condition, the other three in familiar
attire, smiled graciously upon the missionaries. With them
were six other royal ladies, sufficiently if extraordinarily
clad, one in a red velvet gown with a long train, one in
black brocade, two in purple silk, and two more in what
appeared to be men's shirts and a piece of *tapa*. None of
them wore shoes. They were all tall and all very substantial, their weights running from two hundred to four
hundred pounds. The eldest of these ladies and also one of
the most colossal was Kaahumanu, who had been the favorite wife of Kamehameha the Great and was now *kuhina*

nui or queen regent. She alone was haughty in her greeting to the missionaries, extending only the little finger of
her right hand to them. The other queens greeted with
smiling decorum these strangers who had come across the
world to save them from the pangs of hell, and invited
them to sit in Kaahumanu's sitting house while the men
talked.

Meekly the white women followed their hostesses
through a grove of coconut trees to a thatched grass hut,
larger than any of those that surrounded it, and entered
through a doorway to find themselves in a curious enclosure without windows. There were many of the hand-
woven *lauhala* mats laid one on the other. On these the
large queens dropped heavily, inviting their guests to follow their example. The missionaries were a little constrained; their speech in the native tongue was halting;
they felt self-conscious.

Mrs. Bingham swallowed hard and, leaning forward,
said earnestly, "We have come to tell you about God."

The imposing queen regent silenced her brusquely. "We
have only now finished with many gods. We have destroyed the images and forbidden the people to worship
the gods of their fathers. There have been fierce battles—
the cousin of Liholiho and his wife were killed defending
Kukailamoku, the fierce war god. Now the old gods are
pau. What do we want with new gods? The gods bring
sorrow and pain to our people. We will speak of other
things. Where are your children? Have none of you children except this one woman?" indicating Mrs. Chamberlain whose three young huddled about her.

Mrs. Bingham flushed. "Only Mrs. Chamberlain has been
married long. We others married just before the ship
sailed."

Kaahumanu subsided with a grunt and ignored the ladies.

Kamamalu, Liholiho's favorite wife, leaned over and spread out the green-and-white muslin of Constancy's dress. She looked at it, her head on one side, and fingered the white fichu collar. "I wish to have such a dress," she said emphatically.

"I would give you this," began Constancy apologetically, "but———"

Kamamalu let out a sudden whoop of laughter. She leaned over and slapped a sister queen jovially on the considerable thigh nearest her. *"Aia!"* she shrieked. "The little one would give *me* her dress *so* big to wear—" and she measured off an infinitesimal size in the air with hands that were delicate and graceful despite the overfat arms. "You shall *make* me a dress—as you made one for Kalakua," she beamed, and summoning an attendant she poured forth a flood of Hawaiian that made the visitors realize how slowly their hostesses had been talking to their guests. The woman fled out of the door and in a moment was back with a length of blue-and-white calico in her arms.

"This was a present from Captain Grant when he stopped last time," the queen said proudly, "and you shall make it for me." She thrust the bundle into Constancy's arms with a nod of satisfaction. Two of the other ladies immediately sent their attendants forth and were presently commissioning their guests to turn dressmaker. The missionaries meekly agreed and set about measuring their taskmistresses.

The ice was broken; the queens, with the exception of Kaahumanu, who sat in dignified silence pretending not to look at the visitors, chattered. The *kuhina nui* concentrated her attentions upon a small black lap dog from

which she occasionally plucked a flea and, to the horror
of the missionaries, quickly popped it into her mouth.
The other queens waxed childish. They wanted to see the
hair of their guests and commanded them to take it down.
In some embarrassment the white women complied with
the request.

The queens, again with the exception of Kaahumanu,
shook out their own thick manes to their knees and began to comb them. There was not a little chagrin in the
chaste breasts of some of the white women as they were
forced to pluck forth the pins from their hair and let
down a meager display. Thin flaxen locks straggling to
the waist, indifferent brown hair ending at the shoulders,
even wavy black hair that reached part way to the waist
looked like nothing at all beside the mops of hair displayed
even by the middle-aged Hawaiian women. The queens
were astounded at the disparity between their own and
their guests' hair and frank in expressing their surprise.
However, they fingered Mrs. Holman's long, abundant
light hair, and they exclaimed at Constancy's because it
was the color of honey and fell in heavy ripples below her
waist.

Keopuolani, whose rank was higher than any other
Hawaiian queen's, grew warm and casually tossed aside
the man's shirt that she wore, displaying colossal dark
breasts. Attendants knelt beside the queens, gently waving the gaily feathered *kahilis* to keep away the flies;
others stood in the corners briskly wielding palm leaves
to cool the air. The guests were served with a red wine
which turned out to be claret; they sipped it delicately
and gradually waxed more and more loquacious. Between
the claret and the length of the conversation in the strange
tongue the missionaries suffered some confusion of mind.
Relationships among the people they had come to save

were very puzzling. They gathered finally that young Liholiho, Kamehameha II, was king of all the islands but that he had many chiefs under him. Each island had a king subordinate to Liholiho; Kauai, they were told, had a practically independent king, Kaumualii, father of the George who came with them on the *Thaddeus*. Kaumualii had promised to turn over his island to the Kamehamehas when he came to die. Kalanimoku, a chief, was also prime minister to Liholiho and had occupied the same position in the court of Kamehameha I. Kaahumanu was queen regent and had power equal to Liholiho because Kamehameha had willed it thus, fearing the youth and weakness of his son, who quite often drank too much and did foolish things. Kaahumanu was wise and would be able to prevent the young king from misbehaving too flagrantly.

The missionaries' hesitant questions brought forth the fact that the chiefs all had more than one wife, and some of the royal ladies had more than one husband. They were informed that Kamehameha I had at one time twenty-one wives; at the time of his death he had reduced the number to five. Thus Liholiho, king of all the islands, was the son of Kamehameha by the high-born Keopuolani and not by Kaahumanu, the queen regent, as the missionaries had at first supposed. Kamamalu shared with several other queens the privilege of being Liholiho's wife, but, as she placidly confided to the missionaries, she was his favorite. She went on to explain to her wide-eyed guests that she was his sister as well as his wife and that they had always been fond of each other. To the gentle reproof of Mrs. Bingham, the dark ladies merely said it was the custom and shrugged their mammoth shoulders.

Constancy, struggling to adjust her own intelligence to this casual polygamy and polyandry, striving to imagine how she would feel if there were several other women with whom Jonathan might go to bed, and finding herself quite incapable of fancying Jonathan consorting freely with a bevy of wives, was nevertheless ironically aware of the dilemma faced by Mrs. Bingham, whose conscience bade her reprove and instruct these benighted pagans, but whose common sense forced her to hold her tongue until the missionaries should have the authority bestowed by kingly sanction of their enterprise. It was a relief to all of them when a boy appeared in the doorway and summoned them to the *luau*.

As Constancy walked by Kamamalu's side through the coconut grove her heart quickened its beat. The scene before her seemed like nothing out of life, but something from a book. The water in the bay stretched limpidly blue and lavender and jade green beyond the beach; the coconut palms leaned sharply toward the water, their dark trunks cutting the white sand. Beneath the trees men bent moist, gleaming brown backs over the *imu*, or stone bake oven, and drew forth steaming food wrapped in *ti* leaves from beneath the stones. Women and girls wrapped in gayly dyed *tapa* and lavishly decked with flower *leis* moved to and fro under the trees. The children, brown and lithe and smooth-skinned, innocent of all clothing, tumbled at the edge of the tranquil water, laughing and shrieking as they chased one another both on the sand and in the water; even babies, unsteady on their fat legs, swam as unconcernedly as so many baby dolphins. Here, mused Constancy, were color and laughter and light-heartedness . . . beauty. What, she queried, would these people be like when they had learned to fear God? Could this smiling land learn to breed sober piety? The claret warm in her veins scorned sober piety and defiantly proclaimed her spiritual affinity with the happy thoughtlessness before her.

Mats stretched for fifty feet or more in different shaded spots along the ground. One such space in a central position was distinguished by a display of heavy crockery and knives and forks. To this, royalty and anointed made their way and sat down on the small mats provided for them. Constancy, looking over her shoulder, was childishly disappointed at not being allowed to eat from bowls made of small gourds and coconuts. Dishes seemed dishearteningly commonplace, if unexpected, in this setting. To the right of her sat Keopuolani; to her left Kalanimoku, but he spent most of his time talking to Mr. Thurston.

Keopuolani nodded placidly as she surveyed the *luau*. "It is better that men and women should eat together," she announced to Constancy. "Never before the death of Liholiho's father had women and men dared to eat at one table, but then Liholiho and Kaahumanu said to everyone that the *kapus* were gone, and Liholiho, while the people shook with fright, came to my table and sat down at my side and began to eat the food that had been cooked in the women's ovens, and when he did not die, the people laughed and sang and the women all ran to eat bananas, which were forbidden before."

Constancy, with a continuous clatter of Hawaiian syllables in her ear, painstakingly divested a fish of its green wrapping. The coldly staring eye of the fish disconcerted her; she laid a piece of the *ti* leaf over the objectionable head and, thus able to ignore the eye, tasted the fish. It was delicious.

"*Mi-i!*" she said, nodding vigorously to Keopuolani. The queen mother nodded back, and urged, through a mouthful of pork, "*Poi!*" and pointed to a large bowl of the white mushy-looking substance. By way of encouragement she leaned forward with a grunt and dipped a finger into the sticky mass, drew it forth well coated, thrust it into her mouth, and greedily smacked her lips. Constancy, hesitating even after a hearty "You try!" from the king's prime minister, was determined to follow the example set her when she saw Mrs. Bingham and then Mr. Bingham timidly plunge their forefingers into the bowl and then gingerly lick off the *poi*. In went Constancy's own finger, and she sucked off the *poi* as swiftly as Keopuolani had done. Instantly her face went rigid; she swallowed quickly and with difficulty, and her features puckered ever so slightly.

"You don't like it!" sighed Keopuolani and shook her head.

Constancy was embarrassed. "I never tasted anything like it before," she faltered. "I shall become accustomed to it. The fish is very good, though." She picked up the mug before her place and took a sip of the golden brown liquor it contained. It burned like liquid fire; she choked slightly, and her eyes filled with tears. The queen on her left drained off half a mugful at one gulp. Looking down the length of the board, Constancy saw tears in the eyes of Mrs. Bingham and Mrs. Holman. She raised her eyebrows to see Hiram Bingham, deep in a slow, broken conversation with Liholiho, absently lift his mug, take several swallows, and set it down, apparently unmoved by its strength. Jonathan, sitting on the other side of Liholiho, was blinking queerly.

She paused, fork in hand, to rest her eyes upon the bounty of the feast before them. After months of salt pork and dried beef, dried beans and peas, and sea bread, the sight of so much fresh food sent a pang to her vitals. Every few feet a *poi* bowl, every few feet huge platters of fish *laulaus*, steam rising from the *ti* leaf wrappings, bowls of baked sweet potatoes and baked taro, roasted fowls merely garnishing the giant platter whereon rested a mas-

sive pig already half dismembered. Her eye traveled to a
similar platter at the far end of the board. She had at first
supposed it to contain another pig. For an instant she
scrutinized it and then turned quickly away, having recognized a dog, roasted whole. She grimly turned her
thoughts to other things.

Carefully searching her brain—dulled it seemed to her
by food and drink—for proper words, she asked if the
whole village always ate together. Oh, no, several assured
her at once; this was a special *luau* for strangers. Usually
they ate in the houses—the chiefs even had tables. Constancy sighed: she had liked to picture them all eating together out of doors, as if life were a perpetual picnic.

It seemed to Constancy that they ate for hours and that,
the more they ate, the more quickly the Hawaiians talked,
and the more stammeringly the missionaries talked, the
more frequently the latter resorted to their own language
and appealed to an interpreter for any interchange of
ideas. Jonathan, halfway down the line, was unmistakably
leaning against the broad back of the dusky king and
sleepily saying "*Mi-i*" to everything. Then, just as Constancy was wondering if she could ever rise to her feet
after so bountiful a feast, there was a stir of excitement
among the natives—smiles, nods, and a ripple of exclama-
tory utterances.

From the grove came old men and old women carrying
gourds and coconut shells. They flung themselves upon
the ground, facing the missionaries' table, and began to
beat out a steady monotonous rhythm with their odd in-
struments. Weaving sinuously through the coconut palms
came literally hundreds of young Hawaiians, their feet
moving ever so slightly, their bodies writhing jointlessly,
their arms coiling to the steady beat of gourds covered
with sharkskin. They advanced steadily, their heads

proudly erect, the men grave, the girls smiling, faces remote from the lithe rotation of their trunks, divorced from the serpentine twisting of their arms.

Constancy drew in her breath with a little gasp. "What is it?" she whispered to Keopuolani, although she knew that this must be a dance and therefore wicked.

"The *hula-hula*," said the stout queen matter-of-factly enough, but her eyes were gleaming, she smiled broadly, and soundlessly clapped her childlike hands in rhythm while her mountainous shoulders swayed just perceptibly. "For you," she murmured graciously, "two hundred of the young dance the *hula*, the dance of our people. Never have you beheld anything like this."

Constancy shook her head, smiling faintly, her eyes powerless to leave the dancers. "I have never seen any dance before. . . . It is beautiful." She looked, then, from the dancers to Jonathan, to Mr. Bingham, to Mrs. Bingham, frightened lest they should have heard her. Mrs. Bingham sat, her pale eyes wide and startled as they followed the movements of the dancers; her mouth was open. Mr. Bingham's mouth had folded into a narrow line, the ends turned down, but his eyes lacked their usual fire as they rested upon the dancers. As for Jonathan, he still leaned against his future convert's shoulder and, his eyes wavering over the scene before him, gently waved his mug to the time of the drums. It was quite evident that none of the three had heard Constancy. She drew a small breath of relief, and, after making sure that the Thurstons, Chamberlains, and Holmans were staring in absorption which was disapproving or merely amazed, she returned to her contemplation of the spectacle before her.

The men wore only the *malo*, and around their ankles and wrists were bracelets of dog teeth that clattered as they danced. They had about their necks *leis* made of shells or of sharks' teeth. The girls wore wound about them as a skirt the *pa-u*, one end caught up over a shoulder or in some cases merely tucked in at the waist with a fine disregard for the revelation of shapely brown breasts to the uneasy gaze of the missionaries. These *tapa* garments were richly colored in symmetrical patterns, red, yellow, or black. The girls' anklets and bracelets were of dogs' teeth, but their *leis* were of flowers and *maile* which brought to Constancy's mind the eastern smilax.

Following upon the Gargantuan feast, these inscrutably smiling faces, the swaying undulating bodies, the incomparable grace of the coiling arms, and the monotonous beat of the gourds, all conspired to lull the audience to a wide-eyed torpor. Swaying gently or leaning against one another, natives and missionaries alike sat, content to watch the dancers, thought driven from their heads; and when the dancers were gone and the sun was a scarlet ball dropping over the rim of the colorless, shining sea, grave young men sat before them and sang, at first weird chants that lacked all regular rhythm and had no tune, but after a little there were songs with half-tunes, wistful and haunting, that the performers sang to the queer music issuing from a gourd which a musician held against one nostril.

Then the guests of the feast found their eyelids drooping heavily and uncontrollably. When at last there was no more singing and no more dancing and dark had crept out to a single line of silver at the horizon, the polite suggestion of Liholiho that it was now time for the missionaries to sing startled the company into alertness. They struggled to their feet and gathered, a little group apart, for a whispered consultation. Then they sang, less heartily than usual, two hymns. After the mellow tones of the native singers, the missionaries' voices sounded thin and shrill. However, the natives applauded vigorously and seemed sincerely disappointed when Mr. Bingham and Mr. Thurston assured them that the Family could sing no more at present and was obliged to get back to the *Thaddeus* for evening prayers.

It was not until the Family was safely back on shipboard and prayers had been offered up—a little sketchily and rather disconnectedly—that a question from Mrs. Loomis, who had remained on the ship all day, reminded them that, for all his cordiality, King Liholiho had not told them they might establish themselves upon his islands. The missionaries looked at one another abashed: they had forgotten their mission. They went gloomily to bed, aware that they had erred, but they wasted no time in falling into the deepest of slumbers, for even a New England conscience was capable of only the most perfunctory activity after such a *luau* as the Family had enjoyed that day.

8

Eight days passed. The king entertained the missionaries. The missionaries entertained the king and as many of his chieftains and their queens as saw fit to come aboard the *Thaddeus*. The Family was taken to see the great Heiau where the fallen idols had been worshiped, where there were a few grisly remains of bygone human sacrifices to demons. The ladies shuddered, the men looked stern. They saw men at work pounding the taro root on long wooden boards with a stone pounder to make the *paiai* from which *poi* was made. They saw women weaving mats of *lauhala* and baskets from coconut cords. They witnessed the different steps in the making of *tapa* from bark and were shown the gorgeous feather capes and headdresses of royalty.

The king and his subordinates were unfailingly gracious

and smilingly obdurate when pressed for permission to establish churches and schools. The king showed the keenest interest in Dr. Holman. During the week that followed the landing of the missionaries, the doctor was called upon to treat various ailing attendants and servants of the king. He went at his task with lips compressed and fear in his heart. The son of that English seaman, John Young, who had been detained by Kamehameha the Great many years before to dwell on the island as a chieftain and adviser to the king and husband of a royal lady—this man's son by his royal wife informed the doctor that the death of any chief placed in his care would result in death for the physician. He told the disturbed doctor that the native physicians, who prescribed the same drastic cathartic for every illness and believed more in magic than in medicine, had warned the natives that Dr. Holman would kill them. So Dr. Holman brought his medicine cabinet ashore and set up his clinic with misgivings which he dared not admit to the brethren. He treated cases of colic, he set a broken arm, shook his head over a girl doomed to die of consumption, bathed inflamed eyes, lanced boils, dressed revolting sores, and was amazed at the number of ugly skin diseases current among the poorer people. He saved a small princess from untimely death from the croup and encouraged a squealing royal lady through a difficult confinement. The king watched, approved, admired, and said that he would like Dr. Holman to stay on Hawaii. Dr. Holman said firmly that he was a member of the mission family and could not stay unless all the missionaries were allowed to remain in the islands.

The king stroked his chin and looked sober. He said doubtfully that Great Britain wouldn't like America to get a foothold in the islands, that he had every reason to think that the missionaries wanted to get hold of the land for the American government. Then he said that the missionaries, if they stayed, must settle on Hawaii where he could watch them. The missionaries wriggled in helpless irritation. They wanted to go to Honolulu on Oahu, the site of the fort, the site of the larger foreign colony, the logical place for their greatest efforts, where boats came most often, bringing the most temptation to sin to the ignorant natives.

They reached a deadlock which held until John Young befriended them. In a stirring yet simple address to the temporizing king, he reminded him of the friendship between Van Couver and the first Kamehameha, of the curiosity and respect Kamehameha had shown toward the white God Van Couver had mentioned. He reminded him gently and sorrowfully of how the old chief on his death-bed had beseeched the doctor, stopping over while a vessel was in port, to tell him of the white man's God and Jesus Christ, and how tears of disappointment had stood in the dying man's eyes because the doctor had been a bluff, irreligious man unable to comfort him. These missionaries, he told the young Liholiho, had come to tell the Hawaiian people of one powerful God Who could make them live forever in another, more beautiful world after death. The missionaries had come to teach the natives how to be good and useful, how to read and write and figure so that they would not be cheated by the sly traders. The missionaries, he said last, came for the love of God, wanting no land, only houses to shelter them and enough to eat so that they might teach the ignorant natives the way to God. If they had come to conquer the islands, he asked his sovereign, would they not have brought guns and cannon and left their wives at home?

The king sat lost in thought. Then he raised his head and said slowly and with dignity: "It shall be as you have spoken. The missionaries may teach my people to be good —for one year. Then we shall see. But the doctor and one other man with his wife must stay here. They will be given water, house, fuel, and provisions. The others may go to Oahu."

The king rose and walked away, his eyes bent upon the ground. The missionaries eyed one another in consternation. "How," asked Mr. Bingham uncertainly, "shall we decide which of us is to remain with Brother Holman?"

"Thomas!" Lucia Holman's voice was edged with despair. "Is there no other way? *Must* we stay here alone?"

Her husband forced himself to smile reassuringly at her. "It will not be too tedious. The king seems well disposed toward us, but it would be dangerous to cross him now. If you are unhappy or discontented—feel after staying a while that you cannot endure it—I will take you to Oahu."

Lucia nodded. "Very well, Thomas."

Captain Chamberlain stepped forward. "It looks as if none of us hankered to stay, but somebody's got to. Supposing we put all our names in my hat here and let Dr. Holman pull out one to see who stays."

They gravely followed his suggestion, and there was an audible intaking of breath when Dr. Holman drew forth the single slip of paper. "Brother Thurston," he said.

Asa Thurston bowed his head. "It is God's will!" he said, not uncheerfully. Lucy Thurston's voice quavered a little as she said, "It will be nice for us to have the doctor with us, anyway." And immediately she felt that she had been selfish in her thoughts, for she was not yet pregnant, and there had been unmistakable signs that not only Mrs. Loomis but Mrs. Bingham and Mrs. Whitney were expecting babies.

The other missionaries, relieved that they were spared the necessity of staying on Hawaii, were for the time being quite willing to dispense with the services of a doctor. Only Constancy felt a brief pang of regret when Jonathan's name was not read. She could have endured the isolation of Hawaii and the disadvantages of residence on that island, she felt, for the sake of living with the Holmans and surrounded by these childlike, gracious natives. She felt that, living under such conditions, she might forget for longer periods of time that she was under an irrevocable sentence of damnation. And why, she reasoned impatiently, since it was predestined that she should suffer for all eternity once she had put off her body, should she not enjoy these few moments of mortality vouchsafed her unharassed by the depredations of her conscience, prodded into excessive activity by Mr. Bingham in the pulpit and by the exhortations of her sisters in Christ at their women's meetings?

That very evening the *Thaddeus* was under way again; now relieved of the royal party with its assortment of dogs, the ship seemed airy and spacious to the Family. After a journey of seven days the *Thaddeus* rounded Kokohead, drifted slowly past Diamond Head, and approached the harbor. The missionaries trained glasses or stared without external aid at the countless peaks of the Oahu mountains, blue green in the distance, apple green on the nearer slopes, with shadows of low-drifting clouds dappling the sunlit valleys. Purple haze filled the deep-cut ravines, and a rainbow, bending one end into the sea to larboard of the vessel, arched above them, burying its other end in Manoa Valley. But between mountains and sea stretched a dry plain that showed the sparsest vegetation, and, except for groves of coconuts along the shore of Waikiki, no trees.

The vessel hovered at the edge of the harbor awaiting

permission to enter. No boat could enter without official consent. At last they were free to land. The missionaries were prepared to be met by a group of unclad natives and possibly a dignitary or two with a few oddly assorted garments; they were not prepared for the courtly welcome they received upon landing from a fastidiously dressed Spanish gentleman, whose every gesture bespoke old-world grace and a culture riper than any the missionaries had previously known. He introduced himself as Don Marin, the government interpreter. He was a Spanish settler, he told them, and, with a barely distinguishable gleam of amusement in his eye, a Catholic, and at their service— with a bow. Indeed he spoke truly, for he conducted them to the village, ordered the transportation of their worldly goods, and secured them temporary living quarters in the village.

THE ORPHAN GIRLS gathered around the big table were
clamoring for more molasses to pour over their porridge. It
did not occur to Constancy to send one of the children
for the molasses; she picked up the pitcher and plodded
out of the front door of her grass hut, across the yard to
the storehouse where the six households kept their provisions under lock and key. Sometimes she felt that she
would prefer the natives to be less docile in manner and
more trustworthy. Most of them stole whatever they could
lay their hands on. After filling her pitcher she carefully
locked the storehouse and returned to the riotous children.
She helped each of them to more molasses, saw that the
smallest had mugs of goat's milk and the larger ones cups
of coffee, and then poured out coffee for herself. She was
too tired to eat. Her eyelids kept drooping in spite of her
efforts to keep her eyes open wide. She forced herself to
sit erect in her chair, attentive to the wants of the orphan
children and to their more flagrant breaches of table eti-
quette. Usually she fed only half the number; Mrs. Loomis
cared for the other half, but Mrs. Loomis was now abed
with her first baby.

Remembering the scream that had torn across the space
between the Loomis cottage and her own, awakening her
from sleep, Constancy shuddered. That scream had driven

her from her bed; she had put on her clothes, fumbling at the buttons with trembling fingers, and hurried to offer her assistance. Dr. Holman, down from Lahaina, was there —kind, encouraging, watchful of the frightened Maria Loomis. Mrs. Chamberlain was helping him and soothing Maria as best she could, reminding the younger woman that it would soon be over and she would forget all about the pain when she saw the baby. Mrs. Bingham was told to go home and sleep, for she was within two months of her own time. Constancy, three months from her own ordeal, was thought capable of making coffee for the miserable-looking Mr. Loomis, the doctor, and Mrs. Chamberlain, of heating cloths and water and running errands between the houses.

She had wondered, as she crossed and recrossed the space between the cooking house and the Loomis house, laden with buckets of steaming water or a pot of coffee, why Mr. Loomis couldn't have made himself useful instead of stamping up and down muttering incoherent prayers or sitting hunched in a corner looking as if he had been caught killing sheep. Of course, though, she reasoned repentantly in the next breath, he behaved so because he loved his wife and was afraid she would die. Would Jonathan be so distraught when her own hour was upon her?

Again she reflected upon the unfairness of God. He could so easily have ordained a less painful way of replenishing the earth. It wasn't fair that one apple eaten by one woman should have condemned every woman born to torture. Fear stayed the tide of rebellion that flooded her heart: she might die in childbed, and her child might die, too, and both of them be precipitated into hell because she was an unregenerate sinner. Still, and she stiffened her spine again, she was as strong as Maria Loomis, and surely stronger bodily than the frail Mrs. Bingham. If they could survive the ordeal, she ought to. Her face relaxed as she remembered the new baby, rosy, fat, with tiny wrinkled hands and feet and a funny topnotch of dark hair. Her own unborn, pushing blindly against the wall of its prison, reminded her that there was a baby as well as a night of torture in store for her.

She rose and stood in the doorway, staring out across the rocky plain towards the deep blue, glass-smooth sea, noting sails against the horizon and hoping that if it were another whaling vessel the seamen would keep away from the mission. Watch the orphans as vigilantly as they could, the lure of a swaggering sailor with bright beads or a few yards of gaudy calico to dangle before an acquisitive girl on the verge of womanhood was sure to overwhelm super-imposed notions of propriety. The last whaling ship in port had cost them two girls, who now were wont to stroll past the walled-in missionary settlement wrapped in the bright calico, the fruit of their sin, strutting by to flaunt their ill-gotten gains before the frankly envious gaze of their erstwhile fellows. Constancy smiled, thinking of the drunken sailor who reeled into the mission enclosure one night, loudly calling for rum, to be sent away with a Bible in his hand, his jaw fallen with astonishment. But too many of the whalers saw fit to hang over the wall and jeer at the missionaries, shouting rude obscenities to embarrass the pious.

Hurriedly instructing the orphans to wash and dry the dishes, Constancy stepped into the yard to hail Mrs. Chamberlain, who was just leaving the Loomis house. Mrs. Chamberlain passed a hand over her damp forehead. The day was hot and breathless, and she had been on her feet for hours.

"They're both doing nicely, Mrs. Williams. She had an easy time as such things go. I gave her some breakfast and bathed her as best I could, and now she and the babe are both sleeping sound. So's Mr. Loomis, poor man," she chuckled. "He'll be easier about the next one. Captain Chamberlain took on like that about our first. I'm going in and have some sleep. I'm about beat out."

She turned toward her own house, somewhat larger than any other in the row of thatched buildings, with the exception of the Binghams' house, which served as school as well as dwelling. "They're going to call the baby Levi," she called over her shoulder to Constancy.

Constancy went into the smaller of the two rooms in her house and began making up the four-poster bed which Boki's wife, Liliha, had given her in a moment of generosity. Liliha had it from a trader. When the bedroom was put to rights Constancy found the orphans gathered about the long table in the next room, ready for school. From the large house rose the strains of "Rock of Ages," sung in Hawaiian. Mrs. Bingham's school had begun. Constancy went to the rude cupboard Jonathan had made for her and took down a pile of papers on which were printed the first simple lessons in the Christian faith. She held up one and then another to the class. The orphans shouted in singsong Hawaiian:

"I cannot see God, but God can see me.

"In the beginning God created the heavens and the earth.

"Jehovah is in heaven, and He is everywhere.

"Jehovah sees everything that I do.

"Jesus Christ, the good son of God, died for our sins.

"We must pray to Jehovah and love His word.

"God loves good men, and good men love God."

Then those who knew the texts by heart rose and, with hands twisting calico skirts or folded placidly over stomach, chanted them triumphantly. This much of the day's work over, they took pencils and odd bits of paper and painstakingly wrote their names, the alphabet, both in printing and in script, and while a few of the more advanced carefully wrote out the Lord's Prayer in Hawaiian, the slower or younger children wrote out the lesson they had just been parroting. Constancy moved back and forth among them, guiding a faltering hand, reproving a careless pupil whose lines zigzagged too much or whose work showed smudges and erasures, praising a neat piece of work when she found one. Next they sang a hymn. Then little rolls of calico were brought forth from the cupboard and distributed among the orphans. The little rolls were cut in odd pieces, which, fitted together, made drawers, that the orphans might go their way in decency. The longer the children sewed, the filthier grew the garments. They stabbed themselves accidentally with their needles and their mates by intention, whereupon a loud outcry was made. Constancy sat facing them, plying her own needle in the fine linen her mother had given her before the departure of the *Thaddeus*. She made countless tiny tucks with the smallest of stitches.

"Will it be a girl or a boy," she pondered, "and will it look more like Jonathan or like me? I hope like Jonathan, for he is the most beautiful human being I ever saw, and having Jonathan for a father, the child will be good, really good, and I shan't injure it, because, surely, when these grim brethren mistake me for one of the elect, a small babe will not find me out, and I can love it with none to say me nay, for it is proper that a mother be concerned with her child and lavish devotion upon it."

The grandfather clock she had brought from home chimed eleven times. She folded her work and locked it away. Sternly bidding the children behave themselves and make progress with their sewing while she was away, she went out to the cooking house. Mrs. Chamberlain was there before her and had put breadfruit in the oven to bake. She was basting a kid, plump with a taro-and-sausage dressing, as Constancy entered. Mrs. Chamberlain beamed at Constancy over the kid. "See what they brought this morning," and she tapped the kid significantly with a spoon. "I declare I don't know what we'd do for food half the time if the natives hadn't taken such a fancy to the baby. Just this morning they brought this kid—when I was feeling I couldn't look salt pork in the face—and a bunch of bananas and enough taro for a week. There's plenty of everything here for you and the Binghams and the Loomises for dinner. You're looking sort of peaked, and it's hard for you standing over a stove on such a hot day. You go on in and rest and I'll call you when it's ready to dish up." She paused and looked at Constancy critically. "I thought last night it was too bad you had to lug those heavy buckets of water the way you are, but there was nobody else to do it with the most of the men off to Ewa. You go lie down and let those orphans lay the table."

Constancy pressed her hands against her throbbing temples. "I don't know what any of us would do without you, Mrs. Chamberlain. You take care of all of us when you must be worn out yourself. Since you are so kind, I shall lie down until dinner, and the orphans will do the dishes afterward. Then you must rest, and I'll cook supper for the Family."

She went indoors, told the most responsible of the orphans to lay the table, ordered the rest to continue their sewing, and went into the back room. She lay down upon the wide bed and closed her eyes, but opened them at a sudden flurry of wind that blew a fine stream of dust through the cloth-covered window. She thought of the greater beauty and thick herbage of Hawaii in contrast

to this barren plain thick with dust ready to rise with the
least breeze. If only they were allowed to put up the house
frame they had brought with them from New England!
Life would be so much more tolerable if one had a decent
wooden floor under one's feet and a substantial roof over
one's head.

"Still," she thought, "I'm fortunate in being strong.
Mrs. Bingham has had a cough ever since the last heavy
rain that wet us all so thoroughly, and she is nearer her
time than I, yet she goes about her work untroubled. A
saint's rôle is a curious one for me to ape, surely, and what
good does it do for us to work ourselves to the bone trying
to turn comfortable heathen into good New Englanders?
What do they look like after we get them into these unsightly drawers and shapeless dresses? They were happier,
I wager, before they ever heard of Jehovah and hell, as that
British captain said, and they *looked* so much better in
tapa than in calico."

But against her rebellion there rose up the memory of
the child who attended the school, pretty except for the
sunken place where an eye had once been. Asked how she
lost her eye, the child had said simply, "I ate a banana."
And so she had; at the age of four she had chanced to eat
of forbidden fruit, and in view of her tender years had lost,
instead of her life, merely one eye. No, Constancy's reason insisted, the old way was bad, too. And again a vision
rose up to confront her—the pitiful poverty of the common people, living on a tiny plot of land, cultivating it
with toil and with great difficulty raising taro and sweet
potatoes and squash, cherishing a pig, perhaps, and then
to have the chief's agent swoop down upon them, confis-
cate the newly gathered harvest, and make off with the
pig, often as not just as it was cooked and ready to serve.

"Nothing is ever right on earth," Constancy complained

petulantly in her soul. "The *kapus* are gone without any thanks to us, and as long as we keep our eyes on them the chiefs don't make quite so free with their subjects' property—probably because they don't want the brethren to pray them to death afterwards—but, in return, the whalers hate us, the foreigners, or at least most of them, would like to see us all boiled in whale oil, and the natives we scrub and sew for and pray over will steal the very stays off our bodies if we take our eyes off them for a second." She rolled over, and gradually sleep closed over her brain.

Lehua was tapping her gently but persistently on the shoulder. "Mrs. Chamberlain says come and get the dinner," she said when Constancy unwillingly opened her eyes. Constancy rose to her feet, plunged her hot face into the washbowl of tepid water, smoothed her hair, and then hurried to the cooking house, carrying a platter and followed by Lehua with vegetable bowls.

Mrs. Chamberlain had expertly dismembered the kid and cut slice upon slice of the meat, which was so tender that juices streamed from it. She loaded Constancy's large platter and heaped quarters of baked breadfruit in the bowls Lehua held. "There's plenty of goat milk in the cooler if you send over a big pitcher," she offered.

As they were finishing the meal a shriveled little Hawaiian, clad only in the *malo,* appeared in the doorway, a huge white bundle slung over his back. He dropped it on a mat and sniffed audibly and delightedly, his eyes on the table. Constancy heaped a plate for him, and he sat in the doorway, noisily eating the food with his fingers. Constancy untied the bundle and counted the pieces of washing within. "Forty-eight, forty-nine"—she slanted her eyes suspiciously at the brown back in the doorway, and then with unexpected swiftness she pounced upon the plate he held loosely on his knees and, snatching it away,

held it behind her. "Where," she demanded "is the rest of
my wash?" Her eye fell upon a suspicious-looking bulge
about his loins.

The man wrung his hands; he looked injured; he smiled
placatingly.

"Every piece is there, I swear it by God!" and he raised
a brown claw protestingly.

"Don't lie!" said Constancy sternly. "Give me the two
pieces you stole, or you get no more dinner and I'll give
· my washing to your brother and feed him instead of you."

The man rolled his eyes despairingly and began fumbling
with his *malo*. First he drew forth a small wad of white
which unrolled into a pair of chaste-looking muslin drawers with ruffles on them. "No more!" he protested. Constancy's eyes twinkled, but her mouth was severe. "One
more," she commanded. Regretfully he pulled forth a pair
of Jonathan's socks.

"Shame!" reproved Constancy and handed him back his
plate. He snatched it and removed himself from the room
altogether, sitting crosslegged a few yards from the door,
gobbling up his food before it could be taken away from
him again. The orphans giggled.

Constancy set four of them to clearing the table and
washing the dishes, sent one to inquire if Mrs. Loomis
would care for an eggnog with a dash of rum, and took
the rest with her to prepare for use the flour which had
arrived on the last boat. Captain Chamberlain had sawed
the great solid block that was the flour after the long sea
journey into equal parts, one for each family. Now Constancy's task was to pound the hard cake into powder and
sift it carefully to eliminate the inevitable weevils.

One girl pushed and rolled the now empty flour barrel
from the storehouse to the yard. The others lugged Constancy's block of flour out to where two almost **perfectly**

round stones, hollowed slightly at the top, lay in the yard. Constancy followed with a hatchet and a large sieve. She hacked off chunks of the flour and placed them in the stones. The children found small stones and began to pound the flour.

"Be careful," she cautioned, "don't spill any on the ground. It will be six months before we have more sent us. I must see to the ironing."

She went around the house to the cooking house and placed three sadirons on the stove to heat. She set up her ironing board in the hot little room and went back to get the wash. She sent Mary, the smallest orphan, back from the Loomises now with word that Mrs. Loomis would be pleased to have an eggnog a little later in the afternoon, to fetch a bucket of water from the spring. The water beside her, Constancy began to sprinkle the clothes. "Go on outside and play, Mary," she said to the small brown child. "You've been a good girl today. Come and tell me when the girls finish with enough flour to be sifted."

The child scampered away, and Constancy went on sprinkling and rolling up petticoats, drawers, both masculine and feminine, Jonathan's shirts, his cotton trousers and jackets, her own calico and muslin dresses. When she had finished, moisture beaded her nose and forehead and chin. She mopped her face with her handkerchief and tested the iron with a moist forefinger. It hissed, and she began the weary task of ironing in an overheated room on the hot August day.

Thought receded from her brain; there was nothing in life but the methodical backward-and-forward movement of the heavy iron over innumerable garments, most of them stiff as boards from the starch the missionary wives made from pounded arrowroot and portioned out to their washmen to take with the soiled clothes to the clear

Nuuanu stream where the clothes were washed and scrubbed against the clean stones.

She had ironed three beruffled shirts for Jonathan, a calico dress, two pair of drawers, and a corset cover for herself when Mary ran in to say that the stone bowls were full of flour now. Constancy set the iron back on the stove, told Mary to wash her hands and then carry the ironed clothes very carefully into the bedroom and lay them on the bed, and then set off for the scene of the flour-pounding. For half an hour she cautiously sifted the flour, keeping a sharp eye out for the weevils that occasionally worked through the mesh into the barrel. She returned to the cooking house and finished ironing the more difficult pieces— then called to the two largest orphans and told them to take turns at ironing sheets, towels, and pillowcases. There was more flour to be sifted. She sifted it and, seeing that she had perhaps fifteen pounds in the barrel, told the children to put the rest in a sack to be sifted another day.

Her ears still ringing with the heat, she went into her house, took two eggs from her cupboard, sent Mary for a small pitcher of milk from the cooler, and began preparing the eggnog, beating the yolks with a fork until they were creamy, beating the whites patiently with a wire spoon until they stood in snowy peaks, combining the two, adding the milk a little at a time, and to it all a generous portion of rum. She poured the mixture into a bowl, grated nutmeg over the top, and, cautioning the orphans to behave themselves, took her offering over to Mrs. Loomis.

Maria Loomis lay limp and relaxed on her pillow, the baby nestled in the crook of her arm. She looked very young with her hair in two short fat braids and her face, though pale, healthily round above the uncompromisingly decorous neckline of her white muslin nightgown. She smiled placidly at Constancy. "He is a sweet babe, isn't he, Mrs. Williams?" she asked softly. "Even now I can scarce believe that he is really mine."

She carefully removed her arm from around the moist dark head of the baby and lifted herself a little as Constancy deftly slipped a second pillow behind her head. She took the eggnog and sipped it slowly. "It is a very tasty eggnog," she said appreciatively, "and you were kind to trouble when you have the care of all my orphans now. Maria Chamberlain has been nursing me most thoughtfully while her mother has been busy today, and the doctor came in just before noon to see how we did." She leaned nearer to Constancy and, though they were alone in the house, lowered her voice. "It is strange, is it not, Sister Williams, that a man so tender to the sick—so kindly in many ways—should have the hardihood to set himself up against the judgment of the brethren?"

Constancy dropped her eyes. It was a subject upon which she felt strongly. "Both think they are right," she said slowly. "It is only for God to judge. No man knoweth another's heart." She raised her eyes. "I know only that in selfishness I hope that Dr. Holman will still be among us when my time is come."

Mrs. Loomis nodded. "I was grateful for his presence . . . perhaps, indeed, I am sure that it is Mrs. Holman's influence that leads him away from the true path. He is like a man in a story book in his devotion to her. Elisha says it is not godly to love any human being so well— though if Mrs. Holman were as pious as Sister Bingham, perhaps no harm would come of it."

Constancy knitted her brow. "Mrs. Holman is different from us," she said. "She has been brought up less strictly than many of us, and being delicate she has never grown accustomed to hard work and such inconvenience as we meet here on every hand. It is unfortunate that she should have come, for she is not suited to this life, just as a canoe is not suited to a long journey over stormy seas, but a canoe is very good in its own way for all that. I have great compassion for Mrs. Holman, who is surely unhappy."

Mrs. Loomis looked a little wonderingly at Constancy. "You have a good heart," she said. "You speak the best of everyone."

Her visitor rose in haste. "I must be going back to the orphans," she said, "and it falls upon me to prepare supper tonight. Would Mr. Loomis eat with us, or would he like it better if he were to bring his dinner here and eat with you?"

Maria Loomis blushed faintly. "I think," she said shyly, "he would like to eat here. He is in danger of spoiling me."

Constancy smiled. "It is pleasant to be spoiled when one is ill." She stooped over the small Levi, who had just opened his eyes. She slipped a hand under the covers. "Mischief!" she reproved him and, turning, took a diaper from the near-by table. A little awkwardly she put the dry diaper on him and admired the softness of his skin, the plumpness of his arms, the dimples on each hand. "He is a lovely babe, Mrs. Loomis," she said warmly, as she took her leave. "I will send over your dinner—or you might ask Mr. Loomis to come after it a little after six."

Her muscles ached with tiredness as she went back to the house. The orphans were playing a wild game involving much racing and whooping beneath the hot sun. Constancy let them play, cautioning them to be quiet when they approached Mrs. Loomis's house. She sent off one child to ask Mrs. Bingham to come to her house to eat, and, if Mr. Bingham came back, to bring him with her.

She sent another to carry the same message to Mrs. Chamberlain, and then set about putting the boiled beans into a mammoth baking dish with molasses and water and a thick slice of salt pork buried in the middle of them. The oven was hot; she put more wood on the fire and decided that the beans would be done by six. She washed sweet potatoes and laid them aside ready to put in the oven a little later. She washed and sorted taro tops and set them to soak in cold water until it should be time to put them on to boil. She went to the cooler and, finding a jug of sour milk, decided to make sour-milk biscuit for supper. She counted heads: ten orphans, two Loomises, one Bingham, six Chamberlains, herself, and quite possibly Mr. Bingham and Jonathan would be back in time for dinner. Twenty-two . . . well . . . twenty-five could sit at the big table Jonathan and Mr. Bingham had made. The orphans were commissioned to set the table and to borrow additional dishes and silverware from Mrs. Chamberlain. Mrs. Chamberlain sent back two pint jars of *poha* jam which she had made.

Shortly before six a shadow falling across the door of the cooking house caused Constancy to look up from her stirring of the taro tops in vinegar to see Jonathan.

"Jonathan!" she cried joyfully, her weariness for the moment forgotten. "How glad I am that you came today! I cannot help but fancy you are come to grief when you are delayed."

Jonathan's very features sagged with weariness. "It has been a hard trip, Constancy. We have walked more than twenty miles today, but the chief was cordial and the people friendly. One of us is to go out to preach to them twice a month. They seem eager to learn, so the Lord is smiling upon us."

Constancy moved to the door and called sharply for

Lehua. "Quick, child, fetch a bucket of water for Mr. Williams. Put it in the bedroom. Now, Jonathan,"—and she turned him towards the house—"go and wash, and bathe your feet carefully—they will seem less tired. You will just have time before I take up the dinner. There are clean clothes laid out on the bed for you, and your other boots are on the shelf."

Jonathan smiled a little. "Truly, Constancy, you give orders like a general. I will be glad to obey, though. I could scarcely conduct the singing school with this much dust upon my person." He limped slightly as he went toward the house.

"Mrs. Loomis is delivered of a fine son!" called his wife to his retreating figure. He paused and turned his head over his shoulder.

"Praise God for that!" he said warmly and went on.

Constancy busied herself with dinner, a slight frown puckering her brow. She had forgotten the singing school. She paused, spoon in air. If she were to say she felt ill they would excuse her from attendance. No! Her chin shot upward. Mrs. Bingham would never miss a church service or a meeting of the singing school, even if she were on her deathbed. Constancy would endure the singing school if it killed her. "What Mrs. Bingham can do, I can do," she thought stubbornly. She looked at the biscuits; they were just golden brown on top. The beans were done. She called to Lehua and her helpmate, a tall twelve-year-old whose ten-syllable name had been discarded in favor of the more pronounceable Martha. They carried the food in to the table.

Work as hard as she might, thought Constancy, no one was going to see her sit down at a table looking like a zany. She hurried into the bedroom, quickly washed her face and hands, shook out her hair, gave it a few hard brushes and knotted it up again. She looked in the small mirror set above the washstand. Anyway, her hair still shone in ripples if her skin had turned sallow, she thought defiantly. And who could live in this country and keep a milk-white skin? She turned from the mirror and went into the next room.

Mr. Loomis appeared with plates and a tray. Constancy served the two plates, poured out cups of tea, heaped biscuits upon another plate, and put jam in a saucer. She loaded the young man with the well-filled dishes until he protested. He edged nervously away toward his home, uttering thanks in spasmodic jerks, timed to the rhythm of his steps, afraid to lift his eyes from the tray. The missionaries as well as the orphans laughed at his efforts before they were obliged to sober down to the point where Mr. Bingham could properly begin his lengthy and devoutly spoken grace.

Constancy sat pushing her food about her plate, now and then forcing herself to chew and swallow a mouthful. All color had drained from her face. Even her lips were white. The heat, the lack of sleep, the constant activity of the day beat upon her will. But she sat upright, giving her attention to her guests and to the wants of the orphans. Later she superintended the clearing of the table and the disposal of the food that remained uneaten, and then marshaled her orphans toward the large room in the Bingham house that served both as schoolroom and meeting house. If she narrowly saved herself from napping thrice during the hour's singing, and twice failed to see an orphan scratching in such places as the missionaries had deemed improper for scratching, no one was the wiser. The missionaries were much more concerned with watching the derelictions of the governor of Oahu who, having tippled too freely before coming, was inclined to be boisterous during the first part of the evening and insisted upon sleeping audibly during the latter half.

At nine o'clock Constancy shooed her charges homeward. Five of them stopped at the Loomises' to retire to their mats; five accompanied Constancy to her house and prepared themselves for the night (here, too, passed on mats spread out in the large room) with as little noise as could be expected. Jonathan, who had waited to greet the dignitaries who had attended the singing school, was just a little aggrieved to find Constancy sunk in so deep a slumber that she failed to wake up even when he stumbled over a chair in the darkness.

2

On the 26th of December, Jonathan rose in the dark to find Constancy moving about the dim room. She moved heavily, slowly. Her child might be born at any time now. Jonathan paused in his dressing to look at her for a few seconds as she brought in a candle from the next room, shielding the flame with her hand, her face momentarily lighted in the candle flare. Her face was calm, stern, strong.

"She is a good woman," thought Jonathan, "a pious woman. The willfulness that showed in her once or twice during the voyage has gone. She is a brave woman." And he reproached himself for feeling squeamish in his vitals at the thought of the pain that hung over Constancy. Dr. Holman had seen fit to describe vividly the agonies of childbirth to Jonathan shortly after the accouchement of Mrs. Bingham. Jonathan remembered, too, the gray drawn face of Hiram Bingham after Mrs. Bingham's long difficult labor was done, that ordeal which the frailest of the missionary wives bore without outcry. Jonathan's lips moved involuntarily: "Lord, mercifully grant that Constancy may not suffer so; spare her, for though she is young she has served Thee well."

He finished his dressing and followed Constancy to the cooking house. Mrs. Chamberlain and Mrs. Thurston, the latter lately arrived from Lahaina, were busy with the porridge and coffee.

"There isn't a thing you need do, Sister Williams," scolded Mrs. Chamberlain. "Breakfast is all ready to take up, and you shouldn't be on your feet any more than you can help. If Brother Williams'll hold the pot while I fill it up with coffee, and if you'll send out Martha and Lehua for the porridge, we'll have your breakfast on your table in a minute."

"Thank you—but I fear you pamper me more than is good for me. . . . Mrs. Thurston, did your house leak in the rain last night?"

"A little—but not over the bed." Mrs. Thurston was stirring the porridge. "It was providential that Captain Allen gave us glass to put in the window on the windward side, or we should have been badly off."

Jonathan frowned. "I shall seek an audience with the governor today and try to persuade him that we must be allowed to set up our frame house. Mrs. Bingham has never properly rallied from her confinement, nor is she likely to, so long as the walls and mats in her house cannot dry out thoroughly."

Constancy gripped the door frame. After a moment she turned toward the house. "Since you are so kind as to perform my work for me, Mrs. Chamberlain, I shall go and look after the children."

Mrs. Chamberlain narrowed her eyes and looked after Constancy. "I shouldn't be surprised if you'd have a baby in the house in the next twenty-four hours, Brother Williams," she said decidedly.

Jonathan nearly dropped the coffee pot. His heart seemed to fall into his stomach and lie there, an unbearably heavy weight. "You *really* think so?" he queried weakly. "What—what shall I do about it?"

"Nothing!" Mrs. Chamberlain turned away to hide a grim smile. "She'll be glad enough to get it over. You go about your work and pray and leave her to the doctor and me."

Jonathan's voice was still shaky as he found himself saying, "I don't want her to keep at her work till she drops— the way Sister Bingham did. I want her to take more care of herself."

"Well," briskly from Mrs. Chamberlain, "don't go crossing bridges till you come to 'em. You go and take this coffee in now; you all have to eat, whatever happens, and it may not be today for her after all."

Jonathan strengthened his grasp on the handle of the coffee pot and somewhat disconsolately made his way toward the house. Constancy was seated at the table, issuing commands to the five orphans who went in leisurely fashion about the business of filling the pitcher with goat milk and laying the table.

Jonathan asked a deliberate and thoughtful blessing upon the affairs of the day, beseeching the Lord to give each soul the strength to submit itself to the divine will, to endure the trials that might beset each path with becoming meekness, to use each hardship as spiritual food to sustain grace. He read a short passage from the Bible, and then, casting an eye at the rapidly cooling porridge, bade the children be seated and, seating himself, carved a blessing upon the food. With the "Amen," each child grabbed up her spoon and made a ravening onslaught upon her porridge.

Jonathan ate in silence and then rose from the table. "If

you require my presence, Mrs. Williams," he addressed
Constancy formally, since most of the orphans had picked
up a good deal of English, "I shall be in Brother Bingham's
study for an hour or more, going over certain matters
with him and Brother Thurston. I shall stop in to see how
you are doing before continuing to call on the governor."

He took his hat from the top of the cupboard and made
off toward the Bingham house at the far end of the line
of mission houses. Constancy had merely nodded at his
statement; she had not spoken, but the firmly set mouth
had relaxed into a smile. It occurred to him as he tramped
over the wet earth that it was pleasant to have Constancy
smile, and that she did it less frequently than she had in
the first few months of their marriage.

Mr. Thurston and Mr. Bingham were in the large
schoolroom, where Mrs. Bingham sat in a stiff-backed
rocking chair facing a group of perhaps forty children
and adults who made up the mission school. The children
of Don Marin were here, the hybrid children of foreigners
who had settled in Honolulu and taken native wives, but
the majority were grown natives, many of them parents
of pupils in the same room. Beside Mrs. Bingham's chair
was a rude cradle in which lay the month-old Lydia Bingham. The baby stared blankly up at the roof, soothed to
quiet by the gentle jogging of the cradle by a little native
girl. Mrs. Bingham, thin to begin with, was cadaverous in
her appearance since the birth of little Lydia. Her skin
gleamed yellowish white and stretched painfully over her
bones; there were hollows as dark as bruises about her eyes.
She coughed intermittently, a dry, hacking little cough,
and looked apologetic whenever she did it.

The pupils were supplied with battered copies of Webster's spelling book, the shorter catechism, a few New
Testaments, and stray sheets printed in Hawaiian, labored

translations of various psalms, proverbs, and parables. These last came from the printing press which had been set up since August. The pupils kept up a mumbled drone as they studied. One by one, old and young came up to stand beside Mrs. Bingham and read aloud the passage just studied.

The men stood behind Mrs. Bingham's chair for a few moments, watching the performance with satisfaction, and then withdrew to the second room of the house. This room served both as bedroom and study.

"You have done a good work here," said Mr. Thurston slowly. "It is gratifying to see the enthusiasm of the grown natives for learning. I cannot but feel dispirited at the thought of how little we accomplished at Kailua."

Mr. Bingham regarded him with somber compassion. "It has been a grievous disappointment that our plans have come to naught on Hawaii . . . but none may do aught but praise your own and Mrs. Thurston's efforts. We could not predict the defalcation of the Holmans, nor the degeneration of William Kanui into drunkenness and unholy behavior, nor the removal of the court from that island. But with the king established on this island, there will be work for all of us here, and when time has passed, it may be possible to reëstablish the station at Kailua."

Mr. Thurston strummed absent-mindedly on the table. "You may not regard it as an unqualified blessing to have the king and his followers here. While Kamamalu and Keopuolani and several of the women are tractable and truly interested in attaining salvation, Liholiho is wedded to his lusts—to pleasure in any guise—and Kaahumanu distrusts the missionaries. Were the little prince to rise to power, our difficulties would be cut in half, for he is an affectionate lad—quick to learn, studious, and grateful to Mrs. Thurston, who was his teacher. He has shown intelligence and judgment in his reception of the Scriptures, and the seed of faith is already sown in his bosom."

Jonathan sighed. "The governor, here, is more disposed to lusts of the flesh than to the cultivation of the spirit," he said. "He attends meeting—unless there is dancing to distract him—but he frequently comes staggering and roistering with spirits. He sets a dreadful example for the humble who come to be enlightened."

The two older men shook their heads gloomily, and Jonathan went on. "The traders cheat him flagrantly, and he will take no word of advice—and that although he admits that when he drinks with them he overpays them in sandalwood for whatever he purchases. They are children in foolishness and hardened sinners in other ways—and yet there is true piety in many a brown breast in Mrs. Bingham's school and evidence of earnest determination to put off heathen ways."

Mr. Bingham fumbled among the papers in a drawer of the table and drew forth a long sheet covered with unformed writing. "It is true that we have much to discourage us in these islands," he granted, "but on the other hand we may rejoice in such a response as this from Kaumualii on Kauai. Brother Thurston, this is the first letter this heathen king ever wrote. It came shortly after the Whitneys and Ruggleses began their efforts on Kauai."

He passed the long sheet to Mr. Thurston, who scanned the quaint combination of English and the first attempts at spelling Hawaiian names:

Atooi, August 1820.

DEAR FRIEND

I feel glad that you good people come to my Island to do good for me. I thank you. I love them. I take good care of them. I give them eat, drink, and land to work on. I

*thank all American folks—they give my son learning—
he know how read, write, all American books. I feel glad
he come home—he be long time in America. I think dead
but some man speak no. I very glad you good people come.
I love them. I do them good. I hope you do good Owhyhee, Owahoo, and all the Islands.*

Except this from your friend

TAMOREE

Mr. Thurston laughed. "That's very encouraging. His
heart's in the right place, if some of the difficulties of our
language are too much for him. Brother Whitney wrote
to me that the king and the queen come to school regularly and work side by side with the humble. They are
truly diligent in their pursuit of learning. But," and he
sighed, "for one such willing convert, there are a hundred
slothful or suspicious."

Mr. Bingham leaned forward, his eyes smoldering. "One
great task that is plainly assigned us is to wean these people from the dance. That wretched practice is a formidable enemy to our purpose. In July there were days given
over to it—with several hundred of the youth of the island
displaying themselves in unashamed nakedness—pander-
ing to the lowest instincts of the watchers. It is lascivious,
something that menaces the morality of the onlookers no
less than it debases the performers."

Mr. Thurston made a slight gesture of helplessness.
"What can we do—as yet? Have you attempted to reason
with the chiefs about it?"

Mr. Bingham permitted himself a grim smile. "Yes, and
received a palpable thrust. Brother Williams and I expressed our desire to the governor that the people might
shortly learn better things than *hulas* and the barbarous
native songs. That was on the occasion of these July

dances. And the governor, with recognizable supercilious-
ness, expressed his desire that we should soon learn the native tongue more perfectly and so be able to teach them
what they need to know."

"There was, of course, some justice in his criticism
then," broke in Jonathan. "The tongue presented great
difficulties, and we were forced to give all sermons through
interpreters. At first even the teaching in Mrs. Bingham's
school had to be accomplished through an interpreter, but
that remark of Boki's spurred us on, and we have been able
to dispense with interpreters. Every sermon is now
preached in Hawaiian, and Mrs. Bingham and Mrs.
Loomis and Mrs. Williams are able to deal with the pupils
and the orphans directly. But, for all that, when a chieftain desires the *hula* to be performed, nothing is allowed
to interfere with the carrying out of his wishes, even if he
demands the services of the pupils during school hours."

Jonathan rose to his feet and changed the subject with
some abruptness. For some moments he had been unable
to get Constancy out of his head. "I would suggest that
we proceed to Boki's house and petition him to be allowed
to set up our house. With two nursing mothers in our
midst, and with Mrs. Williams about to give birth, it may
well prove disastrous to continue living in floorless, flimsy
grass houses which never dry out between rains. These
benighted souls may, after all, be appealed to through their
sympathies. Once these are enlisted, they are kindly."

Mr. Bingham nodded and rose. "It is well that we should
make the effort. Also, the governor may be interested in
seeing Brother Thurston." He reached for his hat, and the
three men started down the yard toward the fortress
which enclosed the homes of royalty on Oahu. Jonathan
stopped as they were about to pass his house.

"If you will pardon a moment's delay, I should feel happier to look in upon my wife, whose condition as you know is uncertain."

He left them talking before his house. As he entered the door, Constancy sat at the head of the table conducting the sewing period of the five orphans capable of managing a needle. A three-year-old little boy, a newcomer whose parents had died of pneumonia within the last month, sat playing with some spools on the mat at Constancy's feet. Jonathan addressed her with the formality he always preserved in company.

"We are going now to call on the governor, Mrs. Williams," he said stiffly, but his eyes searched her face imploringly. She returned his gaze unfalteringly, but her hands gripped the edge of the table until her knuckles showed white through the tanned skin. "Tell Liliha," she said a little breathlessly after a second, "that I am unable to sew on her red satin dress at present—that if she is in haste to wear it, I will turn it over to Mrs. Thurston and Mrs. Chamberlain to be finished. Otherwise, I shall be glad to finish it—after the child is here and I am about again."

"Constancy!" The rigidity of her features drove Jonathan to forgetfulness of the orphans. "Do you feel well? Would you rather I stayed with you?"

She relaxed her hold on the table, and her face softened. "There is naught wrong with me, Jonathan. You know I am subject to queer aches and pains these days. You must go with Brother Bingham and Brother Thurston. It is to our advantage that you secure permission to erect the house."

Jonathan still looked questioning, but he nodded finally and withdrew. The three men proceeded toward the fortress, nodded gravely to the guard at the gate in the thick walls, and advanced to the doorway of Boki's house. After telling them to seat themselves, the governor ignored them. He sat on a pile of mats and was engrossed in a game of cards with one of his attendants. Resignedly the missionaries sat upon the uncomfortable chairs that seemed so out of place in a native hut, and awaited Boki's pleasure.

Liliha, Boki's favorite wife, lay upon a pile of mats close to her lord, fondling a small white pig. She raised herself on one elbow and regarded Jonathan disapprovingly. "Where," she demanded, "is my new dress? Two weeks now has your woman been in making it!"

Jonathan experienced a rush of anger; he was suddenly outraged at the selfishness of Liliha and other royal ladies in demanding dress after dress from the overworked missionary women. "Mrs. Williams has much work to do," he informed the indolent Liliha. "She cannot lie about all day petting hogs, and she is ill. Her child may be born before another day. She sent word to you that she is unable to sew upon your dress until she is well again. If you are in haste to wear it, she will give it to Mrs. Thurston and Mrs. Chamberlain to finish."

Liliha toyed with the pig's tail for a second before answering. Then she smiled graciously. "I will wait. Your woman sews better than the others. I am sorry for her. Take to her my love and say that Liliha will come to visit the child at once when it is here."

Jonathan's face grew kind. In spite of her selfishness and vanity, the woman had excellent qualities, he decided. Boki finished his game of cards the victor. He emitted a roar of laughter and gave his opponent a clap on the shoulder that would have felled a lesser man. The defeated player scratched his head and reluctantly pulled a pouch from his *malo* and extracted ten Spanish dollars. Making a wry face, he presented the money to the governor. The brethren looked away, their mouths thin slits of disapproval. Boki snatched up a bottle of rum and took a mighty draft. He was ready to grant the missionaries an audience.

The brethren inquired for his health. He inquired for theirs and for the health of their *wahines*. Their *wahines* were not well, Mr. Bingham explained sorrowfully. They were not accustomed to live on the ground. Grass houses were well enough in dry weather, but with the rainy season come, the damp made them ill. Ill, they could not work so hard to teach the natives, they could not ply the needle so industriously to make beautiful dresses for the queens. They might die. They needed a house such as they had lived in in America, a house with wooden walls and roof and a wood floor. The mission board had sent the frame for such a house; would the governor allow the missionaries to build a proper house and so safeguard the lives of their ladies?

The governor scratched his head and then shook it and then took two more gulps of rum. Regretfully he explained that Kamehameha had never allowed foreigners to build a house on the islands except for himself. Kamehameha's son was coming to Honolulu and would be king over all. It would not be possible to build a house without Liholiho's consent. They must ask Liholiho when he arrived from Maui and abide by his decision. He was sorry for the *wahines*, but he could not help them. The visitors must stay and eat with him, and he would hear of the king and the news from Kailua and Lahaina from Mr. Thurston.

The missionaries bowed to his words about the house and accepted his invitation to dinner. No meal at the mission establishment was ever held back. If a member of the family were not on hand at seven in the morning, at twelve noon, and at six at night, it was taken for granted that he was eating elsewhere.

They had finished a heavy meal and were about to take their leave when a shadow fell across the doorway of the eating house of the governor. "Mr. Williams," the frigid tones that Mrs. Holman had adopted for use with the brethren since they had so openly frowned upon her cut across Jonathan's well-fed complacency, stinging him to sentience, "Dr. Holman was summoned to wait upon your wife an hour ago, and I was dispatched to find you. If you are finished with your meal it would be well for you to attend Mrs. Williams."

Jonathan flinched at the scorn in Mrs. Holman's eyes and was then indignant. How dared she reprove him as if he had run away to have a good time when Constancy needed him? But the thought of Constancy in the throes of childbirth wrenched a groan from him. "I will make haste," he muttered, and then stiffly and belatedly, as he grabbed up his hat and strode out of the door regardless of the ceremony due the governor, "Thank you for summoning me, Mrs. Holman."

She hurried to keep up with him, her gaze softening as she perceived his agitation. "She will not be delivered for some hours yet, but she will be more content to know you are there," she said more kindly.

Jonathan grasped her arm and shook it unthinkingly: "Is she suffering greatly? Is it going hard with her?"

Lucia Holman shook her head gently. "It is always hard —but so far she makes no outcry. She admits now that she has been in labor since early morning."

A hollow groan escaped Jonathan. "I should not have left her!" he said wildly. "But she assured me that she was well. . . . Forgive me, Mrs. Holman. I must hurry," and he went bounding down the rocky footpath that led from the fort to the mission, his coat tails writhing behind him as he ran.

He rushed through the main room without seeing Mrs. Loomis with her baby and Mrs. Thurston, and into the bedroom. There he stood gasping for breath beside the bed. Constancy's eyes were closed, and her face was like a mask, he thought, and then was conscious of his heart sinking heavily again to the pit of his stomach as he observed a curious convulsive motion beneath the covers. The motion subsided, and Constancy opened her eyes to stare dazedly into his face.

"I stayed up till dinner was over and the dishes done," she muttered. She blinked hard, and her eyes were suddenly troubled beneath Jonathan's stricken gaze. "Jonathan, go into the next room," she said firmly. "Dr. Holman and Mrs. Chamberlain will take good care of me. I am happy knowing you are here in the house." Seeing his expression, she added gently, "It will distress me to see you worried. If it becomes too bad for me to bear, I will call you. Now *go!*" for she felt another pain begin to worry at her loins.

"Yes, go!" urged Dr. Holman, offering Constancy his hand, which she grasped violently. Jonathan took one more look at the death-mask face now beaded with perspiration, and, with a small moan, stumbled from the room, dimly conscious that Mrs. Chamberlain propelled him and patted his shoulder, saying, "There, there—it'll be over before you know it. Keep up your courage."

He walked blindly past the two women and sat down on a bench, his head in his hands, straining his ears in horror of the scream he expected to tear at his nerves. Mrs. Loomis was jogging her baby on her knees. "Poor thing," she was saying compassionately, "she's so young a creature, too—five years younger than I, but I forget it often because she's so quiet and sure in her ways—far beyond her years."

Mrs. Thurston agreed. "It is God's grace in her—she is one of the true anointed. . . . And to think some of us doubted that she could bear the trials of the life. When we know now how one that is older and should be steadfast has weakened——" she articulated severely and then broke off abruptly as Mrs. Holman came into the room.

Mrs. Holman's wide eyebrows raised a little. She was accustomed to hearing a conversation trail away upon her entrance to a room. "Is there aught I can do?" she asked courteously. Mrs. Chamberlain thrust her head in from the bedroom. "See that there's plenty of water on to boil," she ordered and vanished.

Again Jonathan buried his head in his hands. Still the scream he was expecting failed to come. They were right: Constancy was but a child in years. Had he done wrong to marry her and bring her to a life of hardship where she had not even a good roof over her head or a substantial floor beneath her? He clutched at his thick white hair. "Lord, Lord," he prayed in his innermost soul, "take her not unto Thyself, for she is needed here. She is good and has Thy mission more deeply in her heart than I dreamed possible. Not even Sister Bingham has labored more zealously than she. Thou knowest, Lord, that I did not consider foremost her qualifications for the field. I looked upon her with desire because she is fair, and before she acknowledged Thee before the brethren. Visit not my sins upon her . . . for Thou knowest she is a better woman than I am a man."

A touch on his shoulder startled him. He looked up to see Dr. Holman standing over him with a tumbler half full of a dark liquid with a pungent smell. "Drink this," ordered the doctor brusquely. "You can't go to pieces this way. Why, your wife's bearing up better than you are!"

Jonathan swallowed the whiskey and blinked hard. The doctor regarded him quizzically. Jonathan remembered uneasily the difference in his own bearing on the last occasion when he had met the doctor. Then Jonathan with Brothers Thurston and Bingham had formed a committee to offer verbal chastisement to the doctor for his hardihood in transferring from Hawaii to Maui to placate his wife and against the orders of the brethren, and for his singular lack of all signs of repentance—a lack which allowed him to say boldly that he counted it no sin that he had seen fit to cherish his wife, and that the brethren might find belatedly that it would have been well had they thought at least as much of their wives' happiness as they did of putting drawers on a lot of natives who were quite happy without them.

The doctor spoke again: "You are doing her no good sitting here reproaching yourself for not considering her more. Go and build the fire for Mrs. Holman and carry in a kettle of water. My wife is nearing her own time and should not overtax her strength." He turned on his heel and went into the bedroom.

Jonathan dazedly passed a hand over his eyes as he walked heavily out of the house. The largest kettle on the stove was sending forth little clouds of steam. He silently put out his hand to grasp its iron handle and instantly dropped it with an involuntary cry of pain. Mrs. Holman averted her face to hide a smile, but she handed him a pad and asked solicitously after his hand. He mumbled that it was nothing and with the help of the calico pad made off with the kettle.

He lost track of time as he sat on the bench between demands for hot water. He was mutely indignant when

Mrs. Loomis took her baby and went home, and when Mrs. Thurston set about preparing supper just as if nothing extraordinary were taking place. In his heart he charged Mrs. Thurston with cruel indifference, and loathed her when she and her husband, just arrived on the scene, sat down to eat in apparent tranquillity. He stiffly refused to join them, though they urged him that it was his duty to eat. Mrs. Chamberlain bustled out, her hair straggling, her face flushed and moist, and swallowed a cup of coffee and hurriedly ate some ham and fried sweet potatoes. She stopped to address Jonathan before returning to the next room: "You'd be much more sensible to eat something, Brother Williams. You aren't helping Sister Williams any by sitting there looking like a death's-head and denying yourself food. If you don't go straight over to that table and eat your supper, I shall walk right in and tell your poor suffering wife that you're more trouble than she is, and then she'll have that to worry over."

Jonathan sprang to his feet. "Don't you do it, Mrs. Chamberlain," he gasped, and then rather sulkily, "I shall endeavor to eat a few mouthfuls."

Mrs. Chamberlain nodded cheerily. "That's a good man," she said approvingly and hurried into the bedroom.

Dr. Holman came out for a hasty meal. He ate quickly and in complete silence, but as he rose from the table he spoke to Jonathan: "It will be over shortly now, Mr. Williams." He added kindly: "A first child nearly always takes a long time, but Mrs. Williams has displayed admirable courage."

Mrs. Thurston and Mrs. Holman went about the task of clearing away and washing the dishes. Time dragged heavily on for Jonathan. Still he awaited the cry that did not come, his nerves tense to the point of agony. He sat on the bench gripping its rough edges with his hands. Suddenly a strange animal began a curious noise that sounded to Jonathan like "Ooh-la-ah!" on a rising scale. The noise irritated him; he wished it would stop. But Mrs. Loomis, who had resumed her seat near him, said, "Bless her heart! I know how glad she feels to hear that cry!"

It dawned upon his confused mind that his child was born. He leaped to his feet and ran shakily into the bedroom to stop aghast at the blood-soaked sheets and bedding that Mrs. Chamberlain was stripping from the bed. His knees wabbled, and his heart clamored that Constancy must be dead; but Constancy's voice reassured him:

"For goodness' sake, Jonathan, go outside till they get me fixed up."

He slunk out to stamp up and down the larger room till Dr. Holman summoned him. Mrs. Chamberlain sat washing the blindly protesting baby, making little clucking noises to it, but Jonathan ignored them. He rushed to the bed and flopped to his knees beside it. "Oh, Constancy!" was all he found to say, but Constancy smiled wanly and stretched out her hand to him.

"Your courage was God-given, Constancy," he said; but Constancy's green eyes stared enigmatically at the coverlet. She knew that the origin of her courage was in her sinful pride, born of her desire to equal Mrs. Bingham.

"See, Jonathan," she said as Mrs. Chamberlain placed the baby beside her. They both bent their heads to study the small bundle: the tiny head upon which the down lay soft and dark as a shadow, the button nose, the puckered-up brow and mouth. Constancy raised serious eyes to Jonathan's face. "I should like to call him Samuel, Jonathan."

Jonathan smiled lovingly upon his first-born. "The Infant Samuel," he murmured. "Well named!"

Constancy said nothing, thinking of a very different

Samuel who had written three poems more beautiful than anything Constancy had ever read.

3
(FROM THE JOURNAL OF CONSTANCY WILLIAMS)

Sabbath, January 21, 1821. At services this morning the painful matter of the Holmans was dealt with by the brethren. A sorry thing, or so it seems to me, and one that the brethren may regret when time has healed their tempers. A letter of excision to Dr. Holman was read. They were content to suspend Mrs. Holman, pointing out in great detail all her faults—vanity, weakness of will, selfishness, stubborn pride, etc., the while Dr. Holman sat, his mouth as compressed as Brother Bingham's, his arms folded tight across his chest and a look upon his face that suggested to me that he would fain have pummeled the holy brethren, nor would I have blamed him. Mrs. Holman stared straight into the faces of her accusers and did not change her expression except for a flashing of her eyes when they listed the crimes for which the doctor is excommunicated: walking disorderly, slander, railing, and covetousness.

How those women who have been attended in childbirth by the good doctor could sit looking down their noses at such a time! Mayhap when their next babes are born with no kind doctor to encourage them through the ordeal, they will remember their hardness now. I did shake both of them by the hand after services, thereby receiving some sharp and censorious looks from the other members of the Family. The doctor grasped and shook my hand so heartily that it tingled for some moments, while Mrs. Holman whispered that I had best say naught lest she weep in the presence of her enemies.

The rains continue, and I worry lest a cold fasten itself upon my Samuel's chest. He is indeed a sweet babe and lies in the cradle we procured from Captain Martin, cooing and thrusting with his small fists. His eyes, which first appeared to be blue, are changing to a color nearer green, but he is to have dark hair such as Jonathan had before the fever turned it white. At the next communion the three babes born to our Family will be baptized. They are thriving well so that there is not need to hasten.

Mrs. Loomis told me in confidence that she feared she was imperiling her soul by loving her babe overmuch, and asked me did I never feel guilty of loving my Samuel more than it is proper to love a mortal born to sin—even with that love which is Jehovah's due. But with some ambiguity I did say that my feeling for God was one thing and my feeling for Samuel so different that there was no danger of the one melting into the other. She, poor innocent, sighed and called me a strong soul.

February 5, 1821. The king, his queens, and a few lesser chieftains, with all their retinue, arrived early yesterday morning from Lahaina. There was a deafening uproar of cannon that all but shook us from our beds. They came on the barge *Cleopatra* which the king purchased on credit from Captain Suter, and for which the captain will exact many a load of sandalwood. The men were exceedingly drunken, and when the brethren went to pay their respects, Liholiho was in a stupor; but Kamamalu, evidently feeling that he must make some sign of friendliness to his visitors, lifted up his lifeless hand and presented it to each guest in turn. Today, somewhat recovered, the royal party visited our establishment. The king and some of the queens showed great delight at the feather beds, and jumped upon them, bouncing merrily in the air. They pronounced our crudely made furniture very good, and Liholiho, after hearing the pupils of the school recite, expressed some sorrow that he had not been more diligent in learning to read. In audience with the king today, the brethren entreated permission to set up our frame house and received a negative answer until Kamamalu, out of pity for the discomforts we endure or mayhap out of gratitude for all the dressmaking she has had free, pleaded with the king. Then he said reluctantly, "Do it, but when you go away take everything with you." We are much relieved.

February 26, 1821. An heir was born to Kalanimoku and Likelike during the night. We were apprised of the fact when cannons were fired, as we later were told, directly outside the mother's door. I trust the poor babe will not be permanently deafened by such a rude reception. The criers are rushing about collecting dogs and pigs for a *luau*, and the ceaseless dancing continues. They still pay tribute to the *akuah* or god of the dance despite all the objections of the brethren. The governor, the king, and anyone appealed to make the same response: "It is only in play," and the brethren are in perpetual chagrin. Today Jonathan was even more outraged because, instead of laying flowers or leaves before it, the master of the dance took a cudgel and beat it severely; he told Jonathan that he considered it responsible for the rain that threatened to spoil the dance.

March 10, 1821. The town is gone mad with an orgy of mourning for Likelike. She died some days ago, not long after her babe, who survived the cannon salute by only twenty-four hours. The mother suffered a high fever after the death of the child, for which she was treated by repeated drenchings in a none too clean pond. She died raving in great pain. It was piteous beyond my power to describe. The Family is gloomy and shocked at the extravagance of the commotion raised at her death. Kalanimoku, her husband, was prostrated, and Boki, who was once her husband, led the mourners. It seems that Kalanimoku's former wife eloped with another for a time, and he was so angry that he burned down most of the village of Honolulu. Although he recovered his wife in time, she died shortly after the reconciliation. He promptly took Likelike away from Boki, and Boki in turn took Liholiho's wife away from him, to replace Likelike. It seems an odd custom, this informal seizure of another's wife. It is undoubtedly a judgment upon Kalanimoku that both wife and child should now be stricken down, but I am amazed at the ruthlessness of Mr. Bingham in rubbing it in at this time. To honor the dead, many of the people cut off their side hair, making bare spots above each ear. Some burn their faces with blazing bark so that they will bear scars always, and still others knock out their own teeth. After the first day or two, the mourners waxed drunken and hilarious. It is not a pleasant sight.

March 21, 1821. We have been busy about the third quarterly examinations in our school. The thirty pupils now in attendance have progressed well in their ability to read from the New Testament, to spell from Webster's book, and to read from the Decalogue. They answered questions in Watt's First Catechism glibly, and the premium for special performance was a Bible. Several officers from visiting whaling vessels as well as a number of the chieftains attended. All were impressed and generous. We received donations of two barrels of whale oil, twenty pounds of soap, a barrel of molasses, and three bolts of calico, besides a gift of fifty dollars from Captain Allen.

Now we are having a ten-day vacation from the school, and Jonathan with Mr. Bingham and Mr. Thurston are on an expedition with the boys of the school across the Pali to carry the Word to the ignorant savages beyond the mountains. I must worry over Jonathan's safety till I see him again, for his mind is ever on eternity, and when brooding he forgets the material world altogether, so that I see him in my mind missing his footing on the perilous descent from the mountain.

I am thankful for a little leisure now, and am at liberty to attend and play with Samuel to my heart's content. He is a merry babe, and I am reluctant for the time to come when he must be made aware of the precariousness of mortal life. A little daughter has been born to the Holmans. I went to see Mrs. Holman, and she told me privately that if any more of the brethren or brethrenesses, as she is wont to call the sisters, come to pray over her or exhort her to repentance, she will scream aloud. She says quite cheerfully that if she must go to hell, she prefers to go in peace, and that she has decided that there must be some very pleasant people in hell. She amazes me; she is either courageous beyond belief or else so benighted that she cannot grasp the reality of hell. But I do enjoy being with her.

October 1. The Holmans have left to return to America after going around the world with Captain Porter. The Family is not a little displeased that they left in such excellent spirits. The sea captains and a white settler on Maui, a man of substance, contributed largely to their comfort with both money and luxuries. They made much of Mrs. Holman and the fact that she will be the first woman to sail around the world. I think she enjoyed putting on a few airs for the benefit of the Family. Her eyes twinkled whenever she raised them at the last meeting, and she was wont to boast that when the vessel arrived at Macao, where the Holmans will await the ship's return from Canton, she has the privilege of staying wheresoever she will and of making any purchases she sees fit with no cost to herself or the doctor. There is much talk among the members of our Family about how insensible she is to the injury she has done and continues to do the cause of Christ.

December 26, 1821. Samuel is one year old this evening. He has already taken his first steps alone. Perhaps I am prejudiced in his favor, but truly he appears to me more beautiful than any of the other babes. His black hair curls so softly, and his smile is so roguish, his lashes so long and curling, and his flesh so plumply firm and dimpled. I am worried secretly lest I am forced to neglect him in carrying out the work of the mission, and in my heart I know well that his welfare is more important than that of all the community beside . . . save Jonathan. I shall be busier yet in March when my new baby shall be born. Mrs. Loomis is already the mother of two. Little Amanda was born three days ago. She said the pains were much easier to bear this time and over with much sooner. It is well. Mrs. Bingham will be having her second babe soon. Mrs. Thurston has never recovered from her first confinement, and is troubled by a racking cough. She seems a little better now, and her husband pursues diligently the treatment recommended by her doctor in the United States. For my own part I regret that Dr. Holman is across the world from us.

The Family is much elated that Kaahumanu has professed her love of Christ. Shortly after she married this last time she was ill unto death and is only now recovered. Mrs. Bingham cared for her most tenderly and worked with her together with Mr. Bingham. Kaahumanu is a

great power, and the lot of the missionaries should be
easier with her ranged on their side. The king continues
unregenerate.

March 30, 1822. Our second child was born on March
21. She weighed eight and one half pounds at birth and we
have named her Miriam for Jonathan's mother. Her hair
is palest gold, and her eyes so far are blue. Samuel is greatly
interested and calls her "Beebee." She seems well and
strong, but I am glad nevertheless to be in a house once
more and not be obliged to worry lest she catch cold from
a damp earthen floor.

A box of baby clothes arrived from my mother addressed to me, but they were taken in with the mission
supplies and, since we are regarded as one Family, sharing
all things in common, the baby clothes were distributed
with a fine impartiality between the seven families, so that
I had only four diapers, one dress, and one pair of knitted
boots from the box. There are drawbacks to a policy of
share and share alike.

September 1, 1822. Jonathan gives much time attempt-
ing to teach little Samuel the Lord's Prayer, but the child
will not be serious. He chuckles and squeals, to Jonathan's
great distress. Jonathan thinks he should be punished for
disorder in church, but I will not be severe with a babe
of twenty-one months. Truly it is a trial to carry the baby
in my arms and keep one eye always on young Samuel
beside me in meeting—lest he rap some worthy Christian
over the skull with the spools I give him to play with, or
chatter to himself in the midst of the sermon.

The Family feels greatly encouraged at a recent letter—
her first, I believe, as she has only now learned to read and
write—from Kaahumanu from the other island, where she
has been zealous in burning idols and advising the people

to learn quickly from the "long necks," as she has always called the missionary women because of the type of bonnet they wear. This is her letter, which she wrote to Kamamalu from Waimea on Kauai:

"This is my communication to you: tell the *puu A-i o-e-o-e* [by which she means posse of long necks] to send some more books down here. Many are the people few are the books. I want 800 Hawaiian books to be sent hither. We are much pleased to learn the *palapala*. By and by perhaps we shall be wise. Give my love to Mr. and Mrs. Bingham, and the whole company of long necks."

We have traveled a long way in her good graces since the time when she would extend no more than her little finger to us in greeting. Kaahumanu has great power among the people here, and she has a much stronger character than the king. Since her interest in our cause is so evident now, we hope that she may become worthy of baptism and reception into the Church before much longer.

It has eased the lot of our men to have the English missionary, Mr. Ellis, and his assistants here. The Tahitian language is similar to the Hawaiian, and the experience of these men in the Society Islands has made them invaluable. Mr. Ellis has sent for his family and will remain with us in this field for a year. After four months with us he preaches more eloquently in the native tongue than do any of our ministers. The chiefs like him, and it has been by special invitation from Kaumualii that he remains with us.

February 18, 1823. We toil ceaselessly; our labors grow heavier with the passing of time, and I rarely find a moment to call my own. Mrs. Loomis' health was breaking with the strain of cooking for the entire Family in the house and our frequent guests, so that now each woman cooks for her own family. To accomplish what must be accomplished each day, we must rise at half after four in the morning, that the children be fed and bathed, that the house be put to order, prayers held, and a hundred things done before school begins. I who used to be vain of my looks scarce have time to look in the glass, and my skin is burned a deep tan like leather. I am again with child. This one will be born in the summer, July or August. I feel ailing much of the time. Little Miriam has taken her first steps and is a pretty babe. Sammie thinks so, too, and says "pretty, pretty," most admiringly to his little sister. Sammie still refuses to learn the Lord's Prayer, even though his father waxes impatient with him. I worry lest it be the mother's sin in the child. I love the child with a frenzy that gives me fear for his safety, especially since the sad death of the little Bingham boy when he was but sixteen days old.

Were a child of mine to die, I could not be so tranquil as the Binghams have been. They trust the Lord, and I cannot. Theirs was the first Christian burial to be held in the islands, and the chiefs were impressed with the dignity and the restraint of the service, so that when a little girl relative of Liholiho's died, the king and Kaahumanu asked humbly that she be given a burial like that of the Bingham child. Liholiho was so affected that he took Mr. Bingham off to Puuloa with him to serve as teacher for himself and his little brother, and he has allowed the Sabbath to be proclaimed holy throughout the island. Thus the seventh day of the week is as free now from work and from play as ever a Sabbath at home—except when boisterous sailors come in to port and profane the day. The brethren are greatly encouraged, for we can now list twenty-four chiefs, twelve male and twelve female, who are decidedly friendly to our cause.

May 8, 1823. Much has transpired since last I wrote. Mr. Whitney has been ordained as a regular preacher. The Chamberlains with the consent of the board secured passage and returned to their old home. We grieved to lose them, but none could deny their right to go. They came to instruct the natives in farming, and found land conditions such that the Captain's experience in America was useless; and their children, who picked up the native language so glibly, were endangered by the exposure to the lasciviousness and vulgarity that is voiced and enacted continually among the misguided natives. Mrs. Chamberlain has been a mother to us—though she is too young in years for such an office, and I shall miss her many kindnesses.

Keopuolani has grown godly and put away the younger of her two husbands, and it is expected by the brethren that she will be fit before long for reception into the Church. The last Sabbath in April the second company of missionaries to these islands arrived here on the *Thames* from New Haven. The company numbers five ordained ministers: Reverend Artemas Bishop and wife, James Ely and wife, Joseph Goodrich and wife, William Richards and wife, Charles S. Stewart and wife. We rejoice that there is a physician in the company, Dr. Abraham Blatchley with his wife. Mr. Levi Chamberlain comes as Superintendent of Secular Affairs, and Miss Betsy Stockton, a Negress teacher who was born in slavery, and four young men from the school at Cornwall—one Tahitian and three Hawaiians. Mrs. Thurston is overjoyed to discover that Mrs. Bishop is none other than a girlhood friend of hers.

The brethren now hope to reopen the field on Hawaii and enlarge the stations on other islands. The newcomers were impressed with the orderliness and decorum of their reception by royalty. Their welcome into the new thatched house of the king, which is built on the stone quay at the harbor, a house with latticed windows and neatly furnished with tables, chairs, etc., the walls hung with engravings and mirrors, the chiefs clothed, the queens decorously attired in dark silk dresses and seated upon proper furniture with dignity instead of sprawled on mats picking fleas off their dogs—all this was very different from our own reception. It made me feel that the Family has in one way or another accomplished a good deal in their three years of residence here.

The newcomers arrived in time to see the latter part of an amazing celebration to commemorate Liholiho's accession to the throne. The festivities began on the 24th of April, although May 8th is the anniversary of the actual day. These celebrations represent a curious blend of Christian and pagan custom. Beginning with divine service at the church, all proceeded to a great *luau*, presided over by Liholiho and his five wives. One hundred guests— chiefs, shipmasters, and missionaries—sat at the long table, and all the rest of the townsfolk crowded as closely as the imposing guard in their feathered war cloaks and helmets would allow. The most spectacular part of the whole celebration was the procession which passed through the streets. The parade was headed by Kaahumanu, mounted grandly on a whaleboat on a vast wicker scaffold which was supported on the heads and shoulders of a column of men in war dress and drawn by seventy subjects. Kaahumanu wore a crimson silk gown and a towering feather helmet and sat under a scarlet silk umbrella.

Kalanimoku and Naihe, as her statesmen, stood on either side of her. They too were splendid in gorgeous feather helmets and silk girdles and supported *kahilis*. Back of this remarkable carriage were Kinau and Kekauonolii, who, since they are of lesser rank, were not accorded quite so unusual a conveyance; but they did very well, carried in double canoes by their faithful subjects.

Pauahi rode proudly through the town on a four-poster bed. Kauikeaouli, the little prince, and his sister Nahienaeana were ensconced in a carriage made by lashing four narrow field bedsteads together and draping them royally with tapa and yellow cloth. Governor Hoapili, who is the prince's stepfather, and Governor Kaikeoewa, the princess's guardian, trudged after them in the capacity of menials, bearing respectively a calabash of fish and *poi* and a whole baked dog on a tray—all as a sign of respect to the higher rank of the children.

To my mind the climax of the whole affair occurred at the end of the procession, when Pauahi with a great display of spirit leaped from her four-poster, set fire to it, then stripped off her dress (which I had been at great pains to make a few days previously) and cast it into the blaze, whereupon all her attendants did the same. Pauahi did a dance around the bonfire, clad in a single undergarment. This was reported to be a gesture of symbolic significance, performed to commemorate an incident in her childhood when she was saved from the flames.

The Family was much disturbed over the waste of good material at this point of the festivities. Most of the dresses were of fine silk. I was most annoyed to think of the care I had expended in making small neat stitches on Pauahi's frock, but the sight, taken as a whole, amused me more heartily than anything has in a long time, though I saw fit to keep my face as straight as possible. This has apparently been the bravest celebration ever held in the islands.

August 15. Our second son, Jonathan Seymore Williams, was born on August 2. He weighed seven pounds and has eyes so dark a brown that they look black. I believe he is more like his father than the others. I am still weak and have persuaded Jonathan to bring back John Akana to look after the two elder children. He demurred because the Family has agreed to have no natives with children who are old enough to talk, as it seems necessary to shield them from all speech with the natives. But John is back and gleeful at being with the babies. Truly I think he loves them well and would do them no harm. They are happier and better with him than with anyone else who could care for them while I am ill. I love my children, but it is in my heart to wish that I may not have others until these are old enough to take care of themselves. I fear that I am liable to sloth.

4

The fall advanced. At Lahaina, Keopuolani grew in piety and declined in health. She had accompanied the two new missionaries to their station on Maui and remained that they might be her spiritual tutors. These men, Mr. Stewart and Mr. Richards, ever cautious of acknowledging the unsure, postponed her baptism until the sixteenth of September, an hour before her death. Then it was Mr. Ellis, the English missionary, who performed the ceremony. The Family piously rejoiced that she died a Christian, her last words entreaties to her son to care for the missionaries and to serve God always. Also, the Family was secretly relieved that she would have no opportunity to degenerate from the pure grace that distinguished the hour of her baptism. She was buried without undue frenzy, and the funeral sermon was an elaboration of the statement, "Blessed are the dead which die in the Lord."

Kaahumanu, impressed by the example set by her sister queen, applied herself diligently to her lessons, her haughtiness dissipated by an influx of the Christian spirit. She yearned for baptism, but her teachers were determined to make sure that she was not undergoing a merely temporary seizure of faith. She wept and placed herself unconditionally in their hands.

In November the king and his favorite queen engaged passage on Captain Starbuck's American ship *L'Aigle* to sail across the world and parley with George IV of England. Liholiho spoke vaguely of wanting to see foreign countries and of not wanting to know less of the world than many of his humbler people who had sailed the globe. The American settlers and tradesmen wondered uneasily just what he was up to. They remembered his first unwillingness to allow the missionaries to establish themselves permanently upon the islands. The traders wondered if he could be shrewd enough to know that they cheated him shockingly and were rapidly stripping the islands of sandalwood—thus far the islands' chief resources. They all remembered the imposing ship-of-war the English king had delivered to Liholiho in 1822, in accordance with a promise made to Kamehameha I. They could not easily forget the kingly present since the *Prince Regent*, bristling with brass guns, could be seen almost any day rocking in the harbor. They realized how surely the Americans were assuming control of the islands and pondered the probability of England's objection to such a state of affairs. It was rumored that, in gratitude for the shining *Prince Regent*, Liholiho had written to George IV formally placing the islands under his protection. The ministers of the Lord searched their hearts for guilt in their dealings with these misguided natives; they found none. They searched their minds for misjudgment, and wondered, silently for the most part, if they had been unwise to war so openly on so many old customs—if they might better have waited a year or two to enforce the Sabbath laws.

The king heeded neither questions nor advice. He prepared himself for departure, and on November 27th he and his train went on board. Accompanying Liholiho and Kamamalu were Governor Boki and Liliha, the minor chiefs Kekuanuoa, Naikekukui, Manuia, and James Young, and the king's secretary, John Rives, that Frenchman whose departure the American settlers watched with undisguised pleasure. The population, brown and white alike, turned out to see the royal departure, the brown grief-stricken, the white impressed in spite of themselves by the youth and innocence of worldly knowledge of these sovereigns setting forth on a perilous journey, and moved at the behavior of Kamamalu, who, at the final moment, raised her arms above her weeping subjects and bade farewell to the land she had always known, in poignant phrases:

"O skies, O plains, O mountains and oceans,
O guardians and people, kind affection for you all.
Farewell to thee, the soil,
O country for which my father suffered, alas for thee!"

And then addressing the spirit of the great Kamehameha, who, dying, had entreated her never to leave his son, she spoke with a dignity that surprised the missionaries, who had regarded her as a careless child:

"We both forsake the object of thy toil;
I go according to thy command.
Never will I disregard thy voice,
I travel with thy dying charge
Which thou didst address to me."

And they were off, gazing their last upon the islands through tears, but fortunately ignorant of the solemn, unenviable state in which they were to return.

The missionaries settled down with sighs of relief. Kalanimoku and Kaahumanu were acting regents, and both were approaching that state of grace which warranted baptism. The king had named his little brother as his successor in case of a mishap, and the missionaries were fairly confident that the child who learned of Christ and mouthed his letters at the knees of the missionary wives would never be the trial to them that his self-indulgent brother had been.

The year ended; 1824 began. A few new babies were born to the mission family. Kaahumanu grew in grace and humbly took her place with the lowest of her subjects at the school examinations which celebrated the fourth anniversary of the missionaries' arrival. She competed with her subjects and emerged from the trial honorably successful. Kaumualii, king of Kauai and good friend to the missionaries, sickened and in May died a Christian death that was rewarded with a Christian burial, his earthly remains being placed beside those of Keopuolani. His son George, whom the missionaries had brought with them on the *Thaddeus*, caused considerable excitement by initiating an insurrection on Kauai, a rebellion against the central power, but he was quelled and brought to Honolulu virtually a prisoner and never allowed to leave Oahu again.

On the 9th of March, 1825, Jonathan rushed home in the middle of the morning with tidings from England. He found Constancy in their upstairs room in the mission house. She laid her finger upon her lips as he entered the room, and he saw that Samuel was lying in the big bed, his eyes closed and brilliant circles of crimson on either cheek, but for the moment he disregarded his child.

"Constancy!" he whispered. "Come out here in the hall!"

With a backward glance at the sleeping Samuel, Constancy followed her husband to the stair hall, closing the door after her.

"The king and queen have been dead these eight months, Constancy!"

"What . . ." Constancy eyed him blankly, her mind still on Samuel.

"The *Almira* arrived this morning bearing word. They had scarce reached England before they fell ill of measles and in a few days were dead."

"Oh . . . poor things!" Her attention was caught. "It is as if Kamamalu had some premonition—you remember her words at parting. They were so young—so glad to be alive, Jonathan!"

Jonathan shook his head gloomily. "I would that I might think of them as partaking of bliss," he sighed, "but the young king was ever putting pleasure before duty. Had he only embraced the teachings of Brother Bingham when he had the opportunity, and not decided to put off his reformation for five years! Could he have known that he had only a year to live when he said those vain words! For who can say at what moment death will strike him— be he man or woman or suckling babe!"

Constancy shivered. She laid the work-roughened fingers of her brown hand on Jonathan's arm. "Jonathan!" her voice was urgent. "I am worried about Samuel. He could not eat his breakfast, and he does naught but lie there half asleep, his skin burning to the touch. It would be well if you were to summon Dr. Blatchley."

Jonathan went into the bedroom and stooped over the bed, laying his long, nervous hand on Samuel's dry, hot forehead. The little boy opened his eyes, green and long like his mother's. "God wuz mean," he mumbled to his father's incredulous ears, "to drown all the babies and mothers and kitties. He isn't near as good as Mother."

With a little cry of alarm, Constancy slipped to her knees beside the bed and clapped her hand over the child's mouth. "Sammie—darling! You're too sick to know what you're saying!" And to Jonathan, "Go for the doctor. Do you want your son to be stricken in this state of mind?"

Her words shocked Jonathan into action. He groaned and rushed away. Constancy frowned at the dust that swirled through the window at each gust of wind. For three days a dry, cold kona wind had been blowing, pushing clouds of dust across the arid plain to invade each crack and cranny of the flimsy walls of the mission house, coating floors and furniture thickly with dust. Samuel coughed, and his mother's eyes shifted from the dusty window to his fever-flushed face. His cough was hoarse and throaty. He made a wry face.

"I want a drink—please!"

Constancy uncovered a gourd of water and poured out a mugful. She supported his back with her arm as he drank. He smiled at her.

"It would be nice for you to rock me, Mother. Don't you think it would be nice?"

She wrapped him carefully in a blanket and gathered him into her arms. She sat down in the cane-seated rocker that Kaahumanu had given her and slowly rocked back and forth, Samuel's curly black head pressed into the hollow of her shoulder. "Say the poem 'bout the caves of ice," he muttered drowsily, and Constancy began half under her breath:

"In Xanadu did Kubla Khan
A stately pleasure-dome decree:
Where Alph, the sacred river, ran
Through caverns measureless to man
Down to a sunless sea."

She rocked more and more slowly, her voice diminishing as his eyelids grew still. Through the back window she heard the faint reverberations of a roar that must come from young Jonathan, but beyond frowning she paid no heed. Barely reaching the ear of Samuel came the final words of the poem,

" .   .   .   .   Beware!
His flashing eyes, his floating hair!
Weave a circle round him thrice,
And close your eyes with holy dread,
For he on honey-dew hath fed,
And drunk the milk of Paradise."

A little sigh escaped Samuel's lips. Constancy tightened her clasp upon his body, and warm pride expanded her heart. He loved the music that lay in poetry as much as she loved it . . . and he was so little. Maybe he would be a great poet when he grew up. She bent her head so that her mouth rested lightly upon his curls. He lifted one plump, dimpled hand to pat her cheek.

"I love you best of all the world," he murmured, "and after you I love Kitty, and after him Miriam and Baby and Father." His eyes flew open, and he grinned up at her impishly. "You know, Mother, I don't like God one bit . . . not the God Father always talks about. But I like the God that loveth all things both great and small like in the story about the albatross."

Constancy rocked harder, holding the small body tighter. Fear rose in her throat. She swallowed before she could speak. "Sammie, you mustn't talk like that about God. He'll be angry with you. You know there is only one God."

But Sammie smiled sleepily, eyes half shut. "I like the albatross God better anyway . . . but I love you best because you're nicest." He patted her cheek again and drowsed in her arms.

Constancy rocked gently, her eyes fixed broodingly upon the face of the sleeping child. She knew him for the most sensitive and the most beautiful of her children. In her heart she acknowledged that her love for him was different from the easy love she bestowed upon his little brother and sister. She raised her eyes as Dr. Blatchley and Jonathan came into the room. The doctor was a sober man, although he was not yet past youth. He took the sleeping Samuel from his mother's arms and laid him on the bed. He held the plump baby wrist and bent his head over Samuel's chest, listening for some time. He laid his hand on the white forehead and smoothed back the black curls. Samuel's breathing was audible all over the room.

"A cold has fastened on his lungs, Sister Williams," the doctor said gravely. "This weather—so much dust in the air—is conducive to colds, and colds easily turn into pneumonia at such times. I have just returned from attending two native children afflicted with it."

Constancy's eyes opened wide at the word pneumonia. "Sammie . . . *he* hasn't pneumonia, Doctor!"

The doctor looked again at Sammie's brilliant cheeks. He shook his head. "Tomorrow I can judge better. Keep him out of the draft and put flannel about his lungs. Give him water to drink, and if you can get some oranges from Mr. Marin, the juice of them would be suitable. And re member, Sister Williams, that the Lord regards each sparrow's fall."

He left the room and went down the stairs, followed by Jonathan. Constancy's eyes were bitter as she watched them go. "Regards them!" she thought. "But what consolation is that to the sparrow?" She tiptoed to the rude chest Jonathan had made her and found a small flannel sacque belonging to the last baby. It was large, to be worn over his other clothes; it would do for Sammie. She unfastened the sleeping child's cotton nightdress at the neck and slipped it from his shoulders, putting the baby's sacque upon him next to the skin and fastening it securely across his chest. She drew the nightdress back into place without wakening him and smoothed the covers beneath his chin. She regarded him intently, her eyebrows a straight line. His breath seemed easier. She smoothed the bedclothes once again and noiselessly left the room. She must send Jonathan to ask some oranges of Don Marin.

In the yard her two younger children left their play to come and clutch at her skirts. Her eyes were vacant resting upon them. Samuel was her child; these two she had forgotten. Nevertheless she laid a hand on each tousled head.

"Hungry!" said Miriam imperiously. Little Jonathan tugged at her skirts, imploring her to take him up. Absently she lifted him to her shoulder and gave her free hand to his sister. She could cook them each an egg—and there was goat's milk and there were some cold biscuits left from breakfast for them. She took them to the basement dining room and placed them on chairs. The Loomises, with their brood of children, were already eating at the long table.

Mrs. Loomis pushed forward the large milk pitcher. "There's enough here for your babies, Sister Williams," she said and poured out mugs of the rich milk for each of them. Constancy nodded and went up the stone steps into the lean-to they used for cooking. In a few moments she returned with boiled eggs and a plate of cold biscuit. She went to the cupboard to get the children's, silently waiting upon them, restraining Jonathan gently when he tried to cram half a biscuit into his small mouth at one bite, spreading jam on their biscuits. Mrs. Loomis watched her thoughtfully. "We grieve that little Samuel is ailing," she said. "I will keep an eye on the children for you this afternoon, or put them in charge of one of my girls."

Constancy's eyelids flickered in the direction of the speaker. "That is kind," she said. "It is not good for the little ones to be around the sickroom." She poured herself a cup of milk and drank it quickly. She wondered if Jonathan would return hungry from his long walk to Don Marin's home. It was nearly one o'clock. Surely they would want him to eat with them. If he came home hungry, he must feed himself.

"Sister Williams!" Mrs. Loomis's small voice broke in upon her thoughts. "You didn't ask a blessing upon the children's food!"

Constancy stared at her for a second, uncomprehending. "Oh," she said dully, "I forgot. . . . It's too late now —the food is all eaten."

Mrs. Loomis was timid but persistent. "I know your heart is up in the room with Samuel, but I don't think it is well for the children to think their elders are negligent."

Her husband raised an eyebrow at her. "Now, Maria," he said mildly, "if I remember aright, when our Amanda had croup, you forgot to feed the baby at all."

His wife blushed. "That was very reprehensible of me," she said meekly, "but it is better that they go unfed than that they be fed with food that has not God's blessing upon it."

Constancy shrugged indifferently and made no response. She began removing dishes from the table. Before leaving the room she spoke over her shoulder: "I shall ask Martha to bathe the children, and if you will be so kind as to let them have their afternoon sleep with your children, I shall be greatly indebted to you."

Her duties in the kitchen accomplished, she hurried back to Sammie. She stood at the foot of the bed and scrutinized his face. His cheeks were brightly flushed, and although his eyes were closed, he tossed restlessly in the bed. It seemed to his mother that his breathing was more rasping than when she had left him. She moved to the head of the bed and placed her hand on his forehead. His eyes opened, abnormally bright with the fever. "I'm too *hot*," he protested. "I'm all burning, Mother."

His mother carefully sponged his face and hands with cool water and laid a wet cloth upon his forehead. "Does that feel better, darling?" The effort to speak brought hot stinging tears to her eyes. She blinked them away, busying herself for a moment in the other end of the room so that she might keep her back turned to the bed. Samuel's voice rose hoarsely:

"Sit over here, Mother, where I can see you . . . and don't go 'way! Will you, Mother?"

"No . . . not till you are all well again, darling." She thought: "Will he be all well again? He is so sick . . . and children die . . . and are shut away in boxes in the ground . . . and the Binghams said, 'It is God's will. Thy will be done.' But they didn't love their baby the way I love Sammie to have said that."

"Mother, say some po'try to me."

"Yes, darling." She thought: *"Full fathom five thy father lies*—No, not that! . . . *Underneath this stone doth lie* . . . *Oft had I heard of Lucy Gray* . . . Have I nothing but death in my head? No . . . this will do:

"Where the bee sucks, there suck I . . ."

She held his hot little hand in hers and repeated the words to his closed eyes and his half-smile.

Time had no meaning for Constancy. Her world was the upstairs room in the mission house, where Samuel lay, his breath rasping and his hoarse, tortured voice asking for water, for poetry, muttering inconsequently about drowned babies and kittens, about a palm tree that grew at the foot of his bed, right out of the floor, and bloomed with blue flowers and pink. Miriam and little Jonathan had for their mother no existence. She acknowledged only one child. The grown Jonathan, she ordered peremptorily to bring orange juice or fresh water, or to empty the chamber. The doctor came twice each day. Him, Constancy turned seeing eyes upon, eyes burning with an intensity of hope or despair, her brain assimilating his words, her hands quick to do his bidding.

When Jonathan came to peer into the shadows that enveloped the bed and stayed to pray for the child's recovery, Constancy stared at him with enigmatical eyes. When Jonathan volunteered to sit up at night with Samuel while Constancy rested, she brushed aside his offer impatiently. She could lie down beside the child and doze for an hour at a time between the times when she must heat alcohol to rub on his chest or give him the weak solution of aconite for his fever.

Jonathan regarded her, bewildered and a little hurt. Constancy had never spoken impatiently to him till now.

"Constancy," for a reason he could not have defined, he stammered, "—do you pray—as you sit beside him? Do you remember that it is in God's hands and implore His aid?"

Constancy turned away to heat the alcohol over the whale-oil lamp. "I do nothing but address God on the matter," she said stiffly. "Go down and eat your supper which Mrs. Chamberlain has been kind enough to prepare."

Reluctantly Jonathan withdrew from the room. This was a Constancy he could not recognize. Constancy went back to her chair beside the bed, and her eyes sought the face that had in so short a time lost its roundness, its look of health, and now showed shadows like bruises beneath the eyes, and hollows in the burning cheeks. Her gaze remained unwavering upon his face. She rocked with restrained nervousness beside the bed. Her lips tight sealed, she spoke in her heart to a vengeful God:

"Let him get well . . . let him get well . . . and I will confess before the brethren, keeping back none of my enormities, even though it means being cut off from my children forever. That is more to Your advantage than having me stay a pernicious influence among Your anointed—a hypocrite among the guileless. . . . The moment the doctor says he is out of danger and sure to recover, I will keep my vow. You have no *right* to vent Your wrath for me upon this baby! . . .

"But Sammie is his mother's child . . . only sweeter—more lovable than I could ever have been. . . . Sammie saying God was mean to drown all the babies . . . but it is insane to judge a four-year-old child for baby reasoning! 'To your awful and exquisite torture there shall be no end.' . . . But there is, 'Suffer little children to come unto me' . . . only Sammie isn't like other children. Christ was gentle, but what power has He against Jeho-

vah . . . two . . . three in one, but how can that be
. . . a monster with three heads—a dove and a white beard
and a brown beard. But that's all nonsense; there is only
Jehovah, holding babies suspended over a bottomless, flaming pit, dropping them in to endless torture because their
mothers are liars.

"God . . . let Sammie get well and I'll confess . . .
let him die and—but what can I do to God? A monster
whose pleasure it is to torment the souls of His creatures
with longings which He forbids them to gratify, and to
cast into endless hell the creatures who sin by His own
foreordination . . . a Creator who hates His creatures!
No mother in the world could hate her child . . . it is
unnatural . . . unjust! Nothing that I can do . . . except to make . . . to try to make a covenant with a monster to spare his life. Jonathan!"

He stood beside her. His face, too, was drawn. He knelt
at the side of the bed and prayed aloud. "Lord, if it be
Thy will, spare us this child who is our first-born and dear.
Spare him that he may grow in grace before being taken
from life. Or, Lord, if Thou must slay him, mercifully
grant that his hard, child's heart be softened and his stubborn spirit molded to Thy will."

Constancy grasped Jonathan furiously by the shoulder.
"Go on out!" she said fiercely, although she spoke almost
under her breath for fear of waking the child. "If you
must pray in such fashion, go elsewhere to do it. The child
has the most generous spirit, the tenderest heart in this benighted household. He's too delirious to know what you
say when he *is* awake, but if his mind clears, I *will* not
have you bothering him while he is so ill. Wait till he is
well to try to cow him—and if he doesn't get well . . .
you have spoken often yourself of the futility of eleventh-
hour reformations."

Jonathan stared in stupefaction. "I have naught but the child's good at heart," he stammered, "but . . . I will go elsewhere. You are overwrought, Constancy." At the door he turned back to say, "It may comfort you, Constancy, to know that the Family are all praying earnestly on Samuel's account."

Constancy clasped her hands tightly together; her eyes hardened. "Yes," she said softly above the sleeping Samuel, "they doubtless pray, 'Spare this child of sin if it be Thy will, yet if he must die, let his death be an example to our thoughtless children that they take heed of their souls!' They sicken me! There is no warmth in their hearts. You will not like to listen to me, Jonathan, so you had better go and join your prayers with theirs."

Jonathan flinched. "Constancy! You have been tried beyond your strength," he protested. "This is not yourself speaking, but I shall try not to disturb you further." He went down the stairs, tears stinging his eyes.

Constancy turned back to her study of Samuel. She sat close to the bed, steeling herself to endure each rasping, hard-drawn breath.

"My beloved, I have loved you too unconstrainedly . . . with too much of idolatry, and the Lord is a vengeful God, and uses you as an instrument of torture to me for disregarding Him. He is a cunning God . . . for what would His fiery pit avail Him as punishment for me if you were well and happy? There is worse pain than flames can bring, but only a demon God would force a loving mother to countenance the suffering of her child."

She knelt beside the bed and laid her cheek against the hot, thin little hand that only a few days before had been plump and dimpled, and set her will against Jehovah's.

"I shall bear his pain. The sickness shall leave him and enter me. He shall not be destroyed! You cannot terrify me or break my spirit. . . . It is a coward's way to attack me through another, deliberately to destroy an infant for its mother's sin! Let his sickness fall upon me and leave him."

Over and over, her heart, her will, and her tired brain mumbled the words, until Sammie stirred and shivered, and muttered, "Cold, Mother . . . cold!"

She felt his hands and face and knew that the fever had left him. She felt of her own forehead and laid her hands against her cheeks, trembling with fear and hope, but there was no fever in her. Foreboding weighed down her heart. With unsteady hands she gathered Sammie into a blanket and held him in her arms, rocking him back and forth. There was no sickness in her, only the tired, drugged feeling that had been with her since Sammie had fallen ill.

She scrutinized the shrunken face on her arm. The flush had gone, leaving it chalky white; there was no trace of color in the small soft mouth. She reached to the table, poured a little brandy from the bottle into the glass of water that stood there, and, with a teaspoon, began to pour a few drops at a time between Sammie's lips. He swallowed a little, but most of the liquid slipped off the spoon and ran down the blanket.

"Cold," he whispered again, fluttering the blue-shadowed eyelids. Blindly she reached for another blanket from the bed to wrap about him. Slipping her hand beneath his covering, she began desperately to chafe the small, icy feet. She remembered that the fire must still be burning in the bake oven in the cooking house, and rising, staggered down the stairs with her burden.

In the cooking house, still holding Sammie against her shoulder, she managed one-handedly to lay more wood upon the embers and to pull a small stool near the fire. She sat down, holding Sammie closer to her body. The heat in

the small room brought drops of moisture to her forehead.
But again, sleepily and as if from far away, he murmured,
"Cold! . . . Wuz it so cold in the caves of ice, Mother?"
And his eyelids flickered just once as he looked up at his
mother with green eyes grown twice as large since his ill-
ness.

Fear clutched more strongly at Constancy's throat, so
that she could not speak and could only rest her face
against the top of Sammie's head and sway back and forth
upon the stool. Again her hand sought his feet and began
to rub them, for their coldness persisted for all the two
blankets and the now roaring fire. Across the yard from
the meeting house drifted dolefully "Nearer, My God, to
Thee." Constancy shivered and pressed the wasted body
more closely to her, drew her stool closer to the fire, and
sang defiantly to drown out the hymnal wail from the
church:

"Ride a cock horse to Banbury Cross,
To see a fine lady upon a white horse.
Rings on her fingers and bells on her toes,
She shall have music wherever she goes."

Doggedly she went through all the nursery rhymes she
could remember, and Sammie smiled faintly, and the tiny
frown that had gathered between his brows vanished. His
breathing was quieter now, barely perceptible as she bent
over him. While her lips formed the words, "Mary, Mary,
quite contrary, How does your garden grow?" her brain
pleaded again: "Let him get well, and I promise never to
see him again. . . . I will confess my abominations . . .
tell them all that I am an impostor . . . a hypocrite—
happily!"

A remoter portion of her memory taunted her with the
lines Jonathan so often read aloud from a madman's ser-

mon: "To your exquisite horrible misery there will be no
end . . . when you look forward you shall see a long forever . . . a boundless duration before you, which will
swallow up your thoughts and amaze your soul . . . and
you will absolutely despair of ever having any deliverance,
any end, any mitigation, any rest at all. You will know
certainly that you must wear out long ages . . . millions
of millions of ages; and then when you have so done, you
will know that all is but a point to what remains."

Her lips went on singing Mother Goose while the demon
within her brain accompanied her with a soft mouthing
of Jonathan Edwards's conception of eternity for those
who were not the Lord's elect, till her brain reeled dizzily
in the overheated room, and her senses, benumbed, were
not aware that now there was no sound of breathing at all
from the small body she held in her arms.

It was not until Jonathan and then the doctor stood beside her—it was not until the doctor lifted the still bundle from her arms, and Jonathan, his face suddenly lifeless, murmured, "Thy will be done"—that awareness swept
over her with a sharp agony that wrung one piercing cry
from her and then left her insentient on the floor, unconscious of the decorous expressions of sympathy from the
sisters of the Family, who at length carried her upstairs,
undressed and put her to bed, and nursed her through the
wild fever that beset her brain, wringing from her again
and again in the next few weeks the words with which
Jonathan Edwards had frightened sinners in Enfield. These
women, too, washed and prepared the child Samuel in his
home-made coffin, and with the aid of prayer endured the
sight of the small box being smothered away in the ground,
while the mind of Samuel's mother wandered far from
her fever-ridden body in the upper chamber of the mission
house to explore the gray corridors of limbo.

PART III

SALLY lay rigid on her narrow bed in the little room under the eaves. The choking sound came again from the big room where her mother slept. Sally pressed both thin little claws hard against her heart: it hurt so from feeling sorry for Mother. If only Father hadn't had to go off to try to pull the governor out of hell, he might know what to do for Mother. But if Father were here, Sally thought, Mother would just shut her feelings up inside her and fold her lips up tight and make her eyes look as if they didn't see you. Sally wondered if she could ever be as brave as her mother. She didn't believe that she would ever be so old that she wouldn't have to cry when she felt sorry and say wild things when she was angry. She strained her ears for the disturbing sound. If she could only go and get in bed with Mother and tell her how terribly she loved her and not to cry any more! But she was afraid—not that Mother was ever mean, or even cross, but she seemed so far away—as if you couldn't touch her even when your hand was on her. And if Mother were to send you away—providing you screwed up courage enough to go to her—it would be too dreadful to be borne.

There were steps on the creaking stairway. There was the sound of Mother blowing her nose. Through the parting in the curtain that shut the children's narrow little room away from their parents' room, Sally saw her father strike light from his tinder box, and in a moment the dim light of the whale-oil lamp threw his shadow across the floor.

"Constancy," he said, and his voice sounded as if he were a little afraid, too, "I would not have left you this evening if my duty had not made it imperative. It is not easy—always—to follow duty, Constancy."

To Sally, it seemed that her mother's voice sounded as if she had a cold. "You did right, Jonathan. What progress did you make with the governor?"

There was a sigh from her father. "He swears to follow God—that nothing shall turn him from the path of righteousness again. But you know how weak he is. An attack of acute indigestion, brought on by greed, and a recollection of my last sermon on the pains of hell struck fear to his heart just now—but in health again and with a persuasive companion in evil at his elbow—he will forget. It was a bad day for the mission when Kaahumanu died. Kinau is a good woman, but she lacks the force and the influence upon the chiefs that Kaahumanu exerted."

Weights pulled down Sally's eyelids, but her mother's voice, strangely sharpened, caught her back from the boundary of sleep:

"Jonathan! No more of our children are going to leave us! I will never send another child of mine from home. It is cruel—cruel to send children scarce past babyhood across the world—to die! Miriam—these seven months dead—and we unwitting! Dead at Christmas, and we keeping holiday unknowing. And you remember how bitterly she cried at going? How every letter showed yearning to come back—bespoke loneliness and unhappiness? It was cruel! And now there is Peter, still on the sea—not

yet ten years old, and he has always been a delicate child.
I dare not think of him. Even Jonathan, who has ever a
stern sense of duty beyond his years, speaks longingly in
every letter of the day when his schooling shall be over
and he may return. I tell you in all earnestness, Jonathan,
Sally shan't go next year!''

Again there was the frightening, agonized sobbing of
her mother, and the murmur of her father's voice promising that none of the children now at home should be sent
away, reminding her that Miriam's aunt had spoken of the
child's willingness to die, her confidence that she would
see her parents in heaven.

Sally's eyes opened wide in the darkness. How could
Miriam be willing to die? She herself would be terribly
afraid to die . . . but then . . . she wasn't good like
Miriam. She could remember five years ago, before Miriam
and Jonathan sailed away to Boston to go to school, how
good Miriam was, how she really liked to read the Scriptures and never minded sitting quietly about the house on
Sunday and not making any noise. Did Miriam really like
living with God, and did she have a shining halo to wear
around her head, and did she just go around praising God
all day? Didn't she ever want to run and jump and yell
and swim, or do anything that was fun on earth? But of
course Miriam was fifteen now, and when girls got that
old they didn't seem to want to do anything much anyway.

Slowly, a feeling of comforting inner warmth spread
through Sally's veins. She smiled sleepily. "I shan't have to
go away now. I won't have to leave Mother.'' And then
the less pleasant thought came to her: "If Miriam hadn't
died, I would have to go away next year . . . so I
shouldn't be too happy over not going . . . but oh . . .

I should have died . . . I couldn't bear to go so far away
and stay till I grow up!"

Sleep lay heavily upon Sally's eyes. At the persistent
touch on her shoulder she mumbled crossly till she felt
herself being shaken. Then her eyes flew wide. The dingy
light from the whale-oil lamp edged through the doorway
from the big room. Her mother, fully dressed, leaned over
her. "Up, Sally! Five o'clock already! You'll not have the
children ready for prayers if you don't hurry, child."

Sally sat up and laid her cheek for an instant against her
mother's hand, remembering how sorrowful her mother
was over the death of Miriam away off in Concord, and
pondering on how her mother's words might be stern, yet
her voice was always soft and kind. Her mother drew her
hand away, her lips tightening; but the next second the
hand returned to lie lightly for the length of a breath
upon Sally's tangled red-gold head. "Be quick, child," she
said and hastened away downstairs to put the porridge on
to cook.

Sally yawned rather noisily and jumped out of bed. She
sniffed at the moist air that blew in little flurries down the
length of the close little room under the eaves where the
children slept. The air always smelled good during a rain.
She pattered across the floor to the washbowl and pitcher
and vigorously scrubbed her face and neck, her rather
scrawny chest and thin arms and hands. She pulled on her
long white stockings and stepped into her black slippers,
slipped quickly into the starched white calico pantalettes
and ruffled petticoat that lay over the chair back, and
pulled a green-and-white calico dress over her head,
struggling with the fastenings till she stood a miniature
woman, her skirts nearly as long as her mother's.

She went to the cot at the far end of the room and

thrust her head around the edge of the bed-ticking screen that modestly sheltered eight-year-old Matthew from the idle gaze of his sisters and incidentally shielded them from his equally idle gaze. Matt's tousled yellow head burrowed further into the pillow as the dim light struck at him. Sally peered at him for a second and then pounced.

"Shame, Matt! A great boy like you to be sucking your thumb!" she cried in outraged tones. "Even little Silly knows better!"

The offender jerked his erring thumb out of sight and grinned sheepishly at his sister, but he made no attempt to bestir himself from his bed. Vigorously Sally threw back the covers, pulled his brief nightshirt down over his legs with a mature "Tut, tut!" and hauled his unwilling self from the bed, administering a hearty smack to his small behind. "Be quick, or you'll be late for prayers, and Father said he'd whip you next time you came late. Be sure you wash your ears and your neck well!"

She turned to the wider bed where seven-year-old Faith and the baby, Priscilla, not yet five, slept. Priscilla, or Silly, as the family called her, was humming an almost noiseless tune to the sad-looking rag doll that always slept with her. One of her dimpled fists clutched the doll to her chest, and her black curls rested on the doll's unsightly face. Faith screwed her brown eyes tight shut in pretended sleep, but she could not quite prevent a smile crinkling up her face. Sally, with a chuckle, lightly played her fingers over her small sister's ribs, and Faith bounced out of bed squealing, "Don't you tickle me, Sally, or I'll die!"

"Get up, then, and be quick about it! And you, Silly, leave your doll to sleep some more and I'll wash you both. Up!" She drove her two charges over to the washstand where Matt was absent-mindedly massaging his chin with a practically dry washcloth. With a muttered ejaculation

of impatience, his sister snatched the cloth from him, wet
and soaped it thoroughly, and scrubbed his face and ears
mercilessly. "You are naught but trouble to me," she
scolded. "Faith can make a better work of washing herself than you! For shame! Now," hastily drying his shining chubby face, "see if you can get into your trousers and
shirt by yourself, and be thinking of the verse from the
Scriptures you must know if you are to have any sweet-
ening on your porridge." She shoved him towards his end
of the room and turned more gently to the little girls.
"Say your verse, Faith!" she commanded, busying herself
with the brush and comb over the tangled heads.

Faith folded her tanned little hands over her stomach
and said in singsong, " 'Behold, happy is the man whom
God correcteth: therefore despise not thou the chastening
of the Almighty.' "

"That is well done," approved Sally and turned to Priscilla: "Now, Baby, do you remember the text I taught
you last night?"

Priscilla assumed the correct position and said solemnly:
" 'Apply thine heart unto 'struction, and thine ears to the
words of knowledge.' "

"Say '*in*struction,' Baby," commanded Sally, and Silly
patiently repeated, "*In*struction."

Sally buttoned up their blue calico dresses and went
over to Matt. He was scowling and struggling with buttons. "Here, child," in the grown-up tone of her mother,
"what a mess you do make! There you are proper now
. . . tell me your text."

Matthew varied the position by clasping his hands be-
hind him, standing with his legs braced, his feet far apart.
" 'Be not among winebibbers,' " he began loudly, 'Among
. . .' Oh, Sally, what is that word?"

" 'Riotous,' " prompted his sister. "Begin all over again,

and do try to remember. It makes Father angry to have you careless."

Resignedly he took a fresh start. " 'Be not among wine-bibbers, among riotous eaters of flesh: For the drunkard and the glutton shall come to poverty: And drowsiness shall clothe a man with rags.' "

"It will do," sighed Sally. "Now go downstairs quietly to the dining room, and if the other children are there, mind you behave yourselves and make no noise till prayers be over and grace be said. Oh!"—for she had put up her hand to her head and discovered that in her concern for the children she had neglected her own hair. She snatched up the comb and courageously yanked out the snarls, and then brushed it smooth with a few hard strokes. It hung, a waving mass, to her waist and was unbound by any ribbon, for the home board did not consider hair ribbons an essential to the welfare of its exiled children—at least no hair ribbon had appeared in any of the boxes of supplies that had reached the islands.

Sally hurried downstairs after the children to the big dining room in the basement, where the Williams family had their morning prayers before breakfast. The other families who lived in the mission house had their prayers in their own rooms, breakfasting a little later. The children sat on a bench, their mother on a straight-backed chair. Their father stood before them. Instead of reading them the usual fairly long chapter from the Bible, this morning their father repeated, without need of the Bible, only the Twenty-third Psalm. His voice was calm, but his eyes burned. Sally knew he was thinking of Miriam who had died seven months ago of typhus—with none of her family knowing till yesterday when the ship came.

" 'The Lord is my shepherd; I shall not want,' " chanted Jonathan Williams.

" 'He maketh me to lie down in green pastures: he leadeth me beside the still waters.

" 'He restoreth my soul: he leadeth me in the paths of righteousness for his name's sake.

" 'Yea, though I walk through the valley of the shadow of death, I will fear no evil: for thou art with me; thy rod and thy staff they comfort me.

" 'Thou preparest a table before me in the presence of mine enemies: thou anointest my head with oil; my cup runneth over.

" 'Surely goodness and mercy shall follow me all the days of my life: and I will dwell in the house of the Lord for ever.' "

Sally, stealing a glance at her mother, saw her sitting stiffly erect, her hands clenched tightly together in her lap, her face set firmly as if it were carved from rock, her eyes staring straight ahead, not seeing anything. Sally acknowledged with a pang that for Mother there was no comfort in the words that made Father's face glow. She knew that Mother would rather have Miriam here in Honolulu with them than wearing a halo up in heaven. Her heart ached unbearably for her mother—and a little for herself, though Miriam didn't seem quite real to her any more—it had been so long since Miriam had been at home. And while her father, kneeling now, launched into prayer, "Merciful and Almighty God, Who didst lay burdens upon Thy faithful in loving-kindness, incline our hearts before Thy will. Give us the spiritual grace to say in truth, 'Not my will but Thine be done' . . ." and a great deal more in the same vein, Sally, her hands pressed tight against her heart, was praying fiercely and mutely, "O God, please don't let Mother feel so bad. She is so good, and she shouldn't be treated so. Let her feel better about Miriam, and please, God, don't let any of the rest of us die. It isn't fair, and don't have any of the other mission children be sent away to be educated so far from home. I can't bear the way they cry when the boat goes. Peter was just terrible. Amen."

Her father, his prayer finished, addressed the four children seated primly before him: "Ponder well in your hearts the happy death of your sister, who, though a child in years, was not only resigned but joyful to be casting off the dark veil of the flesh that stands between mortal man and God. Let her holy death be a lesson to you, and may the sorrow you feel for her loss be cast out from your hearts at the thought of her eternal bliss. Pray earnestly, my children, that you may be sanctified by the thought of her bright example."

He glanced at the clock, and his eyebrows shot upward. He nodded to Constancy, who rose to fetch the porridge and biscuits and coffee to the table. The children rose to their feet to deliver their verses from the Bible. First Priscilla and then Faith recited glibly. Sally clasped her hands together in an agony as Matthew plunged out boldly, " 'Be not among winebibbers,' " and then cast a tortured look in her direction. "Ri-ot-ous," she mouthed noiselessly at him. His eyes traveled back to his father's face. " 'Among riotous eaters of flesh: For the drunkard and the glutton shall come to poverty: and drowsiness shall clothe a man with rags.' " He beamed triumphantly upon his father, whose lips twitched, although his voice was solemn: "A well-chosen text, Matt; though winebibbing is haply not among your faults, you are overinterested in what goes in your stomach and have been known to prefer your bed to being on time to prayers. Now, Sally, you tutored your charges well today; have you done as well by yourself?"

"I have learned the first six verses of the Nineteenth

Psalm, Father." She clasped her hands over her flat breast and looked out through the small window just above ground level to repeat lovingly:

" 'The heavens declare the glory of God; and the firmament sheweth his handywork.

" 'Day unto day uttereth speech, and night unto night sheweth knowledge.

" 'There is no speech nor language, where their voice is not heard.

" 'Their line is gone out through all the earth, and their words to the end of the world. In them hath he set a tabernacle for the sun,

" 'Which is as a bridegroom coming out of his chamber, and rejoiceth as a strong man to run a race.

" 'His going forth is from the end of the heaven, and his circuit unto the ends of it: and there is nothing hid from the heat thereof.' "

Her father smiled approvingly and nodded. "Why did you choose those lines, Sally?"

Sally considered the matter for a moment. "Because they seemed passing beautiful to me, Father."

Her father frowned thoughtfully before answering. "They are indeed beautiful, child, but think not in vanity to judge of the Word of God that 'this part is more beautiful than that,' for verily all are of a piece."

Her eyes on the floor, her attitude demure, Sally whispered a dutiful "Yes, Father," but her brain pondered: "Why should God not have had His moments for writing less well than at others? For even with Father, there are times when words flow easily and other times when they come haltingly." And she thought of God in robes of gleaming white, an aureole flaming about His awful head, bending over a desk such as Dr. Judd had in his office, rapidly making the odd Hebrew characters she had seen in Father's Hebrew Old Testament, and writing with a goose-quill pen. She said nothing of her fancy, for she knew by experience that Father was likely to take offense at informal speculations about the behavior of God.

After breakfast Sally washed dishes while Faith and Priscilla were sent upstairs to make the beds. Matt went out to empty the wastebasket in the small pit where rubbish was burned and to take the table scraps to the dozen chickens the Williamses kept in a tiny coop and yard. Constancy tied a cloth over her head and set about sweeping the part of the house her family used. Sally, her hands plunged into the steaming suds, wished that her mother saw fit to keep a native to do the harder housework as the Judds did. But for the last year her mother had asked for no outside help except when windows had to be washed. She and the children did all the work except the washing.

As Sally dried the last dish, her mother came in to place the broom in its corner. She was frowning thoughtfully. "Put the taro on to boil at fifteen minutes after eleven, Sally," she said, "and you had best run over to the school while the children are studying their lessons, for Noah has promised me a fair fish in return for the books he has had of us, and if it is not to be had we must have fried ham for dinner. Do you wish to try your hand at a deep apple pie, child?"

Sally had made biscuits before, but she had never been trusted to make a pie with the precious dried apples that occasionally came around the Horn to the exiles. "Oh, Mother," she cried, pleased. "I am sure I can do it—I've watched you so often. I will be most careful that the apples be not spoiled, and we'll have cream with cinnamon in it over all. . . . Mother—must I sew this morning?"

Constancy shook her head. "No—it is not necessary that

you slave always, Sally, even though you are a missionary child and supposed to set an example of industry to the community. See that Silly practises writing her letters and learns her reading lesson, and Faith must work her sums till all are correct and study well her chapter in the Bible. Matt is still weak with his multiplication. Drill him somewhat on the nines and the sevens, and see that he studies his geography. I need not tell you to study your own lessons, need I?" And with a quick shy gesture she stooped to lay a kiss on the top of the red-gold head. Convulsively Sally flung her arms about her mother's waist and laid her head against her breast. She heard her mother say a little breathlessly, "You shall never be sent away from me, Sally. You shall stay by me and be my comfort, whatever the brethren say." Abruptly she disengaged herself from Sally's tight embrace and was gone to her teaching in the schoolhouse across the yard from the church.

Sally, a smile hovering about the corners of her mouth and lifting it out of its usual seriousness, climbed the stairs to the big room where the children did their lessons. Silly and Faith were romping hilariously under and over the furniture. They sobered as their sister appeared.

"Get to your lessons!" she commanded. "Are you both to grow up sluggards and idlers to shame our mother and father?" she scolded. Silly's forefinger stole into her mouth, and she sheepishly sidled across the room to the bookshelves to get her lesson book. Faith made a face at her sister and shrugged her shoulders impishly. "Don't try to act like a grown-up woman, Sal," she teased. "You're naught but a child yourself." She flounced across to her own books and sat down on a stool beside the window. Sally scowled and then giggled. "Snip!" she said good-humoredly, and then, "Where's Matt all this time?" She poked her head out the window over the *kapu* yard where the mission children played and where the natives were forbidden to enter lest the contact with primitives corrupt the souls of the white children. The walled yard was empty.

"Oh, dear!" moaned Sally. "If he has gone into the other side and is talking with the natives with Father home!" Scarcely were the words out of her mouth before she heard her father's voice from the study downstairs. "Matthew! Come here at once!" And in an instant there was the sharp spatting sound that she knew was her father's heavy ferule belaboring Matt's behind. A loud uproar arose instantly, and Matt came rushing up the stairs sniffling and hiccoughing and roaring in rage and pain. He flung himself headlong into Sally's arms, burrowing his head into her shoulder.

"Oh, Matt!" cried his sister ruefully. "Why will you be so bold as to go into the natives' runway and flaunt your knowledge of the tongue right beneath Father's nose?"

Matt sniffed and gulped before he could answer. "I for-got Fa-Father was h-home still . . . and George's fa-father was t-t-telling me about the p-puppies they ha-have. And he's going to g-give me one! And it's si-silly not to let us t-talk with the natives when Father and M-mother spend all their time fussing with them." He sniffed and let out one final roar of chagrin and went on, "And when they talk the language before us and make us go to church where it's all Hawaiian . . . they must think we're awfully stupid if we don't learn it."

He paused out of breath with his long speech. Sally pulled out her handkerchief and mopped his face and helped him to blow his nose. She patted him consolingly. "It does seem queer," she agreed soberly, "but they think it's for our good, and it makes them happier to think that we can't understand the natives because the natives make jokes of things we mustn't talk about. Of course we know what they're saying, but I don't think we ought to worry Father and Mother by letting them know that we know. You see that's one of the reasons why they always send the mission children away to school way across the world—so they won't be con-contam-i-nated by the evil licentiousness of the benighted heathen—at least that's what Father says it is." She hugged him as he gave a quivering sigh, and kissed his ear. "Now do be good, Matt," she begged, "and don't get into any more trouble today to worry Mother with. She said for you to study 'specially your multiplication tables."

Keeping one eye on her charges, ready to leap up to help them from time to time, she settled herself to learn her irregular Latin verbs for the day to be able to recite them to her mother after lunch. If the children didn't need too much help, she decided, she would be able to finish both the six sentences of composition and the long paragraph of translation from Cæsar's commentaries on his Gallic wars before noon. She sighed, remembering that she had four more algebra problems to do before Father came home in the afternoon.

At nine o'clock, seeing the children bent over their work, Sally tiptoed from the room and down the stairs. She took a large pan from the pantry shelves and crouched down beside the wooden cask where the dried apples were kept. She liked the soft puckered texture of the dried fruit as she plunged her hands in the cask to fill her pan. She poured water over the fruit and set the pan aside for the apples to swell. Then she sorted the taro, cut the tubers from their tops and scrubbed them vigorously.

"All's ready now," she thought, "so I shall have time to do my translation and the algebra after I make the pie. I had best be after the fish, and I hope its head is cut off and its in'ards gone, for I do hate to see them staring at me. I wish people didn't have to eat dead things, though I like meat and fish as well as anyone, once it is cooked and on the table."

She ran around the corner of the house and made her way towards the girls' school, waving her hand to Lizzie Judd, who peered from a window across the way. "We're 'most through with our lessons," she shrieked across the road to Sally. "Can you play in our yard?"

Sally shook her head, midway between regret and pride. "The children are behind with their lessons, and I must bake for dinner—maybe this afternoon . . ." she called and ran on.

"Our mother doesn't make us cook," Lizzie's shrill voice floated after her. "Polly gets our dinner!"

Sally turned and stuck her tongue out at Lizzie and shook herself irritably. "Lizzie can make me awfully riled sometimes," she thought as she went into the room of the school where her mother taught a class of forty girls. Her mother nodded toward a basket in the corner and went on with the recitation she was hearing. Sally grasped the basket and tiptoed out, conscious of the whispering her entry had set up among the children.

"Sally!" Her mother's voice called her back. Constancy smiled and held out a letter. "I forgot for the moment. Mr. Chamberlain received a bundle of letters from Kailua early this morning, and here is one for you from Lucy."

Sally took the letter and hurried home with it, a little disappointed that it was from Lucy Thurston and not from one of the Richards children from Lahaina. Since Lucy with her sister Persis had been received into the Church at the last general meeting, her letters were likely to be filled with pious exhortations to her undedicated little friends to love Jesus and pray for redemption.

Dropping upon a hassock in the kitchen, she tore open
the sheet of paper, fastened together for purposes of mail-
ing and bare of an envelope. No letter was to be disregarded when letters were so scarce. She read:

Kailua, April 25th, 1837.
MY DEAR LITTLE FRIEND: ("H'mph!" grunted Sally, "I'm
just as tall as she is, if I am five years younger!")

*There is word that a boat will leave for Honolulu this
evening, so I must write a few words to one whom I love
and pray for each day, wishing her a contented and profit-
able birthday (though I fear this letter will not come until the day is gone or much before we ourselves arrive. Our
boat leaves in three days). I look forward to seeing you at
the General Meeting next month, but realize always that
we must ever be prepared for death, and hope that, if God
should will us not to meet again on earth, we may meet at
His throne. Oh, my dear little Sally, Persis and I and the
Ruggles children all pray earnestly that God may move
your spirit at the general meeting to profess openly your
love and trust in Him. Love Jesus, and consider how bene-
ficial an influence your coming to God would have on
your little brother and sisters.*

*Our kind father took us on a long walk in the moun-
tains yesterday and taught us the genus and species of
many plants. It was a most enjoyable and* instructive ex-
*cursion. Give my love to your dear mother and father and
the little ones, and remember, dear Sally, that you are ever
in my thoughts and prayers.*

Your affectionate friend,
LUCY GOODALE THURSTON.

Sally folded up the letter and tucked it into her pocket.
Lucy was very, very good, but her letters weren't very

exciting. A frown puckered her brow as she measured out
flour and salt and lard for the pie crust. The general meeting of missionaries from all the islands was to begin on
May 3rd, and most of the missionaries would be arriving
in a day or two. She liked the excitement of having the
children from the other islands to talk to and play with,
even if there was extra work and cooking to do, but—
and she deliberately faced the matter—she did not like the
way they all kept at you to confess yourself a real Christian before all the meeting. Mr. Coan was the worst. She
shuddered at the recollection of the last meeting, when
Mr. Coan had applied himself to the children, taking them
in groups, or, in special instances of difficult children (like
herself), he would back the child into a little room alone
and pray and reason, his eyes never leaving the face of the
victim thus cornered, his resonant voice rising and falling
in impassioned prayer and exhortation that the little sinner might repent and come to God. And Sally—the more
she was urged to love God and consider the pangs of hell,
the harder grew her heart, till it felt like a lump of iron in
her body. When she was alone, and rain had fallen so that
the trees and grass looked fresh and green, and the sky
was blue with small puffs of cloud skimming across it, her
heart was never a lump of iron, but so full it almost over-
flowed with a feeling of love for everyone—God, too; or,
when Mother kissed her or smiled just for her, she felt
loving and good, but no sooner would anyone begin to
plead with her to love God than she was sure that she
didn't love Him at all.

"When I am big and have children," she vowed, rolling
out the crust, "I'm going to leave them alone about God,
and I'm not going to frighten them to death about hell."
She nodded decisively as she lined the deep pan with thin
crust, heaped it with the apples, covered the fruit with

sugar and sprinkled it with nutmeg, and then pinched down the upper crust with its neat perforations. She went out to lay more wood on the fire and then popped the pie into the bake oven. She hurried back to the family living room upstairs to finish her lessons.

2

After dinner, when her father took up his hat and announced that he was driving with Dr. Judd to Waikiki, Sally thought happily that her mother might take the children walking down by the waterfront and perhaps let them go bathing. Her face fell when her mother came downstairs tying on her sober black bonnet.

"Oh, Mother, must you go out?" she cried, disappointment written plain upon her features. "I had hoped you might take us to the beach this afternoon."

Constancy shook her head. "The *kuhina nui* sent for me. She wants me to make her a dress of some new silk that arrived yesterday. But if I get through in time, perhaps we can go down by the water." She stood at the back door shading her eyes and looking out to sea. "Sally!" There was a swift change in her voice. "Look! Isn't that brig nearing the harbor your Uncle Nathan's?"

Sally dragged up a chair and, climbing on it, peered into the distance beyond the masts of the *Clementine*, the drifting prison where two Catholic priests, Father Short and Father Bachelot, were confined by order of the king. She could see the white gleam of sails. A moment more and she was able to see the entire brig. "It does look like the *Mary Ellen!* Oh, Mother, I'm sure it is. Do hurry so we can go down to the water by the time it gets in!"

Her mother nodded. "It will be pleasant to see Uncle Nate again. He is a fine man, Sally. Never forget that he is a great-hearted man and a wise one—even though he is not a professing Christian. Well,"—and she straightened her bonnet—"I shall try to get away from her soon."

She was gone, and Sally perched on a high stool and peered out to sea. It was exciting having her mother's uncle a sea captain who came in once a year with grand presents for everyone. She called to Faith and Silly, at play in the *kapu* yard, and to Matt upstairs, still muttering over his lessons: "Faith, Silly, Matt! Come see!" Matt came rushing down the stairs, and his sisters left their play. "It's Uncle Nate's ship!"

Matt let out a whoop. "What'll he bring us this trip, Sally?" he roared in loud eagerness.

"Shame, Matt," reprovingly, "to think of presents right away!" But she blushed, because her own thoughts had hovered about the subject of presents, too. "Mother said she'd hurry back from Kinau's and take us down to the boat."

The two Bingham children who were too young to be sent away to school came running to look seaward, too. It was Sally's duty to keep an eye on these children on afternoons when their mother was busy at the school.

A sudden clamor in the road, the noise of some sudden riot, took the children scurrying to the front yard. They saw the British priest, the only Catholic priest who had escaped banishment from the islands, walking down the street, pursued by a small crowd of half-grown Hawaiian boys, who were yelling far from complimentary salutes in their native tongue. Across the way the little Judds, Lizzie and the younger twins, hung over their gate, their eyes and mouths so many O's. Encouraged by their audience, the native boys sent a small flurry of pebbles after the priest. Most of them struck harmlessly enough against his robe until he turned in angry remonstrance and a larger stone struck him on the side of the head. He staggered for a step or two and threw up his arm to shield his head.

Sally burst through the gate of the mission yard and flung herself into the midst of the native boys with an avalanche of abuse in the language she was supposed not to know. "Cowards!" she screamed shrilly, dancing up and down. "Lower than *poi* dogs! Shame, for so many of you to band against one who does nothing to you! Go home, every one of you. You call yourselves Christians! Be glad if God doesn't strike you dead before you can get home!"

Pebbles and stones dropped inconspicuously to the road, and the boys backed away, muttering, their eyes rolling. Sally advanced upon them, shaking her red head menacingly. "Quick! Or I'll *kahuna* every one of you!" She stopped aghast at what she had shouted on the roadway and hoped madly that Mr. Bingham was safely out of the way and in no position to hear the threat she had made.

She turned to the priest, her chest rising and falling with the fury of her outburst. There was blood trickling from a cut on his cheekbone. "Oh!" she cried in pity. "You're hurt! I'm so sorry." She cast a swift look about her: there were only children in sight, and she knew there were no grown-ups in the house at this hour. "If you will come into the kitchen, I will bathe it for you." She held open the gate for him. The priest looked at her curiously, a smile twitching at his mouth.

"Thank you," he said and passed into the mission yard. "Will you not get into trouble with your parents for harboring a—'papist'?" he quizzed her with mild irony as she conducted him into the kitchen and pulled forth a chair for him to sit on.

"I don't know," answered Sally, busy with a cloth and a bowl of water. "It is right that I should help you, whatever happens." She turned to see the five children staring at the unusual guest from the doorway. "Run outside and play!" she bade them sharply. "It is rude to stare." They vanished slowly and reluctantly. She gently bathed the bruise on the priest's head.

"You are a proper little Puritan and believe in following your conscience even if it gets you into trouble, then?"

Sally paused in her labor and met his mocking but not unfriendly gaze. "I am not as good as a Puritan," she said seriously, "and I often would much rather not do what my conscience tells me I ought to do."

"But you don't want even an 'idolatrous papist' to have his head cracked open with rocks?"

She shook her head quickly. "I can't bear to have things hurt!" And then with a glance toward the cooking house. "May I not give you a cup of tea?"

"Thank you, child. It would be refreshing—if it won't incriminate you the further with your parents." He looked musingly after her as she took down the teapot, standing upon the very tips of her toes to reach it from the shelf. After enduring several years of varied forms of persecution because of his religion, it amused him to be entertained in the sanctuary of a Protestant missionary home.

Sally came back, the tea made. "The kettle was still boiling from dinner time," she explained. "How much sugar do you take?"

"Two teaspoons," absently. "You are kind to trouble yourself for a person your family would like to see put off the islands."

Sally raised her eyes in protest. "They *wouldn't* like to see you put off the islands. Father doesn't want the papists to mislead the natives," she explained ingenuously, "but he says he thinks it wrong to persecute them so bitterly; and Mother is kind to everyone and says we do not understand you well enough to judge you."

"That is liberal enough," said the priest seriously enough, but humor lighted his face for an instant. "And it is nature for them to be pig-headed about their faith. Everyone is. To a Catholic there is only the one Church. We reach God through the intercession of the Blessed Virgin and the holy saints. You try to see God through the crooked and tortured reasoning of that madman of yours, John Calvin, who cowed the ignorant into taking his ravings for the Gospel." He drank down the rest of his tea and rose to his feet. "But there—I mustn't speak against your faith when you are kind enough to offer me hospitality." Smiling, he held out his hand. "Will you shake hands with the enemy, child?"

Sally slipped her thin little hand into the priest's substantial one. "My name is Sally Williams, and I don't think you are my enemy." She grinned fleetingly. "You tell me if those boys bother you any more and I'll scare the fear of God into them."

Father Walsh chuckled and then absently gave the Protestant child a Catholic blessing before he set forth once more into a hostile world.

No sooner was he out of the house than the children rushed in: Three Williamses, two Binghams, and Lizzie Judd from across the way.

"Sally Williams!" shrieked Lizzie. "Whatever will the brethren say when they hear you've had a papist right in the mission house? You'll catch it from your father when he gets home!"

Sally looked coldly at Lizzie. This was one of the days when Lizzie got on her nerves. "It doesn't matter one little bit to me, Lizzie Judd," she said with great dignity, "what the brethren say. My parents don't think it is right to persecute the Catholics, even if they are misguided, and your own mother said she felt that way, too. I heard her say so to Mother." She hesitated and then thrust her pointed chin higher in the air. "If you want to find out what the brethren will say, why, you can go and tell them all about it. You always did like to tattle, anyway."

Lizzie sniffed. "Miss Pert!" she said loftily and then, in a flash, thrust out her pointed red tongue at Sally and ran out of the house.

Matt burst forth admiringly, "Oh, Sally! Weren't you scared to speak to a papist? How'd you know he wouldn't run off with you?"

Sally answered sharply: "Don't be silly, Matt! Why on earth should he want to run off with me?"

Matt's eyes rolled toward the door. "Lizzie told us that they kidnaped children and took 'em home to torture them till they would bow down and worship graven images."

Sally "h'mphed" disgustedly. "That Lizzie Judd tells more lies than any child of respectable folk should. Don't you believe any such tommyrot from her or anybody else. That's just super—superstition!"

Faith edged closer to her sister and looked fearfully over her own shoulder. "But, Sally—aren't ghosts superstition, too?"

"Ye-s!"

"But you were scared last year one time when Mother had you take some fish over to Mrs. Judd after dark. You know you were scared that a *lapu* would get you. You came running home all out of breath and cried and told Mother you felt a *lapu* breathe on the back of your neck."

Sally blushed. "I was younger then . . . and Martha had been telling me a lot of foolish stories about evil spirits of the bad, dead people. And she said that if you carried fish after dark, the *lapu* would be sure to chase you and twitter in your ear and breathe down your neck. But Mother said it wasn't true, and Father wouldn't let Mar-

tha work for us after that because of her telling us all that
stuff."

She gathered up the cup and saucer and spoon the priest
had used and paused in the doorway. "Anyway, don't you
children believe any silly stories about the Catholics. They
believe in their religion just like the brethren believe in
ours, and anyway I thought that Father Walsh was a nice
man. So there!" She disappeared into the pantry and then
came back to say, "And there's no point in your telling
Mother and Father about this. If they hear about it and
ask me I'll tell them all about it, but there's no sense in
going out of your way to tell everything you know."

It was half-past three before their mother returned
from the palace, a bundle of wine-colored silk under her
arm. Sally had all of the children scrubbed and combed
and their hats on, but her eagerness changed to concern
when she saw how tired her mother looked.

"You look so tired, Mother! We don't have to go down,"
she began.

But her mother shook her head, smiling a little. "I'd
rather go, Sally. I guess I'm getting old to get tired for
nothing. Just wait till I wash my face and smooth my hair
and we'll set off." She hurried upstairs, and Sally looked
after her sorrowfully.

"I'm no better than the little ones," she thought repentantly. "She's feeling just as bad as ever about Miriam,
and she's had to go on about her work just the same. But
she *isn't* getting old. She—she's *lovely*, even if she has to
wear the horrid old clothes that the board sends out to us.
I wish I were older and more good so I could help her
more."

Constancy came back, her burnished hair in shining

even waves over her ears, showing beneath the curved brim of the black poke bonnet she had worn for four years. "Come, children," she said. "We must hurry. The boat's just pulling in, and it would never do for Uncle Nate to have none to meet him."

They hurried along over the rough path to the waterfront and arrived in time to throw their arms around the big, sun-burned, blue-coated captain as he jumped from the small boat to shore.

"Ah, Connie!" he cried, giving his niece a hug and kissing her heartily. "It's great to be seeing you after these months on the water! You're still good to look at, child, but they've been wearing you out. You look done in!"

"No, no, Uncle Nate!" She was half laughing, half crying, and clinging to his arm. "I'm just getting old with the rest of them for all your flattery. But I'm so *glad* you came. I've needed you."

He patted her shoulder with a large brown paw and turned with a genial roar to the children. "Here, you young scalawags! Can't you let an honest seaman have a word with your mother that you don't go hanging on his belt and tearing the clothes off him?" He lifted first Silly and then Faith high in the air while they shrieked with glee, and, setting them down, he swung Matt clear over his shoulder, turning him completely upside down. He greeted Sally a little more respectfully. "Here's my girl! Connie, this one's your child, all right, but for her red hair, and that suits her well enough. Hi!" and he was off shouting orders for his chest to be brought to the mission house and cheerily promising to hamstring and skin alive the sailor he put in charge of the Hawaiian, who was to bring it in an ox cart, if the chest failed to appear before dark.

"How long can you stay, Uncle Nate?" asked Constancy. "I hope you'll not think you have to be off in a week this trip?"

"Only so long as it takes to do my business with the king," he said.

Constancy's face lightened. "Then it will be some time! The king's at Lahaina, and not even this squabble about the two priests whom the British and French consuls say must stay, and the governor and Kinau keep out on the *Clementine*, has brought him back yet. But I imagine he'll arrive by the end of June."

"He'd better. He owes me three thousand in sandalwood for the furniture and silks and knickknacks he asked me to pick up for him in China. I was more interested, Connie, in the knickknacks I picked up for you and the children."

"What'd you bring me, Uncle Nate?" yelled Matt, bursting out of bounds.

"Oh, Matt!" in scandalized chorus from Sally and Constancy. But their uncle chuckled. "Let the boy alone. It does me good to see you've made no little godling out of him."

"Uncle Nate!" reproved Constancy gently; but he merely chuckled again.

The sea chest came while Sally and her mother were laying the supper on the table. The captain straightway opened it up before their wondering eyes. "The supper be blowed!" he twinkled when his niece murmured that the children should contain themselves till the meal was eaten. "Their digestion will suffer from anticipation if we make them wait so long. There's none of your long-faces around to shake their heads if we put a bit of pleasure before business this once."

Constancy shook her head at him, but she obligingly dropped into a chair near the chest and took Silly on her lap. "Make haste, then, but you spoil these giddy children."

He unroped the chest and flung back the heavy cover. He rummaged in high good humor among its assorted contents. "Here's something for the babies!" and he pulled forth two richly clad Chinese dolls and laid them in the outstretched arms of Faith and Silly. "And here's for you —to match your eyes!" He flung a string of jade over Sally's head. Silently she fingered them. Lovely, lovely . . . the color of the water near the shore.

"Oh, Uncle Nate!" she whispered.

He handed Matt a miniature junk and a bright toy sword and a tiny temple carved from ivory. With a wicked grin he handed a small white jade figure, perhaps five inches tall, to Constancy. "Her name's Kwan Yin, Connie, and she is merciful. Thought you might find her pleasant to have around."

Constancy touched the figure wonderingly. "She is beautiful, Uncle Nate. This stuff she is made of—so—so pure a substance, so lovely to the touch. She's so fragile and precious-looking."

"She is," he assured her. "You might look through all China before you find another like her. But here!" and he drew forth lengths of brocade and other silk, and heaped them over Constancy's lap. Soft rose, jade green, honey color, and white, the materials tumbled over one another. "There, now," he chuckled. "You and the small girls here can deck yourselves out so gayly you'll be read out of meeting."

His niece passed her hand lovingly over the shining softness of the silk. "The brethren and sisters may caution us not to be made proud by our fine plumage, Uncle Nate, but they all know too well the dearth of any kind of cloth over here to quibble over its color and texture. You have been all too lavish—as usual, Uncle Nate. You spoil us badly. But now, truly we must lay these things aside and eat our supper." She folded the silks carefully and put them on a towel at the far end of the long table.

The captain settled himself at the table with a sigh of pleasure, as Constancy bore a baked omelet in from the oven, followed by Sally with a plate of biscuits.

"There's something on the ship for Jonathan," he said. "It was too big to get off today. It'll be along tomorrow— Chinese desk affair, more like a cabinet. Thought he might have some use for it."

Constancy's face lighted with pleasure. "He will be so pleased, Uncle Nate. We have so little furniture, and what we have is rudely made from odd pieces of ill-matched wood, and Jonathan has a love of beautiful things that gets little gratifying in a country like this. I wish he could have been here to see the children's pleasure. He went off with Dr. Judd to make the rounds at Waikiki and is likely not to return till late."

The captain made a droll face at her. "I'm not too sad, though, Connie, to have a chance for a visit with you alone for once. These three times my ship has stopped here I've had to talk at you over a dozen families. . . . By the way, where are they all?"

"There was a supper and social gathering at the big Chamberlain house this evening. You know we had a rein-forcement of thirty that arrived on the *Mary Frazier* two weeks ago. We had three of that number quartered with us, and Mrs. Bingham took care of five, having more cots to spare, but my three have been out at Ewa, looking over the field there, and I think they cannot be back for two days more. It is well to have more help in the teaching especially—it will give some of us older ones more time to attend to the wants of our own children."

"You don't have much time for frivolity, do you?" The captain's mouth went down grimly. "You people chose a dour God to follow."

Constancy's eyebrows lifted warningly. "Hush, Uncle Nate . . . the children . . ."

The children were all in bed except Sally, who was privileged to stay up an hour longer than the others. She was left to finish her algebra problems. Constancy turned from tucking in Matt.

"Uncle Nate, if you are not too tired, we might walk down to the shore . . ."

He laughed. "D'you think I can't keep up with a thin little wench like you just because my hair's going gray? After all there's only twelve years' difference in our ages if you are my niece. But I should think *you* might be glad of a chance to sit and fold your hands for a time."

"I like to get out in the air." They went together down the stairs. She went on, "It's curious that people living in a land made for life in the open should have to spend so much of their time indoors as we missionary folk." She sighed.

Her uncle took her arm and walked beside her down the path that led to the shore. "Connie," he said, perturbed, "what are you doing here with all these pious folk, girl? I swear I can't fathom it to this day. . . . Why, I remember you a girl with a head for nothing but story books and poetry and a fair amount of mischief! And then, over-night, here's Constancy a good girl with her life dedicated to converting the heathen, married to a parson with white hair and eyes that burn holes through you and not a thought in his cranium except for the salvation of souls!"

Constancy walked in silence beside him. He went on after a pause: "The whole belief is so unlike you, child! You were always a gay thing—full of life and harmless pranks as a colt—and here you take up with a crew that won't hear of any good in this world and ignore everything that's natural and good for man and will make him happy—all for fear of landing in hell. And nobody but a maniac could ever have cooked up such a system of damnation as theirs. Let me tell you, child, back in the states there are fewer and fewer folk who swallow this thought of a God Who treats his creatures worse than the worst villain alive would treat the orn'riest cur dog. You don't really believe this truck, do you, Connie?"

Constancy's voice reached his ear, small and fearful and stifled: "No . . . I don't think I believe *anything* any more . . . not a single solitary thing! But I've got to pretend I do as long as I live . . . I guess."

"Well," ejaculated her uncle blankly, "I'll be hamstrung! But"—and he came to life suddenly—"what in the name of all the gods are you doing here wearing yourself out and denying yourself to life these eighteen years if you don't believe any of it?"

Constancy shrugged. Her tired brain thrust forward little tendrils of explanation. None of them seemed adequate. Nineteen years ago she looked upon young Jonathan Williams and found him beautiful, and loved him so much that she perjured herself that she might be his wife. Sammie . . . so many years ago, saying "He's a mean God to drown all the kitties and the ladies and the babies . . . I shan't worship him. I love the nice God that liked the albatross." Sammie dying, and she half mad with the thought of small beautiful Sammie tortured forever and ever because his mother was a sinner, because a baby not five years old refused to have any dealings with a God

Who would destroy kittens and babies. The long weeks of fever and the sudden return to life from the swirling delirium; the cool awareness within her brain and heart that the God of the brethren did not exist . . . simply because she herself had ceased to believe in Him. The blessed slipping of the burden from her shoulders and the shouldering of this lighter burden of pretense and subterfuge for Jonathan's sake, Jonathan, who had long ceased to be godlike to her but whom she loved with such deep, pervasive tenderness and compassion as none of her children since Sammie had drawn from her. Jonathan trusted her to reassure him and encourage him on this thorny way he had chosen in defiance of his youthful blood so many years ago; Jonathan trusted her to be a sacrificial offering to duty, a passive, never responsive partner to those rare moments when necessity drove him grimly to her arms, thus allowing him to escape a subsequent conviction of sin. Jonathan was forlorn in his chosen world and must cling to his illusion of her strength.

Aloud she said: "Jonathan needs me, Uncle Nate. I became a missionary because I loved Jonathan, and he depends upon me—as much as a child would. I believed . . . when I married him. Growing up as I did—when there was no thought of anything but this kind of faith anywhere around me—I could scarcely help believing, but I hated it all. Then when Sammie died—twelve, nearly thirteen years ago—I just stopped believing anything." She pushed her hair back from her forehead. Words came so hard. Love and caution had for so long set a guard upon her tongue—almost upon her thoughts. She thought now, "How could I have gone on believing—with Sammie dead —without going mad! The awful fear down deep always that some thoughtless word, some act, will expose me— a heretic in the inner circle—and make me an outcast from Jonathan—and he couldn't bear not trusting in me."

Her uncle was speaking violently: "My God! What a life you picked for yourself! You've iron in your soul, Connie, or you'd break. How do you put up with it?"

"I'm accustomed to it now—one becomes accustomed to just about anything in eighteen—nearly nineteen—years." Her inner voice went on: "Yes, one becomes accustomed even to seeing one's children growing up with so little of the happiness that every child ought to have, denied their mother's time—even her presence—because she is duty-bound to put the interests of other people's children before her own."

And as if his sharp blue eyes saw into her brain, Uncle Nate was saying: "You've made your own bed and may get some satisfaction out of lying in it uncomplainingly, child, but your children—how about them? Knowing this stuff rammed down their throats is all wrong, can you abide to see it?"

"Barely," she replied, almost inaudibly. "It is part of the price I have to pay—but I think I comfort myself with the thought that each new generation is removed from the old—that my children will think for themselves —perhaps." She thought: "Oh, Sally, I was so proud of you and such a weight rolled from my heart last year, when you sat during all those intolerable exhortations at the general meeting, with your little face so grim and unyielding. Matt—so impulsive, so headstrong—do I delude myself that you are not the stuff from which stern men of God are made? Jonathan—so serious, so thoughtful— I don't know . . . will he always be content with the answers in Watts' Catechism? And Miriam . . . Oh, my poor baby, so good and so gentle . . . yet you were merry, too! How can a mother tell what her children really think?

"Uncle Nate!" Her throat contracted; she swallowed, and tightened her clasp upon his arm. "I couldn't tell you before—not with the children happy over their gifts—but yesterday word came to us that Miriam died . . . typhus . . . last November." She ended with a sob.

The captain's arm encircled her, and he paused to lay his cheek against the top of her head, murmuring angrily phrases of comfort in her ear. She heard snatches of words rumbling past her, "Madness to send mere babies across the world from their parents . . . cruel . . . unnatural . . . poor child!"

She straightened up. "It has been horrible—horrible—sending them away. Jonathan and Miriam went together—more than five years ago! Peter went away three months ago when the Richards boys left. The boys will be grown men when I see them again—*if* I see them again. Miriam . . ."

In the dim light, her uncle could see her hands clenched, making tense little hammering motions before her. In jerky torrents words poured from her: "Our own children are the last to be considered. . . . We leave the house early in the morning to teach native children to read and write and to mouth the catechism. . . . We mothers are at the beck and call of any woman in the palace who wants a new dress. We must teach the children of the chiefs in our spare hours. We never have a moment we can call our own! And *I* . . . don't even have the consolation of thinking I am pleasing God by denying every natural impulse. Oh, these poor wretches!" She whirled upon him. "They're frightened to death of the tenderness they feel for their own children—there's too much joy for them in the love they have for their children, and they mistrust joy and agonize for fear God counts their love idolatry. They have to go out of their way to show God that they really do *not* put their children before Him. I used to think these people were fiends . . . without natural feelings, but they aren't fiends. The Binghams are the sternest of the lot, and their sense of duty compels them to send their children away for fear they may be contaminated by the influence of the natives, by their parents' enforced neglect of their education. They do it, but it nearly kills them. Mrs. Bingham is an invalid—only her will keeps her alive and allows her to work as she does. She looks like death for months when a child of hers leaves. Even Mr. Bingham, as austere a man as ever walked the earth, goes about in a daze for weeks after the boat goes. How can any flesh-and-blood parent feel otherwise? *Babies* sent off across the world . . . and no way of knowing for over a year whether they even arrive alive! What more does anyone need to know of hell?"

Her uncle groaned in sympathy and outrage. "Connie, child, is there naught I can do to help you? Come, child, pack every last child on my ship and I'll take the lot of you back home where you belong!"

His words brought Constancy up sharp. She made a sound that was midway between a sob and a laugh. "Oh, Uncle Nate, how good you are—and how impractical! I shouldn't let myself go in this fashion, but . . . I've been pent up for so long I just had to say it. I shouldn't foist my troubles upon you, though. There's naught to be done about what is in the past, but no other child of mine is to be sent away. Sally was to go this fall, but Jonathan has agreed that she need not. She would have gone with Peter, but I couldn't do without her here—she is such a responsible little thing and such a help with the children."

She caught his arm again, and they resumed their walk along the edge of the water. He spoke stubbornly: "You say the word, Connie, and I'll take the whole lot of you

back. . . . Lord! How human beings will torture themselves for a silly notion—when all they need to know is
that they are here for a few years—that the world is beautiful—in spots, at any rate—and that happiness is good
for anyone. And here these brethren of yours, not content
with making themselves uncomfortable, come over here
and scare the natives out of their wits with their talk of
hell. Trying to make Puritans out of the easiest-going race
on earth! Here you have them dressed up and smoothed
down, the higher-ups all sitting on chairs when they are
happier lying on mats, teaching them that man was made
for the Sabbath, scowling them out of countenance when
they break over and dance or drink or try to have a good
time in their own way! It beats me, Connie. And the
deuce of it is that you missionary folk really make yourselves more miserable than you do these poor devils."

They were silent for a moment. Then, "It *is* tragic,"
Constancy said slowly, "to stop and think of what . . .
what impoverished lives the missionaries force upon themselves—all from a sense of duty—and how hard they are
upon anyone who can't follow the pattern the leaders lay
down for the rest. Take the Holmans who came out with
us. He was the only doctor in the first years—only
twenty-five when he came, and his wife was about the
same age. It was really his good work among the sick
natives that put the rest of us into the good graces of the
chiefs, but he was in love with his wife—solicitous of her
to the point of going against the decrees of the Family for
her comfort—so the Holmans were excommunicated—
sent back in disgrace—for no better reason than that they
were young and human and loved each other. Poor young
man, he died a year or two after they reached America—
and I heard that she has married again."

The captain "H'mphed" loudly but made no other

comment. They walked on a few paces without speaking, until a small chuckle burst from Constancy. "Then take those poor wretches they sent out to the Marquesas!" she said. "The Armstrongs and the Alexanders and the Parkers. There had been tales of what a fine race of aborigines hungering for the true faith was to be found there. The Armstrongs and Alexanders had been here a year or so and had a child each. The Parkers were new arrivals, utterly inexperienced, newly married. Off they went with a native servant Mrs. Bingham sent along with them to help make their lives more bearable. When they stopped at Tahiti a local missionary gave them a cow—luckily for their children. When they reached their island their captain wanted to take them back. The natives were savages. There were no white settlers. The natives were sufficient unto themselves. They weren't docile like the Hawaiians. They managed their own affairs quite competently— didn't quarrel among themselves—only with other tribes. They were industrious and self-contained—and skeptical. When the missionaries would explain about Christ, the natives would grunt and say 'It's a lie,' and go on about their own affairs.

"They warred a good deal with hostile tribes and killed and ate their captives right under the noses of the missionaries. Only one native was a real friend to the missionaries; he was a man of rank, and he forbade his people to molest them. Then he died and the natives hung his corpse up in a tree near the missionary settlement and brought offerings of food to it. You can imagine the result after a few days of exposure in a tropical country. The poor missionaries lived a ghastly life, expecting to be made into soup at any moment, now that their one friend was dead.

"Then a missionary from the Society Islands visited the island and assured them of the futility of their work and the increased danger to them since their friend had died. Another thing that frightened them to death was the interest the natives took in the white children; they were always pestering the missionaries to give them the babies. Mrs. Parker had a new baby born there that the natives particularly wanted. She told me that there was a chance of their wanting to bring him up as a chief, but there was an equal chance that they wanted him for a stew. Anyway, when two whaleships came to the island, the sailors lined up with rifles and the missionaries, the women holding the babies under their aprons, marched on board and sailed back here."

"How were they greeted?" queried the captain laconically.

Again there was a little chuckle from Constancy. "As if they were criminals! Would you believe it, Uncle Nate, the brethren had a powwow and censured them dreadfully. They had failed in their duty; they were failures, weak, selfish—I don't remember all the things that were said about them. The women of the Family were a little more lenient—because of the children. The brethren shuffled the three families off about the islands—they did make one abortive attempt to make the Parkers go off to some other outlandish island, but Mr. Parker was riled and refused outright, so the brethren sent the Parkers over to the new station at Kaneohe . . . as far from what little civilization we have as could be. They had no floors in the hut they had to live in, and the ground was so uneven Mrs. Parker couldn't rock the baby's cradle. When they asked for some boards to set the cradle on, so the baby could be rocked properly, word was sent back that they couldn't have any boards to rock the cradle on because they had failed in their duty!"

The captain let out a roar of laughter. "They're still here, aren't they? Were they ever forgiven?"

"Well, after a time—when their own account of the affair had reached the home board back in Boston and been mulled over, a letter came from the board saying that they had done right to return. The scandal died down then, though some of the missionaries still cold-shoulder them a bit."

"But, Connie," his voice was serious, "do you think in your heart that the missionaries have done enough good to balance the harm they do to one another and to the natives?"

Constancy's voice sounded weary as she answered: "It's hard to answer that question—hard to know. In one way the natives are better off than they were when we came. I know how you feel—I feel the same way about trying to stamp out the natural gayety of the natives—and it can't be denied that they are dying out rapidly—every census shows fewer Hawaiians born. The death rate is ahead of the birth rate. Those things are bad, but, on the other hand, the poor people have more rights. The chiefs aren't quite so ready to take away the little the poor have, and Mr. Bingham with the help of the other brethren is slowly getting the king around to apportioning the land and giving permanent titles to it, so that no one can be put off on a moment's notice, destitute. I think that will be definitely arranged in a year or two more.

"You've asked a hard question. On the face of the matter I'll admit freely that the natives are so simple and likable and the missionaries so unlikable. Yet . . . you can't live with the missionary families as I have and not realize how awfully *good* they are. They are ruthless in dealing with one another if they think anyone has lapsed in duty —yet they are utterly selfless. They're appallingly sincere;

they cheerfully endure living on top of one another—with no privacy, putting up with the worst inconveniences imaginable without complaint, and with persecution from most of the foreign population and the whalers who come in and find missionary-induced laws to interfere with their pleasure."

The captain was frowning thoughtfully in the darkness. "Constancy," he said slowly after a pause, "I can't make these people over for you—much as I'd like to—but maybe I can make life a bit easier for you. I've got a plan that might make life pleasanter for you and for me as well. You know I do a good deal of business here now—have to stop off once and sometimes twice a year for several weeks. I'd just as soon have a place of my own here. Now if I were to build a house and wanted you to keep it for me and live in it so I could have a place to come to, the brethren couldn't object to that, could they?"

Constancy gasped. "Oh, Uncle Nate! . . . But wouldn't it take a lot of money?"

"Well—not enough to ruin me. It'd make life a deal pleasanter for me, and you would like it, wouldn't you?"

"Would I like it?" Constancy threw back her head and laughed shakily. "Uncle Nate! Except for a year or two in a grass hut when we first came—before they let us put up the frame house—we have lived under the same roof with anywhere from one to five other families with from two to six children a piece—with walls so thin that anything you say upstairs can be heard in the cellar—one cooking house, one dining room to the lot of us, and everyone getting in everyone else's way all the time. Normally we are packed into the house, but when visitors come from other islands or a new company arrives from the States, we can't draw a deep breath. We have to tuck them away in odd corners and feed anywhere from half a dozen to twenty or thirty extra people.

"Some of the younger ones are arguing to have the Family idea, with everything community property, discarded—have each family receive a definite salary, however small; but a few of the older ones are against it. They think we'd get material-minded if any one family had a complete set of cheap crockery all to itself!"

She broke off apologetically. "I'm talking too much, Uncle Nate—but you see there is a good deal pent up inside after all these years. You asked me how I would like to have a house to call my own!"

He patted her arm. "You say anything you like to me—it'll do you good to get it off your mind. I take it that if I build a house, then, you'll be willing to move into it." He gave an amused little growl of laughter. "Now where'd you like to live—Manoa, Nuuanu, Waikiki?"

"I think . . . at Waikiki," she answered slowly, "right by the water's edge. The children could bathe and play and have more pleasure there, and," she added frankly, "there aren't any other missionaries down there. Oh, Uncle Nate, life would be so much easier!"

"*Will* be, *will* be, Connie," he said loftily and laughed delightedly. "The king owes me a lot of money, and he'll be glad enough to give me a good strip of land in place of some of it, I fancy."

They turned slowly toward the mission house. Constancy rubbed her cheek against her uncle's shoulder.

When they reached the house and climbed the stairs to Constancy's living room, they found Jonathan seated before the table that served him as a desk, his large Bible open before him, but his head buried in his arms. He sprang up as they came into the room.

"Constancy, I was worried about you," he began, and then, recognizing the captain, sprang forward with outstretched hand. "Ah, Captain! You're a welcome visitor here with everyone of us from the oldest to the youngest! I'm sorry not to have been here when you arrived."

The captain shook his hand. "Glad to see you, my boy," he boomed. There was compassion in his feeling for his nephew by marriage, and a touch of reluctant admiration. "I've been taking a stroll and having a talk with Connie that's been a pleasure."

Constancy had been looking at Jonathan solicitously the while. "You are worn out, Jonathan," she said pityingly. "Have you been letting yourself get discouraged again—just because you discovered a backslider or two at the beach?"

He shook his head somberly, dropping into a chair and motioning the captain into an ingeniously contrived rocker which showed four different kinds of wood in its construction. "It's more than one or two, Constancy. I fear we have been guilty of neglecting those poor creatures at Waikiki—one house after another showed the very filth and squalor we have thought to overcome. One house had a young girl—scarcely older than our Sally, but a bold, forward creature—and a sailor, too drunk to be sensible of our reproaches. His purpose there was all too obvious——"

With an effort he broke off and turned to the captain. "But we do wrong to burden you with our worries, sir. Constancy, I think tonight we should be justified in having a glass of the wine that Captain Brown presented to you on his last voyage."

Constancy rose with alacrity. "An excellent idea, Jonathan," she said demurely and went to the small wall cupboard, taking the wine bottle and three small glasses from

its shelves. "Because of the example we must set the natives, we seldom touch liquor of any kind," she explained
to her uncle. "Some of the Family have indeed signed
pledges, swearing they will never touch anything containing alcohol again, but we feel that temperance is more
worthy than complete abstinence." She poured the dark
red liquid into the glasses and handed them to the men and
then filled her own.

The captain lifted his glass toward his niece. "To you,
Connie, and to our secret which I will leave you to share
with Jonathan."

After a few minutes he rose. "Now it is nearly ten
o'clock, and I know how early you must arise in the morning, so if you will show me where you wish to put me, my
dear, I shan't be keeping you awake later."

"I'm putting you on a couch in the dining room, Uncle
Nate—every other nook and cranny is sacred to a missionary for the next few weeks—till the general meeting
is over. Tomorrow we shall have most of them arriving
from the other islands, and we already have those from
the *Mary Frazier*." She lighted a second whale-oil lamp
and preceded him down the stairs.

When she returned, Jonathan was standing before the
washstand making his nightly ablutions, a quaint figure in
his short calico nightshirt that showed his legs, long and
thin as a crane's. She undressed quickly, washed, and
slipped the long-sleeved, high-necked nightgown over her
head, brushed out her long, dull gold hair and braided it
with quick, deft gestures, peered into the little slanting-
roofed room where the children slept, her lamp held high
to make sure that all were covered, blew out the lamp,
and slipped into bed beside Jonathan.

"Jonathan," she said scarcely above a whisper, "it is
wrong for you to reproach yourself with the laxity of

every native on this island. There is much accomplished
here to find favor with God. It is not possible to move
mountains all in a day, and it is the fatigue you suffer
that allows you to despond. A night's sleep will bring you
new hope."

Jonathan sighed and moved his head so that his cheek
lay against her shoulder. "You are right—at least in
part—" he admitted, "but I feel that we have not given
the attention we should to the settlement at Waikiki.
Those souls weigh heavily upon me. The natives are children who must be watched and guarded from their own
worst impulses."

Constancy stirred slightly and put an arm around him.
"Jonathan—I think within a year we may do something
about them. Uncle Nate is going to build a house at the
beach—that he may have a home to come to—and he
wants us to live in it and keep it for him. You see—between us, we should be able to effect some change there."

Jonathan sat up excitedly. "So that is the secret! Constancy, his coming now is a blessing." His mind leaped
ahead. "With a house to ourselves, you can take into it
some of the children from these hovels and train them in
Christian living—and together we can work among them
constantly and patiently. With a house provided for us,
the board should finance a church and a better school
there. Constancy—what should I do without you, my
dear!"

He bent to kiss her forehead and then lay down, his
face turned to the wall.

THE settlement of Honolulu grew. Gradually stone and
adobe or frame houses appeared where formerly grass huts
had stood. The islands, ravished at last of sandalwood, continued to attract whalers. Hawaii did an increasing trade
in goatskins and cattle hides, salt, tobacco, sugar, *kukui*
oil, and arrow root. More schools and churches appeared.
The Catholics continued to be persecuted until in 1839 a
French warship called—after King Kamehameha III had
forbidden absolutely the teaching or practice of the
Catholic religion anywhere in the Hawaiian kingdom and
had made life miserable for such Catholics as he could
ferret out. The Protestant missionaries, harboring no love
for the Catholics, nevertheless cautioned the king against
their persecution, but the king, only recently rid of the
idols of his fathers, was suspicious of the plaster saints of
the priests. Captain Laplace of the French frigate
Artemise, in the summer of 1839, descended upon the
king with a treaty demanding the free practice of Catholic worship in Hawaii and the free gift of land for a
Catholic church in Honolulu; it prohibited the further
persecution of native Catholics and required twenty thousand dollars from the king as guaranty of good behavior.

The *kuhina nui* and the governor, with a long look toward
the frigate with its polished guns trained upon the city,
signed the treaty. Kamehameha, returning from a pleasure
jaunt to Lahaina a little later, stroked his chin and agreed
that they had acted wisely.

Within three years, another French battleship arrived
in Honolulu. The king, being questioned, nervously vowed
that the terms of the treaty had been upheld. The captain
looked skeptical but withdrew. There was reason to believe
that not only France but Great Britain and the United
States were beginning to realize the importance of Hawaii
both as a strategic point in the Pacific and as a coming
agricultural country. The king, subtly besieged from three
points, suffered confusion. During this difficult period,
first the Reverend William Richards and later Dr. Gerrit
Parmele Judd resigned from the mission to become advisers
to the king. Dr. Judd formally renounced his American
citizenship and became a subject of the king. The advisers
worked slowly but surely towards recognition of Hawaii's
independence by the three major powers which menaced
her freedom. There were parleys between the king and
foreign ambassadors. The official visitors waxed wroth at
the shrewdness of the counsel offered by the two ex-
missionaries and demanded their silence. A system of foot-
tapping was inaugurated: it proved quite as effective as
the older, more open means of communication and remained undiscovered by the visitors. One tap on the king's
toe meant that it was permissible to agree to a demand;
two signified refusal.

In 1847 Great Britain, through the connivance of the
British consul, Charlton, sent a commission to seize the
Hawaiian government. Again guns were trained on Honolulu. Alarming rumors of the approach of a French battleship had reached the king's ears. Of the two, he pre-

ferred the British. He yielded. Up went the British flag; all Hawaiian flags the English could lay hands upon were destroyed. Even the king's schooners were taken over and their names changed to the more suggestive *Albert, Adelaide,* and *Victoria.* The invaders recruited from the natives a colorfully uniformed "Queen's Regiment." The recruits were proud of their uniforms, but the Hawaiian government complained bitterly at being forced to support them. Dr. Judd, as king's deputy, resigned by way of protest, and, with no reason to trust the interlopers, made off with the government records to the Royal Tomb, where, in calm hiding, he went on with his work of state, surrounded by the bones of the Kamehamehas and using the lid of Kaahumanu's coffin as a writing desk. For months the British ruled Hawaii with a high hand. Captain Paulet, commander of the British battleship, and Kamehameha III both sent ambassadors carrying letters to the governments of Great Britain and the United States. These, combined with the diplomacy of Admiral Thomas of the British navy, restored the islands to the king in July of 1843. But it took Mr. Richards three years of sailing about the globe to secure the full recognition of Hawaii by the three great nations.

In 1840 the Binghams, driven at last by the steady failing of Mrs. Bingham's health, left the islands, to return after twenty years to their native New England. Before leaving, the Binghams, remembering their own sternly repressed but no less bitter grief at exiling their children from home, gave to the mission family the tract of land at Punahou which had been given Mr. Bingham by the governor—this to become the site of a school wherein the children of missionaries might receive, without separation from their parents, all but a college education.

The early '40's saw the division of public lands, the

making permanent of titles to land. Strictly communal life for the missionaries was ended shortly after the departure of the Binghams. Thereafter the missionaries received meager but individual salaries in return for their labor. By 1852 the government of Hawaii was organized, naturally enough with the king and the chiefs at its head, but with a detailed constitution granting generous rights to the people, a treasure board, which managed systematically and economically the matters of taxation and revenues, an executive branch of the government consisting of five departments—Departments of the Interior, Foreign Relations, Finance, Public Instruction, and Law. The law courts were being efficiently organized. Dr. Judd served the king not only as Minister of Finance but as general adviser, tactfully gathering around his sovereign such men to occupy the other posts as could be relied on for wisdom and ability.

I

1845

Constancy stood at the mahogany dresser in her bedroom and peered intently at her reflection in the mirror. This was the woman her son would see. She tried to remember how he must remember her. She had been thirty-two when he sailed away with Miriam. She shut her eyes and looked back through the years. She had worn an old black silk bonnet when she went to the boat with him, and a green calico dress with great awkward sleeves and a tight waist—not so different from the bodices worn now, but the skirt was skimpy. It was a faded, much-washed dress, and the bonnet had seen four years of service. Those were frugal days. She looked down with quiet pleasure at the heavy folds of her black silk dress. Ten yards of material just in the skirt, she thought complacently. She turned sideways and regarded her silhouette. The long tight sleeves with their frilled white cuffs, and the tight bodice with the frilled white collar, caught with the jade pin Uncle Nate had brought her from China, became her. She was as slim as she had been at twenty. She smiled grimly at her reflection. A life of deceit and being forever on guard was evidently good for the figure. She was glad that she had not spread out as Mrs. Whitney and Mrs. Bishop and some of the other women of her generation had—though having a child every year or year and a half for the first twelve years of marriage was enough to make any woman shapeless.

She bent nearer the mirror to look at her face and shook her head. Her hair that used to be shining and honey-colored was different. It was still heavy and had a wave in it; she dressed it carefully, brushing it hard, but the color of which she had been secretly proud had changed. It was more like light brown now, not much of any color, and there were wide white streaks in the part that covered her ears and went back to form the big knot at the base of her brain. No double chin, though, and her neck didn't look like a plucked chicken's, either—not yet. Her skin fitted smoothly over her bones, a golden tan in color, but there were three wavy lines across her forehead and a fine crisscross pattern of wrinkles at the outer corners of her eyes. Her firmly set lips were no longer red but a faint pink. She sighed. "I'm drab-looking, and I'm old, and he'll be expecting me to look as young as I did thirteen years ago."

She turned away and picked up the black straw poke bonnet lined with white silk and with white ribbons to tie under her chin, and adjusted it carefully. Just then Sally danced in at the door.

"Mother, darling! Please come! I'd weep buckets full of tears if the boat docked before we got there." She broke off and paused, her head on one side to study her mother. "You look awfully beautiful and distinguished," she sighed.

Constancy laughed a little self-consciously. "Foolish child!" she said amiably and turned to scrutinize her eldest daughter. "The dress looks nice on you," she conceded, studying the lines of the yellow muslin with its jade-green ribbons that she had just finished making the day before. "Are the children ready?"

As they left Constancy's bedroom, they met Faith tripping down the hall, resplendent in pale pink muslin and a quilted pink bonnet worn far back on her golden brown curls, her brown eyes snapping with excitement. "Do I look nice?" she burst forth. "Do you suppose he'll like me?"

Her mother's lips closed in a straight line. "If you thought about your lessons half as much as you think about your looks, I wouldn't be having calls from Mr. Dole on your account."

Faith looked sideways at her mother. "Mother, dear, you know a family couldn't be expected to have six children all be angels! You've got Sally and Silly and Jonathan and Peter to be good. You wouldn't appreciate them so much if Matt and I were angels, too."

Her mother's lips relaxed a little. "Get along downstairs and find your sister."

All three went down the broad shallow steps to the lower hall. Silly, white as to hat and gown, the only touch of color being in her black slippers, sat still and abstracted, staring out over the jade green and lavender streaked water. Her lips were moving noiselessly.

"Silly!" Her mother's tone was unusually sharp. Silly

sprang to her feet, her ivory white cheeks turning pink.
Her gray-green eyes were clouded. "Have I kept you
waiting, Mother?" she asked gently. "I'm so sorry."

Constancy shook her head impatiently and was immediately ashamed of herself. "Why should I be so irritated,"
she questioned herself, "when I catch her praying to herself at odd hours? I'm brutal to the child." Aloud she said:
"No, dear, but come along now. Your father has been
waiting with the carriage these last five minutes, and Matt
is ready with the wagon." She looked the girls over
thoughtfully. "There is room for all of you in the carriage
going down, but coming back one of you must ride in the
wagon with Matt and the baggage."

"I will," offered Silly instantly.

Faith twitched a slim shoulder. "You won't, either," she
said abruptly. "I will. You're all in white and will soil lots
more easily than I will."

Constancy recognized the fact that Silly's saintliness
got on Faith's nerves, too. "Better let Faith ride with
Matt," she said. "Come now, or we'll never get there."

Constancy had decreed that her house should face the
ocean rather than the footpath which, with years of usage
by the Williams family, had now become a recognizable
wagon road. Hence she and her daughters went out
through the kitchen to the driveway. Jonathan, frailer
than ever, but stiffly erect in the driver's seat, held the
reins. The two sorrel geldings drowsed in the heat. Faith
climbed in beside her father. Constancy sat in the back
seat with a daughter on either side of her.

"Matt went on ahead." Jonathan remarked over his
shoulder. Constancy nodded. Old Bess plodded along
slowly, and Matt, ever tender with animals, hated to hurry
her.

The carriage jogged along the rough volcanic road

through the coconut palms, on across the dry dusty waste where no trees grew but only scraggly grass and an occasional clump of cactus. After a time they saw the ship within the harbor. Faith clutched her father's arm convulsively: "Oh, do hurry, Father!" she implored. "It would be *dreadful* if he reached shore and found nobody to welcome him!"

Her father turned and surveyed her mildly. "The horses are wet now, going at this pace, Faith. It would be cruel to make them go faster on a day like this." And he resumed his contemplation of the road ahead.

Constancy consoled her daughter. "It takes a long time for the small boats to be drawn to land, Faith. I'm sure we shall be there in plenty of time."

Constancy was scarcely less excited than Faith, and Sally, holding her mother's hand, kept squeezing it till it hurt. Only Silly sat in tranquillity, a faint smile on her lips, her eyes vague.

At last Jonathan drove up to one of the hitching posts near the water's edge, and, climbing out, tethered the horses, leaving his family to clamber out alone, their voluminous skirts gathered tightly about their knees. The wagon stood near at hand, and Matt was pacing up and down at the edge of the water. The family hurried to join him. They strained their eyes to see into the small boat that was being towed to shore by natives.

"He probably won't be on the first boat," warned Constancy, to spare the children disappointment. Her heart rose as she saw some of the other white residents and many of the natives gathered on the sand to watch the boat. Only she could expect a son on this boat. Then she felt a spasm of pity for those who must wait a year, or two years, or perhaps six before they could welcome back a young man or woman who had gone away a child.

The little boat drew nearer. Half a dozen men and a woman could be distinguished now. There were not often women aboard these ships—unless a consul were arriving with his family, or a new company of missionaries.

As the boat was run part way up on the sand, Constancy moved forward, peering at the occupants of the boat. Could one of these strangers be her Jonathan? That tall young man . . . no, his hair was blue-black and curly, and Jonathan's had been brown and straight, once he was past babyhood. Those two . . . obviously seamen. That tall broad-shouldered boy with brown hair? Her heart skipped a beat. No, it couldn't be, for he was helping the woman from the boat . . . so carefully . . . they must be newly married. But where was Jonathan?

The last tall young man, the young woman's hand held fast in his, was staring eagerly into the faces of the crowd. His eye lighted on Constancy and then on Jonathan. He dropped the hand of his companion and bounded forward. "Mother!" he said, and there was a wailing note in his voice. "Don't you know me? I'm Jonathan!" And he flung his arms about her, and she found herself standing on tiptoe to kiss this young giant with a brown thin face and a prickle of beard on his chin. Tears streamed down her cheeks, but she was laughing, too.

"How could you expect me to know you!" she scolded. "Shooting up into a giant overnight!" For now the thirteen years were canceled, and it was as if she had waved a chubby little boy off to school in the morning to have him return in the evening a man.

Over her head, Jonathan addressed the older Jonathan: "Father?" and, his left arm still holding his mother, he held out his right hand to his father. The white-headed Jonathan, who had stood, thirteen years earlier, grim-faced and dry-eyed to see a tearful little boy depart from his home, could now release his stern control, and there were tears in his eyes, too, as he shook hands with his son and awkwardly patted his shoulder.

Suddenly shy, the three girls hung back, but young Jonathan turned upon them the smile that had such power to light and soften his serious face and kissed each one in turn, calling each by her right name: "Sally? . . . Faith? . . . And Silly? And to think Silly wasn't even born when I went away . . . and where's my little brother? This young monster?" He laughed and placed a hand on either shoulder of Matt, who at sixteen was six feet two and never quite able to cope with his long arms and legs.

"Little brother be blowed!" grinned Matt. "I'm taller than you are by an inch!"

Jonathan turned and put an arm around the young woman who had been standing there at the side, smiling out of pleasant gray eyes at them all this while. "Mother," he said, "I have brought you another daughter. This is Mary. We were married just a week before we sailed——" He paused, and a shadow crossed his face at the blankness in his mother's eyes. Almost instantly, however, Constancy smiled and held out both hands to her daughter-in-law.

"My dear," she said, "you are very welcome. Of course it is a surprise to realize that the little boy I sent away is grown up enough to be married—but I am happy for you both." And she gave Mary a quick little kiss. "Here is your new father, Mary, and Matt, and Sally, and Faith, and Silly. I hope Jonathan had you prepared for such an array of us."

Mary rather timidly kissed her father-in-law's cheek and then kissed each of the children, even Matt, who grinned widely and turned red about the ears. "You are very kind," she said hesitantly. "Jonathan assured me that you would be—but I could not help feeling an intruder—until I had seen you. But Jonathan," and she beckoned to the stranger whom Constancy had first mistaken for her son, "you must make Mr. McGuire known to your family."

Timothy McGuire, who had been standing a little to one side, looking with lively interest upon the scene, stepped forward with alacrity, hat in hand. His dark clothes, by some miracle, looked as if they had come direct from a skillful tailor's iron and had never been exposed to an ocean voyage. His linen was snowy and unwrinkled, his boots as shiny as boots may be. He was a very beautiful young man, both in his person and in his clothes. His hair was a careless and extremely becoming profusion of short black curls, and his eyes, Sally thought, the bluest she had ever seen, with the most extraordinarily long and curling black lashes.

"This is Timothy McGuire, Mother," Jonathan was saying. "He is from Boston, and he paints wonderfully well. He became so interested in our talk of the life here that he is going to stay for a time instead of going on with the ship to China. He has been a good friend to both of us on the tedious trip and has the happiest nature of anyone in the world."

They all shook hands with him, and Constancy, liking his half-teasing, half-beseeching smile, impulsively offered him her hospitality. "If Mr. McGuire can put up with a large and noisy family, he is welcome to stay with us for so long as he is pleased, Jonathan." She turned with a smile to Timothy. "Our house has the virtue of always having room for one more, and we shall be happy to have you with us."

Timothy's face brightened. "Your invitation gives me more pleasure than I can say, Mrs. Williams, but I should hate to be a nuisance to you in any way—you know a painter is not the neatest kind of guest to have in your house."

The elder Jonathan, who had been studying the young man's face rather seriously, spoke cordially now: "Think nothing more of that side of the question, Mr. McGuire, for we are accustomed to giving shelter to missionaries with seven or eight children for weeks at a stretch, and it will be a pleasure to us to entertain a friend of my son's."

So the matter was settled; Timothy should stay with the Williamses at least until he decided just what he wanted to do with himself. Then there was much shouting and turmoil over getting the trunks and bundles, Timothy's canvases and big easel, loosely tied together, and a large crate or two into the wagon.

Constancy was frowning over the problem of arranging her charges for the trip home, when Sally advanced the suggestion that Jonathan and Mary and Silly ride home with them in the carriage while she and Faith and Mr. McGuire follow in the wagon. Constancy hesitated; it seemed scarcely courteous to put a guest in a wagon when there was a carriage. But Timothy McGuire, after a keen and approving glance at Sally, eagerly seconded her plan of journeying. He was most solicitous in assisting the girls to the broad seat of the wagon beside Matt, and then perched himself gayly astride a trunk behind them.

"Jonathan," said the elder Jonathan to his son, picking up the reins and clucking to the horses, "is Mr. McGuire a man to be—well—trusted with your sisters?"

Jonathan looked at his father in surprise. "Why, Father! Timothy McGuire is twenty-seven years old. He wouldn't be interested—except in condescension and kindness—in such youngsters as the girls. He is merry and light-hearted but a very generous-souled man, and those who know about such things have praised his painting both in Boston and in Paris, where he spent several years."

"Is he of the faith, my boy?" persisted his father.

Jonathan the younger squirmed mentally. "He is a Christian, Father, but at home he attended the Church of England," and he added privately, "When he saw fit to attend any church!" Then he blushed, for he had been ordained a minister of the Gospel only a month before he had left Boston, and the ease with which he still fell into evasion embarrassed him. He laughed to cover his confusion and turned his head to address his mother. "Mother, Father is already suspecting poor Timothy of having romantic designs upon—Sally, I think it must be, since she is the eldest! As if a man of his age and ability and experience would consider paying suit to a child like Sally!"

Constancy's hand rose to her heart for a second. She remembered the conspicuous guilelessness of Sally's tone when she had suggested that Timothy ride in the wagon with the children. Sally was nineteen. At nineteen, she herself was married and on her way around the Horn to Hawaii. But children stayed children longer nowadays, she argued. Sally had no thoughts of marriage yet—surely. She answered, "Sally is indeed still a child in feeling and experience of the world, but," and maternal pride rose strong within her, "I see no reason why Timothy McGuire or for that matter the President of the United States should not be pleased by any attention shown him by Sally. She is as pretty and sensible a girl as you could find anywhere!"

Jonathan the younger and Mary both laughed delightedly, but Mary patted her mother-in-law's hand reassuringly. "You are right, Mother," she said, "Sally is a lovely girl—indeed, I never beheld so much beauty in one family before; it is a pleasure to look at any one of your children."

Jonathan the elder spoke curtly from the front seat: "I pray that you will not speak so to them. I make no plaint of their looks, but their souls are of greater import, and, with the exception of Priscilla, have not fared so well as their faces."

Mary turned the subject discreetly. "Priscilla, or Silly as you call her, is the one who professed her faith when she was but seven years old, is she not?"

"Yes," said Constancy shortly. But Jonathan turned his head over his shoulder, his eyes smoldering with pride. "Ah, Mary, it was a proud day and a day of thanksgiving in my heart when this infant rose—and we had received no intimation of her intention of doing so—and defended her purposefulness and the unshakable conviction she had of the grace of Jesus Christ and the infinite wisdom and mercy of God as many a grown teacher of the religion could not have done. Nor has there been any lapse on her part. Already at thirteen, her life is dedicated to the service of others, to prayer, to loving-kindness, and her joy in meditation and pondering over the Scriptures is a thing to rejoice a God-fearing man's heart."

Mary stole a glance at Silly and saw her lips curve in a smile and her eyes grow starry at her father's praise. Her attention was diverted to Constancy, however; she was surprised at feeling Constancy's hold upon her hand tighten to painfulness. She turned to see Constancy's face drawn as if in pain, her teeth biting savagely into her lower lip. "You're ill, dear Mother," she cried in distress. "Is it a sudden pain in your heart?"

Instantly Constancy's features relaxed. "It was a twinge —indigestion, no doubt, but gone now," she said calmly enough, but the pain had no relevance to digestion. She was thinking, "My poor Silly, with the terrible weight of your consecration to bear, worrying lest the joy you find in playing the piano be offensive to God—what will become of you?"

She brushed thoughts of Silly from her mind and gave her undivided attention to her new daughter-in-law. "You must tell me about yourself, Mary," she said with a smile. "How long have you and Jonathan known each other, and when did you decide to marry?"

There was an irrepressible burble of laughter from Mary, and Constancy's heart went out to the girl. "There is a story to our knowing each other," Mary said, still smiling. "My father is a minister at New Haven and has always invited the theological students to our home. Jonathan came first in his first year at college, and at dinner I inadvertently tipped the gravy down his waistcoat. I was so confused that I ran out of the room. Though he begged through my mother that I think nothing of it, I could never bear to show my face when he came to the house. It wasn't till last year, with Jonathan a senior, that we met again—and then it was quite the other way. Quite unintentionally he evened the score between us." She chuckled and stole a sidewise glance at Constancy. She lowered her voice discreetly and placed her mouth a few inches from her mother-in-law's ear. "You see, I was strolling along the road toward home after attending tea at a neighbor's house, when a horse and rider at full gallop came thundering along. They startled me so that I leaped aside and slipped and tumbled over backwards into the ditch!" She giggled. "I stuck there, head downwards in the weeds and mud, with my pantalettes waving from the midst of my inverted hoops."

A glint of amusement appeared in Constancy's eye.

"And what," she inquired, "did Jonathan do about that?"

"Oh, he was much distressed and jumped off his horse and down in the ditch beside me in a twinkling, not knowing just where he should lay hold to get me righted. But finally he grabbed me by the feet and pulled me into the road, and I, seeing this young man I had been at pains to avoid for nearly four years—and seeing him at such a time—was paralyzed with mortification, and he was disconcerted, too, recognizing me in spite of the mud in my hair and on my face. But he suddenly, in the midst of the most profuse apologies and self-condemnation, burst out laughing, and I laughed, too—till the tears came—and he put me up on the back of his horse and led me home. Somehow we have been the easiest and most natural of companions since."

Constancy reached over and took the girl's hand, smiling over the story and wondering at the same time how her Jonathan would have been affected by such an introduction twenty-six years earlier. "I feel sure that you are the right wife for Jonathan," she said, "and don't ever let him lose the gift of laughing with you—there is *never* enough laughter in life."

Mary's gray eyes widened slightly at the low vehemence of the older woman's tone. "Oh," she protested, "he won't! We think life is *lovely*—and we aren't afraid of anything that may happen to us as long as we can be together. Once I got that idea into Jonathan's head, all has been well. You see, he wouldn't ask me to marry him at first because he knew he must return here, and he remembered how hard life was for you when he was a child and what grim, dreadful lives the missionaries had to live. He couldn't bear to bring me to such hardship."

Constancy was touched that her child should have noticed the hardness of life for his parents when he was so

small. "Jonathan is a good boy—and kind," she murmured, half to herself. "But tell me how you overcame
his reluctance."

Mary flushed and looked downward. "You may think
I was overbold . . . but he didn't speak and he didn't
speak . . . yet he came again and again to the house and
couldn't seem to take his eyes off me. I knew he wasn't
paying court to any other girl. He looked so miserable,
too, that I just couldn't bear it any longer, so . . . so
. . . I . . . I'm afraid I tempted him . . . just a little,
so that he kissed me before he had time to think whether
it was wise or not, and then he made a fearful to-do and
groaned that he could never marry me and his life was
ruined. And I said why not, if he weren't hiding a wife
somewhere already. Then it all came out, and I convinced
him that life was probably not so wild and primitive here
by now, and that even if it were, I would be miserable and
maybe die if he left me behind, so unless he wanted my
death on his conscience, he had better stop acting so foolishly. Are you dreadfully shocked, Mother?"

Constancy chuckled. "No! I'm glad you had the good
sense to behave as you did. If Jonathan had stuck to his
intention and come back without speaking, he would be a
sighing, dolorous, lovesick calf, no good for anything. I
don't think you will find things so difficult as we did when
we came—even if they want you to go to one of the other
islands. I'm hoping that the brethren will be content to
let Jonathan stay with his father at the beach. It is a new
field, you know, and we need more help than we have
with the school."

Her new daughter-in-law pleased her well. She retained
her clasp on the small, square hand as they jogged along
the rough road. A little later, when Mary's fingers tightened about her own, she attributed it to an impulse of

affection, rather than to the spirited denunciation of the new sect of Unitarians Jonathan the elder was launching from the driver's seat.

2

Although the brethren were desirous of sending young Jonathan and his bride to Lahaina to begin their work in the islands, they discarded the plan after Jonathan's father, at the close of a particularly impassioned sermon upon the consequences of sin, collapsed with a heart attack in the pulpit. The doctor, overtaken on his way home to Nuuanu after he had attended services at Kawaiahao, frowned at the spectacle of Jonathan, lying blue around the lips and his face gray-white in bed, told him sternly that he would be a dead man within six months unless he suspended his labors or most of them, and prescribed a month in bed with absolute rest and a careful avoidance of excitement of any kind.

A subdued Jonathan meekly promised to obey, but in the next breath groaned hollowly: "What of my church? Who will preach during this month—with my son who has been helping me going to Lahaina in three days?"

A consultation followed, and young Jonathan was told that he was needed to aid his father at Waikiki and that he should assist his wife with the language with all haste, as she would be needed as a teacher in the school. Young Jonathan gravely bowed to the will of the brethren, but his heart rose at the thought that Mary, after all, need not be thrust into an alien group to live in a hovel and wear herself out with the fight against cockroaches and dirt—a fight so much more arduous in a grass hut than in a fine coral stone and timber house such as his uncle had built at Waikiki.

While the elder Jonathan lay in bed, Constancy spent her days beside him, leaving the school to Sally, who, with the help of Jonathan and the two young native teachers, carried on the work. Young Jonathan remembered a good deal of the Hawaiian language from his forbidden knowledge of it in childhood. Now he studied diligently and talked with the natives at every opportunity. Each morning at seven o'clock Faith and Silly mounted Ned, one of the sorrel geldings, and Matt mounted Dick, the other, and the three set off around the mud flats for the school at Punahou.

Young Timothy McGuire was left largely to his own resources during the daytime. He was in the second month of his visit. November was at hand. He offered to find other quarters, but Constancy pressed him to stay, saying that one more person made no additional work and that he was company for the children. So he continued to inhabit the sixth bedroom in the big house, the one which the captain occupied on his infrequent visits. He swam daily and on several occasions bumped his head badly in his efforts to master a surf board. He wandered through the native village, his painting paraphernalia under his arm, and made gaudily impressive studies of an old man pounding *poi* and of a mammoth Hawaiian woman weaving mats.

He yearned to paint a young *hapa-haole* girl, sprung of a transient union between a visiting sailor and a native girl. He wished to get her upon canvas as he had seen her one day, dancing a solitary *hula* in the clearing before her grandmother's hut, the old crone beating out the monotonous accompanying rhythm with calabashes. The girl wore a skirt made of the long *ti* leaves, and anklets and wristlets of creamy white flowers, and the *lei* about her neck swung between the small, rounded breasts. Her skin was

pale brown with a golden cast, and her hair hung in shining black ripples below her hips.

Seeing him staring at her, she made no pause in the sinu-
ous movements of her dance, but smiled steadily, enigmatically, and disturbingly into his eyes until she had finished with the customary lithe bow, bringing her face
down to the backs of her outstretched hands. Timothy
clapped softly and said, "*Mi-te! Mi-te!*" vigorously nodding his approval and wishing that he knew more than
half a dozen words in Hawaiian.

Conversationally the two did not progress very far, for
Leilehua knew very little English; what she did know she
had picked up from the sailors, and it had more to do with
the activities of darkness than of daylight. With many
gestures and much flourishing of his canvas and palette,
Timothy signified that he would like to paint her, and she
giggled her willingness. He conveyed by many extravagant gestures the idea that he would come back soon, and
then took himself off toward the Williamses' house, a
broad grin on his face as he reflected upon the nature of
his new friend's English vocabulary.

That night he made discreet inquiry concerning her,
saying first that she was a colorful type and he would like
to put her on canvas. The response from his white-haired
host startled him.

"The woman's a Jezebel!" Jonathan rapped out. "She's
a disgrace to the community, a wilful harlot, encouraging
every youth she can lay hands on to sin. She's a child of sin
herself. Her mother was like her—free and bold with the
sailors from every visiting ship. This girl is the child of
such a union. We've tried kindness—we've done everything we could—to make her see the error of her ways. I
found her in sin with a sailor six years ago, when she was
no more than ten or eleven, and when I reasoned with her

she laughed and blasphemed! She persists in wearing indecent clothing and goes in swimming in none at all. She's a
menace to the community, but her grandmother was wet
nurse to one of the Kamehamehas, and there is no pro-
hibiting her the village. Never think of trying to paint
her, my boy! In this world you can't touch pitch without
being defiled!"

Timothy was round-eyed at the outburst of his host.
"I hadn't supposed she was old enough to be such a desperate sinner," he mumbled. "She seemed scarcely more
than a child."

"Child!" snorted Jonathan irascibly. "Child of Satan!"

Here Constancy intervened with word that the queen
was interested in having her portrait painted, having called
that morning while Timothy was out, and having been
shown the portraits he had painted of Constancy and
Jonathan, and the half-finished one of Sally.

Timothy accordingly waited upon the queen, and to the
dismay of her clerical advisers produced a picture of her
in a Paris gown that showed rather more flesh than was
usual in these days of missionary dominion. Fortunately
Jonathan was put to bed for a month before Timothy had
finished the portrait, and so disaster from that particular
quarter was averted. After a few days of rest, Timothy
commenced work on the portrait of the king, in which
the monarch was to be as conspicuous for a superfluity of
adornment as his wife had been for lack of it, for the king
was pleased to be painted in a crimson-and-gold uniform,
stiff with gold braid and buttons.

Other requests came in for portraits. Royalty was possessed with the desire to see itself recognizably reproduced
on canvas. Timothy spent more and more of the daytime
hours at the homes of the chiefs, but with the household
busy and Jonathan confined to his bed, Timothy found

time and opportunity to visit the hut where Leilehua lived. And Leilehua was obliging about posing—first, because she was curious about having her picture painted; second, because she liked Timothy's smile and his blitheness; and third, because she wondered just how long this engaging young man would pretend that he was interested only in painting her picture.

Constancy had finished giving Jonathan his sponge bath and had tidied the sickroom. Now she left Silly with the invalid to read aloud from the sermons of his favorite divine and went downstairs. Matt and Faith were swimming; she could see them splashing and could hear their shouts of laughter as she reached the foot of the stairs and looked out across the broad *lanai* to the sea. It was ten o'clock. Sally and Mr. McGuire should be halfway up the Pali by now, she thought, and smiled to think how splendid they looked riding off on the sorrel geldings that morning, Sally's small-boned body erect on the horse, and her high black hat resting so becomingly on the red-gold curls. The plain, tightly fitting basque of the dark green riding habit became her well. Constancy remembered the approval in Timothy's eyes as he watched Sally come down the stairs.

"If he should ask her to marry him," pondered Sally's mother, "would Jonathan be agreeable? Mr. McGuire couldn't fool anyone into thinking he was a deeply religious young man—and Jonathan will think no one short of a St. Paul worthy of one of the girls. Is Sally in love?" Constancy made a face at her own stupidity in asking the question. What doubt when Sally, sitting within six feet of the stove, allowed the rice to burn until the stench rose to the second story? And Sally, who was almost as much of a chatterbox as Faith, was nowadays given to sitting quiet as a mouse, her eyes following every move of Timothy McGuire, and blushing if anyone commented on her unusual behavior.

Constancy sighed. Sally seemed so young to take on the responsibilities of marriage—and yet, she was nineteen. If she were to marry Timothy McGuire, there would be little danger, her mother thought, of her being dismayed by the spectacle of a husband groaning in remorse after giving way to his desire for her.

So deep was she in the contemplation of Sally's future that she failed to hear the approach of a carriage, and a knock at the door startled her. She arose and opened the door at the back of the house. There stood Mrs. Owens, wife of one of the ministers of Honolulu and a teacher in the charity school. Her face was grim, and her mouse-colored hair was strained back from her face so that not a single wisp showed beneath her rusty black bonnet.

"Good-morning, Sister Williams," she said severely and stalked into the parlor and chose the least comfortable chair in the room to sit on. "I hope that Brother Williams is well enough to see me. There is a matter that needs the attention of both of you."

Constancy's heart sank, but her chin thrust forward defiantly. "My husband cannot be bothered or allowed to worry over *anything*, Mrs. Owens," she said with quiet firmness. "It might prove fatal. But if there is anything I can do——"

Mrs. Owens sat up more rigidly than before. "I'm sorry Brother Williams can't be consulted, but that's as may be. Sister Williams," and she leaned forward to fix Constancy with a sharp gray eye, "do you realize that you have been nourishing a *viper* in your home?"

"No!" protested Constancy weakly and thought wildly, "What has Matt been up to? Or is it Faith? . . . surely

Jonathan hasn't been talking like a Unitarian!" Aloud she said a little sharply: "Please be more explicit, Mrs. Owens. I don't understand you."

"This young man—this Timothy McGuire from Boston!" hissed Mrs. Owens and sat back, waiting for this much to penetrate.

"But," gasped Constancy, "what has Mr. McGuire done that is so dreadful? He is a very likable young man, we all think."

Mrs. Owens stretched her long, scrawny neck towards her hostess. "He's been painting indecent pictures! That's what he's been doing!"

"Oh! But how could that be?" She was frankly puzzled. "He has been painting the king and queen—surely——"

"That's just it!" exploded the visitor. "Here we spend our lives teaching these benighted folk decency and modesty and religion, and what does this young profligate do but paint the queen in a garment that leaves her whole bosom *bare!*" Her voice sank to an exaggerated whisper. "It's outrageous, and what does the king do but hang this piece of flagrant indecency in the reception hall so the first thing anyone who enters the palace sees is the queen's bosom!"

Constancy's eyes rolled heavenward. Didn't Timothy McGuire have any sense at all? Or did he do it in a spirit of mischief? Surely he should have realized the feeling of the missionaries about exposed bodies. She turned to the outraged Mrs. Owens.

"It is a pity that he painted her that way," she said sympathetically, "but we must not judge him too harshly. He probably felt that it was not his place to dictate to the queen in the matter of her dress—and we must remember that Mr. McGuire is an artist, and artists do not feel that the human body is anything to be ashamed of. I am

ure that when I explain to him how strongly the missionaries feel on the subject, he will not offend in that way
again."

"H'mph!" The sound was a snort. "That's all very well,
Sister Williams, but there's another thing: at the women's
meeting yesterday, which you did *not* attend, the sisters
discussed the matter and decided that it is not advisable
for you to allow Mr. McGuire to remain in your home
with your young daughters."

Constancy's face was stormy, but her voice was low: "I
think, Mrs. Owens, that Mr. Williams and I must be allowed to handle this matter for ourselves. After all, Mr.
McGuire is my son's friend, and we have known him inti-
mately as a guest in our home for nearly two months now.
If we are satisfied that he is not a menace to our daughters,
surely you have no cause for alarm."

"I don't know about that! There is talk about town
coupling his name with your Sally's, and many are surprised that you consent to having your daughter's good
name jeopardized by a godless young man."

Constancy's eyes narrowed. "And I am surprised," she
said as softly as ever, "that the good brethren and sisters
find time hanging so heavily on their hands that they can
indulge in mischievous gossip." Her eyes flashed, and the
words were out before she could restrain them: "Let all
of you look to the beams in your own children's eyes and
bother less about the possibility of finding a mote in my
Sally's. If Sally finds pleasure in Mr. McGuire's company,
that is an added reason for asking him to extend his visit,
for Sally has had little enough pleasure in her life, what
with drudging and shouldering the responsibilities of a
woman when she was at the age when other children still
played with dolls."

She broke off at sight of the tightened face of Mrs.

Owens. "Please,"—and Constancy's voice was conciliatory —"let us not argue the matter further. Mr. McGuire is a stranger to our ways and to many of our ideas. It is to be expected that he should make mistakes, but he is too courteous, too kindly in his heart to wish to offend. I will speak to him on the subject of the picture as soon as they return."

Mrs. Owens jerked her head towards her hostess. "And there's another thing: letting those two ride off by themselves up Nuuanu isn't wise, Sister Williams. You know Satan lays snares for the young, and it behooves us to be vigilant."

Constancy knitted her brow anxiously. She had been so busy in the sickroom, so worried over Jonathan until he began to show improvement, that she had not thought of chaperons. When Sally said she would like to ride up the Pali with Timothy on Saturday, as he had not been up and was anxious to see the view, Constancy had merely thought that it would be a pleasant outing for them both. Sally had been so tied since her father's illness—what with running the school and helping with the extra work at home. Constancy answered slowly:

"Perhaps it was not proper of me to let them go up the Pali alone—but the truth is, I simply thought a day in the open would be good for Sally. You know she has had the full responsibility of the school since her father has been bedridden. I am sure they know how to behave. I can trust Sally, I know, and Mr. McGuire is too courteous a young man to take advantage of such a situation. It will be all right this once, and next time I shall send a chaperon."

"I *hope* you are right," Mrs. Owens croaked, "I'm sure I hope so, but the young need watching, Sister Williams." She rose to her feet. "If any of us can help you, you know that we are anxious to be of service." She held out a stiff hand, and Constancy took it in a brief clasp. "Be assured that you are remembered in all our prayers."

Constancy followed her to the door, murmuring, "I will tell Mr. Williams. You are very kind," and breathed a deep sigh of relief as her visitor clambered into the red-wheeled cart and drove away. Surely, thought Constancy, Timothy wouldn't make any—advances to a child like Sally without broaching the subject to her parents first! And then she smiled involuntarily, remembering how even the irreproachable Jonathan had stammered forth his plea to her before it occurred to him to consult her parents. And if Jonathan, with his strong regard for duty, could so far forget decorum, what might not impulsive young Timothy McGuire be capable of doing? A little uneasy, she turned toward the kitchen; it was time for Jonathan's eggnog.

3

Sally had leaped to Dick's back without waiting for Timothy to help her and was off down the driveway to the road before he could overtake her. Her heart pounded beneath the snug green cloth basque of her riding habit, and her eyes were brilliant with excitement. She heard Timothy calling plaintively, "Why don't you wait for a fellow? Especially when we look so well together!"

She pulled up Dick to a trot and finally to a walk and said quite severely, although little smiles kept twitching at the corners of her mouth, "We have to hurry while it's cool and the road is level. It's a steep grade up the Pali, and we have to walk the horses most of the way." But she continued at a walk.

Timothy sighed loudly. "You're so sensible, Sally. Don't you ever get tired of being sensible and want to be foolish? Now I should think an intelligent young woman like

yourself would welcome a young man like me after all
these venerable graybeards who spend their lives putting
the fear of God into the natives! But instead of appreciat-
ing me, you look as disapprovingly at me as Mrs. Owens
did when she saw my painting of the queen." He burst
into an irrepressible chuckle at the memory of Mrs.
Owens's outrage.

Sally's smile broadened. "You're a very giddy young
man, I fear," she said austerely, over her far shoulder so
that he should not see the smile, "and I doubt not but that
you will come to a bad end——" She paused abruptly, and
when she continued, distress was in her voice, "but I do
hope you won't! Oh, Mr. McGuire, don't tempt Provi-
dence too far." Confusion overtook her, and she was off
down the road at a gallop, with him crying a protest and
pounding after her, but her horse was the fleeter, and she
rushed on, pleasantly aware that he could not catch up
with her until she chose to let him. They went thundering across the plain until the mission settlement was in
sight, when Sally discreetly slowed down. Timothy pulled
up his horse beside her.

"I believe you're a frightful little tease, Sally Williams,
and not half so much of a Puritan as you pretend. You're
far too pretty." He grinned at seeing the color rush into
her cheeks, staining the pallor of her flesh a deep rose.

"You shouldn't say such things to me, Mr. McGuire,"
she said a little breathlessly. "It is so, Father says, that
wicked young men turn young women's heads. Besides,
it should be more your concern to ponder what beauty
lies in the spirit and less to dwell on the outer vain show."
Again the primness of her words was belied by the twitching of her mouth.

Timothy let out a whoop of laughter, which, as they
were passing the Owens house, brought several heads into

view at door and window. Mrs. Owens hurried down the walk and motioned to Sally, whose heart sank. She reined in her horse and awaited the approach of the minister's wife. "Good-morning, Mrs. Owens," she called politely. "Is your household all well?"

"Good-morning, Sally," in disapproving tones. The woman swept a frigid look up and down Timothy's long figure and then returned her gaze to Sally's face. "Sally, does your mother know you're going gallivanting off with this young man all by yourself?"

Sally flushed with annoyance but answered civilly enough, "Why, of course, Mrs. Owens. She thought it would be nice for me to show Mr. McGuire the Pali. He hasn't yet had an opportunity of going up."

"H'mph!" and Mrs. Owen made a singularly unpleasant hacking noise in her throat. "Well, all I can say is that I'd rather see my Maria dead and in her grave than in the company of the dissolute. There's such a thing as trusting the young too far, and while your mother's a good Christian woman as ever drew breath, she's too apt to trust the untrustworthy. Remember to behave yourself like the daughter of godly parents should."

Sally's eyes grew wider and wider and shifted amazedly from Timothy's face to Mrs. Owens's during this speech. At the end of it, her tilted nose ascended a fraction of an inch. With great dignity she said, "Good-day, Mrs. Owens! Come, Timothy!" and set off at a trot, considerably upset at having called Mr. McGuire by his first name in the stress of the moment, for, although Timothy had, at Constancy's bidding, called all of Jonathan's sisters by their given names, they decorously called him Mr. McGuire.

Timothy came thundering after her, but not till they came to turn from King Street up the rude wagon road that led up Nuuanu toward the Pali could he reach her

side and speak. "Sally!" he implored her. "You won't let
that old harridan spoil our day, will you? I don't think
I'm such a bad fellow as she makes out. After all, your
mother seems to think I'm fit to be sent abroad with her
daughter, and just dispassionately, you know, I'd trust
your mother's judgment before I would hers."

Sally eyed him angrily, but the anger was for Mrs.
Owens. "She's horrid!" she stormed, the color again flood-
ing her cheeks. "Her tongue hangs in the middle and wags
at both ends! She's ever spreading evil about people, and
now she'll probably take the trouble to go out and bother
Mother at the first opportunity, and Mother has enough
to worry about. You have no idea how these brethren and
sisters of the Church make everybody else's business their
concern. We've escaped a lot by living out at Waikiki
these last few years, but every now and then a delegation
arrives to express some very unpleasant sentiments. Either
they've seen or heard that somebody else has seen Matt out
on a surf board without as many clothes on as they think
he ought to have, or Faith has said something flippant or
disrespectful about a teacher or a minister, and some little
tattle-tale has gone home and told on her. Oh . . . of
course not all of them are like that, but in every settlement on these islands there are just enough of these well-
meaning busybodies to keep things upset most of the
time."

"Sally darling, you look beautiful when you're angry,
but let's forget about Mrs. Owens and think how marvel-
ous it is to have a day together—just by ourselves, and in
such a beautiful place!"

"Yes," said Sally, and again, "Yes," but her heart
skipped several beats, and she thought, "in the women's
meetings, they told us girls that if a young man who had
not asked our parents for our hands in matrimony became

familiar, we should rise and leave the room at once, but I'm not in a room, and although it is surely familiar of him to call me 'Sally darling,' I like it and wouldn't want to leave the room if I were in one." But she addressed him rather severely: "The artist in you is strangely lethargic, Mr. McGuire. We are approaching the most beautiful part of the island, and you apparently see nothing of it at all."

"That's because I can't take my eyes away from something still more beautiful," he teased. "But, Sally, why the 'Mr. McGuire,' when you've already committed yourself by calling me aright before Mrs. Owens? You go on calling me Timothy and I'll admire the scenery to your heart's content."

He raised his hand to shade his eyes and peered with a great show of attention toward the dark mountains before them. He reined in his horse in sudden excitement. "By Jove! That *is* a sight! Sally! Look at the shadow pattern the clouds make on the mountains, and did you ever see so many shades of green in your life—and the waterfalls!"

Sally nodded approvingly, but she felt a little piqued at his complete absorption in the scenery. "See," and she pointed with her whip, "how that fall disappears in mid-air, spun out on the wind? Sometimes two or three of them are like that, but today they are all pretty big because of the hard rain last night."

They rode on up the winding bridle path, the tall lush grasses wetting their boots and brushing against their horses' shoulders. The mountains grew more thickly wooded with *ohia* and *koa* and *kukui* trees the higher they went, and here and there in the gorges to their right glistened the white ginger, its cool sweetness rising to their nostrils. A shower of huge raindrops beat upon them for an instant before passing down the valley; they rode on, laughing at the folly of rain and sun together, and the sun

dried their clothes in a twinkling. At a turn in the path a
rude bridge spanned a stream that rushed down the valley
from a waterfall just above the bridge. Sally pulled in her
horse and slipped to the ground. She dropped the bridle
reins carelessly over a broken-off branch of a tree and
beckoned Timothy over to the side of the fall where it fell
churning snowily into the pool. Behind a flat stone grew
a clump of ginger. Placing a finger on her lips, she plucked
a single blossom and laid it on the stone.

"That's an offering to the *akuah*," she said in a whisper.
"The one who lives here is very awful with blood-thirsty
habits, and it doesn't do to neglect him." She grinned wickedly. "But don't mention the matter to Father!" She shook
out the skirt of her habit, her eyes fixed on the offering.
"Mother has told me how awfully pained the brethren
were the first time they came up the Pali and had this
place pointed out to them. And then there's another at the
top. In those days the natives used to leave flowers or taro,
or sometimes bits of *tapa*, but now they seem not to
bother."

Timothy gravely followed her example and laid a single
ginger flower upon the gray stone. "It would never do to
call down bad luck upon us today," he said. "We'll be respectful to all the gods we run across."

Sally bent to pluck a blossom which she pinned to her
collar. Darting a glance at Timothy, she plucked another
flower and put it in his buttonhole. Regarding her quizzically, he deftly secured both of her hands, turned them
over, and dropped a light kiss on the inside of either wrist
where the skin was especially silken and white and the thin
veins showed blue. Sally pulled childishly away from him
and ran back to her horse. "Oh!" she scolded. "What
would Mrs. Owens say?"

Timothy followed her more leisurely. "That you were a

daughter of Jezebel, putting temptation in the way of a good-intentioned young man." He smiled broadly at her.

Sally mounted her horse and started off up the path at a trot which soon subsided into a walk. She held her head very high, and the color stayed in her cheeks for several minutes. Warm waves of feeling pushed their way through her heart and into her throat. "What is the matter with me?" she asked herself scornfully. "Lizzie makes me awfully tired when she blinks her eyes and preens herself around the boys, but maybe she feels the way I do now. I would have been awfully disappointed if he had just gazed upon the waterfall and remarked on the beauty of the scenery when I stuck that flower in his buttonhole. But if he should think I were a bold creature, I should die of shame!"

She rode on ahead by several lengths till she reached a turn that threw before her the whole of the valley, its narrow beginnings at her feet, the downward curve of its embracing arms of mountains, the gradual widening till it lost itself in the level sweep of the town, which lay a pygmy settlement far below, the flat blue glass of the sea spreading beyond the spire of Kawaiahao church.

She turned her horse's head toward the town and awaited Timothy's arrival, indicating the view with a nod. Timothy drew a long breath and stared down the valley to the sea, silent for a moment. His eye appreciated the subtle shading from one green to another. Above their heads a tree struggling upwards from an almost vertical bank spread silver-green foliage; the emerald grass at their feet, with its burden of lingering raindrops, was absorbed into the yellow green of the bushes pushing their way up the sides of the ravine beneath them, and again melted into the dark tones of a parasitic vine that swarmed up the embankment, twining its tendrils about each bush and tree;

just across the gorge, beneath the shower that fell in slanting gray lines upon the far hillside, a dozen shades and
tones wavered and blurred from yellow to dark blue green.

Timothy shifted his gaze from the riotous herbage to
Sally's face. "Think," he said, "if you could have a house
up here—with great windows overlooking all this,"—he
waved sweepingly towards the lush world at their feet.
"Do you suppose there ever will be people living up here?"

Sally shook her head. "Maybe," she said doubtfully,
"but it would be awfully hard getting supplies up, and
somehow a road, if they could ever build one, that would
let wagons come up would spoil it. I like it being wild. I
don't suppose people will ever live much farther up the
valley than where Dr. Judd is building his new home."

She clucked to her horse and plodded on up the steepen-
ing trail. There was an hour of steady, slow climbing before Sally drew rein and waited for Timothy again. She
turned dancing eyes upon him. "Now," she commanded,
"you've got to shut your eyes, and I'll lead your horse,
and don't you dare to peek till I say you can."

"You're sure you won't sidestep me over the edge if I
trust my life to your hands?"

Sally laughed. "I might—it's been done up here before,
but I'd hate to ride all the way down alone, so I'll spare
you this time. Now shut your eyes!"

She led him around the giant needle of rock at the top
of the Pali into the divide and within a few feet of the
edge of the cliff that fell sheerly away a dizzying distance.
"Now!" she said with satisfaction. "Open 'em!"

He opened them and drew an audible breath, while Sally
appreciated his silence. They sat their horses, braced and
statuesque against the fierce rush of wind that assailed the
divide. It was a wind cold and yet soft, a wind that hurled
itself smoothly, swiftly through the narrow pass to lose

itself in the trees below. Timothy took off his hat and let
the wind plow through his hair as he studied the scene below them.

"This is a place for dark, beautiful pagan gods to hold
conclave," he said at last, "or for Satan to offer a reckless
man dominion over time and space. . . . Sally, don't you
feel that you are at the very topmost point of the world?"

Sally nodded gravely. "Dark pagan gods do live here,"
she said quite seriously. "I never feel that Jehovah has anything to do with a place like this. I like to think that the
brethren have only driven the old, terrible, beautiful
native gods to this stronghold, and that they can never
reach them here." She surveyed broodingly the curving
rim of menacing dark mountain that hung over the gentle
green mounds of hill and the sloping valleys below. It was
a mountain that might have been carved from some unknown, unassailable black metal rather than from rock, a
mountain extending as far as eye could see, sharpened to
the cruelness of a knife blade at the top, and falling
sheerly to the bottom of the valley thousands of feet below, its side curiously and rhythmically grooved in vertical
gashes from summit to base. The mind protested at the
violence of the contrast between this forbidding darkness
and the guileless green of the world below, and at the contrast between the calmness of the herbage and the garish
brick red of the earth where it showed in patches against
a hillside. And beyond all lay the tranquil, unwrinkled blue
of the Pacific with its handful of small, oddly shaped
islands dropped here and there near the shore.

Sally slid down the side of her horse and Timothy fol-
lowed her example. She approached the brink of the cliff.
"This is where the first Kamehameha, the one they call the
Great, drove his enemies over the cliff and established his

supremacy on this island." She shivered slightly. The thought of hundreds of brown warriors plunging down upon the jagged rocks beneath always made her feel rather ill. She led her horse to the right, where a narrow and precarious trail began its descent of the precipice. "You can get down there on horseback now," she commented, "but when my father and mother arrived in 1820, there was only the barest suggestion of a footpath, and the only way to get down was on foot with ropes and the help of natives. Mother has told us about how worried she was the first time Father and Mr. Bingham and a couple of the others came over to preach to the natives in the villages on this side. They were gone ten days, and she hadn't the slightest idea whether she would ever see Father again or not. They weren't any too sure of the natives that early, either, and she imagined one of the guides assisting Father over the cliff."

Timothy shook his head. "Your parents were made of stern stuff, Sally. I don't see how they stood it—they were so young to bear such hardship."

Sally nodded soberly. "Mother was just the age I am now. She was married a week or so after her nineteenth birthday, and they sailed almost immediately. You ought to get her to tell you about the voyage and their first sight of the natives at Hawaii. Life is really awfully easy now in comparison—and since Uncle Nate built us our house at Waikiki, we have very little left to wish for—except,"— and she dimpled suddenly—"I do wish that we might be allowed to dance. Father doesn't believe in dancing. I guess none of the missionaries do, but Dr. Judd lets his daughters dance and they say it is such fun."

"It *is* fun. I'll teach you to dance, Sally." He made the offer with considerable enthusiasm.

Sally shook her head sorrowfully. "Thank you. I wish I might, but it would hurt Father and cause gossip among the people here."

"But, Sally, what if you were to marry a man who wanted you to dance? Would you obey your husband or your father?"

Sally's green eyes glinted impishly, but her tone was innocent. "Oh, that question won't cause any complications for me. I'll probably marry a missionary's son and be a minister's wife myself."

Timothy straightened up indignantly. "I'm damned if you'll be any minister's wife!" he protested vigorously. He slid an arm about her waist and dropped a swift kiss upon her mouth. He laughed at the widening of her green eyes. "You've a devil in you, Sally—only a very small black imp, but it would make a very poor minister's wife of you. On the other hand, I think it would help you to be perfect as a painter's wife." He disentangled his arm from his horse's bridle, leaving the animal to wander about at will, and took Sally into a more convincing embrace. Her tall black riding hat dropped from her head and rolled slowly to the edge of the precipice and over. Partly released at last, Sally promptly buried her flushed face in Timothy's shoulder, weak with the glow that spread from her heart to her throat and went pulsing blindly through her head. Yet when he strove to raise her head again, she pushed him firmly away, shaking her head violently.

"What's the matter?" he asked, injured. "My God! I love you and want to marry you at the first possible moment, and I thought you felt that way about me!"

Sally continued to back away; she gasped, "I do, I do! But I'm not used to this—I didn't know kissing was like that! I feel awfully queer—and if you kiss me again right now—I'll—I'll burst!" Her face was flaming, and she sud-

denly turned her back squarely upon Timothy, disconcerted by his broadening grin.

He bounded to her side and hugged her in genial and
quite unloverly fashion. "Darling!" he laughed. "You're a
blessed infant! I think it's going to be lots of fun being
married to you. We can leave kisses till after lunch—food
may sustain you in the face of more. Do you suppose we
can find a little shelter from this fiendish wind back of
that rock?"

Sally moved slowly over to the concave rock and sat
down in its meager shelter, leaving Timothy to tie the
horses rather tenuously to small shrubs and get the pack-
ages of lunch from behind the saddles. While Timothy, in
high spirits, devoured large quantities of the excellent food
Constancy had prepared for them, Sally nibbled abstract-
edly at a sandwich, a half-smile shaping her mouth.

"Timothy," she said, when he was momentarily silent,
delving into a fresh package of food, "you make marriage
seem something—gay and happy—light-hearted! And here
everybody speaks of it as being something with dreadful
responsibilities—something to be taken awfully soberly
and prayed over a lot."

Timothy paused, an apple turnover halfway to his
mouth. "That's because the Calvinists—and all these missionaries are Calvinists—are afraid for their lives of anything that gives pleasure. And since love can be one of the
most . . . pleasurable things that can happen to anyone,
they surround it with a lot of silly superstitions." He took
a large bite of the pastry and waxed eloquent. "Jonathan
and I have talked a lot about it. You see, these people left
New England just before the tide turned so strongly
against Calvinism, and predestination, and infant damnation, and all that rot"—with an airy wave of the hand.
"The very group your missionaries once belonged to in

New England is now chiefly Unitarian. It was just suddenly driven home to them how awfully silly it was to
think God would be so fiendish as to permit man's fall
and then throw him to hell for it—or, if you want a pro-
founder argument, that man, a finite being, could possibly
commit anything like a big enough sin to merit infinite
punishment for it.

"I tell you, Sally, everywhere but here Christians are de-
veloping a far cheerier outlook than they used to have
even a quarter of a century ago. These folks over here
have just stayed where they were, sheltered from the new
doctrines and new thinking that has swept America. Why,
look at Jonathan! He doesn't believe the old stuff any
more, though he is mighty careful not to upset your
father, but you don't catch him preaching about the fires
of hell, do you? I think this generation of missionary stock
is going to come back from being educated with greatly
modified notions, and probably the next one will be still
more liberal."

He stopped for another large bite of the turnover. "As
for all this foolishness about not enjoying the bodies supposedly wished upon us by an all-wise God—why, Sally,
my child, it shows a mean spirit in accepting the gifts of
God not to get all the pleasure we can out of them."

Sally was eyeing him wonderingly. "That last bit of reasoning of yours sounds specious to me," she said after a
moment, "and I suspect that it is a case of the wish being
father to the thought, but I think I agree with you about
the rest. Timothy . . . you know I didn't become a member of the Church until I was sixteen, and the brethren
thought it was scandalous. I just never felt the way they
said you were supposed to feel, and I always doubted quite
a number of things. I've never told it to a soul, Timothy,
but when I did join, it was just because Father was griev-

ing and worrying over my hardness of heart. I couldn't bear it—with him walking up and down for hours at night and praying over me and that kind of thing. He's so good —I just couldn't hold out any longer, so I said I felt the way I was supposed to feel and they received me into the Church. Sometimes I think Mother guessed, because she didn't seem awfully happy over my going in, and she asked me two or three times if I was sure, and said that I shouldn't think of pleasing anyone but just of whether I really and truly believed."

"Didn't I tell you you'd make a bad minister's wife?" His eyes danced. Then he sobered. "You know, your mother interests me. She's an amazing woman to find in a missionary establishment. Do you know that she never talks about religion to you? The rest bring in a quotation from the Bible every other minute, and I've never heard a word out of her. I'd like to be able to see the inside of her mind. I admire her tremendously, Sally. . . . Maybe," and his eyes twinkled, "I fell in love with you because you look a bit like her."

Sally whirled eagerly at his words. "Oh, Timothy! Do you really and truly think I look like Mother? I've always thought she was the most beautiful person in the world!"

He studied her face, his head on one side. "Yes—you look a good deal like her—the bone structure of your face is like hers, and you have the same green eyes—only yours aren't grown-up eyes yet, and hers look as if they knew everything. I think I like red hair better than yellow hair, though hers must have been gorgeous when she was your age. By the way, do you think she'll mind her favorite daughter's marrying a dissolute fellow like me—wasn't that the word that old girl used?"

"I think Mother will be agreeable," answered Sally, a

little troubled; "we must tell her first and let her break it to Father. He may not like it because you aren't more religious. You know, Timothy, you just don't give the impression of being an awfully holy young man, however demure you try to look."

He doubled up with mirth and, when he had recovered himself a bit, pulled Sally over into his arms and tightened his clasp when she set her arms about his neck. This time it was he who brought the episode to a close. He set Sally upon her feet and dusted the burrs from her skirt. "I've got to take you home, Sally," he said firmly, "or I might forget to, and then we'd have the Royal Guard led by Mrs. Owens after us." He pulled the watch from his vest pocket. "Jove! It's three o'clock! Now get your hat and we'll be off."

Dazedly Sally put her hand up to her tumbled hair. "It fell off—you know—before lunch, and I haven't seen it since." She laughed merrily. "It must have blown over the Pali. I'll have to ride home bareheaded and chance Mrs. Owens's guessing how it came to be lost." She walked over to Dick, lifted the reins over his head, and this time waited to be helped up, smiling complacently when Timothy retained her hand long enough to kiss it. She headed her horse towards Honolulu and set off down the trail, wondering if anyone had ever been so happy before. Always to be with Timothy, loving him and knowing that he loved her. A vision of their life together stretched before her down the winding path, a sublimely unnatural life from which no discordant note should ever rise.

4

Constancy glanced again at the grandfather clock. The time was a quarter to seven. "Faith," she said decidedly, "run and tell Eliza we can't hold dinner back any longer. They'll just have to do with something cold."

With Faith out of the room she turned to her daughter-in-law. "Mary," she said, and her voice was troubled, "do you think I did wrong to let those two go off by themselves today? Mr. McGuire—I know so little of him, except that he is a very attractive young man. He wouldn't —take advantage of the fact that there was no chaperon, would he, Mary? I can't help worrying when they are so late."

Mary rose and put her arms around her mother-in-law. "I shouldn't be at all surprised if Timothy took this chance to propose to Sally," she said seriously, "for I think he is in love with her, but he is a well-brought-up young man, however gay and careless he may seem, and I am sure he would observe the larger proprieties with a young girl like Sally—especially when she is his host's daughter."

Constancy patted the girl's shoulder. "I can't seem to help having foolish fears when any of the children or even their father is out later than I have expected." She stopped to pick up a dropped stitch in her knitting. "You think, then, that he is really interested in Sally? I had wondered —and, to tell the truth, I was afraid that she had given her heart away to someone who thought of her as a mere child."

Mary laughed lightly. "Don't worry—anything as pretty as Sally could be as young as Faith and Timothy McGuire would regard her as being of marriageable age. . . . Listen! Isn't that horses' hoofs?"

Her mother-in-law drew a long breath of relief and rolled up her knitting. "Yes—there they are! Mary dear, will you run up and tell Silly to come down for dinner? She is with her father. You might tell him that I will be with him as soon as dinner is over."

She went to the *lanai* to greet the tardy riders. Matt was there to take the horses to the barn. Sally tumbled hurriedly from Dick's back and flung her arms around her mother. "Did you think we had fallen over the edge, Mother? We got to talking over lunch, and somehow it was three o'clock before we got started back. And now we're starved!"

Her mother looked questioningly at Sally's hair falling unrestrained about her shoulders. "You do look like a wild Indian, child. What did you do with your hat?"

Sally's hand fluttered up to her tumbled curls. "Oh, it blew over the Pali——" and she ended with a stifled laugh.

Timothy cleared his throat. "I'm awfully sorry we are so late, Mrs. Williams, especially since it is the first time you let us go off together. I'm afraid we're making a bad impression, but it's Sally's fault for being such an engaging companion, and the Pali's for being the most beautiful spot on earth."

Constancy gave her daughter a little push toward the house. "Run upstairs and smooth your hair, Sally, and hurry! Dinner is on the table. Mr. McGuire, you can wash in the kitchen if you wish. You're both a great worry to me. I was beginning to see you with all your bones broken at the bottom of the precipice." Her tone was stern, but she smiled, and Sally pressed a quick kiss on her cheek before running up the stairs to her room.

Just as they finished dinner and were considering leaving the table, Timothy addressed his hostess somewhat formally: "Mrs. Williams, I should be glad of a few words with you. I should be glad if Jonathan and Mary, and of course Sally, stayed, but"—and his teeth flashed wickedly as his glance swept the three youngest members of the family—"you three children run along and play hop-scotch for a while."

Faith leaped to her feet, her eyes snapping and her nose in the air. "Who wants to hear what you have to say, any-way?" she said loftily and departed with great dignity. Matt shuffled to his feet and out of the door, but turned to throw back, "I know what it is without being told. The whole town says 'It's a scandal and a disgrace the way that Sally Williams and young Mr. McGuire carry on!'" He mimicked Mrs. Owens's voice so felicitously that Timothy burst into a roar, and Jonathan followed suit. Silly arose quietly and left the room without expressing any opinion.

"Well," and Timothy leaned forward toward Con-stancy, "Matt was right. Would you mind having me as a son-in-law, Mrs. Williams? Sally proposed to me today, and I accepted on the condition that you had no objec-tions."

"Timothy!" Sally burst forth wrathfully. "You ought to be ashamed of yourself, telling such an awful fib!"

Jonathan and Mary shared Timothy's delight at the re-sponse his effort had evoked. Constancy shook her head reprovingly. "Shame on you, Mr. McGuire, teasing the poor girl so—when you know she blushes so easily." She looked from one to the other. "Sally . . . have you any idea what you are about, child? You don't just admire Mr. McGuire's beautiful black curls and his long eyelashes and his painting, do you?"

Now it was Timothy's turn to look discountenanced. "Oh," he mumbled, shifting in his chair, "Mrs. Williams, you make a fellow feel a dreadful donkey!"

Constancy shot him an amused look and turned back to Sally. "You know you are very young and haven't had much experience with anybody but missionary folk. Are you sure you aren't just dazzled by the first young man you've known from the outside world?"

Sally lifted her hands in protest. "Mother! You know it isn't that way. And I'm older than you were when you married Father. Have you forgotten the way you felt?"

Constancy's eyes rested for a moment on the tablecloth before her. "No," slowly, "I haven't forgotten. I just don't want you to make a mistake. I want to be sure that you will be as happy as it is possible for a human being to be. As for you, Mr. McGuire, are you sure that you haven't been hasty? Sally has had a very different upbringing from your own. She is apt to seem strait-laced—narrow—prudish to you at times. Have you patience and affection enough to recognize and understand the difficulties that will arise from the difference in your outlook? Are you really ready to assume the responsibilities of marriage and family life and give up a good deal of the playing you do —and"—she hesitated for a second and then went on calmly—"and confine your attention to Sally?"

Timothy shifted in his seat once more, conscious of four pairs of eyes on him. "I'll admit," he said awkwardly, "I've thought first of having a good time, but that was before I knew Sally. Truly, all I seem to care about now is Sally, and if ever I make her unhappy—why, I hope somebody shoots me!"

Constancy smiled, and there was a tinge of irony in her smile. "That is all I want to know, but Sally's father will undoubtedly wish to know more. Did I understand that you were a member of the Church of England?"

Timothy flushed. "I was confirmed when I was a youngster," he muttered; "as a matter of fact I haven't gone to church much in later years—until I came here. Of course, I shan't interfere with Sally's practice of her own faith." His eyes twinkled as they rested on Sally.

Constancy rose to her feet. "I should advise you, in talking to her father, to omit mentioning that you seldom attend church. I will talk with him and see how he feels about it. When," and her eyes sought Sally's face, "did you want to be married—if your father consents?"

Sally glanced at Timothy. "Timothy wanted it to be right away, but I thought it would be nice to wait for Uncle Nate. He ought to be here around Christmas time and stay through January. I thought early in January."

Her mother sighed. "So soon? That's not two full months. Well—I'll see what can be done about it." She left the room and slowly mounted the stairs.

The rest straggled into the living room. Mary's arm was around Sally, and she kissed her warmly. "I'm awfully glad for you both," she said. "I hope you'll be as happy as Jonathan and I are." Faith pounced upon Sally. "Sally Williams, I think you're too mean for anything not to tell us. You aren't so much older than I am as to treat me as if I were a baby!"

Timothy chuckled and patted her on the head. "Don't you think we might break the news, Sally, or is your father likely to forbid the bans?"

Sally smiled with assurance. "Mother can talk him around. He'll do anything she wants. Faith darling," and she flung her arms around her sister, "don't be cross when I'm so happy! Timothy and I are going to be married when Uncle Nate comes next time. Isn't that wonderful?"

To her dismay, Faith's face crinkled up as if she were going to cry. "Oh, Sally!" she wailed. "I can't bear it if he takes you away to the other side of the world! And he will —I just know it!"

Sally's face puckered in perplexity. She patted Faith's heaving shoulder tenderly. "He isn't going to carry me off! And anyway we will live here for a long time yet, a

year or two anyway, and then we shall travel—all over—
to Paris and London and Rome, and in between times we'll
live in Boston and you can come and visit us. Won't you
like that?"

"I might," sniffed Faith, "but it probably won't happen. By then I'll be married to some whey-faced missionary's son and washing diapers for the rest of my life—
there'll never again be an appetizing-looking man around,
I'm sure."

Jonathan protested at this. "Faith!" he said sharply. "If
you don't get a more civil tongue in your head, no missionary's son would risk taking you as his wife. Besides," and
he suddenly sounded aggrieved, "you have several brothers who are sons of a missionary."

Faith buried her nose in Sally's shoulder. "I know—I
know—but you're all nice to look at. Even Matt's face is
all right, though he seems to have too many hands and feet
—but the other missionary folk are all so *unappetizing*. I
like *beautiful* people—like Mother and Father. And I
notice you didn't pick out a wife that looks like Mrs.
Owens, yourself, Jonathan Williams, so there!"

Jonathan glanced at Mary, and his face softened. He
contented himself with a compassionate, "You're a giddy
little thing, Faith, but of course you're only a child."

Suddenly Silly stood tall before them. Her gray-green
eyes were enormous and shining strangely; her mouth
trembled. "Sally," she said, "you mustn't marry Mr. Mc-
Guire. You'll fall into dreadful sin if you do!"

Timothy's jaw dropped. "Why—Silly!" he said,
astounded, "I didn't know that you disliked me so!"

Silly's glance swept him calmly. "I don't dislike anyone,
Mr. McGuire. I pray for you every day—but I think you
are light and heedless and have hardened your heart to
God, and your influence upon Sally can only be evil—for

she is not deeply religious herself. She won't raise you—
she isn't strong enough—she'll sink to your level."

Timothy looked troubled and amazed. "But, Silly—
really I'm not such a bad sort—and I'm awfully fond of
Sally and wouldn't hurt her for the world."

Sally put a hand on either of Silly's thin shoulders.
"Silly," she pleaded, "try to understand, Baby, I love him
dreadfully—and we aren't either of us sinful—we just
want to be happy."

Slowly, inexorably, Silly shook her head. "There is no
true happiness except in the constant awareness of God's
infinite grace. If I loved anyone of different faith or of no
faith, I would die before doing what you are doing."

Sally gave a laugh that was more than half a sob. "But,
darling! You are still a child—you aren't yet fourteen!
You'll feel different when you are a few years older."

Again Silly shook her head and unobtrusively withdrew
from Sally's touch. "I shall pray for you both," she said
and went upstairs.

Timothy looked uneasily from one to another of the little group around him. "I—I didn't know the child took
her religion so seriously. Is there—anything I can do about
it to make her change her opinion of me?"

Sally and Faith both made faint sounds of negation.

"She's been that way ever since she got converted—
when she was seven years old," cried Faith mournfully.
"She got the share Matt and I ought to have had."

Jonathan was looking uncomfortable. "You know, there
was a time when I wouldn't have said anyone could be too
religious—but she does seem to carry it a bit far. It isn't
natural in anybody as young as she is."

Sally looked despondent. "The day after her conversion," she mused, "Silly took the doll that had gone to bed
with her every night since she was two years old and

burned it—because she told me that she loved it with an
idolatrous love. What can you do with a child like that?"

"Father thinks she's as near perfect as anything human
can be," said Faith, "but I've always felt that Mother
wished she weren't so pious. Her lips always make a narrow line whenever she comes on Silly muttering prayers."

Timothy turned to Jonathan a bit ruefully. "Well, old
boy, do you think I'm an unfortunate addition to the family? So far the pros and cons are about equally divided."

Jonathan laughed and shook his friend's hand heartily.
"I think you're a bit of a scapegrace, but I don't think
you're any menace to the community. If Sally wants you,
I guess the rest of us can make out."

Half an hour passed before Constancy came hurrying
downstairs. "Your father has agreed," she cried, looking at
Sally and thinking, "Thank God, if there is one, that Sally
needn't spend her life training natives to live in a way
they'd rather not live and that she'll be with a man who
doesn't think pleasure sinful." "But," she continued aloud,
"he wants to speak to both of you the first thing in the
morning before church."

Sally and Timothy looked at each other like fellow cul-
prits. "We'll be very careful and think several times before we say anything," Sally volunteered, and her mother
looked relieved. Constancy turned to take up her knitting.
She had thought so little of her children marrying, and
here Jonathan had surprised her, and Sally would be married before she knew it. She wondered if Peter would surprise her by turning up with a wife when he came home.

From time to time during the rest of the evening Constancy's gaze wandered from her knitting to the corner
where Sally's bright head and Timothy's black one bent
over the chessboard. An unconscious smile hovered about

Sally's mouth, and her cheeks were pink, her eyes starry. A swift pain assailed Constancy's heart whenever she looked at her daughter.

"It's frightening to see anyone so happy," something in her protested. "She's a child—even if she is as old as I was when I married Jonathan. She seems younger now than she did when she was a little thing of ten doing more housework than she should and being a mother to all the children. She looks as if she were so confident of the future —as if she thought nothing could ever destroy her happiness."

She shivered uncontrollably. "I was never that carefree." She closed her eyes, remembering the war waged in her breast between love and fear . . . in the few days of her engagement to Jonathan—the fierce flame of her ardor for the tall, white-headed, burning-eyed youth dedicated to the service of Jehovah, a flame that some instinctive feminine wariness controlled and disciplined lest it offend her unworldly lover; and the appalling sense that she had sold her soul to Satan that was shut away tight in her heart and torturing her. She opened her eyes and stared at her daughter again, just as something Timothy had said caused Sally to raise her head and shake it at him with a severity that was ruined by the low ripple of laughter that escaped from her hard on the heels of the reproof.

Constancy pressed her palms to her eyes and realized that she had a persistent pain in her head. "Love ought to be like that," she thought, "happy, unashamed. . . . Why couldn't it have been like that for Jonathan and me . . . instead of his being on guard against it as if it were a wild beast caged inside of him waiting to destroy him? . . . and then my being torn in two between my . . . wanting it to escape . . . and my pity for him when it did." She looked at her future son-in-law, a rather wry smile twisting her mouth. "He won't lose any sleep lamenting his inability to withstand the joy of the flesh"—her eyes narrowed—"if he can just manage to confine himself to Sally. He's so heedless . . . used to having whatever he wants without thinking about anybody else, and if they lived where women weren't all convinced they'd burn forever in hell if they gave a sidewise glance to another woman's husband . . ."

She deliberately shut off her thoughts, folded up her knitting, and arose from her chair. "Good-night, children. All this excitement seems to have given me a headache, and I'd best go to bed."

5

1848

Constancy sat putting the hem in Faith's wedding dress, her swift needle dexterously catching only one thread of the yellow muslin at each stitch. Her head bent over her work, and a faint frown traced two vertical lines between her eyes. A sudden flurry of April rain spattered through the northern windows of the big living room. Constancy made a move to rise and lower the windows, but Mrs. Owens, hemming napkins beside her, waved her back.

"You sit still, Sister Williams," she ordered. "It's easier to drop a napkin than a dress." She hurried to the end of the room and lowered the windows. Returning to Constancy's side, she picked up the waist of the yellow dress, scrutinizing it right side and wrong. "You're a clever seamstress, Sister," she said somewhat grudgingly.

Constancy smiled faintly but did not look up from her work. "I've had plenty of practice to make me one," she said, "what with all the dressmaking I used to have to do for the queens, and all the clothes I've had to make my own children, and all the orphans I've sewed for and taught to sew."

Mrs. Owens nodded. "Yes, you folks who came first bore the worst of the trials of missionary life. I guess it's the will of God that you should live in more style than the rest of us now." Her sharp eyes roved quickly about the big room with its Chinese rugs and teakwood tables and desk and chest brought from the orient by the captain.

Again the slight frown traced lines up Constancy's forehead. "You know, Mrs. Owens, that we owe this pleasant home and nearly everything that's in it to my uncle. It is his property, and, agreeably for us, he wanted us to live in it and care for it for him while he is away and make a home for him when he is here."

"Some of the rest of us could do with rich uncles, I guess!" A thin short laugh announced to Constancy that Mrs. Owens had made a joke. She smiled absently. "However," her visitor went on, "it is a missionary's business to bear hardship and privation cheerfully. I just hope that Faith will be able to support the burdens of married life with the proper spirit and can reconcile herself to the humbler way of life that must be my Luke's. Funny, Faith never struck me as the kind of girl that would make a good minister's wife, but of course I pray that I am mistaken."

Constancy's lips tightened rebelliously. "Yes!" something within her jeered. "If you were mistaken, you'd be so disappointed you'd burst!" Aloud she said, "Faith was a heedless child, but everyone has noticed the change in her in the last few months. She is so sober and quiet we scarcely know her." A sigh escaped her. She could not banish the ache in her heart for the change wrought in Faith A silent

protest rose in her breast whenever Jonathan expressed his
satisfaction in this new, sober, too quiet Faith who had
suddenly replaced the most wayward and mischievous of
any of her children. Once Constancy had gone so far as to
say, "There is something unnatural in this, Jonathan. I'm
afraid something we don't know of has hurt her—something has happened to her to make her like this." But Jonathan had regarded her in perplexity and said, "Why, Constancy, she is a woman now, and God has at last entered
her heart. I rejoice that such a blessing has come to her and
that young Luke Owens has seen fit to want to marry her.
I have hopes now that she may be as proper a wife to a
minister of the Gospel as you have been." And Jonathan
had smiled at her with a warmth that wrung her heart
even while sardonic reflections passed through her brain.

While Mrs. Owens sewed on in silence, Constancy went
over once more wearily and profitlessly that period of time
which had seemingly wrought the change in Faith. Less
than two months before, Luke had arrived one morning at
a gallop on his big, lumbering horse and, stammering with
earnestness, asked if he might have a word with Faith.
Wondering a little, Constancy had called Faith from the
kitchen and left the two alone in the living room. Had the
young minister heard of something outrageous Faith had
said about him or about some of the other sons of the missionaries who had begun to show her attention? Had he
come to reason with her about her sins?

Scarcely half an hour later she had seen the lanky young
man, who, although he was now twenty-four, still gave a
juvenile impression of having outgrown his strength, climb
upon his horse and overheard him say agitatedly, "I advise
you, Faith, to give this matter earnest attention in your
prayers, and to consult seriously with your parents, and I
shall return Monday evening."

The next moment Faith rushed into the hall and hurled herself in a spasm of giggles upon her mother. "That great gawk thinks I should *marry* him, Mother!" she gurgled. "Fancy *me* being a dutiful daughter-in-law to Mrs. Owens!" and she had seemed about to fall into hysterics. Constancy had smiled grimly but had given her daughter a little shake. "Shame on you!" she said. "If he cares for you, you mustn't hurt him. He is probably all the more sensitive for not being as prepossessing as some. Of course, there's no need for you to marry him! Personally I find it hard to imagine you a minister's wife under any circumstances—but you must be kind."

Faith had looked up at her mother with a twinkle. "Of course I am kind!" she protested. "Very kind—although I nearly split—he was so serious and so embarrassed—but I looked sober as a judge and said he surprised me very much and that I didn't think I was old enough or staid enough to marry anyone yet, and was too frivolous to make a suitable wife for a minister—but the poor lummox couldn't see that I was just trying to be polite about saying no—he protested that all I needed was the love and guidance of a devoted husband!" She made a face and said wickedly, "Wouldn't you love to have that whey-faced piece of piety calling you Mother and pecking your cheek at meeting and parting?"

In spite of herself, Constancy had laughed, but now, in recollecting the incident, she frowned the harder. There had been lunch that day, and then Timothy had come over to say that Sally had passed a bad night and would probably sleep all afternoon and would Faith have pity upon his forlorn state and go swimming with him. The two had gone, bickering as usual and laughing a good deal —they had always been on bantering terms with each other. After they had gone, Constancy put on her bonnet

and walked the half-mile through the coconut grove to
the small frame house that Timothy had built for Sally,
and, finding Sally asleep, had quietly set about putting the
house to rights. After Sally awakened, she was very merry
and fearless over the prospect of her first baby, but her
mother knew how she hated to be alone and stayed chat-
ting with her till Timothy returned. Then she had hastened home. It was dinner time, and Faith had not come
to the table but had sent down word by Silly that she had
stayed in the water and on the beach too long and had a
raging headache. The next day Faith went to meeting as
usual in the morning and at night, but she seemed very
quiet and listless. Monday she spent the day as usual, teaching the small children at the school. At the dinner table
she had suddenly said, with a perfectly wooden face, that
she was going to marry Luke Owens as soon as possible.

Constancy was still aghast. Jonathan looked astonished
and pleased. Silly was quietly approving. Young Jonathan
and Mary both looked stupefied. Only Matt said disgustedly, "Why on earth do you want to do that?" whereupon his sister had said shortly, "It's none of your business."

Luke had come after dinner and received his answer before the family. His sallow face flushed violently—pre-
sumably with pleasure—and his eyes nearly popped out of
his head, as if he found the answer he had received a little
incredible, too. Mystified as she was, Constancy had felt
that they ought to leave the two alone, but Jonathan sat
obtusely on, making conversation with Luke until nine
o'clock came and Luke rose to go. He shook hands all
around, and then sidled up to Faith and kissed her cheek
while Faith stood like a statue—with no more expression
on her face.

Since then Faith had been as quiet and withdrawn as

Silly. Constancy shook her head helplessly. To all her timid attempts to get an explanation of her sudden change of heart, Faith replied, "It seems best," and there was nothing further to be got out of her.

The sense of foreboding—for so long an alien to Constancy—now oppressed her continuously. It had threatened her briefly when Jonathan was taken ill, but he had improved and been so well since rallying from his first hard attack that she had ceased to worry over him. But now the half-formed suspicion that could never rise quite to the surface of her mind—the vague feeling that Timothy might have had some share in the metamorphosis which had overtaken Faith and was driving her into marriage with the dullest and most humorless of the missionaries' sons—and a recollection that Silly's piety was growing more and more pronounced—these things weighed upon Constancy's spirit. They sent fleeting thoughts of the potency of the jealous, formidable God Who she thought was fully foresworn in the dreadful period following on Samuel's death so many years ago. Fear struck at her heart: was this vengeful Deity attacking her cunningly and treacherously through her children? She dropped Faith's wedding gown; her right hand pressed hard against her heart to stifle the pain.

Her musings were interrupted by Mrs. Owens. "I declare I don't see why Faith was so set on a yellow wedding dress. It doesn't seem right for a young girl to be married in anything but white. Of course it's a pretty enough dress."

Constancy shrugged a little impatiently. "She wanted yellow—said she preferred it to white—and a girl ought to have her say about her wedding dress, since she has only one wedding."

"It'll be hard on Faith having to live at Lahaina,"

croaked Mrs. Owens. "Life's a lot harder there than here, and anything will be a comedown for her after this house."

Wishing that Mrs. Owens did not always irritate her so profoundly, Constancy rose mildly to the defense of Faith's future home. "Oh, Lahaina has progressed in the twenty-eight years we've been here. Not many of the *haoles* live in grass houses any more, and nothing is so unbearable if you have a good roof over your head and a good floor under your feet and real windows. Last summer when the girls and I were visiting there, it seemed a pleasant enough place to live. . . . Wouldn't you like to see the wedding cakes, Mrs. Owens?"

She led her guest to the kitchen, where a huge fruit cake in its icing and a smaller white cake for the bride, more elaborately decorated, stood on a table. Mrs. Owens nodded her approval. "Would you like me to come early tomorrow and help with the food, Sister Williams? You're going to be pretty busy."

"No, thank you so much," Constancy's answer came hastily; "you are kind to offer—but really there is very little to do, and Eliza can manage beautifully. Faith's trunk is all packed now, and Matt will take it to the boat early in the morning and be able to get back for the ceremony at noon." She paused, her right hand pressed against her cheek. "I wish Peter might be here. It seems a pity that he hasn't been able to attend one of the three weddings among his brothers and sisters."

"When do you suppose he will be back here?"

His mother sighed. "Not till a year from next summer. He finishes reading for the law this year, but he thought it best to stay in Boston for a year of actual practice before returning. He'll be twenty-three, and I haven't seen him since he was nine—almost ten—years old."

Mrs. Owens surprisingly patted Constancy's arm.

"You've had a hard life, Sister Williams, and I for one don't begrudge you the luxury you enjoy now."

Constancy's mouth twitched ever so slightly, but she said quite earnestly, "I'm sure you don't, Mrs. Owens. You are far too good a Christian to be envious. . . . There, isn't that Luke come for you?" as the sound of a carriage and horses struck their ears.

Mrs. Owens bustled into the hall to get her bonnet and shawl. Constancy accompanied her guest to the carriage, arriving just as Luke was handing Faith down. Mrs. Owens laid a stiff hand on the girl's shoulder. "You go to bed early and get well rested for tomorrow, Faith," she said brusquely. "We don't want you to be a peaked-looking bride."

Faith smiled wanly. "I'm far too healthy to be able to look peaked, Mrs. Owens—but I shall go to bed early, thank you." Her mother looked at her keenly. Faith did have magnificent health, but her face showed hollows, and there were dark smudges under her brown eyes.

As the carriage drove away, Constancy put her arms around her daughter, and an uncontrollable impulse bade her say quickly: "Faith, my dear . . . if you don't want to marry Luke, don't do it, child!"

Faith stared at her speechless; Constancy went on rapidly, "Life is hard enough under any circumstances—it would be too awful to be borne . . . living with someone you did not admire and love. Don't think what anybody will say. . . . I'll stand by you."

Faith's eyes stared brilliantly into her mother's eyes for a moment; then the light went out of them. Very gently she disengaged herself and said dully, "You are mistaken, Mother, if you think I am unhappy about marrying Luke. I . . . want to marry him, and I want to make him a . . . suitable wife, and be useful . . . in *Lahaina!*"

Her faint stressing of the last word caused her mother's eyes to open wide. "Faith! Are you sure you aren't marrying Luke . . . just to get away from home . . . from Honolulu?"

Faith was unprepared for the question. Her mouth trembled till she pressed her fingers over it hard and said in a despairing voice, "Don't keep questioning me so! Can't you see that I've *got* to do this?" She broke away from her mother and ran upstairs, leaving Constancy staring after her with grief in her heart.

6

In the next few weeks Constancy was kept from too much brooding over Faith's plight by her concern for Sally as the latter drew near her confinement. Constancy, who had faced her own first confinement with unshrinking stoicism and seven subsequent births with quiet acquiescence to the brutal plans of nature for producing babies, flinched at the thought of her daughter bearing a child. She insisted that Sally and Timothy move into the big house the first of May and stay until the child should be born. She hovered anxiously about Sally for the two weeks that elapsed after the first of May before young Timothy was born with no undue suffering on Sally's part.

Constancy kept a shrewd eye on Timothy during this time, and observed with compressed lips the silence that fell upon Sally on the five occasions when Timothy mounted his black horse and, gayly announcing that the king desired his presence, made off for Honolulu. On these occasions he arrived home long after midnight; once, going downstairs to let the cat out, Constancy passed him coming in and smelled liquor on his breath. She observed that he clung to the banister as he mounted the stairs. Her heart sank.

Everyone knew that the king loved to drink and that he loved a good drinking companion. The concerted efforts of the missionaries to close the breweries had merely resulted in the king's closing the ones he himself did not patronize. Even Dr. Judd, powerful as his influence upon the king was, had been incapable of persuading the jovial monarch to give up drinking or gambling. Constancy's heart sank still lower. Could Timothy be gambling with the king, too? And if, as was practically certain, Timothy was an habitual member of the king's revels, the other missionaries were sure to know about it before long. Experience told Constancy that they would not be content to gossip about it among themselves: the matter would be brought up at the next general meeting, and there was Jonathan, who, apparently, had no suspicion of the state of affairs.

When Timothy was with Sally, he was as solicitous for her comfort as even Constancy could wish. She had to admit that Sally was usually responsible for his going off with his easel and painting materials during the daytime. Questioned by her mother, Sally laughed lightly. "He is so concerned about me, Mother. You would think that no one had ever borne a child before! He hovers around me like a mother hen with one chick and acts as if every breath I drew might be my last. It's good for him to get away from me—and when he is painting he doesn't think of anything but his painting."

But when Sally's night of labor was upon her, her husband was very much on hand, getting in the way, clutching at Constancy's skirts as she hurried back and forth between the kitchen and Sally's bedroom, groaning aloud

when, in the last hours, Sally's piteous cries sounded be-
lowstairs, where Timothy had been banished by Sally's
own orders. He sat, abjectly miserable, his face in his
hands, only half aware of Jonathan seated by the lamp
reading the Scriptures and stopping now and then to
mutter a prayer. Silly fetched and carried for her mother,
her lips moving ceaselessly. Young Jonathan strode about
looking harassed, partly on Sally's account and partly on
his wife's account, for Mary's first child was to be born in
July. Matt, sent hurriedly for the doctor at eight o'clock
in the evening, returned near midnight with the disheart-
ening news that he had been called out to Ewa on an acci-
dent case and could not be expected before the next evening.

Constancy set her lips and resigned herself to the task
of bringing Sally's child into the world unaided. It was a
task she had accomplished often enough both among the
natives and among the white women of Honolulu, but it
was a different matter when the woman in question was
her own daughter, and the daughter who was nearest her
heart.

At four in the morning Constancy appeared on the
landing of the stairway and announced wearily: "It's all
over, and the baby is a boy—nine pounds. Timothy, you
can see her for a minute, but don't let her talk much."

Timothy bounded up the stairs to sink beside the bed
and burst into loud and unrestrained sobs—greatly to his
mother-in-law's surprise. But Sally merely laughed, a
small but amused chuckle, and weakly stroked his bowed
head and told him to cheer up and look at his son. Timothy stared curiously at the small red urchin with a tuft
of black hair and said thoughtfully, "Jove, did we all look
like that once?" And, turning to his wife, he said auto-
cratically, "Sally, that's the last child we're going to have.

I can't go through another night like this." Sally smiled at him maternally and perhaps a little ironically before falling asleep.

Again Constancy was too busy to have time to think. Sally and Timothy stayed in the big house until small Timothy was three weeks old and Sally felt strong enough to manage him alone, with the fourteen-year-old niece of Eliza to do the housework. There was the general meeting, which Constancy attended with dread, but no mention was made of Timothy's association with the king: the brethren were too concerned over the matter of preparing a letter of excision for one of their number who had defied them to the point of marrying a native woman on Maui.

No sooner was the general meeting over and the school closed for the summer than Mary's daughter was born. This time there was a doctor present, but Mary fared less happily than Sally and was weak for some time after her confinement. Constancy was kept extraordinarily busy well into August. Each ship brought a brief, impersonal letter from Faith at Lahaina, signed "your loving daughter." The letters told her family that, although she lived in a grass house, she had a wood floor, and the thatched roof had as yet let no water in during the rains. Once she mentioned receiving a great deal of advice from the wives of the other missionaries—much of it on matters that seemed to her to concern them very little, "but," she wrote, "I try to bear all with patience, knowing they mean it for the best." In none of these letters could Constancy find a trace of the Faith she had known for nearly nineteen years.

In September, when the school opened, a bitter argument arose between the two Jonathans. It began with young Jonathan's decision that Mary should not resume her duties in the school while little Deborah was so small, and ended with the elder Jonathan's discovery of the appalling fact that his son considered John Calvin nothing but a deranged fanatic and believed no longer in hell. The discovery brought on another severe heart attack, and Jonathan senior was sent to bed for two months.

Constancy, who had known for some time that Mary's father was a Unitarian minister and that Jonathan had grown away from the austerer features of his childhood faith, had been trusting foolishly in young Jonathan's compassion for his father to avert catastrophe. Now she realized how vain her hopes had been: deception of any sort was foreign to her eldest son's nature. He had long been chafing at the bonds laid upon him by his agreement to spare his father. Even Mary had been in league against him, shrewdly arguing that he could do much more good dispensing the kindlier faith from the pulpit under the guise of Calvinism than by renouncing Calvinism openly and being denied the pulpit altogether.

Now Constancy lived in a nerve-racking atmosphere. Her husband gazed gray-faced and haggard-eyed into space for hours on end, or, whenever she entered the room, implored her aid with burning eyes. "Constancy!" and the cry was for succor. "What must I do? Must I denounce my own son for a heretic and have him put out of the Church?" And he would groan and twist in his bed. Often she heard him muttering, "God, if it be thy will, let this cup pass!"

Constancy's task was to soothe him as best she could, striving to convince him that Jonathan was at the age when unrest and questioning were natural and that it would be wrong to take him too seriously. "Wait, my dear, until the next general meeting before you commit yourself. After all, he is your son, and your lenience is forgivable. It seems to me that you owe him and yourself that year. Besides—he preaches no subversive doctrine from the pulpit—he just chooses to emphasize the loving-kindness of Christ rather than the awfulness of hell." And finally Jonathan agreed to let the matter rest—at least for the present—while he prayed with renewed vigor that his son might see the light.

7

In the first days of Jonathan's illness when Constancy's presence was demanded in the sickroom, young Jonathan and Silly struggled along with the school. Timothy had extricated Sally from the schoolroom a year and a half earlier. After a month of Jonathan's illness Constancy was back in the school for most of the day, and Mary took her place as nurse to the elder Jonathan. The sick man was fond of his daughter-in-law and enjoyed watching her play with the baby. Mary was a natural nurse who could keep the patient cheerful without resorting to the fatuities generally thought suitable for the sickroom. Even Matt was drafted into service for the school and made to conduct classes in gardening and the care of chickens, goats, and horses.

The Williamses believed firmly in a practical course of instruction for the natives. The children in their school were taught to read and to write; they learned elementary arithmetic and the essential facts of geography; they memorized a small book, the title page of which bore in Hawaiian the following inscription: *The Evangelical primer, containing A Minor Doctrinal Catechism; and A Minor Historical Catechism; to which is added The Westminster Assembly's Shorter Catechism, with Short Ex-*

planatory Notes and copious Scripture Proofs and Illus-
trations; for the use of Families and Schools, by Joseph
Emerson, Pastor of the Church in Beverly. But the pupils
were not taught astronomy, botany, higher mathematics,
or rhetoric. On the other hand the girls were taught to
sew, not only how to make small neat stitches, but how to
cut and fit and finish any and all articles of clothing
needed by the average family; they were taught to cook
and to keep house. The boys were taught gardening and
poultry husbandry, the general care of animals in sickness
and health, and elementary carpentering.

Thus any child who passed through the Waikiki school
could be trusted to respond promptly, if asked, "What is
the general character of the natural heart?": "It is enmity
against God; it is deceitful above all things, and desperately wicked." He could define "Effectual calling" as "a
work of God's Spirit, whereby, convincing us of our sin
and misery, enlightening our minds in the knowledge of
Christ, and renewing our wills, He doth persuade and enable us to embrace Jesus Christ, freely offered to us in the
Gospel." He could also be trusted to grow handsome vegetables, to delouse chickens, to feed them in such fashion
that their laying powers would be improved, or, if the
child were a girl, she could be counted on to prepare an
edible meal or make a proper dress.

November found Jonathan up and about. Life went
smoothly through November and December, although
Jonathan had been disturbed to discover on one of his
tours of the native colony that the *hapa-haole* girl, Leilehua, was pregnant. Sally was blooming and so was the
baby. The families united for a large Christmas dinner,
and Constancy's troubled heart became tranquil.

One day in January, Jonathan started off to make a call

or two in the native village, mentioning that he might stop to see Sally and the baby before returning. Cautioning him against overtaxing his strength, Constancy watched him make his way through the coconut grove. It was nearly five o'clock when, seeing Matt drive hurriedly out of the yard in the wagon, she was moved to wonder where he could be going without a word to anyone. Then Mary came in, her face very pale and tears in her eyes, to tell her that Jonathan had had another heart attack just as he reached Sally's . . . that it had been too sudden for him to suffer, and that they would be bringing him home as soon as Matt could get there.

Constancy stood tall and erect, staring at Mary's tear-stained face. "He is dead, you mean," she said matter-of-factly and went to stand at the door, her face expressionless. Dispassionately she watched the small procession approach. She saw Matt on the driver's seat, his young face painfully screwed up. Sally sat on the floor of the wagon. In the instant of the wagon's arrival Constancy saw that Sally held her father's head in her lap, and the face she turned to her mother was ashen, the eyes wide with fright. Timothy, carrying the baby, walked behind the wagon with Jonathan. Timothy handed the baby to Sally across the motionless figure in the wagon; then, with Jonathan's aid, he lifted the long, frail body out of the wagon. Constancy saw that they had put a handkerchief over his face. Without thinking, she snatched it off, saw the wide-staring, death-dulled eyes of her husband, the fallen jaw and bared teeth, and screamed. Astonished at the sound, she looked sharply about her until her eyes fastened on Sally's terrified face. "Hush, child!" she said sternly. "Death always changes them—it even changed Sammie!"

Sally, starting to falter, "But—*I* didn't scream," stopped in amazement. She had never before heard her mother mention the name of the brother who had died. Constancy was giving orders calmly. "Carry him up to our room, Jonathan—and Matt, put Old Bess away and get a bite to eat. You'll have to ride in to town on some errands to-night."

She followed as Jonathan and Timothy made their slow way up the stairs. They laid the body on the bed. Jonathan put his arm around his mother's shoulders. "Don't you want Mary—or Sally—with you, Mother?"

Constancy shook her head. "No. . . . I can do for him what needs to be done. Please leave me alone with him."

The two men shuffled to the door. "Wait . . ." She hesitated a moment, frowning as if she were thinking hard. "Jonathan, you had better go with Matt . . . about the coffin, you know, and tell them at the mission to let others know . . . Mr. Owens should preach the services, and they must be held here at your father's own church. . . . Oh, yes, he will be laid in our plot at Kawaiahao, but leave room between . . . Sammie's grave and his . . . for me. Remember!" and her voice was sharp. "The grave isn't to be next Sammie's, but one removed!" She walked swiftly to the door and shut it after them.

Outside the door Jonathan and Timothy eyed each other uneasily. Timothy shrugged one shoulder toward the closed door. "Do you think it is . . . all right to leave her alone with him like that?"

Jonathan hunched his own shoulders miserably. "I don't know what else we can do. . . . You know, I don't think she knew that she screamed out there in the yard. . . . She's usually so controlled . . ."

They tiptoed down the stairs, and Timothy went over to where Sally sat holding the baby. She held him so tightly that he was whimpering, but she paid no attention. Timothy bent over her.

"I have to go home for a few minutes—I'll be right back." His voice sank to a whisper: "And, Sally . . . don't ever tell anybody . . . it wouldn't do any good, and we didn't know he would come along just then. It's awful, but it would be even worse if the rest of them knew."

Sally spoke dully through stiff lips. "I wasn't going to tell anybody."

Timothy patted her arm. "We'll get out of this place just as soon as I can get us passage," he murmured and went out.

He started toward his house at a stride that shortly became a run. The house was dark; he groped for the lucifer matches, found them, and lighted the lamp. He held it high, so that it shone on the picture he had been finishing when his father-in-law had chosen to surprise them with an ill-timed call. The flickering light found an answering gleam in the shining whiteness of the body of the woman depicted on the canvas. He bent nearer to scrutinize his handiwork, nodding in involuntary pleasure at the subtle difference in tone between the warm whiteness of the woman's flesh and the delicate rosiness of the infant that tumbled over her, burying his fists in the masses of her red-gold hair.

Constancy sat dry-eyed through the long funeral address, in which the Reverend Mark Owens reviewed painstakingly Jonathan's life of labor in the islands, referring to him reverently as one of the Lord's anointed ones. Women she had worked with side by side in the early years, both in the school and in the kitchen of the old mission house, stole curious glances at her, slyly avid for any sign of emotion, any sign of abandon to the grief they knew she must be experiencing.

But Constancy, deathly weary from her long night of service to Jonathan, sat, brain and heart numb, only one far corner of her mind conscious of the words of the minister. Her glance swept the row of her children. Timothy and Sally were sitting hand in hand, Sally's face tearstained, Timothy's jaw squared belligerently against the emotional strain of the long service. Jonathan's shoulders drooped miserably. Dispassionately Constancy reflected, "I don't think he felt any real tenderness for his father, but he feels sorry and remorseful now to think that he had that argument with him and wonders if he isn't in some way responsible for this."

Mary's attention was divided between the sermon and the baby sleeping in her arms. Matt lounged in his stiff-backed chair, his long legs curled around the chair legs, his features twisted into a furious scowl. Constancy sighed. She knew from past experience that the scowl meant that Matt was wanting to cry and hated himself for the softness. She knew, too, that he was feeling horrid because he hadn't loved his father more. Silly sat erect, her eyes fixed on the sallow face of the minister, heedless of the tears that rolled down her cheeks and wet her white frock. Her thin hands twisted and writhed on her lap. Constancy looked away. Silly, she acknowledged now, was the only one of her children who had really loved her father. Her heart smote her. Jonathan had been such a dutiful father, so concerned for their welfare, yet so fearful of erring by being more lenient than the Lord would approve, so timid of earthly bonds which might trespass upon his obligations to Jehovah, that the children never seemed to feel comfortable in his presence. Only Silly was different. Constancy surveyed her youngest daughter through narrowed eyes and thought with sudden clairvoyance: "It isn't because Silly saw through Jonathan's disguise of austerity to

the sensitive kindliness underneath, but that she adored
the disguise, the adamant armor of the man of God. She's
hard—for all her piety, she has no patience with weakness,
and I think she would have less for her own than for other
people's."

Constancy's mind suddenly veered around. Could Jonathan's disembodied spirit see into her mind? Impossible to
think that all of Jonathan lay in the black-painted coffin;
that shrunken, gray-faced image had nothing of Jonathan
in it. She shifted uneasily in her chair. Jonathan was so
good, and so simple, so unsuspicious where he had once
given his trust. Whatever the system of rewards and de-
merits in the unknown world beyond the ugly miracle of
death, Jonathan must fare well . . . and it would not be
well for him to see in his widow's mind the lie she had
lived for nearly thirty years. The truth about his wife
would be a poor reward for Jonathan to receive.

At the side of the grave she felt herself being pushed
toward the coffin. She went a step or two before she understood that they meant her to look upon her husband's
face for the last time. She raised her hand to her breast,
palm outward as if to fend off a blow. "No!" she said
sharply. The minister, after one swift look at her face,
murmured his last benison over the body, "Ashes to ashes,
dust to dust," crumbling the dark earth above the casket.
"Into Thy hands, O Lord, we commend our brother's
spirit," Constancy heard him say. There was the sound of
earth falling on wood, and she turned away, her eye falling upon the carving of the small stone above her first-
born's grave, the stone with its defenseless lamb surmount-
ing the one word "Samuel" and the dates of his birth and
death. She remembered how distressed Jonathan had been
because she wanted a kitten rather than the symbolic lamb
carved upon Sammie's stone, and how gentle he had been

in his refusal, thinking her illness had made her irrational. Clearly as if it had been a day or a week ago, there arose the picture of Sammie's curly dark head and his long green eyes that tilted so unexpectedly when he smiled, and the memory of the confiding affection with which he curled in her lap, snuggling his head into the hollow of her shoulder while she read to him or recited fragments of poetry. There was, sharper still, the memory of Sammie's thoughtful decision to love only the God Who had loved the albatross.

Those watching the tears drop painfully from beneath her lowered eyelids could not know that they were shed for a child dead twenty-four years, and that for Jonathan, covered now with earth, there was only the tearless anguish that made her heart a burden in her body, and the bewilderment of her brain induced by the sudden removal of her only reason for enduring an alien life and living a lie for more than a quarter of a century.

8

Constancy continued to follow automatically the established pattern of her days. She rose at six to help Eliza with the breakfast, attended family prayers, which young Jonathan now conducted, at seven, breakfasted, instructed Eliza in regard to her day's work, and hurried to school at eight o'clock, where she taught the larger girls in sewing and geography and arithmetic forenoons. On two afternoons a week she supervised the larger girls in her own kitchen, teaching them to bake bread, cakes, and pies, how to make *poha* jam, how to cook such vegetables as the garden produced—whatever a cook in the Hawaii of the middle nineteenth century needed to know. The remaining three afternoons of the school week she spent visiting the houses of the native village, carrying medicines and food to the sick, advising them as diplomatically as possible in matters of cleanliness and hygiene, prescribing for the ailing, and frequently assisting at a difficult birth.

Too, there was the matter of Sally's departure to distract her. It seemed so sudden a decision. She had not known that Timothy would want to leave so soon. She had realized that he would not always be content to live on the island, but she was not prepared for Sally's abrupt announcement on the twelfth of January that Timothy had engaged passage for them on Captain Brown's ship the *Dolphin*, just in port and preparing to sail on the seventeenth. The ship was to stop for a few days at San Francisco before beginning the long journey around the Horn. Timothy spoke fluently of his need to reach Boston in time to arrange for an exhibit of his work the next fall. Sally, to Constancy's hurt surprise, seemed anxious to go. Constancy tried to reconcile this eagerness to leave the home of her childhood with Sally's early horror of being forced to leave her family. She put the change in her down to the force of her love for Timothy, to the inevitable substitution of new love for old when a girl reaches womanhood and begins a new family life.

Then there was Matt, suddenly bent upon sailing with Uncle Nate the next time the *Mary Ellen* stopped at the island. He confessed that he and his great-uncle had talked of it many a time, but that he had feared his father would object to his becoming a seaman. There were Jonathan and Silly, both suddenly clamoring to take into the big house as many of the larger girls from ten to fifteen years of age as would be allowed to leave their parents. The two argued with some reason that the greatest lapsing into lamentable heathen ways came when the girls were in their early teens and were left in the midst of a careless native family that thought little enough of irregular relations among the young and accepted a clerically unsanctioned birth in the family as casually as they did the arrival of a litter of pigs.

"If they can live beneath our roof, Mother," Silly pleaded, "they will be safe from temptation, and they will have the privilege of seeing how pleasant and how noble is a truly Christian home!"

Jonathan had argued a little more practically, "Our business is to keep these young people moral, and the first step is to make it impossible for the girls to be anything else—to keep them apart from the boys and men until they are sought in marriage. You know, Mother," he had argued, "it is not right that we should have this great house with six large bedrooms and, when Matt goes to sea, only three of them in use. We can easily have six cots in each bedroom, and eighteen girls could stay with us, and——"

But here his mother had interrupted him dryly: "You forget, son, that this house belongs to Uncle Nate. It is making a little free with it to turn it into a reformatory without consulting him. You must wait and discuss the matter with him when he arrives."

Two days before Sally was to set sail, Constancy was putting on her bonnet, preparatory to setting out on a round of visits, when Eliza's pink calico-clad form appeared in the doorway of her bedroom.

"The Jezebel waits for you with her child of sin," she announced disapprovingly.

"Who?" Constancy was for an instant bewildered, and then remembered that Eliza had told her of the birth of Leilehua's baby. "Oh—I'll come down at once." She left her bonnet on, thus hoping to curtail the visit. Wondering a little at the call, for Leilehua was not given to haunting the missionary preserves, Constancy hastened down to the hall and found the girl sitting in a straight chair, holding the baby negligently on her knees. It was wrapped in what appeared to be a red skirt.

"Don't rise," said Constancy kindly, seeing the girl slide to the edge of her chair. "What a fine baby!" She picked up the red bundle and looked at the small face. "Another sailor," she thought to herself, observing that its skin was very fair. She sat down on a low chair and laid the baby over her shoulder. Leilehua looked at her sharply from tilted, liquid brown eyes; she smiled ingratiatingly, and Constancy noticed that she was fair enough to have red lips.

"You like the baby?" Leilehua asked eagerly.

Constancy nodded and smiled, thinking of how the men who did not seek favors of Leilehua condemned her so bitterly; she wondered if they never envied the swaggering sailors and the thoughtlessly animal natives—if spite never tinged their censure of this sleek, half-wild girl. Hadn't Jonathan said once, "Her kind is a menace because Satan makes her fair and gives her an evil lure that troubles even a moral man."

Leilehua rose swiftly to her feet. "You can keep her," she said airily and was making toward the door, the gaudy red calico garment she had donned in honor of Constancy swirling about her slender brown legs.

"Wait!" commanded Constancy sternly. "You can't give your baby away! Women who have babies must look after them. I will show you how to care for her and give you some clothes for her to wear—but you must keep her."

Leilehua shook her head. "There is nothing to feed her —except *poi,* which makes her cry." She shrugged her shoulders. "I have not the money to give her to a poor woman to suckle."

"Why can't you nurse her yourself?" Indignation was in Constancy's voice.

Again the shrug and a half-smile. "Too much *pilikia,*" softly; "I have not the time." She came a little nearer to Constancy. "But if you do not wish to take the baby, perhaps your daughter would like to care for her together with the little brother——"

"What do you mean?" demanded Constancy angrily, but realizing in the next breath that her question was purely rhetorical. Again the amused smile on Leilehua's face. "Because Teemothy liked me very much just before his son was born," she murmured. "You say she is a nice baby, so perhaps Meesus Teemothy will like to have her." She smiled blandly upon the white woman.

Constancy tightened her hold on the scarlet bundle and set her teeth firmly together. "Why do you think the baby's father is Mr. McGuire?" she asked stiffly. "You know other men."

"At the time," remarked Leilehua amiably enough but stifling a yawn, "there was no other man for it to be . . . but if you will look upon the toe that turns away from the great toe . . . it is just like Teemothy's toe. Where else should my baby get such a toe? See, all of my toes are alike." She held up one slim brown foot and then the other, flexing the perfectly shaped toes like a cat.

Constancy snatched back the red skirt from the baby's feet and looked carefully at the tiny feet. The middle toe on the right foot curved sharply away from the great toe, a miniature crescent contradiction. Constancy held the small foot in her hand, staring at the mark. She remembered Sally bending over her own new-born baby and saying with a laugh, "Timothy was sure that the baby would have the McGuire toe. He and his father and his grand-father all have a crooked toe. You'd think a crooked toe was a mark of beauty. He'll be disappointed that young Timmy hasn't it."

Constancy looked narrowly at the girl before her. Her lip curled involuntarily at thought of a female creature of any sort who cared no more for her offspring than this. She spoke scornfully: "I will take the baby—if you never, as long as you live, come to see her, or bother me or any-one who cares for her. She must be as if she had never be-longed to you—as if she had no blood of yours in her veins. Do you understand?"

The syllables of the Hawaiian tongue fell slowly and dis-tinctly from Constancy's lips. Leilehua was suddenly wreathed in smiles. "Thank you," she said graciously. "She is yours; I do not want her."

Constancy stood up, the baby in her arms. "If you ever try to get her back or to get to know her, even," she said levelly, "or tell anyone whose child she is—who her father is—I shall take you to the judge and you will be fined and put in prison to work hard for a long time. You know that is what happens to women who will not care for their children." She glanced quickly about her to make sure that there was no witness to her prevarication. "If you do any of these things, I will tell the judge that you left your baby out to starve, meaning it to die, and he will believe me—not you."

The girl's eyes rolled in her head. "I shall do all that you say! Everything shall be as you wish!" she protested glibly and backed hastily out of the door.

Constancy's eyes dwelt compassionately upon the small form in her arms. Suddenly she frowned and went swiftly into the kitchen, where Eliza was washing the noonday dishes.

"Eliza," she said, "I am taking this poor child to bring
up. You know the mother is not fit to care for her. I do
not wish even my sons or daughters to know whose child
she is. It is enough to say that she is an orphan." She paused.
Eliza looked up and nodded. "They will learn nothing
from me," she said briefly. "You are good to the Jezebel."

Constancy turned to the kettle and tested the water in
it with her finger. "Get me the tub we use for Deborah's
bath," she said and busied herself with unwrapping the
soiled red skirt from the baby. "And Eliza, while I bathe
her, you go up and get a diaper and little shirt and nightgown from the baby's things."

The baby screwed up her face and set up a thin, pitiful
wail. Constancy's heart smote her. "Poor lamb!" she murmured compassionately, as she gently soaped the small
slippery body. "Just a minute now, and you shall have
some milk. It's not your fault, poor thing."

Her mind strove to grasp the problem of Timothy's behavior, the while she ministered to his child, dressing it in
the soft clothes prepared for her son's first-born, mixing
milk with a little boiled water and sugar, pressing the nip-
ple over the bottle, and feeding the hungry baby. She
counted back nine months from January: April . . . and
she stopped aghast. This baby had been conceived, then,
during those last weeks before little Timothy was born.
She remembered how Sally had encouraged Timothy to
go off painting so that he shouldn't worry about her as her
time drew near. Constancy stared, unseeing, at this token
of Timothy's faithlessness. Was his love and concern for
Sally, then, all a lie? Or was a man bereft of the fear of
God free of all restraint, all loyalty, all decency?

Her face puckered in distaste at the thought of Timothy desiring Leilehua when he had Sally as a wife. Possibly
it was only because of Sally's condition, but . . . even if

Jonathan had not been dedicated to his religious faith mind, body, and soul, she argued, he still would have abided by his marriage vows. Her imagination failed to picture Jonathan sauntering cheerfully (or for that matter, even fearfully) off to lie with any other woman while his wife was awaiting a confinement.

Perhaps it was the atmosphere of the islands. . . . At the general meetings there was always talk of resisting the temptations of the land. Was this what the brethren had meant? Perhaps Timothy would be different in the chastening atmosphere of New England. But Sally . . . Constancy's heart misgave her. She was sure that Sally had no suspicion of Timothy, just as she was sure that Sally looked upon Timothy as a cross between a god and a delightful child. She drummed her fingers upon the baby's bottle in exasperation at the helplessness of her position. There was nothing at all she could do to help Sally except bid her godspeed and hope that she would never discover Timothy in iniquity. Her shoulders drooped dispiritedly. Was there nothing for her daughters between the charming and deadly irresponsibility of Timothy and the deplorably dull piety of Luke Owens?

Already the small boat that was to carry the voyagers out to the ship was sliding into the landing. Constancy stood on the sand holding little Timothy on one arm. The uneasy silence of prolonged partings fell on the group that surrounded Timothy and Sally.

"Oh!" cried Sally as if a sudden pain had besieged her, as if the significance of the moment had just dawned upon her. She began kissing them all, Jonathan, Mary, Deborah, clinging for a moment to Silly, who hugged her spasmodically and unexpectedly and then turned away from her family to cry. Sally flung her arms around Matt, whose face was working and whose big hands clumsily patted his sister's shoulder. "Anyway, Sal," he gulped, "I'll be coming to see you when I sail with Uncle Nate."

Last of all, Sally turned to her mother and with a despairing cry buried her head in her mother's shoulder. Constancy strained her favorite daughter fiercely to her breast, speechless, great tears rolling unheeded down her face. They had no words for each other. Sally raised her head, and the two women stared through tears into each other's eyes before their lips met in a hard, unhappy kiss. Constancy was unaware that Timothy kissed her cheek before leading Sally to the little boat where an oarsman waited to carry her through the water and establish her in the boat. Timothy, with the baby held rather negligently under one arm, sprang in as the tide receded, and the boat was off, leaving the little group on the shore gazing silently after it.

9

Within a week of Sally's departure an epidemic of measles broke out among the natives at the beach. Constancy, making her round of visits, found two children burning with fever, their eyes watering, and their chests dotted with the bright red spots. She remembered that other epidemic of measles in which ten thousand had died. Particularly she remembered how the ignorance of the natives had led them to death: they had leaped into the ocean to cool their fever, driving the eruption inward.

She bade the mothers of the two small victims to keep the children in bed; the huts were dark enough so that she had no fear for their eyes. She told the mothers to wash the children's eyes frequently with water that had been boiled, and to come to her back door for milk. "No *poi!* No bananas!" she said forcefully and continued with her round of visits, cautioning parents, telling them what to do and, more important, what not to do if their children took the dread disease. Frightened with recollections of the plague that had swept away the population in '48, they promised to obey her. She went home heavy-hearted. She bathed, changed all her clothes, and even washed her hair before approaching either of the babies.

Jonathan brooded over the matter. "There's no help for it," he announced at last. "Mary must take your place in the school. If you spend all your time watching over these poor wretches, you may save many if not all of their lives and keep the disease from spreading beyond the village here."

Constancy remonstrated. "Certainly I must devote my time to the natives, but I should not advise Mary to try to teach. These children are likely to come down with it, and Mary might bring it to the baby. . . . Have you had measles, Mary?"

Mary shook her head. "However, there isn't much danger of a grown person getting them is there?"

Constancy raised her eyebrows. "Most of the deaths in '48 were among the grown-ups. Silly and Matt both had them, so they are safe."

Mary thought hard. "I know," she said brightening. "Until this is over, I can teach out under the trees. Surely in the fresh air there won't be any danger."

Jonathan's relief appeared on his face. "That's what you can do!" he said with great satisfaction, but Constancy looked gravely from one to the other. "I hope it will be all right," she said slowly. "For my own part, I'd rather shut the school entirely than have you run the risk of catching anything like this. Measles go hard here—especially if you are past childhood."

But they laughed at her. The next day Mary resumed

teaching, holding her classes on the broad *lanai* of the big house and leaving the babies in Eliza's care. Constancy went ceaselessly back and forth among the native huts, finding three more cases of the disease, two children and one adult. Dr. Hollingsby came from town three times a week to make the rounds of the village, but Constancy's was the heavier and the more responsible task.

The first week passed to the second, and a month went by. Leilehua's old grandmother was among the dead, two other old women, one young married woman, one father who had been struggling to care for three young children since the death of his wife a year earlier, and one husband and wife who left two children. Constancy tightened her mouth and brought the five orphans home with her. She dared to hope that all who were going to catch the disease were now in the throes or on the way to recovery. She was worn out with the long hours of active service to the sick, service which included bathing the patients, washing their clothes, and preparing their food. The day she brought home the last two children she found Mary coughing with every breath, her eyes watering, her skin dry and hot to the touch, and her breasts painfully swollen with milk, since she had not dared to nurse the baby with the fever upon her.

Constancy straightened her shoulders, thrust back her fear into the recesses of her heart, and took command of the situation. She gave the two orphans to Eliza to scrub and then put Mary in the downstairs bedroom and sent Jonathan for the doctor.

Through the days that followed, Jonathan and Silly and Matt with one native teacher ran the school and cared for the orphans. Constancy devoted her entire attention to Mary, leaving the care of the two babies to Eliza. Mary was a very tractable patient, a very apologetic one, but in spite of her efforts to be as little trouble as possible, she caught cold one night when the wind veered and blew from the south through the window by her bed. At the doctor's next visit Mary was definitely very ill. He shook his head gravely as he listened to her rasping breathing and mouthed "Pneumonia" to Constancy. Constancy's eyes darkened in fear. To her pneumonia meant death: Sammie had had pneumonia. Hourly all night, in response to the doctor's orders, she heated alcohol and wet the hastily improvised cotton-batting pneumonia jacket with it and wrapped it about the alternately shivering and burning patient. She continued the treatment the next day and the next night until, at four o'clock, when she came in with a fresh supply of alcohol, she found Mary lying more quietly even than was her wont and saw that she was dead.

Constancy's eyes followed Jonathan. No words, no gentlest touch could arouse him from the blazing-eyed abstraction that had fallen upon him with Mary's death. His mother could not put him out of her mind for a moment, with all the extra work of caring for five orphans, one of them a baby in arms. Silly and Matt struggled with the school for the week after Mary's funeral. Jonathan seemed unaware of the school. When Sunday came Mr. Owens was called to conduct the services. Conscientiously and heavily he reminded Jonathan that it was not given mortal man to understand the ways of God, that it was God's will that Mary should be taken. Jonathan stared at him wildly and said nothing at all.

All day Jonathan wandered up and down stairs, in and out of all the rooms of the house. At night he went out, and Constancy, straining her eyes through the darkness, could make out his tall form striding up and down by the water's edge. Her heart was wrung with pity for him and with a sense of her own helplessness to offer him comfort. Sometimes at night Silly would follow him out to the waterfront, and then Constancy would see the two of them walking slowly, apparently in utter silence, along the sea wall.

Weariness weighted down Constancy's spirit, weariness and stupefied acceptance of the deluge of sorrow that had so suddenly been loosed upon her home, just when she had been basking in the peace and comfort of their life in the big house at the beach. She was too numb to feel emotion on her own behalf now—even when a letter came in her mother's tremulous writing to announce that her father was dead. Similarly she felt nothing of pleasure when a letter came towards the end of February from Faith, telling of the birth of a daughter whom she was naming Constancy. Faith's mother wondered a little at the enclosure of a sealed note which Faith asked her to give Uncle Nate as soon as he arrived; she placed it under a vase in his bedroom in readiness for him and forgot it.

It was the tenth day after Mary's death when Jonathan at last broke his silence. He came quietly into the room as Constancy was heating the milk for the night feeding of the two babies. On impulse Constancy laid little Deborah in his arms and handed him the warm bottle. "You feed her while I attend to Elspeth," she said matter-of-factly and cuddled the plump olive-skinned baby in the bend of her left arm.

Jonathan did as he was told, and after a moment began to speak. "I have been in sin, Mother," he said so quietly that his mother glanced at him in surprise.

"Yes?" There was surprise in her tone.

"I feel that it is because I wandered from the true faith —to embrace an easier, laxer one, that God has seen fit to visit His wrath upon me."

Constancy's heart sank. "But, Jonathan!" His reasoning put the Creator's action in a very bad light to Constancy. "Isn't that line of reasoning inadequate to explain the thing from Mary's point of view?"

Jonathan explained patiently, "Mary was innocent. She was as good as it is given a mortal to be—so that death is a boon to her. It is only upon me that punishment is inflicted—in order that I should see the error of my ways."

His mother's lips tightened into a straight line. "If Mary had been consulted, son," she said, "I think she would have elected to stay here on earth and look after her new baby —and you." It was on her tongue to remind him that Mary was a Unitarian and therefore, according to his logic, could not be innocent, but she stifled the words.

"No . . . no!" he knit his brows a moment and then went on eagerly: "You see, I have been acting a lie for this last year or two—preaching a false doctrine from the pulpit of the true faith, the faith that brought you and Father across the world. That is my sin, and now I must make what restitution I can. I must confess this matter and profess my repentance before the mission board."

"After all, they do not know that you have ever faltered in the faith," reasoned Constancy, without much hope, however, of reaching him with such an argument. "Do you feel that you *must* take this step? You know you are unstrung with grief at Mary's death, child. You may feel different about it in a month or so. Isn't this matter between you and God—rather than between you and the brethren?"

She gazed down unseeingly at the dark little head on her arm and tipped the bottle a little more. The thought of the emotional clamor, the exhortation, the violent prayers that would arise among the brethren at any such demonstration on Jonathan's part filled her with distaste.

Reproach filled her son's eyes. "Mother," he cried, "I thought *you* would understand! How could you countenance deception and hypocrisy such as I would be guilty of if I did not confess all frankly before these men of God?"

Irony turned Constancy's mouth downward at the corners, but her voice was very earnest and very gentle when she spoke: "My dear, I have not lived among these men of God for nearly thirty years without learning that they are human and liable to the mistakes of other men. Their greatest mistake has been to conceive of God as a—monster —capable of such cruelties as no man living would be guilty of; and consequently they act in fear sometimes, rather than in loving-kindness, and they so easily mistrust the most innocent happiness. I cannot feel that they are qualified to judge you in this matter."

Jonathan was staring at her in amazement. "Mother! You sound like a—a heretic!" His voice sank to a whisper.

Constancy smiled at him sadly. "Do you think me a heretic, son? For thinking it a mistake not to credit God with at least as much pity and kindness as you or I have in us?" She busied herself with changing the babies and then went on slowly: "Of course, you are a grown man, and you must decide this matter for yourself, but I suggest that you wait for the general meeting, at least, before you take any decisive steps. You are unstrung now. Give your mind time to regain its composure. I want you to be comforted, my child. I have grieved with you and for you these bitter days, but I do not want you to act hastily."

Jonathan handed his daughter to his mother and stood up, gaunt and haggard. "No man may look to anything but God for succor!" he said hoarsely. "Silly—young as she is—understands my plight, but you—my own mother —fail me." He turned and rushed from the room.

Constancy pressed Deborah to her breast, her hands clenched in the flannel jacket the baby was wearing. Tears of grief and mortal hurt gathered in her eyes. "I don't think that I can bear anything more . . . I don't!" she said aloud and started at the sound of her voice. With compressed lips she put the babies in the wide cradle that held them both, blew out the lamp, and crept into bed, to find herself trembling, every nerve in her body on edge. Her will deserted her, and she wept hysterically, smothering her face in the pillow so that she would not disturb the babies or Silly, who slept in the next room.

10

Looking out to sea one morning shortly after her talk with Jonathan, Constancy saw a ship rounding Diamond Head. She strained her eyes to see if she could identify it and then called, "Matt! Matt! Your eyes are sharper than mine—isn't that your uncle's ship?"

Matt came running with the excited whoop of a ten-year-old. He peered toward the ship across the smooth stretch of green water and the white rim of foam that indicated the reef. "It must be!" His voice was tremulous with feeling. "Wait—I'll get the glasses." He rushed into the house and in a moment came back with the field glasses. A moment of adjusting them to the distance and he whooped again and seized his mother around the waist. "Oh, Mother! It is!" A sudden change came over his features. "Oh—what if he shouldn't want me, Mother?"

Constancy smiled at him a little wryly. Her heart reached out to keep him with her; her intelligence forced her to approve his eagerness to depart. "Don't worry about it, son. It isn't likely he would change so suddenly. Hasn't he been talking about taking you with him for three or four years now? You'd best hurry and hitch up the team if you want to get down by the time he anchors."

He leaped off the *lanai* and was running toward the barn, but he stopped short to fling over his shoulder, "Hurry and get your bonnet on!"

Constancy shook her head. "I'm too busy with the babies, and I've got to help out at the school today. You'll have to meet him alone, and you explain how I really can't get away. He'll understand, and anyway it'll be nice for you to have a talk with him alone."

She looked after him a trifle wistfully. This would be the first time she hadn't been at the harbor to meet the captain. It seemed to her now that she had depended upon his visits to the island as she might upon a powerful tonic, to fortify herself against the pattern of her days during the rest of the year. It was so comforting to be with a person who knew her, and, knowing her, loved her. The thought suddenly disturbed her: "The woman Jonathan loved never existed except in his own imagination. I never was that person even for a moment! And even a hint that I am not wholly one in spirit with the brethren makes young Jonathan look stricken. Sally loved me without thinking about my theology . . . loves me," she corrected the tense and then shrugged. There was that moment of parting. . . . "But Sally is absorbed in her husband and in little Timmie. I don't think she is really conscious of anyone else. Faith would be surprised if she knew I was unorthodox . . . but I don't think she would think the worse of me for it—though she is so different now that I can't say for sure. And Silly would shrink from me as if I were a leper, I verily believe. Bless Uncle Nate!"

She turned away from her study of the sea and went in to begin the business of bathing the three babies and putting them away for their morning naps before going over to take charge of the sewing class at the school. She was glad that the other orphans were large enough to be in school. She scarcely knew whether the tiredness that seemed never to lift from her body and mind was occasioned by the weight of recent sorrows or by the sly creeping on of age. "Nonsense," she told herself decisively, "I shan't be fifty till September, and I'm perfectly healthy. It must be the weather." For it had suddenly turned warm and sultry with no breeze blowing.

The captain stood over Constancy that afternoon, his face quizzical as he watched her administer bottles to the two small babies and milk in a cup to the ten-months-old orphan. "Are you never to get clear of all this, Connie?" he asked at length. "I thought you were through bringing up children, and then I come home to find you with a grandchild and all these little savages on your hands."

Constancy shrugged in answer and said: "They were here—with no one else to look after them. What would you have me do? Besides—would you call Elspeth a little savage?" She raised the half-sister of Sally's son for the captain to inspect. The baby smiled sleepily and closed her eyes, the long silken lashes lying on her skin that was old ivory beside the milk-white of Deborah.

The captain stared at the small hybrid. "Jove!" he said. "She's mostly white, I'd say offhand. What're you going to do with her?"

"She's three quarters white," said Constancy slowly. "I'm bringing her up just as I shall bring up Deborah. Perhaps she'll marry a white man—that happens here occasionally, you know—look at Mr. Bishop. More than one good missionary would have been pleased to have him for a son-in-law, but he chose to marry . . . royalty . . . as prepared for wifehood in the Puritan tradition by Mrs. Cooke."

"She and her husband the ones who bring up the royal children on the New England plan?"

Constancy nodded. "When she turns them out they are prim and proper and well behaved as any Salem offspring. Occasionally there are lapses after they are out from under her eye, but we don't mention them." She finished with the babies, adjusted the shades, and shooed her uncle out of the room. "Come down on the *lanai*—and we may be able to pick up a breeze."

She sat in a low rocker, her mending basket in her lap, frowning over the threading of a needle. Her uncle regarded her questioningly. "I want you to go back with me, Connie," he said abruptly. She said nothing. "Your mother's alone now, Connie," he reminded her. "She's ten years older than I am, and I don't feel as young as I used to—that's why I've been anxious to train in Matt to take my place when I give out. Your mother's too old to run the farm alone with just a hired man. You ought to be with her."

His niece placed the thread through the eye of the needle, but the frown lingered. "I thought she'd sell the farm and go to live with Sis in Boston."

The captain laughed. "You evidently have forgotten your mother. Mary Ellen's still got plenty of spirit if she is seventy-two. She'll be gracious and even grateful to anyone coming to live with her—so long as she's the lady of the manor and has the reins in her own hands—but she wouldn't be caught dead living with one of her children in any house but her own. Don't you see?—she'd really feel old and useless then, as if she were there on sufferance. Besides, Sis's husband is a wealthy lawyer, and they move in fashionable society and put on a good many airs. Your mother's too downright and impatient of tomfoolery to stand such a life. It's your duty to go and stay with her and take Silly along with you. Maybe she'd get over some of this religious folly of hers. What the girl needs is to fall in love."

The sewing fell from Constancy's hands; her eyes focused on the reef. "I wish I could go with you, Uncle Nate," she sighed. "Mother must be so lonely—though she's so proud I don't suppose she'd ever admit it. It seems strange to think of her in her seventies. She was forty when I married and left home—and she looked younger. She was so straight and slim and looked so proud and was so kind. I can't think of her as being old." She paused for a moment and then went on. "I can't leave now. If Mary hadn't died, perhaps I might have. But now—you see how Jonathan is. It's turned him fanatic. He's got this notion that Mary's death was a punishment meted out to him— for being lured from the Congregational faith to the Unitarian. He's awfully miserable, and I couldn't leave him now. And then there's Silly. She would be immeasurably shocked if I were to suggest leaving here. She's bound up in the business of making—little prigs of little heathens. She'd think I was running away from duty to a life of ease and luxury and wouldn't go with me. Then there are the babies and the orphans. Silly and Jonathan have all the piety in the world, but they aren't awfully practical or useful when it comes to details." Her eyebrows quirked humorously. "Their minds are too much on the other world to be good at planning proper meals for babies or remembering to feed them on time."

She closed her eyes and saw the orchard that rambled away from the south side of her childhood home toward the meadow. Now the apricots would be in bloom, and in

a few weeks the peaches and plums—more gaudily—and
then at last the frozen beauty of pear blossoms and the
warmer loveliness of apple blossoms. It was hers to see
spring come in New England—if she chose. She opened
her eyes, and the vision fled. The red and pink hibiscus at
the end of the *lanai*, the giant-fingered leaves of the breadfruit tree, and the slanting coconut palms leaning out over
the wall to sea oppressed her. They disappeared in a mist.
She rubbed her eyes childishly and angrily.

Observing her emotion, her uncle changed the subject.
"How did Faith happen to marry this pious young missionary, Connie? I can't make it out for the life of me."
He was troubled by the note of urgency in the letter Faith
had written him, imploring him to stop at Lahaina to see
her when he left Oahu.

Constancy sighed heavily. "I don't know. . . . It's
tragic, Uncle Nate, that however much we love our children and they love us, we can't reach them when they are
in trouble. There is an awful reserve that no amount of
sympathy or love can penetrate. I can't help feeling that
Faith made a frightful mistake in marrying Luke Owens.
You know how full of life and harmless mischief Faith
always was, and how she poked fun at the gawky young
ministers-to-be who came courting her—she called them
'whey-faced sons of missionaries' and shocked her father
and young Jonathan dreadfully. Then just overnight she
changed and said she was going to marry Luke Owens.
And, Uncle Nate, she had made more fun of him than of
any of them! I just can't understand it. She's never been
the same since that day. She's been more like a statue that
has the power to move and speak. It just isn't Faith any
more." Again her work fell into her lap, and her hands lay
listlessly upon it.

"I don't know . . ." Her uncle hesitated and then went

on firmly: "She may not have wanted me to say anything to you, Connie, but I shall anyway. She asked me—in fact she begged me—to stop at Lahaina on my way—said she *had* to see me. She sounded desperate, Connie. I hope I shall be able to help her in whatever way she seems to think I can."

·His niece drew a long breath. "I'm glad you told me, Uncle Nate. I'll admit that I was a little curious about the note she enclosed for you. You'll let me know what the trouble is after you have seen her? Promise me to send word from Lahaina."

"Of course, Connie, of course," he soothed her. "And you can be sure that anything in my power shall be done to help her, whatever it is that she wants of me. In the first place she's your daughter—that alone would be enough— but I've always been fond of her for her own sake. I liked her spirit."

The captain's business in Honolulu detained him for two weeks; then he set sail with Matt for Lahaina, leaving Constancy saddened at the parting with her son and anxious for word of Faith. Ten days passed, and missionaries from the other islands began arriving for the general meeting. Two families were quartered with Constancy, and she was kept busy attending to their wants, keeping her orphans out of mischief, and caring for three babies. In these days she left the school entirely to Jonathan and Silly, except for the cooking lessons she taught in her own kitchen on two afternoons of each week. She was forced to listen again and again to well-meant and tactlessly expressed sympathy from her visitors and other missionaries from the outer stations who showed what seemed to her a morbid interest in the details of Jonathan's and Mary's deaths and funerals.

When word first came of Faith it was not from the captain, after all. His letter was forestalled by one day by the
descent of Mrs. Owens and a disheveled Luke. Seeing them
drive up, Constancy felt a chill of foreboding sweeping
over her. If Luke had arrived, why was not Faith with
him? Had something happened to this child of hers? She
braced herself against shock; her heart ticked to the words,
"I can't bear anything more!"

She was not left long in suspense. Mrs. Owens, wisps
of grizzled hair hanging dankly down either cheek and her
hat awry, burst into the room, followed by her lanky son.
The visitor's eye swept the room, reproving Mrs. Smith
from Hawaii and Mrs. Hall from Kauai who sat placidly
sewing. "Sister Williams," she said abruptly, "we must see
you alone . . ." Her voice trembled. "All alone!"

The two visiting missionaries looked startled and, gathering up their needlework, scurried silently out of the
room. Constancy motioned the Owenses into chairs and
sat down before them, unable to take her eyes from the
doom-laden face of Faith's mother-in-law.

Luke sat tongue-tied, twisting his hands. His eyes were
red-rimmed, as if he had been crying or else had not slept
for a week.

"Sister Williams!" Mrs. Owens declaimed in an awful
voice. "You must steel yourself for a shattering blow!"
She paused significantly and peered into Constancy's face.
Constancy's hand rose to her heart.

"Faith . . ." she whispered. "Faith isn't dead, *too?*"

Her visitor snorted audibly. "It would be better if she
was! The Lord in His infinite wisdom has seen fit to
chasten you with a graceless daughter, Sister Williams."

Constancy drew a long, quivering breath. At least Faith
was alive. The words of Faith's mother-in-law had an al-

most comfortingly familiar ring. Constancy had listened
to those words or words very similar to them so many
times from Faith's teachers. Midway between relief and
concern, she asked, "What has she done?"

Luke sniffled childishly. His mother glared into Constancy's eyes. "You may well ask, Sister Williams! She's
run away—that's what she's done!"

Again Constancy's hand sought her heart. "Where. . . .
Who with?" she queried faintly. This was more than she
had bargained for.

"With your uncle," bitterly from Mrs. Owens, "which
goes to show that he's no better than I've thought him for
a long time. No righteous Christian would think so much
of gauds and display as that man does—you may talk of
kindness and gentleness all you please. And no Christian
man would aid and abet a woman in running away from a
good husband."

Constancy gasped at the news. She disregarded the
criticism of the captain for the shameless leaping of her
heart at the thought that Faith was away from the
Owenses. Yet in the next breath her eye fell on Luke,
whose pale face was working miserably, and she thought
in surprise and compassion, "Why, he loves her . . . this
is awful for him." She heard herself saying very gently, "I
am so sorry for you, Luke," but after that she had no
words to say to either of them.

Luke unexpectedly broke into a torrent of language:
"Why did she have to be unhappy with me?" he asked
wildly. "I've cared for her ever since we were children—
and she's always teased and flouted me. I thought she'd
changed when she agreed to marry me. She was so quiet
and gentle for a time—until the baby was born, and then
she changed. She was like a wild animal! I tell you she

wouldn't let me touch the baby—or her! And that's no
way for a Christian woman to behave to her lawful husband!"

His mother spoke peremptorily. "Be quiet, Luke. Try
to behave as a minister of the Gospel should. Let *me* do
the talking!" She fixed a stern eye on Constancy, who sat
regarding them dispassionately and thinking, "How ugly
. . . how awfully dull and ugly they both are! I'm sorry
for him—he's suffering, but I'm glad, *glad* that Faith has
gotten away."

Mrs. Owen said sharply, "I must say, Sister Williams,
you don't act as much surprised as you ought. I'd hate to
think that you'd be a party to anything as sinful as a
wife's running away from her wedded husband. I can tell
you that if my daughter did such a thing, I'd be in sackcloth and ashes and ashamed to lift my head!"

"I think it very unlikely that either Maria or Milly will
ever place you in a similar position," Constancy could not
forbear saying. "But you are quite mistaken if you think
I was aware of Faith's intentions. I knew that she was
troubled about something, because she wrote to my uncle,
begging him to stop at Lahaina to see her on his way." She
looked soberly at Luke and said carefully, "You have my
sympathy, Luke, in having lost a wife whom you evidently love, and in having to be an object of curiosity for
a time—but, after all, it isn't as if she had eloped with another man."

Mrs. Owens cleared her throat. "I don't think she had
any right to take the baby with her!" she said defiantly.
"I don't think she's a fit person to bring up an innocent
child, and I tell Luke he ought to get the law after her
and make her give the child to him."

Constancy's nerves snapped, and she lost her head. "You
have no grounds for saying that Faith is not a fit person

to bring up her own child just because she was miserable with her husband! Besides, you'd have a hard time getting the baby back when she's taking it to another country and across the world from here. Do you want her to tell the world at large that your son made her so miserable that she couldn't stand living with him?"

Mrs. Owens rose, her chin high. "I can only hope, Sister Williams, that this unbecoming behavior in you is caused by a mother's prejudice, and that it has not its root in sin of a darker hue."

Constancy's eyebrows shot upwards, but when she spoke her voice was mild: "I think you forget yourself, Mrs. Owens, but I understand that it is because of your natural concern for your son." She looked her visitor sternly in the eye, and Mrs. Owens's neck and ears turned a dull red. Constancy was not a member of the First Company of missionaries to the Sandwich Islands for nothing.

Mrs. Owens muttered reluctantly, "I guess I let my feelings get away with me, Sister Williams, but I can't help feeling for my poor son." She cleared her throat and pushed back a strand of hair from her face. "I do think, though," she said doggedly, "that Luke should have the child, and I shall use my influence to persuade him to take proper steps to recover it."

"I daren't!" Luke spoke raspingly. The words seemed torn from him. "She spoke in her letter to me of how it was not an Owens—of how it would be quite useless if I were to try to get it away from her! And what could that mean but that she has sinned?" His high voice broke, and he buried his face in his hands.

Constancy gazed at him stupefied. This was something she must think about alone. She heard herself saying too calmly, she knew, "It is hard for you—you have my sympathy. . . . I trust that your faith in the Lord will sus-

tain you, and through the execution of His labors you will
find forgetfulness of this sorrow." She felt cruel and calloused mouthing such platitudes to him in his real distress,
but for the Owenses, she realized suddenly, she would
never have anything but platitudes.

Mrs. Owens had risen to her feet. Constancy promptly
held out her hand, praying inwardly, "Oh, make her go,
make her go! I know she didn't know about what Faith
said in the letter to this minute. I've got to think this out
. . . how could it be that way? I don't believe it. The
baby was born eleven months after they were married,
and I know she knew no one at Lahaina. . . . I'm sure she
just said that to keep them from trying to get the baby
away from her. But, oh, what a lot of clatter I'll have to
stand at the general meeting when it gets around that
Faith has run away and taken the baby!"

Luke spoke vehemently again: "Mother, if you ever
dare to breathe this to a soul—even to Father—I'll never
forgive you as long as I live!"

His mother's eyes bulged in reproach. "Why, Lukie, I
shouldn't want to spread anything that'd reflect on my
own family."

Constancy was gently heading them for the door.
Finally they passed through it. She leaned for a moment
against the door frame, watching their carriage down the
drive. Her body slumped at the thought of telling Jonathan and Silly. Anyway, she thought, they need never
know that Faith had hinted at an adultery.

Jonathan turned pale and then scarlet with the shame
of his sister's behavior and fell on his knees in the living
room to pray in agonized accents that his erring sister
might suffer a change of heart, be made conscious of her

sin, and repent truly, in order that her soul might not suffer the torments of hell forever.

Silly shrank at the tidings as if her mother had dealt her
a blow. "How could she! How could she!" she said over
and over, and for the remainder of the evening her lips
moved silently in the way that Constancy particularly disliked. From time to time tears rolled down her pale cheeks.

The next morning the captain of an interisland boat
and a friend of her uncle's brought Constancy the letters
she had been awaiting. There was Uncle Nate's terse note:

*I find Faith in a bad way, with her nerves on edge and
saying deadly calm that she'll kill herself and the babe if
I don't take them away from here. I think she means it,
and I take no chances. Her husband goes on a trip of three
days to the mountains tomorrow, and I am to get her
aboard at dark with her belongings. I plan to take her to
your mother. Don't worry. Matt is pleased as can be to
have her go along. The baby favors you.*

She took up the letter from Faith and read:

DEAREST MOTHER:

*It may seem dreadful to you that I am running away
from Luke, but I couldn't bear thinking of having any
more children by him for fear they would be like the
Owenses. This one is like you, I am sure, but I can't risk
any more. Also living with Luke is making me hateful. I
find myself disliking him more and more, and I know that
it isn't really his fault, but I can do nothing about it. I
shouldn't have married him, but I was frightened. Uncle
Nate says he will take me to Grandmother and that she
will like having the baby and me and won't think I am a
black sinner. Please don't stop loving me because I am*

doing this, because really I had to. Living with Luke was like having every day a Sabbath, and you know I couldn't stand that.

Your loving daughter,
FAITH.

P. S. Uncle Nate said maybe the Owenses could get Connie away from me by law, so I thought I'd better make Luke think it wasn't his baby. I just said it wasn't an Owens, which it isn't in one sense, as she looks and I hope acts like my side of the family. But you see I mean it one way, and he's too slow to think it means anything but that it had another father, which couldn't have happened because I don't know anybody at Maui who wouldn't be just as tiresome as Luke.

Constancy dropped the letter and began to laugh. She laughed until tears rained upon her sewing. Jonathan, coming in, reached for the letter, but Constancy snatched it up and tore it into shreds before he could touch it. She went on laughing. Jonathan laid a hand on her forehead and looked nervously into her face. "Silly!" he shouted. "Mother's got hysterics."

Constancy pulled a grave face before her youngest daughter could arrive with a bowl of water to fling at her. "I don't know what's the matter with me, children," she said weakly and apologetically. "I guess I'm tired out and not responsible."

Jonathan placed his arm about his mother solicitously. "You'd best go and lie down for a bit, Mother," he said anxiously, urging her towards the stairway. "No wonder your nerves are unstrung! But with all our prayers in her behalf, our foolish but not really evil sister may suffer a change of heart and be drawn back into the fold."

Very gently Constancy disentangled herself from her son's embrace. "I will lie down for a little, dear, if you will remember to take the babies out for a bit, you and Silly, as soon as they wake up." She went upstairs, conscious only of the necessity for being alone for a time, alone with the unorthodox joy she knew and must not allow to show, joy at her recognition of the old Faith in the last words of the letter she had destroyed.

II

In August of 1851 Constancy suffered again the minor shock of setting forth to welcome a bachelor son at the boat, only to find him a married man. Searching Peter's face, she could find no trace of the frightened, sorrowing small boy who had sailed away to be educated fourteen years earlier. For Peter at twenty-four had the assurance of a successful business man of forty. His manners were charming; he was gracious to everyone and courtly with his mother, but he was a stranger in the house. He treated his stolid, apple-cheeked wife with a cool politeness that kept her perpetually nervous. Constancy, unable to feel affection for her new daughter-in-law, felt sorry for her: she so patently worshiped the distant elegance of her husband.

Within a week of his arrival Peter secured an office over a store on Fort Street. He grimaced over it and straightway set about having it painted and equipped with shelves. Constancy hesitantly asked him if he needed money. He raised a humorous eyebrow.

"My dear Mother, Tabitha would be hurt if I allowed anyone but herself finance this enterprise."

Constancy lifted her own eyebrows. "Has Tabitha so much money, then?"

"Not a great deal in the eyes of some men—but she had fifty thousand in her own right after her father's death and will have as much more, I fancy, at her mother's death." He drew his mouth down drolly. "And it is her pleasure to spend it on me."

Something in Constancy protested. "But, Peter!" She looked at him bewildered. "You didn't marry her just for her money, son!"

Again mockery lay in Peter's brilliant gray eyes and at the corners of his full, beautifully sculptured lips. "Why, Mother," in reproachful tones, "are you insensible of Tabitha's charm and wit?"

Constancy shook her head and said gravely, "I am sensible of the fact that she loves you deeply and is a human being who may be easily and cruelly wounded by your disregard." She looked him straight in the eye. "It is not pleasant to realize that a son of mine would mock at his wife for the very qualities which helped him to deceive her. . . . If she had the wit you desire she would have seen through you, Peter, and had she had charm, others would have been before you."

Peter raised a slender, fastidiously kept hand in protest. "Don't be too hard on me, Mother," he wheedled. "It takes money to get ahead in this world. Don't you think I can remember how you and Father slaved back in the old days, and what awful odds and ends of clothing we had to make do? We can consider Tabitha's money just a loan. I needed some capital. I tell you, Mother," and his voice was suddenly earnest, "I have a plan for making money out of these islands. I don't think most people realize yet just how valuable these islands are. If they did, one of the big powers would have annexed them long since."

Constancy surveyed him anxiously. "What is it you are going to do, Peter? I hope your plan is honest."

Peter raised his head indignantly. "You forget that I am a lawyer, Mother. You may trust me to keep within the law."

And his mother had to be content with that. She was curious about the number of times in a week that he found it necessary to ride into town, at first on Dick, but in a few days on the high-stepping black mare he purchased. It was not for several weeks that she learned that he was engaged in other activities besides the preparation of his law office. There had been a night when he dined with Governor Kekuanaoa; a little later there was a night when he dined with the king. But it was not until Jonathan descended upon her in anguish one night that she realized the significance of these incidents.

She lifted her head from the perpetual mending of socks at Jonathan's "Mother!" to see him striding up and down the living room, his shock of hair, iron gray since Mary's death, waving as his father's shock of white hair had been wont to do, the same burning light in his eyes.

"What is it, Jonathan?" she asked quietly. But she dropped the sock she was darning to give him her full attention.

He wheeled about and stood above her. "Do you know what Peter has been doing?" he demanded.

"I understood that he had been preparing his office for use," she said calmly, but her heart missed a beat.

"H'mph!" Jonathan took a pace or two away from her and then whirled to look in her face again. "He's been wheedling land out of the king, that's what he's been doing!"

"Land?" repeated his mother blankly. "What does he want with land, except maybe to build a house on?"

Jonathan tossed his head impatiently. "I'm sure I don't know, but you may be sure he wants to make money on it. You know the king's been drinking—even more than usual lately—and he listens to all his evil associates. I—I hear that Peter has acquired a hundred acres out on the road to Ewa, and you know the king isn't given to letting more than fifteen or twenty acres fall into the hands of any one person."

"Where did you hear this? Did Peter tell you?"

There was a quick shake of Jonathan's head. "Indeed he didn't! He's as close-mouthed as an oyster about his affairs. I heard it at the mission house today."

"What's this you heard at the mission house?"

They both jumped at Peter's voice. He stood in the doorway, beating his riding crop gently against his boots. "It seems to me that this town displays an exaggerated interest in my affairs."

Constancy looked him sternly in the eye. "Is it true that you have acquired a hundred acres of land from the king?"

Peter grinned teasingly at his mother. "And what if it is?"

"Just this, my son," explained Constancy wearily. "You see, a little while ago the king, in acknowledgement of all the missionaries have done for his people, made it possible for the missionaries all to buy a little land very cheaply—not more than ten or fifteen acres at most. In one or two instances when some missionary had rendered him some personal service which had gone unpaid, he gave him a small tract of land in deferred payment. The hostile element here immediately started tales about how the missionaries were out to get all they could, and how they planned to get the ownership of all the land away from the natives. And this, when none of us was interested in land really—except to have a place for a home and garden and maybe do a little farming in a small way."

Peter had sat down at his mother's side. He began drumming on the table. "But what has all this to do with my enterprise? I'm not a missionary!"

Jonathan turned on him fiercely. "You are a missionary's son! And you are under obligation to your mother and to the memory of your father."

"Don't let's be melodramatic," entreated Peter in a pained murmur.

Jonathan shrugged his shoulders irritably. "Try to be serious for once," he said sharply. "Your grabbing so much land within a few weeks of your arrival reflects upon the missionaries as a whole and lays us all open to criticism."

Peter smiled enigmatically. "Well—you see—the king practically forced the land upon me," he said guilelessly. "The land is to pay a debt of honor." He raised his head and grinned broadly. "The king was short of money, or else he didn't want to part with it, so he suggested some land instead, and just to oblige him, I took it over." He gazed pensively at the ceiling, rocking gently back and forth. "As a matter of fact, I have it in mind to experiment with a little sugar cane."

Jonathan glowered at his brother. "Do you mean to say that you've been *gambling* with the king?"

"Just a friendly game of cards to pass the time," protested Peter and glanced sideways at his mother.

"You're a disgrace to the family! What have our parents done to be cursed with such children as you and Faith?" Jonathan took a turn about the room in great agitation. "I was nearly as black a sinner as either of you, but through the chastisement of the Lord I was brought to see the light. You should pray for like regeneration that you shame not your parents."

Peter raised his slender right hand in a gesture of

fatigued protest. "Please, please, Jonathan," he said gently, "spare us these recriminations. In the first place they are wasted, because I believe nothing at all of what you believe. I believe neither in God nor the devil, in heaven nor in hell, only in the here and now, and I tell you, my dear brother, I intend to wring every last drop of pleasure from this business of living that I can get. I'm going to have wine and women and song, and the only thing that assures you of having all of them is money. Therefore I shall have money."

Jonathan's face was gray, and his eyes were coals of fire. He stretched a trembling arm towards his brother. "Get out of this house, you blasphemous fiend!" he cried in a voice that trembled with outrage. "There is no place beneath this roof for you or any of your breed."

Constancy sprang to her feet, her sewing basket and all its contents scattering far and wide. "Boys, boys!" she said breathlessly. "Jonathan, Peter is your brother. Peter, *why* do you tease Jonathan? Of course you shan't get out of the house unless you wish to, Peter." She turned to Jonathan. "You, Jonathan, forget yourself. This is not your house that you may turn my son out of it. You forget the commands of the Lord you profess to love! Have you forgotten that you are commanded to forgive your brother to seventy times seven?"

Peter patted her on the shoulder. "Don't worry, Mother. I guess I'm the black sheep of the family, but it will be awkward if I stay after this flare-up. It's too late to do anything today, but tomorrow Tabitha and I'll move to the hotel until our house is finished." He walked out of the room and mounted the stairs, humming a little tune, just audible to the outraged Jonathan.

Jonathan flung himself at his mother's feet and buried

his head in her lap. "Mother! It was cruel of you to take his part against me—even if I did do wrong to lose my temper."

Constancy stroked his hair thoughtfully. "I know, Jonathan, but you must remember that Peter is my son, too. A mother can't cast off her children simply because they are not all good as gold. None of you could do anything that would make me stop loving you—at least I don't think there is anything."

Jonathan raised his face to look at her. "You're a wonderful woman, Mother," he said soberly. "But I fear there is more than the usual evil in Peter. It is not meet for a son of a sober family such as ours to get himself up like a dandy, and look at the way Peter dresses, and his finicky concern that every ruffle is plaited just so, and gambling. . . . It is well that Father knows nothing of it."

Constancy went on drawing her fingers through the prematurely gray hair. Her thoughts were away on the *Mary Ellen*, which at this time might be nearing the Horn. "I'm weak as water," she thought, "but I am so desperately tired of smoothing things over and pretending. I wish I had run away like Faith on the *Mary Ellen*. I wish I were where I never had to go to another women's meeting and hear a pack of silly females fussing over whether the Lord will or will not be angry if they let their children draw pictures on the Sabbath."

Aloud, she said, "Jonathan, my dear, I think you take Peter's foibles too seriously. After all, he is very young, and he grew up in a different atmosphere from you. He lived with Aunt Sis, who is gayer than the rest of your relatives. Remember—her husband is a rich man, and they live a fashionable life, but your aunt is as good and kind as any of these missionary women. You must try not to

judge people too harshly for being different from yourself
—but I know it's hard not to sometimes."

12

After Peter and Tabitha went to live at the French
Hotel, life ran more smoothly at the Waikiki house. Eliza
and her husband, who had no children of their own, took
the one little boy among the orphans Constancy had
given shelter. He slept in Eliza's thatched house but spent
the part of the day when he was out of school at the big
house. The four little girl orphans slept in the big bedroom
that had been Sally's. The eldest, Alohilani, a soft-eyed,
nearly inarticulate child of ten, was dependable and took
most of the care of her six-year-old sister and the two
smaller children. The youngest of the four, who began to
run about within a month of her rescue by Constancy,
was mischievous and given to snatching covers from
tables, especially when the covers supported breakable
matter. By spring little Deborah and Elspeth were both
trotting unsteadily about the house and had to be guarded
from falling down stairs and destroying whatever came
within their reach.

Constancy gave up all but her cooking and sewing
classes at the school, and these she gave in her own home
where she could keep an eye on the babies. Only once a
week could she find the time to make the rounds of the
village. Jonathan and Silly, with the help of a native
teacher, recently ordained and being trained as an assistant
to Jonathan, managed the school.

Constancy had breathed a sigh of relief when the general meeting passed without Jonathan's having made a
spectacular confession of heresy. He continued silenter
than when Mary was alive, his face prematurely lined,

and his eyes burning with the light that had lived in his father's eyes. He preached grimmer sermons now: there was less stressing of the gentleness of the Son and more elaboration of the vengeance of the Father; at least once a month there was a sermon which set forth the torments of the wicked in the hereafter with such authoritative vigor that the eyes of the native audience rolled in their heads.

But in the evenings, with the children in bed, Jonathan subsided and listened avidly as Silly read aloud or played to them. He lounged in an easy chair, his long, nervous fingers strumming noiselessly on its padded arms, his eyes closed usually, for he was troubled by headaches. Constancy sat in her low rocker, sewing, and Silly entertained them.

These were the hours when Constancy felt her spirit draw nearer to her youngest daughter. Silly, whose unnatural gravity and austere dedication to religion unconsciously rebuffed her mother by day, laid down her defenses when her fingers played over the keyboard of the huge rosewood piano that Uncle Nate had brought them the year the house was built. Silly, who had no speech for the small exchanges of the family, found a voice through her fingers. Her mother marveled that this daughter whom she had never understood—except reluctantly—could play with such disciplined passion. Sally had played easily, Faith rather laboriously, but Silly, from the first, had played with certainty, giving each note a separate life, giving her listeners a feeling both of security and of excitement. With lessons from an indifferently trained teacher, the only one Honolulu offered in the early days, she combined the exalted seriousness she brought to religion, the painstaking effort and the unequivocal contempt for anything less than perfection. In giving expression to the genius of Bach or of Beethoven or of Mozart, she found relief for the disquiet that jangled her young nerves, the loneliness that weighted down her heart in the intervals when her spirit fell exhausted from the skies.

And Constancy, staring motionless at her daughter's back arching over the keyboard as she wrought the hard clear anguish of a Beethoven sonata, thought wonderingly: "Now I know her for my child! I am in her fingers —in her brain—at this moment. But she doesn't know I am there. . . . If only there were a word—some word that has never been spoken—that I might say—then she would know, perhaps, that we are together."

But the word eluded her, and Silly, arising at last from the piano, her face colorless and her eyes shadowed with fatigue, smiled absently at her mother, with a gentle, "Good-night, Mother, Jonathan," and slowly climbed the stairs to her room.

Other nights Silly would read to the two of them, making her own selection, reading in her low husky voice, not from the works of Jonathan Edwards or Cotton Mather or from any of the thick volumes of sermons that filled several shelves, but from the small mottle-backed volumes of poetry that Uncle Nate brought from the bookstores in Boston. She chose songs from Shakespeare, the *Divine Songs* of John Donne, parts of *Paradise Lost*, the metaphysical yearnings of Herbert and Vaughan, the lighter, sweeter songs of Robert Herrick, the parson poet who would have been so lost in a general meeting of his fellow wearers of the cloth in the Hawaiian Islands, and now there was a volume of poems by John Keats that Uncle Nate had brought to Constancy on the last voyage. Jonathan lay back in his chair, eyes closed, a ghost of a smile lingering about his mouth, and Constancy automatically

went on with her darning while Silly read so softly that
the words were just audible:

"Darkling I listen; and for many a time
I have been half in love with easeful Death,
Called him soft names in many a musèd rhyme,
To take into the air my quiet breath;
Now more than ever seems it rich to die,
To cease upon the midnight with no pain,
While thou art pouring forth thy soul abroad
In such an ecstasy!
Still wouldst thou sing, and I have ears in vain—
To thy high requiem become a sod.

"Thou wast not born for death, immortal Bird!
No hungry generations tread thee down;
The voice I hear this passing night was heard
In ancient days by emperor and clown:
Perhaps the self-same song that found a path
Through the sad heart of Ruth, when, sick for home,
She stood in tears amid the alien corn;
The same that ofttimes hath
Charmed magic casements, opening on the foam
Of perilous seas, in faery lands forlorn."

And when the poem ended, Silly dropped the book into
her lap and sighed, pressing her thin fingers against her
eyelids. "It is music, too," she said half under her breath.
Constancy looked up quickly at the excitement in her
voice. Silly was staring at her with shining unseeing eyes.
"How do people *live* who don't know about poetry?" she
asked, and then, before Jonathan or Constancy could
speak, she jumped to her feet. "Good-night," she called
hastily, and although it was only half-past eight, she ran
up the stairs to her room.

Her mother's heart was beating faster. Her eyes were wide and dark with exhilaration. Could it be possible that this spark that she thought was buried in the small grave back of Kawaiahao church with Sammy was alive in Silly? Silly of all her children? "I must try to be more to Silly," Constancy vowed. "I must make her know that I realize how she feels. I'll have to find words . . . tomorrow."

But the next day Silly's eyes were remote. After prayers, at breakfast she talked with Jonathan about the forthcoming examinations as if they were all in the world that mattered to her, as if nothing were so important as that each of their charges should know by heart so much of the Bible translated into Hawaiian, or so many lines of the catechism.

Sorrowfully Constancy's eyes followed her daughter. She thought painfully, "She is shut away from me by a wall . . . like glass. . . . I can see through it, but I can never touch her. If she marries, will she let her husband through?" But Constancy could not quite imagine Silly aware enough of any man to marry him.

Still, although Constancy could not find the magic word which would destroy the wall between herself and Silly, her discovery that a flame that was not altogether religious burned in Silly gave point and interest to Constancy's days. She brooded a good deal upon the matter of Peter, too. He was flourishing as a lawyer, and he was busy creating a small village on his land.

In the early fall of 1852 Constancy spent a few days at Peter's plantation. Peter and Tabitha had driven out to the beach to see her, but she had not previously been able to visit them in their new house. Most of the women of her generation chose to travel in a carriage, but Constancy elected to ride through town on horseback. She enjoyed riding, and something in her rebelled at too tame a submission to middle age. "As long as my heart and kidneys can stand it, I shall ride," she said grimly, when Jonathan suggested that it might be more tiring to her to ride on Dick such a long way. "And I guess they'll hold out for a few more years!" And in a spirit of defiance she thundered out of her yard at full speed, forgetting to leave her usual last-minute instructions about the care of the house and children.

She could never ride past the old mission house without experiencing a twinge of thankfulness at the thought that she no longer lived there. She wondered how she had been able to stand it in the days when six families inhabited it at once, when there was no such thing as privacy, when every word spoken above a whisper in one room was sure to be heard by the occupants of the next. She hurried by, not wanting to stop for the usual call. It was nearly three, and Peter had assured her that he would be ready to leave for the plantation at three. As she turned up Fort Street to go to his office, she overtook him walking from court. He raised his hat, and his face brightened at sight of her.

"We're both early!" he said, pleased. "Now we can get out before it's too dark for you to see anything." He held Dick's head and gave his mother his hand as she slipped to the ground. After tethering the horse, he and Constancy went, arm in arm, up the narrow stairs to his office.

By putting in four large windows in place of the two small ones that had originally let a minimum of light and air into the room, knocking out a partition to make a large room of two small ones, painting the walls white, and hanging chintz curtains at the windows, Peter had made a pleasant enough place of his office. Constancy smiled at him. "It's a very homelike office," she said. "Even those forbidding-looking law books don't make it seem dreadfully legal-looking. I like it. It's cool and restful-looking."

Peter laughed. "Mr. Symons or Mr. Quennell of Boston would think it undignified, but somehow plush and mahogany and red velvet draperies don't seem very suitable over here. Anyway, I'm prospering these days. Mother, I haven't lost a case yet." He smiled and tapped three times on wood.

"Don't boast!" His mother stood up and drew on her gloves. "We'd best be off if we're to be at your . . . *waiwai alunu* in time for me to see it." She narrowed her eyes as she employed the Hawaiian phrase.

Peter grinned. "What's that? I've forgotten a good deal of the Hawaiian I picked up before I went away, though I can make out most of what the natives say."

His mother flicked her riding crop against her skirt. "It's what the natives call property that was acquired—somewhat dubiously."

He laughed a little self-consciously. "How you do ride me about that land, Mother! You're almost as bad as Jonathan. We'll have to talk this out when we get started on the road."

But it was not until they had left the last house of Honolulu several miles behind them that Peter returned to the subject. "Now look here," he said earnestly. "I wish you didn't so evidently think me a double-dyed villain. I'm not anything of the kind. I've just got a Yankee head for business on my shoulders. Here's all this good land going to waste. Why shouldn't I make something of it? The natives have no sense about it—they don't know enough to do anything with it, and if they did, they'd be too lazy. I tell you, Mother, there's big money in sugar cane, and I'm not the only one to realize it. Look at this gang on Kauai! The business men are beginning to see there's something in it, and some of them are advancing money on these ventures. I don't see why I shouldn't grab what I can as well as the next."

Constancy frowned. "You mean, Peter, that it seems all right to you to buy up these small farms of the natives for much less than they're worth—just because the natives are such children that they let themselves be cheated?"

Again Peter was momentarily embarrassed. "You do ride a fellow, don't you, Mother? Don't worry about the natives. I'm taking care of them. Why, I build them houses with floors in them, and keep them supplied with fish and *poi* and pay them fifteen cents a day to work for me. If they get sick, I'll get a doctor to take care of them. Jove, Mother, I'm no slave driver. I'm not such a bad sort!"

Constancy looked skeptical, but she smiled. "You were a wheedler as a little boy, Peter. . . . I'd almost forgotten. You got around me oftener than you did your father."

Peter flashed his most charming smile at her. "I think I always suspected that you weren't half as stern as you seemed. You never convinced me that you were shocked at the things we said and did that made Father resort to agonies of prayer and exhortation."

"Your father had no understanding of weakness. I don't suppose he ever wanted very much to do anything wrong in his life, so people who did seemed depraved to him." She flickered a look of sardonic amusement at him. "I had no trouble in understanding their impulses."

Peter shot her a teasing glance. "How did you get in such sympathy with the dark spots of the human soul, Mother? Did you once find yourself saying a bad word under your breath? Or were you guilty of wishing the brethren in Bundy? I'd like to know what black sins you've been hiding all these years."

"I don't doubt it, my child," said his mother dryly. "However, I doubt your having the spiritual requirements of a confessor, and the thought of retailing my sins to my son attracts me very little."

She clucked to Dick and was off at a gallop, leaving Peter in a cloud of dust.

It was a little after five when they drew up at the steps of Peter's rambling frame house. The ground about the house looked bare to Constancy, in spite of the hibiscus bushes and oleanders that had been planted against the *lanai* and the young mango trees set out in the yard. A young Hawaiian boy ran forward to take their horses to the stable. He stood stroking Dick's nose while Peter detached the small bundle containing his mother's things for the night from the back of the saddle. Constancy gave the boy a friendly greeting and turned to kiss Tabitha and inspect the baby. Marcia, Peter's first-born, had the dark hair of her father, but otherwise showed merely the usual fat complacency of a well-cared for if overfed baby of six months.

Tabitha had put on weight having the baby and seemed inclined to go on adding to her bulk now that the baby was born. Her straight, fine, light brown hair straggled in wisps across her perspiring forehead. Constancy thought with some malice, "This is what he gets for marrying for money. Serves him right!" But she felt vaguely sorry for Tabitha. Peter, after one look at his wife, said, "Let me have Marcia, Tabitha, and you go and freshen up a bit."

Tabitha flushed a little. "I know I look a sight," she sighed apologetically. "But it's so hot—and somehow you just can't look neat with a baby pulling at you every minute."

Constancy smiled at her and said sympathetically, "I know how it is, Tabitha. You must be tired. Let me take my granddaughter, and we'll look at the place while you get ready for dinner." To herself she thought, "I never could have stood going around with my hair stringing about my neck like that even if I'd had triplets. Peter'll be looking elsewhere if she doesn't look out." But in the next breath she reflected that since Peter wasn't in love with his wife, he probably would look elsewhere even if she took all the pains in the world to please him.

Tabitha looked helplessly from her husband to his mother and said, "Well—I will go, then, if you're sure you don't mind tending Baby. I'm glad you could come, Mother; we've been hoping you'd get out to see us for a long time. Well—you go on while it's still light, and I'll try to make myself more presentable. Dinner'll be ready at six."

They went out through the kitchen, where a native woman was bending over a fine black stove with much nickel on it. She looked up and grinned broadly at Constancy. She was an enormous woman. "*Ai!*" she burst forth in a delighted squawk. "You don't know me?"

Constancy smiled but shook her head, puzzled, and searching her mind for some clue to recognition of the broad brown face before her. "Did you go to school at the mission?" she ventured.

The woman nodded vigorously. "I am Hephzibah!" she said proudly. "Mrs. Loomis gave me the name many years ago because my own was so long. It was when you lived in the grass houses and taught us to live the good life."

Constancy laughed and held out her hand. "You have changed, Hephzibah," she said. "I hadn't seen you since you were a little girl—so high—and so thin . . ." She made suitable gestures.

Hephzibah shook the proffered hand and beamed. "I remember, even if you are old now with the beautiful yellow hair all white."

Constancy felt a small but mean stab at her heart. She knew her hair was white, but it was a shock to be called old. "We all must become old," she said tritely and turned to Peter. "We had best be getting on if we are to see anything before dark."

Peter led the way to the barn. "She's a good old thing. We call her Hep." He chuckled. "You wouldn't believe what a pretty daughter that great bundle of flesh has."

"Does she live here?" Constancy's voice was sharp.

Peter looked at her innocently. "Oh, yes. Her mother's husband went off with a younger woman a few months ago, but Hep and Hagar (they're awfully given to biblical names—these converts of yours) have a hut down the line. See,"—they entered the barn—"the horses for family use have stalls here, but the work horses and the cows use the shelter at the end of the corral."

His mother admired the three horses in the barn, and then her attention was caught by the small man who was loading manure into a handcart. She looked at him closely through the gathering dusk. His garments were shapeless upon his small form and told nothing, but as he turned, a long thin braid of hair swung against his back.

"Peter!" Constancy led her son out of the barn, fearful of hurting the feelings of his stable boy. "Are you taking on these Chinese they have begun to bring in here?"

Peter shrugged diffidently. "Oh—I have three or four from the last shipment. Once you can get them to understand you, they are good workers—turn out twice the work a native does, and they can get along on less. All the

sugar growers are beginning to use them. You know yourself, Mother, that the Hawaiians abhor work and that it's
like pulling teeth to get anything out of them."

Constancy's mouth shut tightly for a moment before
she spoke. "I don't like it, Peter. These islands belong to
the natives—at least they ought to belong to the natives,
but they're being crowded out. First the foreigners get
hold of the greater part of the land, and then they even
employ imported labor. Where will the natives be a few
years from now?"

"They were fools to let foreigners in in the first place.
It was a bad day for the islands when Liholiho agreed to let
the missionaries settle here."

His words stung Constancy. "You have no right to say
that! The missionaries have never been grasping. They
aren't grasping now! The people who are grabbing land
are not the churchmen. Business concerns and individuals
outside of the Church from both America and England
are getting hold of all they can, but except for some of our
misled children, the missionary element is clear of your
charge! I hate to think of how the missionaries, who were
sincere and unselfish, will probably be blamed for cheating
the Hawaiians in the years to come."

Mischief sounded in Peter's chuckle. "Now, now,
Mother! You know that every calumny borne on earth
means the greater glory in the hereafter for the anointed.
I tell you, Mother, I'll make more money than you ever
thought of, and when I'm due for a transfer to hell, I'll
found a home for destitute Hawaiians and make restitution that way. Will that even things up?"

Constancy tapped her foot on the rocky ground impatiently. "It's not a matter of what the Bible or any of the
churches say is right or wrong that bothers me. It's . . .
what seems, to any instincts of decency and fairness that

I may have, wrong and unfair! The brethren came here with the most exalted and altruistic purpose in the world —and though they were blind sometimes, they never debased that original purpose. They worked their hands off for the natives in return for very inadequate food and shelter and the most atrocious clothing in the world."

The baby began to fret, and Constancy paused to jiggle it up and down on her hip. "The whole trouble was that the brethren were pretty simple. To them a soul was a soul, whether it belonged to a people who had been fostered in the most civilized traditions for hundreds or thousands of years, or whether it belonged to a savage, so primitive that he had never even figured out a means of writing. Here came the first mission family and found savages—and they thought, because these people would listen to the religious teachings and parrot Scriptures, that they had the mental stature of a more highly developed race. I think they were wrong. The Hawaiians' only weapon against the trickery of foreigners was the ruthlessness of the savage, their deeply rooted suspicion of anything strange. Now we've pretty well prayed the ruthlessness out of them and they are docile and weak, and one shrewd Yankee or Frenchman or Scotsman can get the better of the lot of them."

Peter listened to her attentively, stroking his chin. "You've done a lot of thinking about all this, haven't you?" he asked, half admiringly. "But," and he twinkled again, "I'll wager you never voiced those thoughts at a general meeting!"

Constancy flushed, and when she spoke, her voice had an edge: "I've had plenty of time to think in the thirty-two years I've been here. You may be moved to do a little thinking yourself by the time you're my age." She chose to ignore the second part of his speech. They were mounting to a knoll behind the barn.

Peter stretched his arm proudly towards the mountains. "See—that field is ready to harvest. They're going to start stripping it next week. It takes the stuff a year and a half to mature, you know—that's why I haven't but about fifty acres at that stage. But see there," and his arm waved toward the sea, "a hundred acres will be ready by spring, and," his voice sank to an awed whisper, "there are five hundred acres coming round next fall! Think of it! After I shipped in mules and proper implements everything went so much faster. If only the United States would take the tariff off sugar, I'd be a power to reckon with in these islands. By Jove! I will be, anyway! Mother! You're going to be proud of your son—even if you do have your doubts now!"

Constancy stood, the baby on one hip, shading her eyes with the other hand to peer through the gathering dusk at the soft green of the sugar cane. "If you squint your eyes a little," she said, more to herself than to Peter, "you could almost believe you were looking at the fields at home . . . in spring . . . with the corn coming up."

Peter laughed incredulously. "Don't tell me, Mother, that you still get homesick for New England after all these years! And anyway," without waiting for a response, "there's more money in these fields of sugar cane than you'd find in a whole state full of corn. I thought I'd be able to show you through the mill, but it's too dark. It's the most modern and well-fitted of any in the islands— none of your primitive methods for me! I'll show it to you tomorrow—all in readiness for the first crop."

They walked back past the workers' cottages, a dozen in a row, one-room huts with thatched roofs. "Well, the poor things at least have floors," observed Constancy compassionately.

Around a corner of one of the cottages, in pursuit of a small kinky-haired boy, dashed a girl whom Constancy judged to be about sixteen. She was slender, and her dark, smooth hair flew behind her at great length as she ran, and a scarlet hibiscus flower fell to the ground. Her dress was of red calico and clung closely to her lithe body. She stopped, abashed, in the midst of the shrill maledictions she was pouring forth upon the small offender, whirled in her tracks, and presented herself all smiles before Peter and Constancy.

"What's the youngster been up to, Hagar?" inquired Peter amusedly.

The girl dropped her eyes and then lifted them demurely, and Constancy thought what remarkable eyelashes she had. "The child of Satan stole a cake my mother had given me," she said mildly, "and I wished to choke it from him."

Peter laughed. "You go and tell your mother I said to give you another cake—and hold on to this one." He patted her on the head. Constancy caught the sudden widening and softening of the girl's eyes at his touch and the sweetness of the smile that suddenly curved her lips. Constancy felt a swift stab of pity for the girl; she wanted to cry out, "Don't feel that way about him . . . you'll only be hurt! And you can't rely on him for a thing!" Instead, she said casually, "Hagar, I have just seen your mother and discovered that she went to school to me at the mission a long time ago—when she was no bigger than that little boy you were chasing."

Hagar flashed the brightest of smiles at Constancy. "My mother speaks sometimes of the years when she learned at the mission, and she speaks always of the beautiful young

teacher with the beautiful yellow hair and the soft voice."
Her eyes swept Constancy appraisingly. "You were young
that long ago," she said candidly, "and except for the white
hair and the lines in the face you would still look young."

Constancy laughed a little shortly. Twice in the same
afternoon had she been reminded of the fact that she was
no longer young. She had a sudden inspiration. "Tell me,
Hagar," she said as diffidently as possible, "would you like
to live at Waikiki? I have a large house to look after, and
Eliza, my cook, needs more help with the housework.
There are three babies in the house that need lots of attention. Would you like to come and work for me?" She
looked suddenly, not at Hagar, but at Peter, in time to see
him give a barely discernible shake of the head. Hagar
stood twisting her hands. "You are good to ask me," she
said courteously, "but my mother needs me here, so I
couldn't go. I thank you very much." She backed away
and vanished into the house.

Constancy was disturbed. She could see nothing but
trouble ahead—for Tabitha, for Peter, and for the girl,
herself. To Peter she said calmly enough, "She speaks excellent English, Peter. Where did she learn?"

"Her mother sent her to the Catholic school. Hephzibah is a good Catholic nowadays. Evidently the Congregational doctrine didn't sink in far enough when you had
her in charge." He eyed his mother mockingly. "I asked
her why she changed, and she said she liked the way the
priests chanted and there was always something to do and
not so much sermon in church, and the Catholics didn't
think it was wrong to dance."

Constancy made no response. She was thinking of Jonathan: Jonathan aware that one of his sons was bent on
seducing (if he had not already seduced) a native girl
after marrying a drab woman for her money, and that

the same son was planning an enterprise built on unscrupulous methods, working against the natives, extracting land from king and commoners by dishonest methods; Jonathan aware that some of the converts to his faith were now converts to Rome, the scarlet woman of Jonathan's symbolic world; Jonathan aware that Timothy had begotten a child of Leilehua whose name alone could distress Jonathan beyond words, and that she, Constancy, was caring for that child of sin as tenderly as she cared for her own granddaughter; Jonathan aware that his youngest daughter had run away from her husband. These things would have been too much for a man of Jonathan's nature to bear. "No," she mused aloud, "he couldn't have stood these things. It's well he isn't here."

13

November began with a *kona* storm that chilled the air and rushed upon the island with a fury of wind and rain, hurling coconuts to earth and beating the hibiscus bushes into gaunt twigs, bare of flower and leaf. The stable began to leak by the end of the third day of the storm, and a good part of the hay was spoiled. The children, pent up in the house, grew unruly and cross; there was no drying of clothes, and what seemed to be an incurable damp settled upon the house at Waikiki and invaded the spirit of all its members. Several nights the thunder rumbled and crashed continuously, and the lightning flared along the coral reef, cutting the heavy curtain of the rain. On these occasions Deborah shrieked in terror till her grandmother took her in her arms to afford the blanched little face a hiding place against a reassuring shoulder. Elspeth, on the contrary, laughed in the face of the storm and stretched out her arms admiringly when the lightning streaked through the house and said, "Pretty! Pretty!" Constancy, murmuring consolation to the frightened Deborah, would hear a despairing howl from the room where the orphans slept, and have to hurry in to comfort the brown children, who, with the exception of Alohilani, old enough now to repress her own fear, hurled themselves under their beds to hide from the frightening din.

After a week of fury the storm abated and the sun stood forth again; the *kona* wind died and a gentle trade wind blew over the island. On the tenth of the month the sand was white and dry once more, and the world was familiarly tranquil. The school had been badly flooded, and until the roof could be repaired and the interior dried out, school was suspended. Constancy sent Jonathan and Silly to town for badly needed supplies, and after they drove away she put the children into their bathing garments and took them down on the beach to play. The older ones tumbled one another about in the water; sprawled out beneath the clear water, their arms and legs threshing, they reminded Constancy of young frogs at play. The babies were less daring and fled at the approach of each swell, half delighted, half scared when their short, none too steady legs failed them and a wave submerged them. With her own shoes and stockings left for safety on the sea wall, Constancy shepherded the children, her long full skirts tucked up about her knees.

Down the beach two native boys flung themselves on surf boards and started paddling vigorously toward the reef. Constancy followed them with her eyes, remembering how the brethren in earlier years had reproved the natives for their love of surfing and sought to turn their attention to matters of head and spirit, how they had remonstrated with the natives on the subject of suitable swimming apparel, insisting that they cover their bodies

from shoulder to knee and try to remember that they were
Christians in the water as well as on land. She remembered
the dismal appearance the docile ones had presented trying to swim in clothes. She had not been surprised that
these docile ones soon surfed less and less, convinced alike
of the indecency of performing in the more sensible *malo*
and of the impractical nature of the garments that covered them decorously. The two youths paddling toward
the reef were evidently among the hardier spirits; they
swam unhampered. Following their progress, Constancy
observed a familiar ship rounding Diamond Head. Her
heart quickened its beat: If it were the *Mary Ellen* . . .

She had not seen Matt since he set off with his uncle on
his first voyage, for the captain had undertaken a voyage
to England before returning to the islands and the Orient,
and two years had gone by since the two had sailed from
Honolulu. She called Alohilani from the water. "Run into
the house and bring me the field glasses from the chest
in the hall! Quick, child!" and she shaded her eyes with her
hands, the better to inspect the approaching ship gleaming white in the sunlight.

The glasses assured her that it was her uncle's ship. This
meant Matt, it meant the sustaining presence of Uncle
Nate, it meant direct word from Sally and Faith. She
caught up Deborah and pointed to the ship. "It's your
Uncle Nate—and your Uncle Matt, darling! Look! In the
lovely ship." Deborah smiled gravely. "Unca Matt," she
repeated.

There was a sharp tug at Constancy's skirt. "Up,
Gramma, up!" Elspeth demanded imperiously. Constancy
laughed and caught her up on her other arm, her back
bent with the double burden. "Unca Matt . . . Unca
Nate!" pronounced the little hybrid triumphantly and
then chuckled mischievously. Constancy hugged her and

made a small face, grimly amused at Elspeth's calm appropriation of the family. She had derived sardonic pleasure from Mrs. Owens's disapproval upon hearing the olive-skinned little urchin lisping "Gramma" to her protector. Secretly it pleased Constancy that Elspeth so obviously preferred her to anyone else in the house, and she knew in her heart that she loved her son-in-law's unlawful child quite as much as she loved any of her own blood.

She was suddenly aware that the ship had ceased its advance. It rocked gently on the waves, and through her glasses she saw a boat being lowered from the side of the vessel. At the same time the pilot from the harbor approached the *Mary Ellen.* It was unusual for ships to lie off Waikiki unless they were to be quarantined. She smiled at the thought that Matt might be so eager to get home that he couldn't wait to come in the usual fashion. She watched while the men swung down the side of the vessel; she saw them supporting what seemed to be a human figure down the side and into the small boat. Her heart dropped leadenly. "Nate . . . Matt . . ." Hastily she put the babies down upon the sand and focused her entire attention upon the occupants of the small boat.

The pilot came alongside the *Mary Ellen,* and for some time there seemed to be parleying between the two boats. Then the pilot set off for Honolulu and the small boat approached the beach. It seemed to move tortoise fashion over the gently swelling water. She strained her eyes to discover identity in the blurs that were faces. "I can't stand anything more," she was saying in panic, but as she said it, she was automatically squaring her shoulders to meet catastrophe, the while her brain ran on wildly, "Sammie, Miriam, Jonathan, Mary . . . I can't bear anything further . . ." And then her protest hung suspended as she recognized Matt waving his handkerchief. She could not

see her uncle, but she perceived the jubilance in Matt's
bearing and knew, with a rush of relief that brought tears
to her eyes, that nothing could have happened to the captain.

She heard Matt's lusty shout, "Mother ahoy!" and then
the seamen had leaped over the boatside and were dragging
it to shore. Matt jumped from the boat and came wading
through the shallow water to seize Constancy in an embrace that left her skirts dripping and her hair awry.
"Mother! God, but it's good to see you!" He held her at
arm's length and then kissed her again. "How are you?
How's everybody? Are you glad to see me?"

Constancy looked up at him and laughed and cried a
little. "Don't be silly!" She said brusquely. "I nearly died
while I was watching the boat come in for fear you'd
managed to break your neck and they were bringing what
was left of you to me. But, Matt! How huge you are!
Why, you're a grown man!" She looked at him, astounded,
and he grinned delightedly.

"Why not? It's a man's life I've been living these last
two years." He puffed out his chest, expanding with pleasure at the approval he saw in his mother's eyes. He had
left, a lanky boy never quite sure of what to do with his
hands and feet; now he had filled out, caught up with his
growth, lost his old air of embarrassed uncertainty. He
turned away to call to the men, "Easy with him there!
Bring him this way!" And Constancy was aware of the
limp figure in the bottom of the boat. As she looked upon
him with concern, the men gently lifted him on an improvised stretcher and came toward her. "Who is it,
Matt?"

"He's a good fellow who took passage with us and was
going to the Orient, but he's been down with a fever for

past a month, and he needs nursing. . . ." Matt was suddenly shy. "Of course if you don't feel up to taking him
in we can send him to the hospital in town, but . . . I
didn't quite like to put him off like that by himself."

"You did right to bring him to me." Constancy was
looking upon the yellowish white face that was so thin
that the skin pulled tight over the bones. The youth of
the sick man, evident in spite of the dark stubble of beard
on his face and the black smudges sickness had left around
his brown eyes, caught at her ready compassion. "Bring
him right in. . . . Alohilani, you take good care of the
children and bring them in before long." She led the way
up the stone steps of the sea wall and up to the walk to the
lanai and held the door for them. "I'll put him in your
uncle's room, and you and he can share your room. It'll be
easier taking care of a sick person in the downstairs bedroom." She hurried ahead of them and turned down the
bed. Then she went to the bureau and took out one of the
captain's old nightshirts. "Here, you get him into this,
Matt."

The sick man had been turning his eyes to follow her
every motion. He managed a faint smile and said haltingly,
so low that she had to stoop for the words, ". . . hate to
be a trouble to you . . . too kind." She laid her hand on
his forehead. It was cool, but he was plainly very weak.
"You mustn't talk," she said kindly. "I'm glad to be able
to take care of you. We'll soon have you on your feet
again."

The men who had carried the stretcher stood awkwardly
about the room, staring curiously at Constancy and at the
pleasantly furnished large room. Matt, bending over the
sick man, jerked his head toward the door. "Be off to the
ship, now!" The men tramped out. Constancy held the

nightshirt and popped it over the patient's head as Matt took off his shirt. She discreetly gazed out of the window while Matt divested him of his trousers.

Matt spoke out of the side of his mouth to her. "We'll probably let the ship lie out here for the time being—the pilot says there's trouble with the sailors from the whaling fleet in town—some brawl or other with a sailor killed by the jailor and the rest of them excited over it. He said there are upward of two thousand sailors in town, and Uncle Nate thought it best to keep our men out of harm's way. Poor devils, they'd been counting on having a good time ashore!"

Constancy whirled about at his first words, forgetting the patient, whose trousers were halfway off. "Oh! Silly and Jonathan are in town today! Do you suppose there's danger of a riot? I wish they hadn't gone."

Matt gave a final tug at the trousers and turned to face his mother, the trousers in his hand, leaving the patient to grope with a feeble hand for the sheet and draw it over his exposed self. "That's bad!" exclaimed Matt in consternation, and then at sight of his mother's face altered his tone. "Oh, well, I daresay that they won't be molesting the ordinary townspeople. They may have a tussle with the constables or the guard, but I don't think we need worry about their damaging Jonathan or Silly."

Constancy's brow was still puckered, but she turned her attention to the patient. "When did Mr. . . ."

"Macaulay, Richard Macaulay," supplied Matt.

"When did Mr. Macaulay's fever leave him?"

"Two days ago, I think."

"Oh—then we must feed him well and often. I'll have Eliza make some chicken broth, and I'll bring you a glass of milk right away. Is there anything you wish?"

Dick Macaulay's thin hand rose waveringly to his chin,

and he looked beseechingly at Matt. "Shave!" he whispered.

Matt chuckled. "Beginning to think of your looks, are you? Well—that's a good sign, I'd say offhand. Mother, you see about feeding him and I'll attend to his looks. . . . Oh, yes, Uncle Nate said he'd be along before lunch to see you—even if he can't stay at the house at night just yet."

Constancy nodded and hurried down the stairs, her face puckered in thought. The clock in the hall pointed to the hour of ten. It would be at least twelve before she could reasonably expect Silly and Jonathan back. She shouldn't worry before then, but the thought of the horde of enraged sailors filled her with anxiety. Marshal Parke was a competent official: he had made something of the local constabulary, drilled the uncouth, lazy constables into efficiency, uniformed them, disciplined them until they could be trusted to carry out orders. There was an amazing difference between these military-looking guardians of the law and the old police force, the members of which turned out or not at an alarm, according to the whim of the moment, failed to report for duty at all if anything more interesting offered, and let the veriest scoundrel escape for a little money. Still, even though the police and soldiers might be able to quell several thousand riotous individuals under no strong command, the thought of the violence and bloodshed harassed her feelings. She compressed her lips and went into the kitchen.

The family was just sitting down to lunch when the sound of wheels sent Constancy running from the table to greet her children. Those at the table heard the fear in her voice as she cried, "Where's Jonathan?"

Silly came into the room, paused in silent surprise at seeing her brother and uncle, and then went to kiss each of them. She turned worried eyes upon her mother. "He's all right—at least he was when I left him. He thought it might do some good for him to stay in town, so he sent me home alone. It's dreadful—the sailors are forbidding-looking, and the governor refused Marshal Parke permission to call out the guard to restore order." She sighed and slipped into her seat at the table, raising the glass of water to her lips.

Constancy's hand was pressed against her heart. "What good could Jonathan possibly do?" she asked bewilderedly. "I don't understand."

"He thought that he might talk with some of the men —reason with them," Silly answered wearily. "I tried to persuade him to come home with me, but he thought it was his duty to stay, and of course he stayed."

"Did you get the straight of how the fracas started?" Matt asked curiously.

Silly nodded. "I think so—you know there's always extra drunkenness and disorder when the whaling fleet is in port. The jail's always filled then. Anyway, this sailor named Burns was arrested for being drunk and disorderly night before last, and he had to be put in a cell with eight or ten others because the jail was crowded. He was still drunk, so he started tearing up the bricks from the floor and throwing them at the door. I suppose some of the others helped, too. The jailor, Mr. Sherman, ordered them to stop, but they went right on, so he opened the door. You know there isn't any light anywhere, and he was afraid of having his head smashed, so he stood in the door and whirled his club in the darkness to protect himself and accidentally hit Burns in the head, and Burns died a little later." She drew a long breath and went on:

"Next morning, when the sailors around town heard, they went wild and descended on the fort to demand that the jailor be turned over to them. Of course Marshal Parke refused and told them he'd have to be tried in court, but they wouldn't go away. They're still hanging around the fort waiting for a chance to do something, though they aren't up to a direct attack because the fort guns are trained on them. Burns's funeral is this afternoon, and everybody's afraid there may be a riot."

The captain shook his head. "It's a bad business. Can't the guard do anything?"

Silly spread out her hands in negation. "I doubt if they could do very much against so many of them, and anyway Governor Kekuanaoa refused to let the marshal take any action. What Jonathan thinks he can do is beyond me. If they get drunk enough they're apt to burn half the town."

Matt jumped up from the table. "I'm going to town and see what's happening. If I can find Jonathan I'll make him come home."

Constancy frowned. "You'd best keep out of it, Matt. The men won't listen to you. Why should they? They aren't from your ship. Thank goodness your men are well out of it!"

"I think your mother's right, Matt," the captain said soberly. "I don't want my first mate to get his head split open in a brawl that doesn't concern him. But," and he brightened up a bit, "I tell you, I'll go and round up Jonathan. You know he's much more likely to listen to me than to his youngest brother!"

Matt looked disappointed and a little sulky. He suspected the captain of being quite unaverse to getting into the thick of the disturbance. "All right, sir," he said unwillingly, "but I don't see why I can't come, too."

The captain rose from the table and laid a hand on his nephew's shoulder. "Never mind, son, if I'm not back by noon tomorrow, you can come after me. Now there's no telling but what a gang of them might take it into their

heads to come out here, and there ought to be a man on the
place."

They all watched the captain setting off on horseback.
Constancy called after him, "Do be careful, Uncle Nate
—we couldn't bear to have you get hurt!"

They went back into the house. Silly's face was very
sober. Matt threw his arm about her. "Cheer up, Sil," he
said. "We've got a sick young man in the house for you
to minister to. You ought to like him—he's got a voice
that made the very whales sit up on their hind legs around
the ship whenever he sang."

"Who?" Silly looked inquiringly at her mother.

"His name is Richard Macaulay, dear, and he's been
very ill with a fever. The fever's gone now, but he's so
weak he can barely talk. We've got to feed him and nurse
him back to strength." Constancy reflected a minute. Silly
was nice to look at and young, and she probably wouldn't
pray over the young man in the first moment of meeting,
and he would like to see her after months of nothing but
men. "Will you carry in his tray and help him to eat the
broth and custard Eliza has made for him, dear?"

Constancy went about her work, putting the two babies
away for their naps, sending the other children out to play,
and discussing dinner with Eliza. No sooner was she
through in the nursery and kitchen than a frightened
young native appeared, imploring her to come to his wife,
who was having a baby. Constancy, accustomed to such
calls, gathered together some diapers, a few baby clothes,
old rags, soap, and such materials as her task called for,
and left, with a hurried word to Silly to keep an eye on
the patient and on the children. Silly nodded. "He ate all
of his broth and most of his custard," she said gravely,
"and now he is asleep."

Twilight was darkening into night when Constancy returned, having helped an hysterical woman deliver an eleven-pound boy. As she approached the house she heard faintly the slow movement from the "Moonlight Sonata" and remembered that Matt had mentioned that the visitor was musical. She entered the house and went into the sickroom. Judging that Silly would not be playing if the patient was not awake, she peered through the gloom and asked if Silly had taken good care of him.

"Very good care indeed," came the voice from the bed, much firmer than it had been in the morning. "She ministers both to the imagination and to the body."

Constancy made a grimace of surprise in the darkness as she said tranquilly that she was glad and asked if he would care for a light. Her fancy leaped ahead; she wondered if romance were again brewing in the house, but her common sense, coupled with her knowledge of her youngest daughter, refuted the idea. Silly was touched by Mr. Macaulay's illness and possibly by his interest in music, she decided, and admitted that her imagination was incapable of picturing Silly in love with anything but religion.

During dinner Matt talked cheerfully of his experiences on the sea, of the strange ports where he had been, of some of the characters he had met on his voyaging; but with dinner finished and the children all in bed, anxiety took possession of the group. Matt, walking along the beach, saw a red glare at the edge of the town and came rushing into the house with the news that fire had broken out in the town.

"It looks as if it were on the very edge of the harbor. . . . My God! If the whalers caught fire!"

"Oh!" There was alarm in Silly's voice. "I saw them—'

two long lines of them—more than two hundred and so close together I truly believe that a person could jump from one to the next. If one caught fire they'd all go. Oh!" Passion leaped into her voice. "How can men be so foolish and so wicked!"

Matt ran back to the end of the grove, where there was only level, bare plain between Waikiki and the town, and watched until the glare grew fainter and finally vanished altogether. He came back to report that the fire had evidently been put out. "Anyway, Mother," he said half defiantly, like the small boy he had been, "if they aren't back here by noon tomorrow, I shall go after them."

His mother smiled wanly. "You may . . . you may, Matt, but I do believe that your eagerness is less anxiety than hatred of missing any excitement. I thought you were grown up, son."

Matt flushed and then laughed ruefully. "Maybe so," he admitted, "but anybody'd rather be on the scene than away from it and not knowing what's happening. Don't be too hard on me, Mother! You know you wouldn't want us all to be saints in the family."

Silly spoke, a little sharply for her: "It isn't kind of you to refer to me that way! You're all always making fun of me. I'm no more saint than the rest of you—only I want to be good, and the rest of you don't care—except Jonathan."

She faced Matt angrily for a second and then ran out of the room, leaving Constancy blank-faced with astonishment and Matt stroking his chin, thunderstruck. "Well, I'll be eternally damned!" he said softly, and then, aware of what he had said before his mother, flushed a deep crimson. Life on the sea did not fit a man for conversation in a godly household, he reflected. His mother had apparently not heard him. "I didn't mean to hurt her feelings," he muttered uncomfortably. "You know she's always been the pious one of the lot—with all her praying and her early conversion. I guess I'd better go and make my peace with her," and he went slowly from the room and up the stairs.

Constancy scarcely heard him. She sat still pondering on Silly's outburst. She could not remember that Silly had shown a sign of temper since she was a baby.

When noon came the next day there was still no sign of Jonathan and the captain. Matt gulped down his lunch and rushed off to town on horseback. Constancy could not tear her thoughts away from the trouble in town. She tended the children and the house absently, leaving the care of Mr. Macaulay, who was noticeably improved, to Silly. She found temporary diversion from her anxiety in rereading the letters that had come on the *Mary Ellen* from Sally in Boston and Faith in Connecticut. Sally's announced the birth of a daughter whom she named Miriam for the sister who had died many years before. "I wish she were a gold and blue and white baby as Miriam was, but she has her mother's red hair. However, she is nice, and I am not complaining. Timmie thinks she is wonderful, but he is a little disappointed that she can't play with him."

Constancy smiled and picked up the next sheet:

I wanted Faith to come and bring her little Connie for a visit before we leave for Italy in the fall, but she can't be torn away from Grandma and the farm. I never imagined that such a harum-scarum child as Faith was would develop such a sense of duty. I think she is happy with Grandma, and her little girl is a charming child. I took Timmie down for a short visit on the farm a few months before Miriam was born, while Timothy had to go to New York to see about an exhibit, and Faith was well and blooming. Perhaps it was wrong of her to run away from Luke, but I can't for the life of me be sorry.

I am as usual happy—so happy that I am almost afraid to speak of it, but I feel that I must to you. The only cloud in my sky is the distance that separates. Please, Mother dear, take care of yourself and don't work yourself to death with all those orphans you have on your hands. I couldn't bear it if you were to kill yourself with overwork before I see you again. Do you suppose you will ever be free to return here—if only for a visit? Grandma speaks so wistfully of you and longs so to see you again. Isn't Silly old enough to keep house for Jonathan and let you get away?

Constancy laid down the letter with a sigh. Perhaps when the orphans were a little older . . . but she shook her head. It was too much to expect of Silly. Maybe in ten years' time . . . but in ten years' time it would probably be too late . . . at least to see her mother. Resolutely she put the thought of returning to New England from her mind and took up Faith's letter.

MOTHER DEAREST:

It was wonderful when your letter came at last saying that you still loved me and weren't angry with me because I ran away. I really couldn't do anything else. I could have stood Luke's piety if he hadn't been stupid. There was just nothing in him to make me love him, and I couldn't stand living with anyone I didn't love and just sometimes felt sorry for. I love it here on the farm, and Grandma is so

good to Connie and me—in fact she spoils Connie dis-
gracefully and cries harder than Connie when C. has been
up to mischief and must be spanked. She tells me of your
childhood and girlhood, and how proud she was of you for
being such a scholar and able to teach mathematics and
Latin to the neighbors' boys who were preparing for col-
lege. It makes me feel lighter-headed than ever by com-
parison, for you know how little of a scholar I am, though
I like to read well enough.

We enjoyed having Sally and Timmie with us. Posi-
tively Sally seems younger than she seemed when I was
little and she was about ten and used to take care of Matt
and Silly and me all day while you were away at the school.
She has lovely clothes and leads a gay life, going to parties
and the opera. She has learned to dance and loves it. It is
strange how differently people live and how much more
they enjoy themselves here than in the islands. They go to
church, but they don't worry about the state of their
souls forever and forever. Even Grandma wasn't a bit
shocked at hearing that Sally danced, and I don't think
she was really so awfully shocked at my running away
from Luke, though she called me a giddy rapscallion. The
neighbors think I am a widow. Grandma said they didn't
have sense enough to be told the truth, and, since I haven't
a conscience like Sally's, it doesn't bother me to sail under
false colors.

The letter slipped from Constancy's fingers and she
smiled, thinking of her mother. She suspected that her
mother had never been as God-fearing as her father. Did
women always adjust themselves outwardly to the code of
the men they loved, and then go on thinking differently
inside themselves?

Through the open door of the sickroom she heard Silly's low, slightly husky voice reading to Mr. Macaulay:

"Fear no more the heat o' th' sun,
  Nor the furious winter's rages;
Thou thy worldly task hast done,
  Home art gone, and ta'en thy wages:
Golden lads and girls all must,
As chimney sweepers, come to dust.

"Fear no more the frown o' th' great;
  Thou art past the tyrant's stroke:
Care no more to clothe and eat;
  To thee the reed is as the oak:
The Scepter, Learning, Physic, must
All follow this, and come to dust.

"Fear no more the lightning flash,
  Nor th' all-dreaded thunderstone;
Fear not slander, censure rash;
  Thou hast finished joy and moan:
All lovers young, all lovers must
Consign to thee, and come to dust.

"No exorciser harm thee!
Nor no witchcraft charm thee!
Ghost unlaid forbear thee!
Nothing ill come near thee!
Quiet consummation have;
And renownèd be thy grave!"

A little pause, and then Silly's voice: "Would you care to have me read you a little from the Scriptures?" Did Constancy fancy it, or was there a hint of amusement in the young man's voice as he answered, "I think it would be lovely if you were to read me the Song of Solomon"?

She heard Silly rise and cross the room and in a minute the reading began again:

" 'The song of songs, which is Solomon's.

" 'Let him kiss me with the kisses of his mouth: for thy love is better than wine.' "

And in the living room Constancy was thinking, "Does the child believe that is all about a union of the soul with the infinite?" The voice went on smoothly for a time but it faltered over the lines:

" 'Thy two breasts are like two young roes that are twins, which feed among the lilies.

" 'Until the day break, and the shadows flee away, I will get me to the mountain of myrrh, and to the hill of frankincense.' "

But it rallied and went firmly on for a space. Then it grew incredulous, as if the reader were finding a new meaning in familiar lines:

" 'How fair and how pleasant art thou, O love, for delights!

" 'This thy stature is like to a palm tree, and thy breasts to clusters of grapes.

" 'I said, I will go up to the palm tree, I will take hold of the boughs thereof: Now also thy breasts shall be as clusters of the vine, and the smell of thy nose like apples;

" 'And roof of thy mouth like the best wine for my beloved, that goeth down sweetly, causing the lips of those that are asleep to speak.

" 'I am my beloved's, and his desire is toward me.' "

Silly read faster and faster, breathlessly. Constancy sat listening in detached amusement. Knowing Silly as well as she did, she thought it unlikely that she would stop before she reached the last word, whatever her discomfort. She did not stop. Her mother wondered if she did not feel that the Scriptures had played her false. At the close, Dick Macaulay's voice reached Constancy's ears.

"That's as grand a love poem as was ever written."

"Oh!" from Silly, breathlessly but defiantly. "You are wrong! It's not earthly love the Song of Solomon is about. It's impious to think so! It's . . . it's . . . symbolism! *Not* what you think at all!"

There was a chuckle from the next room, and the man's voice again: "Why, what a little Puritan you are, aren't you? But I still think it was human love Solomon was talking about and not any mystic wedding of the soul to God. After all, Solomon knew a deal more about earthly love, judging from all accounts of him, than he did about the celestial."

Silly broke in on him in distressed tones: "No! No! You don't understand! The Bible wouldn't be like that. Oh, you're horrid to think that!" And with the clatter of an overturned chair, which she very evidently did not stop to pick up, Silly came running from the room and rushed up the stairs without even a look at her mother. Constancy quietly withdrew into the kitchen, smiling a bit sardonically. She was thinking that it had never occurred to Jonathan, either, that Solomon was celebrating human love.

The matter of Silly and the Song of Solomon was forgotten as the afternoon wore on and night came with no word from the town. Constancy held back dinner till seven o'clock, although she fed the children earlier. Silly shook her head when her mother told her she should eat. "I just can't—when we don't know what has happened to the boys and Uncle Nate! Oh . . . what's that?" For even as she spoke, the sound of carriage wheels reached them.

They hurried out to the *lanai* in time to see the three

men drive up in a strange vehicle drawn by the Williamses' horses. Constancy leaned limply against the pillar at the head of the steps, speechless. Joe came to take the horses to the stable. It was Uncle Nate who came up to Constancy and put his arms around her. "There, there, Connie, it's all right, nobody killed, and only two or three a little bruised—and the whole thing over with! Not a scratch among the three of us, and we're starving to death."

The last of his speech brought back Constancy's composure. "Of course! You must be. Dinner's been ready for more than an hour, so hurry, and you can tell us about everything as you eat."

Jonathan, in particular, looked worn out. "Poor child," said his mother compassionately as she looked at him, "did you have any place to sleep last night?"

He smiled faintly. "Anybody'd think I was ten, Mother, the way you talk. Yes, I got Peter's keys and slept on the couch in his office after midnight, when the worst excitement died down. They ran amuck after Burns's funeral yesterday. Somehow they got the notion in their heads that some of their friends were being neglected at the United States Hospital, and that Mr. Ladd had it in for sailors. So they all descended on the hospital and were going to get even with Mr. Ladd and rescue their abused comrades. Luckily Mr. Ladd got wind of it and cleared out with the money and papers of the place to Mr. Severence's—up Nuuanu—and by the time the gang could get to the hospital he was safely out of the way, and their friends in the hospital said they were treated all right and had nothing to complain of. The sailors were disappointed, I guess, and wanted some excitement, so they went back to town and mobbed the police station—took all the firearms and set the place on fire."

"Oh, dear," breathed Constancy. "Was anyone hurt?"

Jonathan smiled grimly. "No! The officers at the station weren't any of them inclined to be martyrs, and they
didn't put up any fight. The fire department turned out,
but the sailors cut up their hose and made a ring around
the burning building and dared anyone to try to break
through. Nobody dared, so the place just burned down.
Luckily for everybody, the wind was from the south or
the whole fleet of vessels would have gone. It is very wonderful to think of this great example of God's mercy and
loving-kindness in sending this rare breeze to prevent such
loss to these very sinners! Why—their whole year's work
lay in the barrels of oil on those vessels. As it was, the ship
nearest the station caught fire, but the sailors had their
wits about them enough to get it put out in quick order—
before it had reached the part of the ship where the oil
was stored."

"I should think that would have sobered them down,"
commented Constancy.

"It did—some of them, the ones who were gifted with
any common sense at all—but about a hundred of them
were still bent upon mischief, so they went on a round of
the saloons along Nuuanu and chased out the proprietors
and drank up everything in sight. In about an hour's time
they were crazy mad with drink and were shouting about
revenge. Somebody had the idea that it would be a good
thing to lynch Dr. Judd, and others were wanting to do
the same thing for Mr. Armstrong at Punahou. They
divided, and most of them set off up Nuuanu for Sweet
Home. A messenger was sent ahead on horseback by somebody in town to warn the doctor, and he sent his family
to the neighbors but stayed at home himself to greet the
sailors." Jonathan's face lifted, and his eyes glowed with

fervor as he said, "Again God intervened and caused the very sins of these men to defeat them. Drink overcame all but a mere handful of them, and they fell by the roadside to sleep it off. The half-dozen who arrived at Dr. Judd's gate were so befuddled that they could just stagger about in the road and shout a few curses before trailing off again, not quite sure why they had come. And the ones who set out for Punahou evidently succumbed in the same fashion."

He picked up his knife and fork and tackled his dinner. The captain spoke musingly: "Dr. Judd always seems to be the goat in any uprising. I seem to remember that the French have been out for his scalp a couple of times —and now these ruffians. I guess he thinks it's all in the day's work by now."

"But what happened today?" Constancy was a little impatient to get to the end of it. "Why didn't Marshal Parke do something?"

Matt spoke up indignantly: "His hands were tied. That's why! The governor wouldn't let him do a thing! This morning he just couldn't stand to see things going from bad to worse any longer, and he went and presented his resignation to the king. That stirred up things a good deal, and he was asked to reconsider. He said he would if they would let him declare martial law. They quibbled about it, he said, because there were supposed to be some formalities which had to be scrapped, but he went ahead and declared it anyway, and lots of the foreigners and some of the sea captains and officers, and Jonathan here, even, volunteered their services and got into formation while the marshal and his men posted notices all about town to warn people. Then we marched through town and rounded up all the sailors." He chuckled. "All the

fight went out of them when they saw us coming, I can
tell you! All but two or three scuttled along as meek as
Moses. They arrested about two hundred of the worst of
them for trial, and packed the rest off to their ships in care
of their officers, and they can't show their heads on the
streets again this trip. I do wish I'd gotten in on it earlier."

"Shame, Matt!" said Jonathan disapprovingly. "It was
a disgraceful time—there was fear that they would burn
the whole town. That's what they were threatening for a
time. One good thing may come of it, though," he added
thoughtfully. "I believe it will help to bring about a reform in the prison. It's shameful to have a prison and
insane asylum both in the cells of that fort. They have
as many as thirty prisoners in some of the cells at one time,
and there aren't even locks on the door. I've seen myself
how they keep the prisoners in by bracing a pole against
the outside of the door. The place is filthy and a very
breeding place for disease."

Constancy "h'mphed" grimly. "It takes a good while
for reform to set in here!" she said. "If you're talking
about breeding places for disease, what about all these
duck ponds over here in the marshes?" She turned to her
uncle. "You know, they dig the silt out and plant bananas
on the banks and raise ducks in this awful stagnant water,
and families live right on the bank of each little pond,
doing a double business in ducks and bananas. Some day
there's going to be a lot of typhus let loose from those
marshes."

The captain frowned. "Isn't there any health department here?"

"There's a board of health, but it doesn't do anything
that would stir up objection among the natives," said
Jonathan soberly. "Of course there would be a dreadful
hue and cry if they drained out those marshes when sev-

eral dozen families are supported by them, so it has just been allowed to slide."

They arose from the table, and Constancy sent Matt in to settle Dick Macaulay for the night. When he came back to the living room, he was grinning mischievously. "Dick says he would like to speak to Silly for a moment if she is at leisure."

Silly jumped to her feet, her cheeks flaming. "I . . ." *Can't!* she was starting to say, and then, conscious of all eyes upon her, she walked swiftly into the room across the hall, closing the door after her. Jonathan looked inquiringly after her. "What's the matter with her?" he asked mildly, and then with a frown, "I don't think she should have closed the door—the young man might misinterpret it."

"Not when Silly closes the door," said his mother dryly and began to count her stitches aloud. After a very few minutes Silly reappeared, a spot of color burning high on either cheek, and her eyes downcast. She went to the piano. "Mr. Macaulay said he thought he'd sleep better if I played a little," she said a little apologetically, and attacked Mozart's 'Fantasia in C Minor' with a vigor that could hardly be considered conducive of sleep. Matt gave his mother a sidelong look, but her eyes were on her knitting, and her expression was forbidding. He formed his lips to whistle and then thought better of it. With a shrug he settled himself to listen to his sister's music.

The following Monday the school opened again, and Silly was busy from eight in the morning till three in the afternoon. Dick was able to be up in a chair in the living room when she came in from school on the first afternoon. Constancy heard her say, surprise and pleasure in her voice, "Oh . . . I'm so glad to see you up. You *are*

feeling much better, aren't you?" Constancy went upstairs and left them alone. Presently she heard Silly playing
to him.

In a few days the convalescent was able to take short
walks in Silly's company. In the evenings he sang in a
tenor that had none of the thinness or the twang of the
usual untrained tenor, but was full and rich and gravely
sweet. He spoke of the venture that was taking him to
China. A firm of tea importers was sending him out for
a three-year term. He spoke somberly of the loneliness
of life in a far-away part of the world for a young man
alone, and Constancy caught him looking out of the tail
of his eye to see how Silly was taking his statement. Silly
was staring at her folded hands, her features set in grim
lines that indicated to her mother that she was unwillingly
moved. Constancy studied her secretly, wondering if this
unworldly daughter was losing her heart, and, if so, if she
would lose it to the extent of throwing in her destiny with
that of a young man she had not known three weeks
earlier. It was nearing the time when the *Mary Ellen* must
leave for China. They were to embark on Friday of the
fourth week after arrival. After two weeks most of the
whalers were gone, and the *Mary Ellen* had been allowed
to dock in the harbor, and her men had been permitted
shore leave.

On the Thursday afternoon preceding the departure of
the *Mary Ellen*, Constancy, at work in the kitchen, suddenly remembered that she had forgotten to fill the large
reading lamp in the living room and started after it. Silly
was playing while Dick sang "Drink to Me Only with
Thine Eyes." Something in the timbre of the singer's voice,
something in the sweetness of Ben Jonson's lyric, brought
a mist of tears to Constancy's eyes. She paused in the hall-
way as the song came to an end and was just entering the

room when she heard Silly push back the piano stool and say breathlessly, "Oh . . . it's so beautiful . . . I can't bear it!" She paused involuntarily on the threshold of the room, unperceived by the two at the piano. They stood facing each other, Silly's head thrown back and her lips parted. Constancy caught her breath; so did Dick. "*You're* so beautiful . . . I can't bear it!" he muttered, and had an unresisting Silly in his arms and was pressing kisses upon her mouth.

Constancy clapped her hand over her mouth and backed stealthily into the kitchen and dropped into a chair. Would Silly want to rush off to China with Dick with only two days' notice? Her brain leaped to attack the problem of clothes and supplies.

At dinner Silly's cheeks were brilliant and her eyes radiant, and she had not a word to say to anyone. Matt, who suspected how the land lay, grinned villainously and started to address her, but he had only gotten so far as her name when he stopped short with a grunt at the viciousness of a kick on his shin. He looked indignantly around the table, met his mother's warning eye, and subsided, leaning down to rub his injured shin.

After dinner Dick quite transparently invited Silly to look at the moon, and she accepted his invitation quite as transparently, it being a night when the moon could not possibly rise before midnight. Even Jonathan unbent to chuckle as they left the room. "It looks as if Silly's heart were lost to this young man," he ventured.

Matt strolled to the bookcase and remarked flippantly, "If she just doesn't discover that he doesn't know the answer to question eighteen in the catechism."

The captain looked up quizzically. "Love has been known to bridge a gap like that," he said. But Constancy's brow puckered. Surely, she thought, the excitement of love while it is new should thrust religion into the background . . . for the time being, at least. But she was uneasy. Ten o'clock, the usual bed hour came, and the two had not returned. Matt yawned. "Looks as if they really meant to see that moon," he said. "I'm going to bed."

Jonathan looked questioningly at his mother. "Should I . . . call them in, do you think?"

Constancy spoke heatedly. "Don't be a goose! Have you forgotten how you felt?" She was instantly sorry, seeing his face. She went up to him and put her arms around him. "Forgive me, son. I didn't mean to hurt you. Go on to bed, dear, and I'll wait up for them." Jonathan bent silently and kissed his mother's forehead and went up the stairs, dragging his feet. Constancy resumed her knitting, Eleven o'clock came. The front door opened. Silly came in alone; without a glance at her mother, her head held high and her mouth uncompromisingly set, she walked woodenly up the stairs.

Her mother stared after her, bewildered. Where was Dick? And why should they have quarreled so soon? She would have to wait up till he came in. She took up her knitting again. Half an hour went by, and she grew worried. After all, the boy was still far from robust. He shouldn't be out so late. The night was chilly, too. She took a shawl from the window seat, and, throwing it about her shoulders, went in search of him.

The beach seemed the most likely place to find him. She stood on the sea wall and peered through the darkness. A hundred yards or more down the beach she thought she saw a blot on the lightness of the sand. She walked toward it and saw that it was a man lying face downward on the ground. She found herself running toward him, and as she ran she heard great, gasping sobs. Appalled, she knelt be-

side him and tugged at his shoulder. "Mr. Macaulay! Dick
. . . you mustn't lie here. Poor boy!"

He raised himself, startled at her first word, and then
sat up and blew his nose, turning his back on her, painfully embarrassed that she should have caught him in such
a predicament.

"I don't know what you think of me," he gulped over
his shoulder. "I guess I'm still weak. I assure you I don't
usually boo-hoo—even if I am pretty badly knocked up."

Constancy laid a light hand on his shoulder. "Tell me
about it if you care to—it might help a little."

He reached for her hand and clung to it childishly. He
was silent for a minute, as if he didn't know how to begin. Constancy said nothing, sure he would speak when he
could. Finally he burst out furiously. "It's her damned
religion!"

Constancy started and then thought grimly that it was
a good phrase. "I suppose," she said, "that that means she
doesn't approve of yours."

He groaned and pushed the fingers of his free hand
through his hair. "I haven't any! I didn't know she felt so
strongly about it, or I might have been less frank. No! I
wouldn't, either. You can't lie about things like that. I
think you could lie or steal easier than pretend to a belief
you haven't—for an ulterior motive."

"Do you?" Constancy could not forbear querying,
thinking how taken aback he would be if he knew the
spiritual history of the missionary beside him.

"Of course you can't!" he said angrily. "Anyway, you'd
think I was unclean, or had robbed widows—and mur-
dered orphans, the way she drew away from me."

"Oh! Poor Silly!" murmured Constancy. "Don't be too
hard on her. It's a twist in her mind or her spirit. She's

been unnaturally religious, even for this place, since she was a baby. I verily believe she would die rather than go against her conscience, but I thought that love might change her."

Dick shook his head. "I was *sure* she loved me—before dinner! And after—until she suddenly drew away from me, right after kissing me, mind you, and asked, solemn as any judge, 'Are you a communicant?' For a minute I didn't know what she meant and asked her. And she said, 'A communicant of a Christian Protestant church, of course!' I was flabbergasted, and said 'No.' She groaned as if she had a pain and then straightened up and said, still grim as a judge interrogating the prisoner at the bar: 'Do you believe in the redeeming grace of our Lord Jesus Christ?' And I tried to squirm out of answering, but she said, 'Yes or no?' Then I had to say 'No.' And she crumpled all up and cried awfully and wouldn't let me touch her or even come near me, and she kept saying over and over that she ought to have known that anything that made her feel the way she did was wrong, and that this was a snare Satan had set for her soul, and my voice and—" he stammered a little uncomfortably—"my . . . uh . . . body were the bait, and she'd die before she'd get caught now that she knew.

"I tried to tell her that I wasn't a criminal and that I couldn't help it if I just couldn't believe in a white-headed God in a nightshirt and a beard or anything so unthinkable or so repulsive (to me, at least) as a virgin birth and a vicarious atonement."

This time it was Constancy who groaned aloud. "Did you say it *that* way—to *Silly?*" she asked in horror.

"Yes," gloomily, "that was the way I thought it."

"Then there's no hope for you at all, my poor boy."

"That's what she said." His voice broke, and Constancy

could hear him swallow hard before continuing. "She said if I'd been a Baptist or even a Unitarian or a Catholic, she might have overlooked it and felt that God would not blame her for marrying me, but that there was no hope at all for an unbeliever, and she said something about not being able to touch pitch without being defiled!" Ending almost in a wail, he turned suddenly and, flinging his arms around Constancy's waist, buried his head in her lap and sobbed, "How can she be like that . . . when she is so beautiful and loves poetry . . . and can make such music come from the piano? I'd swear there was passion in her . . . and yet she turned from me cold as ice . . . just because I don't explain the universe the way she does!"

Constancy stroked his hair. She felt unspeakably sorry for him, and wished irrelevantly that he had been her son and not had to fall in love with Silly, and thought fleetingly of lost Sammie. "She *has* . . . passion in her," Constancy said determinedly, but she faltered over the word which was not in common usage among the missionaries, "but she'll turn it all into religion and think it sin to bestow it upon anything human—unless maybe a minister—and then she'd think it was all spiritual—probably, and I don't think she'd ever be humanly aware of the kind of minister they make nowadays."

Dick sat up and stared into her face. "Then you think there's not a vestige of hope that she will relent?"

Constancy pressed his hand for a moment before answering. "No," she said with unequivocal firmness, "not a vestige. And though it seems hard to you now, it's better that she shouldn't." Suddenly there was pent-up violence in her voice. "Do you think you could stand it if she weakened now and married you—and then all the rest of her life made you feel that the pleasure she took in your love for her—in moments when she was off guard—was a sin which she must repent in sackcloth and ashes? I tell you a dyed-in-the-wool Calvinist is something beyond believing when it comes to mixing up pleasure and sin! You can take my word for it—I've lived among them more years than you've been on earth!"

She broke off abruptly, annoyed at having committed herself. She stood up. "You can't stay out here any longer unless you mean to give yourself pneumonia and make her sorry for you that way. Get in the house and to bed."

Meekly and wordlessly, Dick followed her into the house.

Constancy found herself yielding Silly a grudging admiration the next day. Her face ashy white, her gray-green eyes darkly circled, she appeared at prayers, stolidly ate her breakfast, and went to school as usual. After dinner she took her place in the living room with the rest of the family. A devil of malice possessed Dick. He brazenly went over to Silly and, before she realized his intention, pulled her to her feet. "Come! My last night—we must give them a song."

"Yes, do!" came heartily from the captain, who had been out all day and was unaware of the turn affairs had been taking. Silly surveyed her lover stormily for an instant and then, with her chin held high, went to the piano. She sat rigidly while he turned through the music, and as he set the music before her, she played without comment through two ballads.

"One more!" he said and slipped another song book before her. Constancy, watching them fascinated, saw Silly straighten her shoulders with a jerk, then set her chin forward, and begin to play the opening measures of "Drink to Me Only with Thine Eyes."

"That's brutal!" everything in Constancy protested.

"She's suffering, and he wants her to—but you can't blame him." She felt that she was committing an indelicacy, but she could not wrench her gaze from them while Dick's voice soared tenderly, heartbreakingly, it seemed to her:

"Drink to me only with thine eyes,
And I will pledge with mine:
Or leave a kiss but in the cup,
And I'll not look for wine.
The thirst that from the soul doth rise
Doth ask a drink divine;
But might I of Jove's nectar sup,
I would not change for thine."

Silly's face was a stony mask, but tears slowly rolled down her cheek and splashed on her sleeve. She went on playing, an automaton. And Dick sang the second stanza:

"I sent thee late a rosy wreath,
Not so much honoring thee
As giving it a hope that there
It could not withered be.
But thou thereon didst only breathe,
And sent'st it back to me;
Since when it grows, and smells, I swear,
Not of itself, but thee!"

Constancy watched, spellbound, while Silly rose, as she had the day before; but now her face was ashen and the tears streamed unheeded from her eyes. She faced Dick and with sudden fury struck him in the face. Covering her own face with her hands, she ran from the room. Dick stood, astounded at what his maneuver had effected, feeling the place on his cheek where Silly had left red finger-prints. For a moment he was speechless, and then he began to laugh—a little too loudly. He stopped as abruptly as he had begun and rushed out of the room to his bedroom and slammed the door after him.

The three men left in the living room had all risen ex-citedly to their feet. If Dick had just been the one to strike Silly, they would all have known how to behave, but with Silly striking Dick, they had no pattern of behavior to fol-low. There seemed no action to be taken which would clear the atmosphere.

Jonathan turned speechless to his mother, a question in his eyes. The captain scratched his head. "Well, Connie," he said resignedly, "perhaps you can throw some light on this performance."

Constancy drew a sighing breath and folded her hands. "It means," she said mildly, "that Silly is in love with a man instead of God. That alone bewilders her, but he doesn't happen to—" she paused and remembered Matt's jibe of the night before—"he doesn't happen to know the answer to question eighteen in the catechism, Matt, and that finishes the matter."

She rose to her feet and rolled up the sock she was knit-ting. "I've had all I can stand for one day, and I think I'll go to bed." She walked out of the room and up the stairs, leaving the three men staring after her.

14

In the weeks after the departure of the *Mary Ellen,* Constancy was to marvel at her daughter's ability to dis-semble her feelings. She was sure that Silly's love for Dick Macaulay had been no light or passing affair. She knew instinctively that only a more than commonplace emotion

could have driven Silly to perpetrate the sensational scene
of Dick's last night, Silly, who since childhood had never
given way to the normal displays of temper of the average human being. But after her brief lapse, Silly lived
behind a mask. If she suffered, she asked no one for sympathy. She taught in the school and conducted a Sunday
School class, she played the piano in the evenings, and she
did her share of the housework. She talked little, but then
she had never been given to light or easy conversation. By
common consent the entire household avoided any refer-
ence to the recent visitor. Constancy was aware that when
Silly went up to her room, closing the door after her, as
early as nine o'clock, she did not go to bed. Rising in the
night to see to one of the children, Constancy was more
than likely to see the pale light from Silly's lamp making
a thin frame of her door. She stood in the hall, shaken with
pity for Silly, but constrained to withhold any evidence
of her compassion. There had always been something in
Silly's bearing which rebuked intrusion.

Just before leaving Honolulu, the captain had insisted
upon transferring the ownership of the Waikiki house and
property to Constancy. "I should have done so long ago,"
he said when she objected. "You know I can't live forever,
and though I've had rare luck with my ship so far"—he
surreptitiously reached out and tapped three times on the
arm of his chair—"there's no point in tempting fate. I
built this house just for you, and I'd leave it to you in a
will if I didn't do this. Making it over to you now is the
same thing in effect and will save a lot of bother by and
by."

The act troubled Constancy, although she realized the
wisdom of it. It brought to mind the fact that if she was
getting old, her uncle was getting older, that he couldn't
hope to sail the seas much longer. She could not imagine

him reduced to inaction. The thought of the captain sitting about in a rocker, whittling to pass the time when he tired of reading, was very disturbing to her. As if he read her thoughts, the captain said with a twinkle, "Don't worry about me, my dear. I'm not going to wring your heart by shuffling about the house in carpet slippers, a feeble wreck of my former self. I'll keep going till the end and probably burst a blood vessel while I'm in a temper over some green hand's stupidity. And when that happens, young Matt will fit into my shoes well enough. He's young, and when the time comes it won't tear at his vitals to give up a fine, trim, sailing vessel for one of those atrocities that run by steam."

He engaged Peter as the lawyer to transact his business and commissioned him to give Constancy the monthly sum of money he had always paid her for caring for the house. He did not see fit to tell her that he had transferred bonds to her name which would yield her an income whatever happened to him. He had accomplished what he had set out to do back in 1837: made Constancy as independent as she chose to be of the missionaries. As long as Jonathan had lived, Constancy conducted classes in the Bible and took a part in women's meetings and taught regularly in the school. At his death she refused the small salary due her from the mission board and felt free of obligation to them. Thus she dispensed with the need of conducting classes in the Bible; gradually she dropped all her work of a more religious nature, justifiably enough, as her duties to the orphans, both of her own family and the natives, allowed her little time. The classes in sewing and cooking for the girls of the school she gave freely and was aware that the brethren could find no fault with her, while, on the other hand, her conscience was not disturbed by any necessity for instructing the young in a faith which was meaningless to her.

In February of 1853 there was cause for some alarm on the island when the ship *Charles Mallory* approached port flying the yellow flag which symbolized smallpox. There was only one case on board, but the men were taken off and quarantined in a vacant house at Waikiki near the Williams home, while the victim was isolated in a grass house belonging to Prince Lot Kamehameha on a small island toward the end of the harbor. There he was ministered to with great caution and a good deal of reluctance by a scared member of the Board of Health. None of the other members of the crew had the disease. When the sick man recovered, the house he had inhabited was burned down; his clothing and all the clothing of the rest of the crew and all the bedding on the ship added to the conflagration. The ship sailed away and tragedy was averted. But people had been terrified—especially the foreign population, who flocked to the doctors to be vaccinated.

This incident was merely an introduction to an epidemic that broke out with fury three months later. There was no connection between the first case in the islands and the plague that descended so soon afterwards, but the two episodes were linked in everyone's mind. As a matter of fact, a sea captain quite innocently brought in the disease on some clothes which he gave to a native woman to launder. Before starting for the islands, he had stayed in a San Francisco rooming house in a room next to one in which a man had died of smallpox. The rooms were separated only by burlap partitions, and the captain's clothes had hung against the flimsy wall. These clothes found their way into the house of two native women in Kakaako, came out clean, and the captain sailed obliviously on his way. A little later the groans of the two women attracted a neighbor who, after a hasty inspection, rushed off to Marshal Parke to report what he feared was the smallpox.

The conscientious marshal took possession of a vacant building on Queen Street and pronounced it a hospital of isolation; he reported the matter to the king and the governor. As the legislature was then in session, the king immediately managed the appointment of a Commission of Health, consisting of Dr. Judd, Dr. Rooke, and Marshal Parke, with full authority to handle the matter as they saw fit.

When it came to transporting the two sick women to their place of incarceration, it rapidly became evident that there was no one on the island who would risk infection. The worthy marshal patiently took horse and wagon and drove after them himself. He asked nothing of anyone which he was unwilling to do himself. Arrived at their hut, there was nothing for it but to carry the two great bulks of corrupted flesh to the wagon himself. The marshal was a strong, sizable man, but he puffed and grunted as he half boosted, half carried one and the other of the two sufferers to the wagon. He drove them grimly away to the improvised hospital, where he had to perform the same Herculean labor again.

A week went by. The cases had been discovered on May 13th. No more cases developed, and the panic subsided. By the first week in June, however, with the two original patients well on the way to recovery, one case and then another was reported. The white population flocked to be inoculated. The natives were a little superstitious about the value of inoculation and held back. Suddenly the pestilence was upon the town. People died more rapidly than they could be buried. The medical men bravely volun-

teered their services in ministering to the living, but they
could scarcely be expected to dispose of the dead. The disease spread from Kakaako; cases were reported in Liliha,
Kalihi, Manoa, Waikiki. All day the Black Maria creaked
from one end of Honolulu to the other in quest of its
grisly load. The constables were drafted into service, and
finally, in desperation, six of the sailors who had been
given prison sentences after the riot of the preceding fall,
and were known to have had smallpox, were offered their
freedom on condition that they give their services to the
Health Commission as buriers of the dead, as ministrants
to the living, as anything the health officers ordered them
to be. The prisoners accepted the terms.

By the middle of June the schoolhouse near the church
and several hundred yards distant from Constancy's house
had been taken over as a hospital, with one constable vali-
antly trying to care for all the afflicted who were brought
in to lie on piles of mats or the occasional couches. Constancy had been afraid that Jonathan's strong sense of
duty might send him to nurse the sick, but at the beginning of the epidemic he was suffering from a severe cold
and congested lungs, which led him to agree, after much
deliberation, that his health, none too good at any time,
was not equal to nursing.

Everyone in the house, including the babies, had been
vaccinated at the time of the first fright about smallpox,
and Constancy, though the sight of the stricken being carried into the building she could see through the coconut
grove, and the worse sight of bodies being removed to the
Black Maria filled her with pity and horror, felt no great
alarm for her own family. The children were not allowed
to play on the school side of the yard, and she would permit no one but herself to drive into town for supplies. One
day of the third week in June, she returned from a trip

to the town, to be met at the door by a pale and harassed
Jonathan. Giving the horses over to Joe, she hurried up
the steps, fear assailing her as she saw her son's face. He
came to her and put his arms around her.

"It's Silly!" he said.

Constancy drew back in horror. "Has she got the smallpox?" Her voice was a screech.

Jonathan shook his head. "No—not that—not yet. But,
oh, I feel sure she will. . . . I shouldn't have let her go!"

His mother seized his shoulders and shook him. "What
do you mean? Where has she gone?"

"To the hospital. . . . The doctor talked to me over
the gate as he came away—he said there was only one man
to take care of twenty patients. He said he didn't know
what they were to do. She heard . . . and . . . the next
thing I knew she was down here with a bag of clothes,
saying it was her plain duty to go and that nothing I could
say would stop her."

Constancy turned on him fiercely. "You *should* have
stopped her! Even if you had to tie her to a post! Have
you no sense, Jonathan Williams? What does that child
know about nursing! How's she going to stand seeing people a mass of horrible sores—when a sick cat has always
made her turn green? How can she stand waiting on them
and touching them? Silly's a child—she's only twenty
years old! And you, a grown man, say you couldn't stop
her from going to her death!"

He looked at her stupefied. His shoulders drooped.
"I'm sorry, Mother. I guess I should have stopped her
some way." He drew his hand in a tired gesture across
his forehead. "It's hard to know what is right. . . . Mor-
ally it is right for Silly to do this, and you know once
she sees her duty, or what she thinks is her duty, there's
no deterring her."

Constancy clenched her hands in irritation. She burst forth uncontrollably: "Oh! If just for once you men of God could season your holiness with a little common sense —with a little plain humanity!" She brushed past him and went upstairs. In her bedroom she found a sheet of paper on the dresser. It read:

DEAR MOTHER:

Try not to worry about me. They need help desperately, and I am confident that God will protect me from harm if it is best. If He judges otherwise, I have no dread of death. I should have liked to see you to say good-bye, but this way is easier. You would have been sure to try to prevent me from going, and I must go. I promise that the doctor will let you know each day how I am.

Your loving daughter,
SILLY.

Constancy threw down the paper and groaned with despair, wishing that she had sent Silly to school in New England, anywhere, so that she would not have been here at this time, wishing Silly had married Dick Macaulay and gone to China with him—even if she were miserable married to an unbeliever. Aside from the possibility of infection, the harrowing of Silly's sensibilities by the ghastly nature of her tasks as nurse in an improvised pesthouse made her mother shudder. She went to her bedroom window and stared through the opening of the grove toward the schoolhouse, and, as she looked, the Black Maria drove up and stopped at the door. Unwillingly and yet fascinated, she watched the two men in the vehicle jump down and carry, on what appeared to be a door, five limp figures into the building. After the fifth trip in, they began bringing out burdens, dumping them with little care in the Maria. Constancy shuddered. Four times the men carried out a human form and deposited it in the wagon. Then they climbed to the seat and drove away.

Four dead in one day, and five new cases that they had been able to ferret out in this one section of town. And she knew how prone the natives would be to hide their sick ones away and keep them as long as possible. No telling how many of the huts farther down the beach hid the stricken ones where the hasty glance of the inspectors would fail to see them.

Distractedly she turned away from the window. There was nothing to do but wait for nine days—or was it ten?—that it took for the disease to develop? She thought, "I'll go mad before so long as that. I'm getting old . . . I haven't the resistance I used to have. I've borne enough for one woman. . . . Is there never to be peace for me this side of the grave?" She shrugged her shoulders despondently, and then squared them to meet the invisible foe as she had been squaring them at fairly regular intervals ever since she had met Jonathan Williams thirty-four years earlier.

Each day she lived for the moment when the doctor called from the gate. Each day she refused to stir from the part of the house that commanded a view of the gate until he should have come and gone. She waited tense and grim until he said Silly was well. "Overworking, of course," he said regretfully. "One man and one woman are bound to overwork, taking care of twenty-five patients. It's still spreading. Every day we find new ones. If a third of them didn't die, I don't know where we'd put the new ones. Even with the other buildings farther down the beach that they've taken over for hospitals, we're desperately overcrowded. God knows when it will end."

He would go, and Constancy would relax for the rest of that day. But after she was in bed she would start up in horror, thinking, "Even at this minute she may be feeling the onslaught!" And she felt in her own body the chills, the pains, the nausea, and the fever which marked the beginning of smallpox. Through the day she was kept busy with the children; she could keep her fancy in bounds. But at night her imagination ran riot in the dark jungles of morbidity and fear. She realized that her anxiety, aside from waxing and waning in the daily cycle, was steadily mounting toward the ninth day after Silly's departure from home. When the ninth day came and the doctor reported that Silly showed no symptoms of the disease, her relief was so great that she dropped to the ground where she stood and cried hysterically. That night she slept soundly through the night for the first time since Silly had placed herself in danger. The next morning the doctor reported that Silly seemed to have a cold, but he said it was undoubtedly because she was overworked and had no resistance.

Constancy's blood chilled in her veins. Her heart was a leaden weight in her body. "It isn't a cold," she said quite steadily. "It's the beginning of the smallpox!"

The doctor shook his head angrily. "I wouldn't say that," he said irritably. He, too, was overworked, with scant time for food or sleep. "She was vaccinated, wasn't she?"

"Yes," said her mother somberly, "but it didn't take—not any more than a mosquito bite. Everyone else in the house had fever for a day or two, but she didn't have a bit —felt just as usual." She left him to enter the house, convinced that Silly was doomed. More than ever, now, her eyes clung to the hospital. She could scarcely tear herself away from the window to attend to the children. Elspeth and Deborah pulled at her skirts and howled in hurt wrath when she failed to notice them.

The next day, too, the doctor tried to reassure her. "She says herself that she feels better, though she is running a fever—but if she had the smallpox there would be vomiting, backache, cramps, half a dozen things she hasn't! She wouldn't be able to tend the patients."

Constancy looked at him unbelievingly. "She has it," she said stubbornly.

The doctor's nerves were on edge. He spoke petulantly: "You might give me credit for recognizing smallpox when I see it! After the last few weeks, you might think I'd know it, Mrs. Williams!"

Constancy looked through him, unseeing, unhearing. "If she isn't better by tomorrow, I shall go to her."

The doctor looked alarmed. "Now, Mrs. Williams, I wouldn't do that, if I were you! You know you wouldn't be allowed to leave—once you had entered the building."

"Come by here as early as you can in the morning," she said tonelessly and turned to go into the house.

She knew that Silly had the smallpox. Now that she was sure that the worst had happened, she felt calmer. She was able to give more of her attention to the children, who promptly forgave her her recent strange behavior and swarmed over her in their usual fashion. After they were in bed that night, she gathered together several changes of underwear and some wash dresses, soap, towels, and several bottles of grapejuice that Mrs. Conde had sent her from Maui. She took a satchel downstairs with her the next morning and left it in the hall while she went into prayers and to breakfast. At ten o'clock she saw the doctor arrive at the schoolhouse. She stood at the window, gazing intently at the building, passively waiting for him to come to her. It was half an hour before she saw him hurry out of the schoolhouse and get into his gig. She went out on the *lanai,* satchel in hand, and stood awaiting him.

He pulled up his horse at the gate, and Constancy walked down the path to meet him. His face was grave. "I am very sorry to have to tell you that Miss Silly has broken out overnight. It is certain now that she has the smallpox." He noticed the satchel. "You understand, of course, that if you go to her, Mrs. Williams, you will have to stay until the period of danger is over, possibly two weeks if you are immune from the disease, and of course you run the risk of catching it."

"I understand," she said impatiently, "and you don't need to worry lest I crawl out a window and run home! I have no desire to give it to any of my household!"

"Then," said the doctor, lifting his hat, "I can only say that your services are needed. Your daughter's illness leaves only one person to care for the sick. I think we're getting it under control—yesterday only two new patients were brought in against the five or six that came in here alone daily for a time." He clucked to his horse and drove away.

Constancy was starting for the hospital when she remembered that she had said nothing to Jonathan or Eliza. She returned to the house, gave Eliza instructions concerning the food and care of the children, and then found Jonathan in his study.

"I've got to go to Silly, son," she said. "Take care of the household for me. I'll be gone several weeks, no doubt, as they need me, and anyway I'd have to stay there until they were sure I wasn't going to catch it myself."

Jonathan rose to his feet, paling at her words. He shivered a little. "It seems *horrible* . . . to think of Silly . . ." He was unable to finish his sentence. His mother nodded.

"That's why I'm going. Try not to worry. The doctor will report to you each day. Good-bye, son." She drew his head down and kissed him gravely, observing with remote tenderness that his eyes were filled with tears. She caught up her satchel and hurried away to the hospital.

She was half conscious of bracing herself for what she would find in the schoolhouse turned hospital, but, even so, her imagination, which had pictured the foul sight of the disease that filled every cot and pile of mats in the three rooms of the building, had not bargained for the foul odor that accompanied smallpox. As she entered the first room where only men lay, nausea assailed her. She walked rapidly through the room, scarcely glancing at the figures on the cots or mats, and went into the next room. She stood in the doorway, and her eyes flashed over the eight women who lay about the room on piles of mats or mattresses on the floor. In one corner she was aware of large brown eyes, vaguely familiar, staring dully at her from a hideously disfigured face. With a start she recognized Leilehua, the mother of Elspeth. But there was no time for Leilehua now. For the moment she thought that Silly was not here. All seemed to be native women, till she espied, almost hidden by a cot, one more pile of mats. In a second she was across the room, peering into Silly's face.

Not as badly disfigured as the others in the room, Silly nevertheless appalled her mother. The one angry-looking eruption on Silly's broad forehead, the three on the cheek turned toward her mother, and a few visible on her neck were the more offensive, as Constancy saw in contrast the face that had been Silly's a few days ago, the creamy pallor with no blemish. These filthy-looking sores were an outrage upon Silly's fastidious cleanliness.

Constancy dropped down beside the mattress, forcing

back the sob that rose in her throat. Silly's eyes opened, brilliant with fever. She put out a hand to her mother and then hastily drew it back; but Constancy had time to see the vile sign of the disease on the back of her hand. Silly's voice came wearily.

"I thought I would be spared . . . I prayed so hard to be of use . . . they need well people to look after them so. God is angry with me, Mother, and now I can't even pray!" Her eyes burned into her mother's heart.

Constancy struggled for a moment before she could find her voice: "You should have given up sooner, Silly. The sooner you begin to take care of yourself, the sooner you will be well."

Silly smiled faintly, ironically, though Silly was not as a rule given to irony. She was thinking that her mother realized little the preponderance of death in this house of pain and vile odors. Her mother bent over her and was sickened at the suggestion of decay in Silly's breath.

"Can't I do something to make you more comfortable, dear?"

Silly moved restlessly. "I'm so miserably hot, and these things itch so! No wonder the natives can't be kept from scratching. If I just had a cold wet cloth over my head, maybe I could go to sleep."

Constancy nodded. "I brought some extra rags and towels along. I thought you might be needing them. I'll wring one out right away." She rose and walked over to a small stand in the corner where a basin and pitcher stood.

Silly raised herself on one elbow. "Maybe you'd better not. That's all we have for drinking water till evening, when Ahana can go after some more. We always run out." She sank back exhausted.

"Bother Ahana!" said Constancy spiritedly and poured some water in the basin and proceeded to wring out a towel. "As soon as I get you settled I shall go to our gate and shout at Joe to bring water and milk and anything else that's needed and leave them outside." Gently she laid the folded damp towel across Silly's head.

Silly motioned for her to bend down. "See if you can do anything for Leilehua," she whispered. "From the look of her, she can't last much longer. She's half in a stupor, and the eruptions have spread into her hair. I'm all right now."

Constancy nodded and made her way to where Leilehua lay supine, only her dark eyes moving from one object to another about the room. A dagger of pity twisted in Constancy's heart as she looked down at her: she remembered how satin-smooth Leilehua's olive skin had been, what untamed loveliness had been hers, and, remembering, she flinched at the revolting eruptions that were destroying the girl's flesh. Swiftly she prepared another damp cloth and laid it over the native girl's forehead.

"*Mii!*" Leilehua muttered.

On impulse Constancy bent lower, forcing back her repugnance to the rank smell of the disease. She spoke softly, so that Silly might not hear: "Your little girl, Leilehua . . . I love her as my own. There is no difference between her and my own granddaughter in my eyes. She is very pretty."

Again there was a faint "*Mii!*" Constancy turned away to tend the other six occupants of the room. Two of the women were showing definite signs of recovery. One other besides Leilehua was obviously marked for death. The rest were in the early stages of the disease, feverish and unable to resist digging at the itching sores, even while Constancy chided them. She went from one to another, giving water, repressing the nausea that attacked her when she was obliged to touch them; bathing them, she smothered as best she could the shock she felt at sight of the great eruptions dotting their breasts and abdomens. The filth of their garments sickened her. She had brought two old nightgowns with her, intending to use them as rags. These she brought forth from her satchel and substituted them for the dirty clothing of two of the women. At last she had done all that could be done for the time being. Silly seemed to be dozing. Constancy tiptoed from the room to inspect the third and last room. Smaller than the others, it was given over to the children.

Ahana, the constable delegated to serve as nurse, was patiently trying to quiet the whimpering of a three-year-old. He looked up in surprise and relief when Constancy entered. "It is hard for the small ones," he said gravely. "For all . . . but most of all for the children."

Constancy nodded somberly as her eyes swept the room where nine children ranging in age from three to twelve years lay. She wanted to find what they had in the way of food and how it was prepared. Ahana told her that the doctor brought arrow root, *poi,* sometimes bananas, sometimes a little fish, and there was tea. The only place to cook anything, even to boil water for tea, was an open fire in a small pit he had made in the yard. Fortunately, he said, most of the patients were too ill to eat.

In half an hour's time Constancy had pitchers of fresh milk, ripe mangoes, eggs, tomatoes from her garden, rice, oatmeal, sugar, dishes and cooking utensils, buckets of water, and as many nightgowns as Eliza had been able to lay hands on deposited at a discreet distance from the hospital, and Ahana went after them. Daily Joe was to bring food, and twice daily he was to bring water. For two hours she was busy feeding the patients who were not too sick

to disregard food. She found some of those who were con-
valescing ravenous; even the very ill were grateful for
milk and fresh fruit. After the meal was over, realizing
that her assistant was falling asleep on his feet, Constancy
sent him out on the *lanai* to get some rest. He told her he
had not had more than an hour's uninterrupted sleep in
three days. Leaving him to his slumbers, she went once
more into the men's room to find that one of them was
very evidently dying.

In a moment of lucidity he looked into Constancy's face
and implored her to "talk to God" for him. Resignedly,
stoically, she sank stiffly to her knees and did what she
thought her financial independence of the mission had
freed her from doing forever more—performed the farce
of addressing a discredited God. She was to address Him
again and again in the days that followed, in fervent eagerness to help in whatever way she could the doomed creatures about her. This first man to make the request of her
scarcely waited for her to finish her plea in his behalf before relinquishing his tenuous hold upon life. Constancy
covered his face, biting her lips to keep from crying wildly,
cursing her softness in being so vulnerable, so weak, in this
position that demanded more control than she felt she
had, in this place that bred death with regularity and frequency.

She went into the women's room. Looking down upon
the rigid figure of Leilehua, she was grateful to her for
sparing her the actual death moment. Twice within five
minutes Constancy covered a dead face. There was nothing to do with the bodies until the Black Maria called late
in the afternoon.

Silly dozed restlessly, turning and twisting in her sleep
and moaning. When she was awake she forced herself to
lie still without complaint. Awake, her eyes followed her

mother about the room. "You're twice as useful as I was," she said. "With all the will in the world I am not a good nurse." With a sudden alteration in tone she said despairingly, "I'm not good for anything in the world!"

Constancy was astonished. "You're so ill, Silly. . . . It may seem that way to you now, but you *must* know better when you haven't a fever," she said earnestly, but she felt shy at so downright a statement from Silly. She was relieved when a fretful crying from the children's room made it necessary to leave Silly. Not as sick as the adult patients, the children naturally complained more, whined, cried, were generally fretful, and demanded more constant attention. Constancy was on her feet without pause until the night was well advanced. The Black Maria brought three new patients to take the place of the two who had died.

Constancy slept fitfully that night, on a thin hard mattress placed near Silly's. She started up from sleep each time anyone in the room turned over. The next day the eruption was more profuse on Silly's face and arms and chest. The doctor said it was bound to be, that it would continue to spread for the next week. Constancy worked day and night. By the third day she no longer felt hysterical when death descended upon one of her patients; she prayed automatically beside the bed of any of the religious, did what she could to allay the sufferings of all, and avoided thinking as much as possible. This last she was not able to do when she ministered to Silly, who became delirious after the third day and babbled a jumble of the Bible, Shakespeare, and personal distress.

When ten days had passed, Constancy had the sense that she was caught in eternity, that she was in a bitterer hell than any the brethren had ever devised, a hell where deadly fatigue, the awareness of suffering in others, filth, and nauseating odors were the only realities. Looking upon her daughter, she realized that when the too bright gray-green eyes were closed Silly was unrecognizable; even the line of her features was changed, distorted, rendered grotesque. Outwardly an efficient automaton, Constancy ministered to her; inwardly pain had numbed her till anguish was merely a heaviness weighting down her heart and sitting stonily in the pit of her stomach. The direct hurt could not reach her. Her composure could survive even when assailed by the spectacle of a distraught Silly bringing herself upright in bed to wring swollen, disfigured hands and moan, "I'm *afraid* to die . . . Mother! I thought I wanted to . . . but I'm not fit! There's a wall that shuts out the face of God . . . and I'm afraid!" and burst into a storm of sobbing that sent her temperature soaring.

Her mother was without words to comfort her. She learned to kneel quietly beside the mats where Silly lay and let Silly clutch her hands until the paroxysm should subside. A voice in her brain implored repetitiously, "Let her die . . . let her die quickly! She has suffered enough to gratify even you," and she failed to recognize the fact that she was addressing as a reality once more the vengeful, crafty God she had once tried to bargain with for her first child's life. But Silly lay and babbled of walls that shut away the face of God for two more days.

The thirteenth day after Constancy's arrival at the hospital, the doctor found her awaiting him on the *lanai*, her arms folded, her face expressionless. "She isn't going to be taken away in the Black Maria," she said stonily. "Joe is digging a grave for her under the banyan tree."

Compassion came to life in the doctor's eyes, but he hesitated. "You know, Mrs. Williams, it isn't possible to hold a funeral at this time. . . . The Health Commission has ordered that all . . . bodies be disposed of in this fashion."

Constancy regarded him steadily, unmoved. "There will be no funeral. The grave is deep. Ahana and I will carry her to it after dark. Quicklime in the grave and the earth deep over her, and the Health Commission has nothing to fear."

The doctor bowed slightly in acquiescence. "And you . . ." he said reluctantly, "if you disinfect yourself thoroughly, it is safe for you to leave now, you know."

Constancy shook her head. "There is no one else to help Ahana. I shall stay as long as there is need of me here."

Silly died on the 18th of July. On the evening of the twenty-first of September the last patient was released. Constancy watched Ahana set fire to the schoolhouse, and while its flames crackled and soared, she walked away to the beach, where she was to find a basket of fresh clothes, left there by Eliza. She discovered the basket. Stripping off her clothes, she plunged into the ocean. When she came out of the water, she approached the basket, took out the clothes and towel she found, laid them on the sand, and took the basket over to where the infected clothing lay. She shut the discarded garments away in the basket and again bathed in the ocean. When she came out and had dried herself, she put on the clean clothes. Picking up the covered basket, she walked back to the schoolhouse, now half demolished, and with the smoke rolling toward her and nearly stifling her, she approached near enough to hurl the basket and its polluted clothing into the flames. She was ready to go home; it was ten weeks since she had entered her house.

At sight of her Jonathan sprang to his feet with a cry.

She felt his arms about her, his lips against her wet hair
and against her cheek, and his tears on her face, and knew
an impersonal sorrow for him. She put up her hand and
touched his tear-wet cheek, vaguely surprised at the prox-
imity to herself of a sorrow that could find so simple an
expression.

"I'll take care of you now, son," she heard herself saying
to him in the tone she used with the babies. "Don't cry."

A little later, when she went up to her room, she set the
lamp down on the dresser and went to look at the two
babies. Deborah slept on beneath her gaze, but as she looked
down at Elspeth, the baby opened wide dark eyes that for
an instant flickered with disbelief in what she saw. Then
she sat up with a lusty shout of "Gramma! Gramma!" and
jumped up to clutch at Constancy's dress. Constancy lifted
her out of the cradle and sat down in the rocking chair
with her. She remembered that Elspeth's mother had died;
that Elspeth should be motherless, even though she did not
know it and need not, seemed suddenly tragic. Her clasp
on the child tightened. Elspeth clutched her about the neck
and kissed her with grave, unchildlike fervor before
snuggling herself in Constancy's arms. Constancy, holding
her foster grandchild in her arms and rocking slowly and
rhythmically, felt the numbness of the last weeks leaving
her spirit and was in some measure comforted.

A few days later, however, Constancy's sorrow and her
perception were given fresh sharpness when, in going
through Silly's possessions with a view to disposing of
whatever had belonged to Silly, she found a small copy-
book, its pages covered with Silly's small prim handwrit-
ing. The missionary children had all been encouraged to
set down their thoughts in similar blank books, which, at
regular intervals, their parents inspected—a course which

moved most of the children to stop keeping journals (unless they kept them secretly) by the time they reached adolescence.

Now Constancy turned through the pages of this journal of Silly's and saw that it began with a date two years old:

"It is my earthly attachments which have power to disturb the peace I value above all else—the fact that those who lack most the grace of God have most of my affection. There is Faith, who has jeopardized her soul by turning her back on duty; and there is Mother who, though she has none of the weakness of Faith and is tireless in the performance of her duty, is motivated, I think, not so much by submission to the will of God as by love of mortal man. Despite the years of her service to the mission, I can never feel sure that she is a deeply religious woman; yet, where I have reverenced my father, humanly speaking, I love my mother more, though I think she believes me to be the least affectionate of her children."

Constancy laid her head on her arms and wept, her heart pierced with remorse, her brain devising savage self-reproach for her blindness. When she was able to resume her reading, she found set forth in the prim, childish hand:

The Body, vile with Eden's primal Sin,
The Brain, Coadjutant of the lewd Snake,
Do well to fear Thee, Lord! (Being no kin
To Thy Stern Majesty) Do well to quake
Before th' abundant symbols of Thy Might:
The surging flood of Thy Benignity
Bestowed upon Thy chosen, and the blight
Lain on the sinner lost in heresy.

But the Soul—infinitesimal part
Of Thee in Me—may dare to love *the Whole—*
Not fear, *as must the alien mortal heart,*
Each jot in excess of th' expected dole.
Thus, though Thy floods submerge me, I implore
Hardily, "Lord, try Thou my soul with More!"

Amazed at her discovery, Constancy hurriedly searched
the pages of the little book. So Silly, who exercised so stern
a control over her emotions in her contact with people,
had poured forth the feeling that could not be dammed
up within her or expressed through her fingers at the piano
in these verses. A dozen pages beyond the first poem was
a second. She read:

Nowhere my eyes or heart may turn
But Thou hast gone before,
Ordering Chaos with Thy Smile,
Thyself the Blinding Door
Through which my soul is free to go
Communicant with Thee;
Thy Radiant, Awful Infinite
Invading finite me.

She stared at the page before her and for the first time
realized something of what faith was to Silly. God was no
stern taskmaster to her youngest child, but radiance,
beauty—something of what she herself found in poetry or
in human love. She turned the pages again. Several months
had gone by with no entry, and then, during the time of
Dick Macaulay's stay, came the entry:

"This new feeling that I have fills me as the perfect
contemplation of God has done before; but it thrusts

from me the will to meditate upon God, and I distrust it while I cling to it, and I believe its very sweetness to be perilous to me."

The next entry was brief:

"I have put him away from me, and doing so is near killing me, which would be disastrous, for I am in no fit state to die."

Only one more page was written:

Lost in this jungle sinister and fanciful,
Where I perceive the tiger lithe and evil,
Potent to slay the soul for all Eternity
That knows him beast and finds him beautiful—
O little bird, charmed by the serpent's eye,
Thou'rt not so doomed as the affrighted soul of me!

The writing wavered and blurred before Constancy's eyes. She sat motionless, unaware of the tears that fell upon her sleeve, pressing the little notebook against her breast so hard that she was dimly conscious of pain, saying over and over, "Poor child! Poor frightened child . . . and I was no help at all." And she sat recriminating herself with a bitterness she had always spared others: "I've been blind, blinder than anyone in the world. I have been a little useful to Jonathan . . . perhaps, and because it pleased me so much to be helpful to him; but I have never been able to lighten a single burden for my children . . . and Silly I didn't even love enough, or try hard enough to understand."

She sat hating herself, devoid of the will to pull herself from the slough of morbidity in which her remorse was submerging her. "There is nothing left for me," she told herself. "Nothing at all. I am of no use to anyone in the world!" But, as the thoughts took form in her brain, she was aroused by Deborah's high little voice at the door: "Gramma! I want my Gramma!" Constancy automatically dabbed at her eyes with her handkerchief and smoothed her hair, snatching back the composure that would enable her to present a familiar countenance to her grandchild.

Going downstairs with the children, she came upon an agitated Jonathan pacing up and down the hall.

"Mother!" he burst forth. "I do think the king is possessed by the devil! You never heard of baser ingratitude!" He ran his long brown fingers through the hair that was now as white as his mother's. "The very man who is responsible for his having a kingdom at all. It would have been twice lost to the French and once to the British but for his labors!"

The perplexity lifted from his mother's face. "Oh . . . Dr. Judd," she said, relieved by comprehension. "Why, what's the king done now?"

"It's unheard of, but some of the trouble makers, while Dr. Judd was too busy about the smallpox epidemic to be much at the palace, poisoned the king's mind—even made him believe that Dr. Judd was responsible in some way for the spread of the disease! And he listened to them and has removed the doctor from office."

"Oh!" There was regret in Constancy's voice. "Poor man—it is a sorry return for his lifetime of devotion! It must be a bitter blow to his pride, too. He was never one to brook much opposition—or criticism. However, he can return to his practice of medicine."

"You don't understand!" Jonathan spoke impatiently and stalked three steps down the hall to whirl on his heel and face his mother again. "It's the principle of the thing! How can you be so calm about it? Here he's given twenty-five years out of his life to serving the king. Wasn't he the first missionary to renounce his American citizenship and swear allegiance to the king, and didn't he do it purely that he might serve the Hawaiian nation more effectively that way? And hasn't it been because of his shrewd diplomacy that the islands haven't fallen into the hands of other nations who realize more and more that these islands are important?"

"Yes, dear," patiently. "Don't get so excited. I'm not criticizing Dr. Judd. I have always admired him, for I don't care too much for meekness in a man. All I mean is that he has done as he did because he wanted to. I think he is a born diplomat—born to wield a . . . temporal power. I don't think for one minute that he would have gotten the satisfaction from his life that he *has* gotten, if he had stayed a simple medical missionary. He is a man who has thoroughly enjoyed being dictator to a king—and he does dislike opposition, my dear. Just why do you suppose he exerted his influence to keep Hiram Bingham from returning here after his poor wife died?"

"If it was because of his influence," responded Jonathan doggedly, "it was for the best. From all I have heard, Mr. Bingham was not . . . a progressive man, although he was an exceedingly pious man."

"Also an exceedingly forceful man, Jonathan. His word was law. You see, he and Dr. Judd are a bit too much alike in temperament and a bit too different in outlook to live comfortably side by side in as small a community as this. But, dear, at any event, I am sorry for Dr. Judd—and for the king. The king is an amiable man—but not an extremely intelligent one. If ever anyone needed powerful, sane advisers, he does. You know he is easily swayed—why, he may be asking Dr. Judd to come back before long." Privately she doubted it. She knew something of the monarch's fondness for liquor and gaming, and she knew more of Dr. Judd's violent disapproval of both. Since the king had now got out from under the powerful thumb of his Minister of Finance, it seemed improbable that he would care to place himself under it again.

Jonathan nodded, a little relieved. "There's something in that. I feel a little better about it since talking with you."

Constancy smiled a little pensively. She had heard those words from the other Jonathan on so many occasions. Apparently she was of some use to the Jonathans of the world. Aloud she said, "You are more like your father as you grow older, son," and observed the look of pleasure on his face.

Her hand felt the hardness of Silly's journal, which she had slipped into her pocket. Sammie, Miriam . . . Jonathan . . . Silly—beloved dead, a shadowy company to sleep in the attic of her mind, lulled by the incessant demands of the living upon her time, but given to clamoring at her spirit in the quiet of the night when the living slept.

She dropped into a chair and took Deborah on her knee, thinking, "How many more that I love must I see die?" She fancied herself living on, on—to senility, while the young, who should live, went down one by one in death.

15

Frequently now Constancy could have believed that she had the elder Jonathan with her again. Her son turned himself to his work with a feverish zeal. Feeling turned him hollow-eyed when the Hawaiian Evangelical Association announced decisively that there was at present no money to rebuild the school at Waikiki—especially in light of the fact that plague had killed a dozen of the fifty pupils, while the removal of several families to the country had taken a dozen more from the roll. It was more important, the association gravely pointed out, to concentrate their resources on the schools in the more populous districts. Jonathan came home and paced the floor, denouncing the heartlessness of those in authority; then, appalled at his own vehement temerity, turned to praying for meekness and humility in the face of adversity.

Repressing a sigh, Constancy offered her house to be used as a school and agreed to teach regularly again. So, from eight-thirty till twelve and from one until three daily, her large hall and her dining room were transformed into schoolrooms.

In his resentment of the king's treatment of Dr. Judd, Jonathan sought an audience with the incorrigible Kamehameha III and reproved him for his conduct and was thereafter forbidden the palace. Report had it that the king was drinking more than the human frame could be expected to endure and that the palace was the scene of unseemly revels. Jonathan agonized over the situation, and always his mother must serve as comforter. He went on periodical tours of the outlying districts of the island, preaching among and questioning the natives, coercing some of them into seeking salvation, but antagonizing more, grieving at the hardness of hearts which had for more than thirty years been unsuccessfully exposed to redemption, hopeless before the evidence that sprang up on every hand to prove that the Hawaiian race was diminishing: the frequency of death in childbirth of the women, the frequency of death among the new-born, the early death of most of the people. He deplored the number of deaths from abortion, but was horrified when his mother mildly suggested that the rigorous laws against fornication might be responsible. Constancy's hands were full. As in other years, she found that she was able to lock her personal sorrows in the background of her mind.

In December of 1854 Jonathan came home from town, his face alight. The king had sent for Dr. Judd to ask forgiveness for dismissing him so shabbily. "He has made his peace with the doctor!" Jonathan said radiantly. "And with God."

Constancy regarded her son's face thoughtfully. "Is the king sick, by any chance?" she asked, remembering how in other days he had been wont to grow exceedingly pious when ill health fell upon him.

Jonathan nodded. "Poor man, he is near death. And he admits that his debauchery is responsible, but his soul is serene." Again the radiance lay on his thin, prematurely lined face.

A new thought occurred to Constancy. "Jonathan," she said, leaning forward, "was it that you couldn't bear the thought of the king's being damned that disturbed you so?"

A shadow fell upon his face, and he pressed his hands against his temples; his voice was full of anguish: "The king . . . and *all* these benighted souls! Mother! The thought of hell is burned into my brain—into my soul! I feel that I must perish if I do not make a personal effort to save every sinner in the world! Have you ever thought how it would be to be safe with God yourself . . . and yet know that there are poor wretches bearing this unfathomable torture?"

"Many times;" irony, unperceived by Jonathan, curled slightly the left corner of Constancy's mouth; "but I had

supposed that you conceived of a state in which your soul
would be so in harmony with God that you . . . would
not be troubled by pity for those who had in God's eyes
merited damnation."

Jonathan flung himself on the floor beside her and buried
his head in her lap. "I can't reconcile myself to it," he muttered. "It keeps me awake nights! I lie and shake with horror—with nausea, Mother—to think of the countless souls
in torment . . . and I wish"—his voice sank to a whisper,
and he raised his head to look Constancy in the eye—"I
can't help wishing that I had continued *blind* . . . as I
was in my careless days of happiness, before Mary's death
made me see the light!"

Constancy cradled his head in her arms. "My poor
child," she said and rocked back and forth, straining his
head against her breast. "My poor child!"

She was relieved when he gave way to irritation. She felt
that it broke the terrific tension of his nerves when he
stormed at the waste of the period between the king's
death in the middle of December and his burial in the middle of January. It was a period when every retainer was
summoned from near and far and two thousand of them
maintained at the expense of the court—housed and fed
and provided with suitable mourning garments. Jonathan
was livid with disapproval when the funeral was finally
held. The late king's coffin, bedecked with crimson velvet
and armorial paintings and resting on the embroidered
cloak of Kamehameha the Great, was drawn on the cano-
pied funeral car by an excessive number of Hawaiians and
surrounded by *kahili* bearers. Jonathan, in company with
others of the clergy and a number of physicians, marched
behind the advance guard of Hawaiian cavalry gaudy in

blue-and-scarlet uniforms and glad to leave the accouter-
ments of mourning to their mounts that stepped nervously
beneath their sweeping black draperies.

Jonathan's mother, sharing a carriage with two other
missionaries who had once taught the late king, was appor-
tioned a place at the rear of the fire companies. Constancy
was fully aware of Jonathan's feelings about the ostenta-
tiousness of the display; she wondered half humorously
what he would have done about the procession which had
celebrated the anniversary of Kamehameha II's accession to
the throne. Remembering Kaahumanu being borne triumphantly through the streets in a whaleboat, and Pauahi
frenziedly plucking off her clothes and burning them in
the street, Constancy felt the present procession to be a
conservative affair—if the infantry, in uniforms as colorful as those the cavalry wore, and the Hawaiian chapters
of Masons and Odd Fellows, in full regalia, did look more
like the adjuncts of a circus than the augmenters of a
funeral cortège. The muted wailing that arose from the
throngs lining the streets, too, reminded her that times had
changed. Could these restrainedly mourning people be kin
to the wild men and women who, at Likelike's death, back
in the '20's, had pulled their hair out by the roots, shaved
the sides of their heads, knocked their teeth out, and
burned their faces with live coals so that they would bear
scars to their graves? She decided, as the procession left
the palace grounds, that it would be well for her to describe a few of those earlier scenes for Jonathan's benefit.

"I must be made of pretty durable material," she
thought, her eye on the gayly waving plumes that decorated each cannon carriage of the artillery. "I've survived
two kings and half a dozen lesser dignitaries younger than
I. Alexander Liholiho isn't quite twenty-one yet, though,
so he ought to survive me. Queer how low the birthrate is

among the members of royalty here—how seldom there is a direct heir. If they don't look out there won't be any more Kamehamehas left. If anything happened to this one, about the only possibility would be his brother, Lot."

Her carriage jolted on over the rough street on its circuitous route to the royal tomb. She wondered if the missionaries would exert as much influence over this determined young king as they had over his uncle, who, however frequently he might lapse from grace, was pretty consistently under their thumb when it came to deciding affairs of state.

She was to remember her thoughts on the subject when, in the days that followed, the young king efficiently plucked all representatives of the missionary element from his cabinet. It was the first cabinet that had not been dominated by the mission. The missionaries were aghast; they were hurt; they shook their heads, remembering how the new king had received his early education from Mrs. Cooke and how he and his brother Lot had been escorted by Dr. Judd to the capitals of Europe and to Washington, where they had picked up ideas of court life totally at variance with any entertained by the older Kamehamehas.

Formality entered Hawaiian court circles. There was much distress in the breasts of the missionaries, and here and there a little amusement when someone was moved in the face of pomp and ceremony to recall the audiences with royalty in the '20's—the queen sprawled on a mat and clad in a man's shirt and a piece of *tapa* (if that), picking fleas off her pet pig, and the king in a *malo,* squatting on the floor playing poker with his attendants and tippling rum from a bottle.

When the young king married the granddaughter of that John Young who had been adviser to Kamehameha I and friend to the early missionaries, there was another

shock in store for the missionaries. John Young's granddaughter, in whose veins ran Kamehameha blood, had been
adopted in infancy by Dr. Rooke, an Englishman, and,
while her education had begun under the Cookes, it was
finished by an English governess in the Rooke home. Emma
Rooke, then, had a profound veneration for the English
and for the Church of England. Thus, although the young
king and queen were married in Kawaiahao church, they
demanded that the form of service be that of the Church
of England.

The king shared his wife's interest in the English and
their way of life. It was rumored that the seeds of his
prejudice against America began on the trip he had made
under the chaperonage of Dr. Judd, when in Washington
a train official mistook the dark young princes for Negroes
and had to be shown their credentials before he would allow them to ride in the white section of the train.

When the hoped-for heir to the throne was born in
1856, plans were at once made for establishing an English
church in Hawaii. The little prince of Hawaii was to be
christened in the new church, but, frail with the blight
that seemed to have fallen upon the Kamehameha line, the
child sickened and died of brain fever a few weeks before
the Right Reverend T. N. Staley and his party could arrive. Again the pastor of Kawaiahao was obliged to swallow his scruples, this time to baptize the dying prince,
using the ritual provided in the Church of England prayer
book. The first Episcopal church, known as the Hawaiian
Reformed Catholic Church, was established shortly after
the bishop's arrival in 1862. The original missionaries reluctantly admitted that their power at court was definitely
a thing of the past. The new church was Protestant; theo-
retically the relations between the two elements were amia-

ble. The missionaries buttoned up their mouths and turned with renewed vigor to the salvation of the populace.

In 1857 the missionaries welcomed the arrival of their own ship; it was called the *Morning Star* and was under the command of the second Hiram Bingham, a man as sternly religious as ever his father had been. The spiritual night which enveloped the islanders of the farther Pacific weighed on the souls of the Hawaiian missionaries. In 1853 they had sent two Hawaiian converts to the Marquesas Islands to found a station. Now, with the *Morning Star* in their possession, they planned a company to carry tidings of salvation with its alternative of damnation to the Gilbert Islanders. In August the ship set sail.

Constancy stood motionless, Deborah clinging to one of her hands and Elspeth to the other, peering after the ship as long as she could identify Jonathan. The eight-year-old little girls stood quietly beside their grandmother, demure small figures in skirts that hung to their ankles and bonnets that tied under their chins. They looked at their toes peeping out from beneath their dresses; they looked out to sea; they took quick upward glances at their grandmother's grim face. Once she muttered "Tommyrot!" with such violence that they both jumped; but the next moment she murmured feelingly, "Poor child!" It occurred to neither of the children that she referred first to the faith which her son was carrying to the benighted heathen and second to the awe-inspiring man who had just left them. Deborah was more afraid of him than was Elspeth. Deborah had to call him Father while Elspeth escaped with calling him Uncle Jonathan. They both had been obliged to go through hours of instruction with him, hours that left them stiff with fright. They had had to know the catechism by heart before they were six.

Elspeth peered around Constancy's skirts at Deborah, her face suddenly alight. Her red lips cautiously shaped the words, "We won't have to talk about God any more." Deborah looked doubtful and cast an upward look at her grandmother. Elspeth shook her head decidedly. "She won't make us," she mouthed again confidently. Deborah smiled and was moved to put both arms around her grandmother's waist and squeeze hard. Constancy looked down, and the grim look softened. "We'll go now," she said.

She climbed into the light one-seater with the little girls beside her and shook the reins over the back of Nellie, the black mare she had bought when old Lucy died. She drove toward the business section of town, her mouth assuming forbidding lines again. She pulled Nellie up in front of the building where Peter had his law office. "You stay here and mind Nellie," she said to the children, who were preparing to clamber down. "I shan't be long."

She mounted the dingy stairway and entered the door with "Peter Williams, Attorney-at-law," on it in big black-and-gold letters. Peter was mauling through papers on his desk. He rose to his feet as she entered and grinned wickedly as he saw the expression on her face. He went around to her and kissed her cheek.

"I'm an unnatural brother, and you're ashamed of me!" he said, holding her at arm's length. "Isn't that what you came to say?"

Constancy's straight brows drew toward each other. "Exactly!" she said, unsmiling. "Have you anything at all to say for yourself?" She looked him indignantly in the eye. "No telling whether we'll ever see him again—going off to that outlandish place!" Her voice trembled, and she jerked away from him and went to look out of the window.

"You were so fond of each other as little boys," she said protestingly. "You cried as if your heart would break when he sailed away to go to school . . . why, you said you loved him better than anyone in the world! Doesn't that feeling you had for him mean *anything* to you?"

Peter came and stood beside her. "I know. . . . I remember how awful I felt . . . seeing his boat move off that day. But, Mother! We were children then! We've both changed too much to be friends now. He thinks I'm a renegade and that there's no good in me because I can't see anything in all this religious business. I can't be with him five minutes without wanting to wring his neck. Now you're good . . . and all that . . . but you don't ram your piety down a fellow's throat. You disapprove of me, but you're fond of me anyway—or am I mistaken?" He slid his hand under her chin and forced her to look at him. She compressed her lips into a narrow line for an instant and shook her head impatiently. "I'm sure I don't see why I should be," she said severely, "but I suppose I am. I'm a silly old woman and don't know any better."

Laughing with an air of secret triumph, he pushed her into a chair. "I'm going to try your patience a bit further, Mother." He hesitated and looked in some embarrassment at the palms of his thin, smooth-skinned hands.

"What have you done now?"

"It's Tabitha. . . . I rather think you may find her when you get home—bag and baggage."

"Oh, Peter!" There was real distress in Constancy's voice. "What have you done to her?"

He flushed a little and then lifted his head to look his mother defiantly in the eye. "Well . . . you see, I brought home a child for her to bring up and she didn't like it."

"Whose child?"

"Well . . . as a matter of fact, mine."

"Peter!"

He avoided her eye. "She's a bright little thing—pretty as a picture, brown curls, big brown eyes, and dimples. She's as full of spirit as a kitten. There's no reason why Tabitha should make such a row. Good God, Mother! I don't mean anything to her any more! Why should she care?"

"You're hard, Peter," Constancy commented quietly. "You married Tabitha for your own purposes—and they weren't exactly noble. Remember she loved you—and you've never been kind to her. She isn't very clever, maybe, but she is clever enough to know when you've ridiculed her, and to know it when you take advantage of her in words. Just remember you owe your plantation to her. Without her money you'd be nowhere. By the way, who is the child's mother?"

Peter took his turn at strolling over to the window and contemplating the view. "Um . . . Hagar. She's going to marry a Chinese clerk in the bank." He laughed shortly, and Constancy thought curiously, "I believe his vanity is hurt by her marrying!" Peter went on, "They'll be having children of their own, and most men aren't enthusiastic about bringing up some other man's brat. Anyway . . . the child's my own flesh and blood, and I'm fonder of her than I am of either of my other two. Marcia and John are *mousy!* I tell you, Mother, I like a child with some spirit."

Constancy rose to her feet. She felt suddenly very tired and very old. "What am I expected to do about her?" she asked wearily.

Peter chuckled irrepressibly. "Tell her it's her Christian duty to bear with me and that she'll rate an extra polish on her halo by and by for being a martyr on earth."

Constancy drew away from him. She felt a sudden aversion for his arrogant good looks. "If Tabitha feels that she can't go back to you, I certainly shan't try to persuade her. Personally I think she's put up with enough from you. Of course she can stay with me, if nothing else offers! A runaway wife and two children more or less don't matter. I have only six children living with me now, and twenty coming to be taught every day. Good-bye!"

She shot him a scornful glance and hurried downstairs. Her displeasure with Peter went deeper than the surface this time. She felt that he was calloused, wilfully cruel. She drove home in complete silence. The two little girls sat tongue-tied beside her, stealing frightened glances into her set face. They were unaccustomed to this forbidding-looking grandmother.

As they drove into the yard, they saw two extra children playing with the members of the household. "Oh! Somebody's come to see us!" chanted Deborah delightedly, and then her tone changed. "Oh . . . it's only Marcia and John!"

Constancy turned on her heatedly: "Don't talk that way about your little cousins! They're good children, and you're unkind to speak that way of them!"

Deborah's blue eyes grew round and filled with tears, but Constancy paid no attention. She got down from the buggy and hurried up the steps toward Tabitha, who came forward, fat and disheveled, her face swollen with crying. She promptly burst into a paroxysm of sobs on Constancy's shoulder.

"There, there!" soothed Constancy kindly enough, although she was frowning at the display before the children. "Come into the house, my dear." And she led her into the little room that had been Jonathan's study.

Hunched lumpily on a settee, Constancy beside her, Tabitha produced a squall of unlovely snorts and sniffles and hiccoughing sobs. Constancy, her face expressionless as it was prone to be when she was experiencing violent distaste for anything, argued with herself: "The poor thing's grief is real enough, and goodness knows, if she cares for Peter her plight is hopeless enough! But she's so impossibly ugly like this. Nobody but a beautiful woman should give way to emotion like this before anyone!"

Finally, as the tears flowed on and on, Constancy was moved to remonstrate. "Come, come, Tabitha!" she said briskly. "You must try to control yourself. I've seen Peter and know what is troubling you. Do you feel that you can't forgive Peter—that you can never bring yourself to return to him?"

Tabitha sat up, her eyes red and bleary, and dabbed at her nose and eyes with a sodden handkerchief. "I don't know! I don't know!" she wailed. "Peter doesn't love me; he doesn't care about me a bit! I knew he didn't feel about me the way I did about him when we were married. He doesn't know it, but I guess I'm smart enough to know he'd never have looked at me even the first time if I hadn't had money."

Constancy's eyelids flickered slightly. She hadn't credited Tabitha with even so much insight. "But, my dear, didn't you realize that you were taking a great risk in marrying a man you suspected was just interested in your money?"

Tabitha wagged her head back and forth disconsolately. "Of course I knew, but I tell you, nobody's *ever* wanted to marry me, not for *any* reason . . . except a perfectly awful farmer back home, and I was so fond of Peter that I knew I'd be miserable if I didn't marry him." She sat staring dully ahead of her, twisting her hands. "I thought if I gave him all my money and did everything he wanted me to do . . . he'd get fond of me after a while . . . but

I was wrong. I guess if they don't love you to begin with, there's not much chance of their getting to later."

Her mother-in-law could stand the sight of the twisting hands no longer. She leaned forward and took them in a firm grasp and held them still. She was choked by the force of her pity for the dowdy woman beside her. She felt that there was no word in all the language which would be of the least use; she sat speechless. After a moment Tabitha went on colorlessly:

"I guess a woman as homely as me hasn't got any right being jealous, but it nearly killed me when I saw Peter smiling around that brown Hagar! And then he'd come in and look at me as if it hurt him to see me—just because I'm fat and my hair won't stay put. I'd try and try to think of something I could say that would interest him— but the harder I'd think, the dumber I'd get and couldn't say a word. I thought the children would make things different, but"—and she raised hopeless eyes to Constancy's face—"that wasn't any good, either, because the poor things look like me. You've no idea how sorry I feel for them."

Something in Constancy rebelled at the abjectness of the woman. "Don't talk that way!" she commanded her with some acerbity. "You've got to have some *pride*, Tabitha! Whatever the Bible says about pride, a woman's just got to have it to stand things."

Tabitha's pale eyes watered at the tone more than at the words. Constancy stroked the pudgy hand impulsively. "I'm sorrier for you than I can say, my dear, and I'll help you in any way that I can. Peter may not love you as he should, but I know that he would prefer you to return to his house with the children." She paused and looked narrowly at Tabitha. "I know also, however, that he has every intention of keeping this child with him. If you go back to Peter you'll have to make up your mind to bear with it."

Tabitha was shaking her head stubbornly. "I can't do it —I just can't," she said tonelessly. Suddenly she raised her head and glared wildly into Constancy's eyes. *"You* try and think what it would mean to you to have children of your own that their father never notices if he can help— unless to tell them to stop doing something—and then see him with a child he's had by some other woman, and see him play with it and pet it and make a fuss over it! I tell you, when I'm away from it, I know well enough the poor child shouldn't be blamed, but when I see her around and know she's prettier and smarter than my lawful children . . . I . . . I want to *kill* her!" She ended on an hysterical note, and collapsed in tears once more.

Constancy put her arm around the hunched and shaking shoulders. She sat quietly for a moment, biting her lip and frowning thoughtfully. "Would you like to . . . take your children and go home to your mother, Tabitha?" she asked hesitantly.

She was answered by a shake of Tabitha's head, and Tabitha's voice, almost strangled with her emotion, quavered, "I just *can't* go home. They all said Peter was marrying me for my money . . . and laughed at me. People are unkind! They'd laugh some more if they knew I'd had to give up and go home to my mother. . . . I just can't face them."

Constancy braced herself before speaking: "You have no need to decide anything now, my dear." She swallowed and went on bravely: "I have a large house, and you are welcome to stay with me for so long as you like, you and the children. This has all been too much for you. . . . After you've had time to rest and think things out, you may want to do something else."

"You don't really want me, either," sniffed Tabitha, "but you're good and kind—and you're sorry for me. Nobody really likes me!"

Constancy stiffened in embarrassment and distaste for the awful humbleness of her daughter-in-law, but she spoke immediately: "Don't say things like that of yourself, Tabitha. It's bad for you, and it makes the person you say them to feel miserable and uncomfortable. I'm not asking you just in charity or pity, child. You could help me here a great deal if you cared to."

Tabitha's face expressed disbelief. Constancy went on quietly: "Do you realize, Tabitha, that I have been working in these islands for nearly forty years now? That I am getting on in years, and that I have the responsibility of six children here in this house—to say nothing of twenty to thirty that I try to teach? Once in a while the native pastor, who was Jonathan's assistant and will be alone here now, helps me out for a few hours, but he is too busy with his church work to be much help. You could help with the little ones. You know I have stopped teaching in Hawaiian in the last few years. Because of trade relations and the changes going on, the natives themselves prefer their children to learn English as early as possible. So . . . you see there would be no difficulty for you there, and you might enjoy working with them."

Tabitha clung convulsively to Constancy's hand. "You're awfully good to me, Mother Williams!"

"Not a bit of it!" The difficulty of making the offer over, Constancy could be brisk and smile. She could scarcely suspect that she was to have Tabitha with her for fifteen years.

WHEN THE *Mary Ellen* came to the islands in the fall of 1862, Matt was captain and half owner of the ship. Constancy, who for the last six years had steeled herself against the day when her uncle would not be hastening with h: first mate to her home from the ship, saw Matt's solitar approach and knew what tidings he brought.

She walked slowly across the *lanai* and held out her arms to her son. "He's dead, then," and there was no rising inflection of her voice.

Matt nodded, speechless for the lump in his throat, and stood with his arms around his mother, his head bent so that his cheek lay on the shining white hair. After a moment she withdrew from his embrace and went into the house. She sat stiffly erect, every feature set in sculptured composure, but slow tears rolling down her cheeks while Matt told her of the captain's death.

"It's the way he wanted to go, Mother," he cried, the lump still bothering his throat. "It wouldn't have been right for him to be sick and die in bed. It *was* right for him to die on his feet—his whole mind and heart on the gale and the orders he was shouting to the men. His heart just gave out all at once, and he was gone in a breath without knowing what happened to him, and he was buried there off the Cape with every man aboard looking as if he'd lost his best friend." He put forth a big hand and laid it over Constancy's two small brown ones clasped rigidly in her lap. "Don't be too concerned for him, Mother. Whatever's beyond . . . I'm sure Uncle Nate's due for the best. Why . . . he was the salt of the earth . . . for all he could make sparks fly when he got in a temper."

Constancy continued to stare straight ahead of her. "I'm not concerned for him." Her voice was so low that Matt had to bend his head toward her to catch the words. "I'm concerned for me. A part of me nobody else knows died with him. It's myself I'm crying for. I've had to wear a mask of one sort or another with everybody I've known in my whole life . . . except with Uncle Nate. To everybody else in the last forty years and more, I've been a missionary, a teacher, a mother . . . a dutiful wife . . . but to him I've always been a person. There was something between us that I've never known with another soul."

She stood up and walked quickly out of the room and up the stairs, leaving Matt shifting from one foot to the other, the awkwardness of his half-grown years back upon him. He was wishing miserably that he could do something —say something—to make his mother feel better. It seemed to him that every trip brought worse tidings to his mother. The last had brought word of his grandmother's death, but his mother had taken that better than she was taking this. He bit his lip at the thought of what he must tell her about Faith. That, in its way, was as hard as breaking the news of Uncle Nate's death. He couldn't remember ever feeling that his mother was really shocked at people's behavior, though; that was some comfort. As a boy, he had often fancied that he caught a gleam of amusement in her eye at something that had upset his father dreadfully . . . for instance, the time his father had left it to a native assistant to prepare the wine for communion, and the native had wanted the wine for private purposes and set out the vilest brand of rum in its stead. His father had taken a sip from his glass and choked, and there had been choking noises and sputtering from all over the church. He was sure that his mother thought that funny deep down inside her. Then, when his father had paced up and down and gotten so upset over some girl's having a baby by a sailor, his mother had never said anything to indicate that she thought it so dreadful. Maybe, though, she would feel different about her own daughter.

He went out on the *lanai* and lifted his sea chest to his shoulder and carried it into his room, thinking, "Mother's had a dog's life, really: always looking out for somebody else and working beyond her strength. There's Tabitha she's saddled with now for God knows how long, and those two shabby brats of hers, and Peter flourishing on ill-gotten gains and playing politics none too cleanly and taking in a new half-breed orphan every year or so that everybody knows is his own. He's a reckless devil, selfish as hell, but I can't help liking him. Anybody else'd be drawn and quartered who was as barefaced about his sins as Peter. Of course he's got money and influence on his side, but you can't expect people to shut their eyes entirely to four hybrid bastards . . . and he may have another one in his house by now. At least he takes them in and brings them up as his own—even if he does go through the monkey business of adopting them in court, I must say he's pretty frank about the thing."

His thoughts went back to Constancy: "She's had eight children and three of them died. I can still remember how she was when we were little. She hardly ever smiled, though she was always good to us. Sally said that was because she couldn't forget about Sammie. Miriam could remember how Mother was when Sammie was alive—how she'd play with them and laugh a lot, but she changed when he died. Then she changed again after we moved out here away from the rest of the brethren. She's gotten old since Father died, and then Mary, and then Silly, and Jonathan got so awfully holy and chased off to some wilder islands for the greater glory of God. It's tough on her being across the world from Sally and Faith. Faith . . . if Mother'd been really stiff-necked like the rest of this gang of missionaries, she'd have disowned Faith when she ran away years ago."

He stroked his chin reflectively, wondering futilely once more why Faith had ever married Luke Owens in the first place.

All day he was irked by Tabitha's presence. It was Saturday, so there was no school. The two elder children of the orphans Constancy had taken into her home after the epidemic of measles had grown up. Alohilani had married. Her little sister was living with her. One of the other younger girls had become housekeeper to Mr. Owens since his wife died of cancer. Only the youngest of the orphans was still with Constancy. Matt was Uncle Matt to this fourteen-year-old child, Kukana, as well as to Elspeth and Deborah. He was fond of the children, but he resented the lack of opportunity for private conversation with his mother with these three and Tabitha's two and Tabitha under foot all day.

It was nearly ten that night when Tabitha finally took herself off to bed, leaving Constancy and her son alone. She led him into the study that had belonged in turn to her husband and to her eldest son. It was a fair-sized room with bookshelves filling every bit of wall space not taken by windows or doors. Constancy set the lamp down on the desk and motioned Matt to one easy chair while she took another. He fumbled for his pipe and then hastily withdrew his hand from his pocket. Constancy smiled. "It's all right for you to smoke, Matt."

He looked relieved. "That's awfully decent of you, Mother. I reached for it without thinking. I hadn't known . . . thought maybe you didn't approve."

"Where's the harm? But now . . . really tell me about the children . . . Sally . . . Faith . . . and their children."

Matt chose to tackle the safer subject first. "Sally's pretty as a picture, Mother. You'd never dream she's nearer forty than thirty. Just as slim as she ever was—and she looks very grand always. Timothy's still proud as punch of her . . . but I wouldn't trust him too far with other women."

"No!" His mother remembered Leilehua. "Neither would I. But does Sally suspect him of philandering?"

Matt shrugged. "Blest if I know! Sally's grown up: she doesn't tell everything she knows by a long sight, nor anything she doesn't want to. I dropped in to call on Timothy at his studio one time, and the door was locked and there was a great tittering and giggling going on the other side of it. I got out as fast as possible. Timothy might not have been embarrassed at finding me there, but I'd have felt seven kinds of a fool to have been found there—sort of as if I'd been the guilty one instead of him." He sent a half-apologetic, half-amused look at his mother. "I guess if Sally knows about it, she figures she comes first and that it doesn't matter what he does on the side. She *looks* happy, and she's awfully proud of the two kids."

"Queer," Constancy spoke musingly. "It doesn't seem possible that Sally should be nearly thirty-seven years old. I can't realize her any way but as she was when she left here. But tell me about Faith and little Connie."

"What's happened to Luke Owens?" The question was

so abrupt that Constancy jumped. "He hasn't died by any chance, has he?"

Constancy darted a quick look at him. "No . . . he'll probably live till he's ninety. Why?"

"Oh," a little too casually, "I just wondered. It seems a pity that Faith can't marry again. You know she's a good-looking woman—the kind a man notices. It's not right for her to be in such a position—and goodness knows I never could blame her for leaving Luke."

"No more could I! But, Matt, I can feel you trying to approach something you find hard to tell me. For goodness' sake, stop beating around the bush and tell me outright what it's about! Are you trying to say that Faith is interested in some man and would like to marry if she were rid of Luke?"

Matt took out his handkerchief and mopped his brow before speaking. "How'd you figure that out?" he asked admiringly. "As a matter of fact, you've just about hit the nail on the head!"

Constancy gave a sardonic chuckle. "Well, when you inquire so solicitously for Luke's health, and then remind me that it seems a pity he isn't underground so Faith could marry again—since she's the kind of woman men notice —what else should I think?"

"Well . . ." He cleared his throat. "It isn't quite so simple as you have it. You see, this doctor from Sedley who looked after Grandmother got . . . interested in Faith. He was at the house a lot during Grandmother's last days—a likely enough young fellow. You see . . . everybody there thinks Faith is a real widow. . . . Grandmother figured there'd be less talk that way. So I guess Dr. Pritchard thought so, too, and that it was all right for him to be courting her." He stopped and shifted uneasily in his chair and seemed unable to get out another word.

"Yes, yes! Do go on, Matt!"

He gulped nervously. "When I went to see Faith this last trip, I had to stop in Sedley, and a fellow who knows me there pops up first thing with the news that Faith . . . has gone and *married* this doctor fellow." Again he paused and mopped his brow. "I tell you, Mother, I guess my jaw dropped a foot, and there stands this landlubber laughing at me as if it's all a joke, and tells me he supposed I'd be pleased, everybody liking the doctor. So I said, 'Oh, yes, of course,' and hurried out to the farm. And there's Faith as bright and beaming as you please—though she did blush when she saw me."

Constancy's eyes appeared to be starting from her head. She put up her hand to her throat. "But Matt! . . . Bigamy's a *prison* offense, isn't it?" she said in a hoarse whisper. "Oh! . . . If Luke Owens should find out and make trouble!"

Matt coughed before he answered: "She isn't a bigamist, Mother, but maybe you'll think it's worse the way it is. She isn't married to this doctor . . . though everyone thinks she is."

"Why . . . how? Why?" Constancy looked her bewilderment.

"They both sat up, cool as cucumbers, and told me how they loved each other, and how, since Luke was likely to live to be a hundred, they couldn't bother to wait around drumming their heels in hopes he would die. So what do they do but say they are going to be married. Then they set off one Friday for Boston and came back on the Sunday with a new wedding ring for Faith and set up together at the farm. It's near enough town so the doctor can carry on from there just as well as not, and not a soul in the country but thinks them properly married."

His mother sat in silence. Matt moved slightly in his

chair and crossed his long legs. "I'd swear, Mother," he said earnestly, "that their feelings for each other are as fine as those of any properly married pair. He's a good man, and Faith wasn't meant to live alone, I guess."

Constancy waved a hand in impatience. She spoke as if she had not heard him: "I'm glad it's that way and not so that she'd be liable to a charge of bigamy. But, Matt . . . if Luke Owens ever found it out! He's just the kind of well-meaning, pig-headed zealot that would go to any lengths to expose them. And then he'd persuade himself that he was acting for the good of their souls."

Matt relaxed, vastly relieved at his mother's reception of the news. "Oh, well," he said more easily, "I guess there isn't much chance of his ever dropping in on them. Why, he doesn't even know where Faith lives, does he?"

"No. But he might find out if he were to give his mind to it, you know." Suddenly an expression of alarm crossed her face. "Matt! He left here three months ago to offer his services to the Union army as a chaplain or nurse or anything they needed!"

"You don't say!" Matt looked alarmed, too, and then settled back in his chair again. "Oh, well, Mother, the fighting isn't anywhere near Connecticut. There isn't much chance of his getting up there. Anyway, maybe he'll get killed."

"Don't, Matt! You shouldn't wish that for anybody! After all, poor Luke can't help being the kind of person he is. He hasn't gotten much out of life. He did love Faith, you know."

"H'm. . . . The doctor said he was offering *his* services to the Union army. He's probably gone by now." Matt looked quizzically at his mother. "There's not much chance of their meeting, I suppose. Anyway, Luke wouldn't know him from Adam, but the doctor would know Luke by name."

Constancy pondered the matter for a moment; it seemed unlikely that the two should meet. Her thoughts progressed to her other son-in-law. "Timothy? He's not thinking of going to war, is he?"

"I don't think so—at least not seriously. He was all in a fever about going to Paris when I saw him, but he did say, come to think of it, that if the war wasn't over by the time he got back, he guessed he'd have to go and see what it was like."

Constancy sighed heavily. "There's so much trouble . . . everywhere, and in everybody's life. Why do they have to go having wars, too? Why can't people sit down quietly and talk things out instead of lining up a lot of men and have them shoot one another?" She rolled up her knitting and stood up. "I'm going to bed, son. You've given me a good deal to think of this trip." She smiled a little wanly and laid her hand on his shoulder. "How about you? I've been half expecting you to bring a wife home with you some trip."

Matt blushed and shuffled to his feet. "As a matter of fact," and he swallowed noisily, "I am thinking of getting married next trip back—and I'll sure enough bring her along, because she says she's going to sail right along with the ship wherever I go. You never saw anyone like her, Mother. She's little and trim—no bigger'n a child, and she kind of swims over the ground with her head up and looks you square in the eye like a man. There's none of your coy miss about her. Uncle Nate thought a lot of her."

Constancy dropped weakly into her chair again. "Have you got anything else up your sleeve?" she inquired with mild sarcasm and then patted his arm. "What's her name, Matt? And where does she live?"

"Her name's Elizabeth Hanson, but everybody calls her Betty, and her father's a sea captain and her family lives in Concord. She teaches school there, and there's not much she doesn't know, I can tell you!"

Constancy smiled at the pride in his voice. She rose to her feet and bent to kiss him. "She sounds fine, Matt. I'm glad for you. You ought to have a wife. Tell her I'll be glad to have another daughter. Now I really am going to bed this time."

He watched her as she mounted the stairs, thinking soberly: "She's a great woman . . . damned if she isn't!" Suddenly he grinned widely. "Lord!" he mused. "What a to-do the rest of the missionaries would make if they could have seen the way she took the business about Faith. Why," —for the first time the thought occurred to him—"to talk to her and be with her, nobody'd ever know she was a missionary!"

2

The Civil War in progress in America gave new impetus to the sugar industry. Peter Williams continued to prosper. His only worry, as far as his plantation was concerned, sprang from the uncertainty of the water supply. For several years he had entertained the desire to establish a conduit to bring water from the mountains, a project which would assure him of proper irrigation. The installation of the ditch would cost him in the neighborhood of $75,000. He could raise possibly $50,000 without crippling himself financially, but the further sum was beyond him—until his great-uncle died and divided his property equally between Constancy and his favorite nephew, Matt.

Immediately it occurred to Peter that his mother might be persuaded to come to his aid. It was a question of whether Constancy's prejudices against his venture, which she still regarded as a form of thievery, would outweigh her inclination to indulge her son. Too, while Constancy's income from the ship could be depended on to take care of her and her household, she might not feel inclined to risk the entire balance of her resources on what might seem to her an extravagant gesture.

For six weeks Peter rode out to the Waikiki house every two or three days, to the distress of Tabitha, who scurried out of sight, herding her children before her, at the first sound of her husband's approach. His proposition was to give his mother an interest in the plantation. He erred in using as an argument the assurance that her support of his scheme would add to her wealth. She did not need to profit at the expense of dispossessed natives, she told him dryly, her mouth curved downward in scorn. He suggested artfully that she could use the profit to counteract in some measure the wrong done her islanders; he airily mentioned a home for the aged, a school, an orphanage, and perceived that he was on the right track. He had caught her attention. After six weeks of his campaign, Constancy yielded.

The ditch was a year in construction. Within three years Constancy was receiving twenty per cent on her investment. She was firmly determined that no part of this profit should be spent on herself. She covered sheet after sheet of paper with figures, and then approached Peter with a terse demand for five thousand dollars. He teased her with the suggestion that she was extracting hush money from him. "Call it what you like," she said shortly. "I want the money." He produced it, and she bought two acres of land across the road from her home and began the building of the Jonathan Williams School, a substantial frame building with three schoolrooms and quarters for resident teachers. It was to be an English school for native children, supported entirely by herself.

Daily she went over to watch the workmen, an enigmatical expression on her face. The members of the Hawaiian Evangelical Association were awed by the magnitude of her gift. They called on her and inquired respectfully after the progress of the new school and were flattered if she took them to see it.

As the years went on, Constancy was at first astonished and then amused at the hint of deference in the manner of her mission associates toward herself. It still seemed to her that she must seem to the grave mission directors a young and not too trustworthy charge. She had frequent need of reminding herself that she had been in the field longer than any of the directors. A number of these men were of second-generation stock. She realized with something of a shock that to them she must appear venerable. Too, she was conscious that they were not wholly indifferent to the fact that she was a woman of means.

When she announced with quiet decisiveness that she no longer felt equal to teaching, the missionaries agreed that she had earned a rest from labor. She smothered a grin: the missionaries were relaxing. She suspected that Hiram Bingham I, were he there, would think she ought to labor till she toppled in her tracks. Sardonically she recognized the fact that her uncle's money in Peter's competent, ruthless hands had purchased her freedom for the remainder of her life. She explained smoothly that when the school was finished, her ward, Elspeth, would teach in it. Elspeth would be finishing the course at Punahou by summer. Deborah, she explained, was going to New England to finish her education and be with her mother's parents who were old now and longed to see their only grandchild. She did not see fit to add that Jonathan had written eloquent letters urging that Deborah be sent out to the Gilbert Islands to keep house for him and join her efforts with his to convert the natives, and that her desire was to put as much distance as possible between Deborah and the Gilbert Islands.

Even the new king rode out to see the school, accompanied by his sister, the Princess Victoria Kamamalu, her purple satin skirts just clearing the ground at her horse's sides. He talked with Constancy so courteously, so amiably, that she wondered at the missionaries who regarded him as a formidable monarch. Kamehameha V had thrown the foreign element into consternation when, upon his accession to the throne after his younger brother's short reign, he had boldly refused to support the constitution devised by his uncle in 1852 and devised a new one investing the king with a more nearly absolute power.

Answering his questions about the school, Constancy reflected that he had the stamp of missionary training without the limitations usually imposed by it. She saw integrity in him and was sensible of his austerely passionate love for his people. He was making a valiant stand for a dying race. His education allowed him to understand the strength of the foreign power in his kingdom and to identify the menace it held for his people; also it allowed him to recognize the limitations of his own people, to appreciate the unfitness of the kingdom for universal suffrage, their unreadiness for the republic that was germinating in the American influence. In his insistence upon guiding the common people, in his determination to protect them against their own impulses, he might be despotic, but he was benevolently despotic.

In taking his leave of Constancy, the king graciously acknowledged her generosity. Constancy raised to his face eyes in which ironic humor gleamed. "It is an obligation, your majesty . . ." She smiled. "Perhaps 'atonement' would be a better word."

The king's teeth flashed in a sudden, very charming smile. "I am inclined to see it as a vicarious atonement, then," he said.

Watching him ride away with his sister and their attendants, Constancy pondered on the distance this king had traveled from the world of the first young Kamehameha monarch she had known, Liholiho, who had died ingloriously of the measles at his first contact with an Anglo-Saxon civilization. She wished Kamehameha V well and hoped that he would live to enjoy a long reign. What, she wondered, had undermined the constitutions of this breed of men that they should die so young? The traders blamed the missionaries with imposing an alien and artificial civilization upon the natives too rapidly, and the missionaries blamed the traders with introducing venereal disease. She shrugged and wondered once again whether the good the missionaries had done the islanders could balance the evil they had unwittingly wrought among their converts.

3

Elspeth, seated on a hassock with school papers strewn about her on the floor, paused with lifted pencil to study the expression on her grandmother's face. She drew her clearly marked black brows together, accentuating their lifted wing sweep.

"Grandma! Is there bad news in your letter?"

Constancy started guiltily and then shook her head. "No, dear," she sighed. "I am just disappointed that Sally has decided against coming to live with us. She feels that her place is in Boston while the children are still in school."

Elspeth rested her pointed chin in her cupped palms. "I wish she would come. She is so lovely in the picture her husband painted of her when she was a girl. . . . I've always wanted to see her, and it would be so nice for you now that you've only me left—except, of course, Aunt Tabitha," she added apologetically. She bent over her papers again.

Constancy picked up the letter and reread it. She was disappointed enough that Sally was not returning to the islands now that Timothy had managed to get himself killed in the first engagement he took part in when, for the sake of the adventure, he had gone to war in the last year of its duration; but her concern was for quite another matter. She read, frowningly:

It was a bad moment, Mother, when I recognized Luke. He looks more like a scarecrow than ever. He was dreadfully shabby, and his eyes have the wildest light in them. I haven't heard such a discourse on hell fire and damnation since Mr. Coan used to corner me and wrestle with Satan for my soul when I was a little girl, as Luke poured forth in my drawing room. He is bound and determined to find Faith and "bring her to see the light." I couldn't help feeling sorry for him, for I think he really cared dreadfully for her. He sounded tortured when he was talking about how she must suffer eternal punishment if she didn't repent. He is a hopeless fanatic, however, and the thought of what he might do frightens me. I stood up to him and told him Faith's life was her own, and that she would never dream of going back to him—which is what he insists she must do to escape hell—and that it could do no good for him to see her. He knows she is on your mother's farm, somewhere in Connecticut, but he doesn't know what town it is near. I refused to help him out. But he glared at me and said he would find her before he died because he was holding evangelical meetings in every town in Connecticut until he should find the right one. When I think of his descending upon them and finding that Faith is living as the doctor's wife—it gives me the horrors! I never wished anyone ill luck before, but I can't help thinking what a happy solution it would be if Luke were to be gathered to his fathers before he reaches Sedley.

Constancy eyed the letter hostilely. It had been like a stone rudely thrown into the placid pool of her recent existence. Relieved of the necessity to teach, and with the children past childhood, she had been living to please herself this last year. She spent more and more of her time in the library, which had once been Jonathan's study. She had indulged in a frenzy of reading: novels, plays, poetry, essays, philosophy, history, and science. Darwin and Huxley had space on her shelves. With conscious intent, she set *The Origin of Species* next to Jonathan's old copy of the sermons of Jonathan Edwards. The tonic skepticism of Voltaire faced Cotton Mather's *Wonders of the Invisible World.* The bloody tragedies of John Ford, Webster's doomed and gallant duchess, Beaumont and Fletcher's ruthless dramas with their strangely sweet lyrics, occupied a shelf. She discovered *Tristram Shandy* and sniffed at Richardson's *Pamela.* She had a tender feeling for *The Scarlet Letter*, which Uncle Nate had brought to her on his last voyage. The suave essays of Montaigne were balm to her mind. Row after row of poetry met the eye. Catalogs from British and American publishers were close at hand, and scarcely a mailboat sailed for the mainland without an order in her neat hand for more books.

Peter, on one of his visits, Peter, who, in his late thirties, had an air of elegant fatigue and an appearance of slightly dissipated urbanity, chuckled over his mother's library.

"Any of the good brethren ever look over your books, Mother?" he queried.

"No!" sharply. "What I read is my own affair."

Peter laughed. "Good for you! But what do you suppose—well, Hiram Bingham II, for instance, would say if he saw *The Origin of Species* hobnobbing with the Edwards sermons?"

His mother's chin rose in the air several notches. "I don't feel obliged to take criticism from any of these young whippersnappers! Do you realize that the Thurstons are the only surviving members of the First Company of missionaries in Honolulu—except myself? And poor old Asa Thurston's tottering on the brink of the grave. It's not for any of my juniors in age or inferiors in point of residence and years of service to tell me how to conduct my life."

She spoke very severely, but her eyes danced. Peter laughed delightedly. "You're a wolf in sheep's clothing, I do believe, Mother! I think you're making up for all the wasted years of your youth in your old age. Now me, I got my wild oats out of the way early, so I'll probably surprise you by going pious in my old age."

His mother regarded him skeptically. "It would certainly surprise me for you to go pious at any age."

"Yes," she thought, laying down Sally's letter, "my life in the last year or two has been very pleasant . . . suspiciously pleasant. I might have known that a calm period in my life always means trouble ahead. Now I shan't be able to get Faith out of my mind. Bother Luke Owens! Somebody ought to shut him up where he can't do any harm! Maybe if Faith'd sell out the farm—quick—and move out West—anywhere out of the country—he couldn't find her."

But she had a hopeless and helpless feeling that Luke would find her no matter where she went. And in the weeks and months that followed, she could not lose her awareness of impending catastrophe.

For a time she really had enough to divert her mind from Faith in Peter's worries. For Peter besieged her with his troubles. The close of the Civil War had brought a slump in sugar prices. The tariff was prohibitive, and the reciprocity treaty that had been dickered with periodically for fifteen years was still hanging fire. Once that got signed, Peter said irritably, everything would be satisfactory. Until then, sugar was a fearful risk. She made little on her investment for a few years, but her profit from Matt's voyages on the *Elizabeth,* the steam vessel he had acquired to replace the old *Mary Ellen,* was great enough to carry the expenses of the school.

Since Matt had bought the *Elizabeth* a steam-propelled vessel, he came to Honolulu three or four times a year. Constancy could never see the *Elizabeth* grunting its way in to port without a pang for the skimming grace of the *Mary Ellen,* but she delighted in the frequency of Matt's visits. She had in earlier years looked forward to visits with Betty, Matt's wife, whenever the ship came to Honolulu. But now Betty was the mother of three children and had given up the carefree life of her early married years to settle down in Concord.

Whatever her occupation, whatever her concern of the moment, Constancy could not rid herself of the foreboding that crouched ominously at the back of her mind. She knew that Luke Owens's mission was a menace to Faith. She pitied Luke, suffering under the frenzied compulsion of his faith; she understood something of the agony that a man of his convictions must endure, loving a woman whom he considered damned. Faith's course in life, Constancy neither condemned nor justified: the older she grew, the less easy it became for her to pronounce judgment upon anyone. She feared lest the consequences of Faith's secret defiance of convention find her out, but she could not find it in her heart to censure her daughter either for the impulse which led her feet astray from the rigorous path of Christian virtue or for the deception she practised. Constancy's desire was that no one should suffer, and she knew the impossibility of gratification for such a desire. She wished passionately to shield those whom she loved from pain, and knew the futility of her wish while she was powerless to discard it.

It was on Constancy's sixty-ninth birthday that the letter she had so long anticipated came. When Elspeth returned from town and dropped the letter into her grandmother's lap with a cheerful "Here's a fine birthday present for you, Grandma," Constancy had to grip the arms of her chair to stay the trembling of her hands. She did not at once pick up the letter; she waited until Elspeth left the room. Then with shaking hands she tore open the envelope and adjusted her spectacles to read:

DEAR MOTHER:

Luke found us at last. He arrived exhausted and ill from exposure in a storm. We put him to bed and took care of him for two weeks before he died. In one of his more lucid moments he said he had been too appalled at hearing I was supposed to be married again to speak out at the time, and when he recovered the use of his tongue, he decided that he should give me the opportunity to confess myself. He exhorted us both to repent until we nearly went mad. I thought at one time he was out of the woods, and I must admit that it frightened me to think of what his recovery would mean to us, but he took a sudden turn for the worse and died. I cannot say truthfully that I was not relieved. We gave him a proper funeral. We said he was a brother of my first husband. So far as I know, no one is the wiser. We can really be married now, but I feel that there is a shadow on us. It has made a most unhappy impression on Daniel's mind. He is not the same, but somber and brooding ever since Luke came to us. He must throw off this mood soon or I don't know what will become of us. Fortunately Connie was away at college and knows nothing of it. I have written to Luke's father—an unpleasant task it was, too. I shall not attempt to prolong this letter. Write to me.

> *Your loving daughter,*
> FAITH.

The letter dropped from Constancy's fingers into her lap. She shivered, thinking: "I'm glad he's dead. It's awful for me to feel so, but I can't help being glad. It's really unbelievable that it should have worked out this way . . . like a book . . . not life. It's well nobody knew he was Faith's husband . . . they might have been suspicious . . . a doctor could so easily help a sick man to die."

She drew in her breath quickly, startled at the turn her thoughts were taking, and pressed her hands over her eyes in an effort to shut out the pictures that flashed before her mind. "I'm an evil old woman. . . . People don't do such things! What a mean mind I have to imagine such a thing . . . but why should the doctor be so downcast? You'd think he'd be relieved, not sorry . . . unless . . . Oh, stop it, *stop* it!"

Tabitha, grown fatter and unwieldier with the years, came puffing indignantly into the room. Constancy welcomed her, for once glad to listen attentively to her complaint that old Eliza had no business to box John's ears just because he stuck his fingers in the bread dough.

Two months later there was a brief note from Faith telling of a journey to Boston and her marriage there. She said nothing about her husband's state of mind. Then there was silence for the better part of a year. Constancy wrote regularly, but her letters elicited no response. Sally wrote as usual but complained that she had only the most meager scrawls from her sister. Then there arrived a letter from Sally which her mother opened with her usual feeling of pleasant anticipation, to receive a rude shock in the opening sentence:

Daniel Pritchard has killed himself. It's terrible to break it to you this way, but there's no gentle way of breaking such news. Why he did it, I don't know. If Faith knows, she isn't saying anything. She's mum as a clam. She seems so far away that it frightens me to be with her. I hadn't heard from her for months—not a word—and the thought of her preyed on my mind worse and worse till I couldn't stand it any longer and packed my things and went to visit her without telling her I was coming. I arrived an hour before the funeral. She hadn't sent word, Mother. Don't you think it queer that she shouldn't have notified me when we've always been so fond of each other?

It was awful, just coming on it that way. My cab driver was a stranger in Sedley, and so I didn't learn from him what had happened. I just walked in and found Faith standing over the coffin, stiff as a ramrod, not crying or even looking sorry, but with her face as grim as Mr. Bingham's at his worst. The shock of seeing the coffin and all the chairs lined up in readiness for the funeral and Faith looking that way started me crying, and she just looked

*around at me for a minute and said over her shoulder,
"What are you crying about?" Then she seemed to recollect herself and made me take off my things and was very
polite and distant. I asked her, when I could, how he died,
and she answered "Bullet," and not another word could I
get out of her. I couldn't make out whether it was an acci-
dent or what it was until the minister and the neighbors
arrived, and the minister talked a long time about how
Daniel had overtaxed his strength caring for the sick in
the recent epidemic of scarlet fever, and how he was out
of his mind and didn't know what he was doing.*

*I stayed with Faith a week, and it was the worst week
I ever spent in my life. She is selling the farm. I believe she
has a buyer in view. Then she promised to come and stay
with me for a while. I think she is numbed with all she has
been through, for Faith was never one to be so hard and
cold with anyone she cares for. I'm hoping that here in
Boston, where she won't be reminded of what has happened at every turn, she will be comforted.*

*She wouldn't let me send for Connie, who was about to
graduate. She said there was no need to upset her. She was
going down to see the commencement as if nothing had
happened, but if she goes with a face like she's been wearing since this happened, I don't see how Connie can help
knowing something is awfully wrong.*

Constancy read on through several more paragraphs,
her mind clutching at the commonplaces contained in
them: Timothy was reading law; Miriam had just com-
pleted school and was engaged to a magazine editor, but
she was going through a stage of humanitarianism that
was a little hard on the family. She came to the end of the
letter and could no longer postpone thinking about its
particular burden.

She rose stiffly to her feet and walked over to the portrait of Faith that Timothy had done nearly a quarter of a century earlier. She scrutinized it bewilderedly. There before her was Faith as she had been at sixteen, seated on a hassock, the voluminous ruffled skirt of her pink muslin dress billowing out on the floor around her, her hands loosely clasped about her knees, her head thrown back. Timothy had caught with rare felicity the gleam of mischief that had been ever present in Faith's eyes. He had caught, too, the merriness that hovered always about the corners of the young Faith's mouth.

Constancy's tightly interlaced fingers dug into the flesh of her hands. Everything that she was protested at the harshness the years had meted out to the gayest of her children. How could Faith sustain her lot? Strange that this giddiest daughter had the stamina to survive, however warped she might be by her experience. Jonathan had found refuge in a fanatic religion; Silly's religion had failed her when she needed it most, and she had been desolate and lost to life before death claimed her. But Faith— what resources had she within herself that she could support with stoicism such malicious buffeting as had been dealt her by a perverse destiny?

The next letter from Sally informed her mother that she had persuaded Faith to accompany her to Europe for a year. Connie had been asked to teach in the college from which she had just graduated. Miriam had married her editor, and Timothy was old enough to take care of himself. The sisters were free to travel.

Constancy, remembering how competently the ten-year-old Sally had mothered her smaller sisters and brother, felt happier about Faith than she had in several years. She was able to sink back into the peace she had known before the disturbing tidings of Luke Owens's presence in New England had shattered her tranquillity. Again her life was quietly pleasant, made up of hours of reading, the easy warmth and understanding that bound her to Elspeth, amusing and stimulating sessions with Peter, whose vagaries of conduct she had come to accept with a shrug and whose unorthodox views she was prone to enjoy.

She had learned to take even Tabitha philosophically by the time the need to put up with Tabitha was effectively disposed of, the agents being a nervous horse and a newspaper blowing across the road at the precise moment when Tabitha drove along on her way home from town. When some natives carried Tabitha's body, with its head rolling grotesquely on the broken neck, into the house, Constancy could not help reflecting that poor Tabitha could not achieve dignity even in death. Looking down at her daughter-in-law, Constancy was unable to put from mind the image of a well-fattened hen with its neck newly wrung. She reproached herself, but the image persisted.

Peter attended the funeral, his face so appropriately composed for the occasion, so properly expressive of bereavement borne with fortitude, that Constancy's fingers itched to box his ears. She was more put out with him when he barely waited to get clear of the burial ground to tell her jubilantly that it looked as if the Reciprocity Treaty was assured at last.

"That's all very well," his mother commented sharply, "but at this time you might show a little concern for the future of your children. Have you no feeling of responsibility for them at all?"

Peter looked injured. "Why, Mother! You never give me the benefit of the doubt, do you? As a matter of fact, I was just thinking that Marcia might come out and keep

house for me on the plantation and get acquainted with
her little brothers and sisters—by adoption."

Constancy eyed him suspiciously. "You're trying to get
me excited, aren't you, son? I suspect that you'd find it
inconvenient to have a girl like Marcia on the place. You
might have to behave yourself."

"Well—if you don't like that plan, how about shipping
the two of them off to New England. Tabitha's mother
would probably like to have them, and John ought to have
his education finished over there."

She nodded. "I'll write to Tabitha's mother. I'm not going to ship them off in the casual way you suggest. If they
prefer to stay with me, they can—or if their grandmother
doesn't sound really anxious to have them. I've always
done what I could for them, but they don't respond very
well. I think they might be happier somewhere else."

But by the time Tabitha's mother wrote that she would
be delighted to welcome her grandchildren, Marcia, very
quiet and of indefinite appearance, announced that she
was going to marry Jeremiah Johnston, a sober young man
just ordained, a missionary's son. With Marcia married
and settled on Kauai, and John off to Boston in Matt's
care, Constancy was aware that Peter came to the Waikiki
house very frequently. She enjoyed seeing him and was
flattered to think that he came so often. In fact, until the
moment when she walked into the library just as he was
kissing Elspeth, it did not occur to her that he was motivated by anything but pleasure in his mother's society.

Constancy found herself stamping her foot in rage. She
heard herself saying more harshly than she had ever spoken
to anyone before in her life, "Peter Williams, are you
utterly depraved?" To her reasoning, Peter belonged to
one generation, Elspeth to another; Elspeth might have

been Peter's daughter as far as age went. He seemed suddenly any middle-aged roué making a fool of himself.

Peter started in confusion. He flushed, but met his
mother's eye, a glint of amusement in his own. "Come,
come, Mother," he protested. "I'm not so bad as all that!
I have no evil designs on Elspeth. I assure you I've proposed honorable marriage to her, and she seems to think
she can put up with me."

For a moment Constancy eyed them both blankly. Els-
peth ran to her side. "Grandma, don't look at us like that.
Is it . . . is it that you don't think me good enough for
Peter?"

"Don't be a little goose!" Constancy's tone was sharp,
but she clasped Elspeth's hand in both of hers. "It's quite
the other way around, my dear. I don't believe you have
the faintest notion of what you'd be getting into if you
married Peter. In the first place,"—she threw back her
head and looked her son in the eye as she spoke—"Peter is
old enough to be your father; in the second place, he
hasn't the remotest idea of what faithfulness is; he has a
house full of supposedly adopted children who are in
reality his own, and from all I've heard, no two have the
same mother. There's no reason to believe that he has it
in him to limit himself to one woman. It isn't pleasant
having to say this about my own son—but I feel that it is
necessary."

Elspeth, to Constancy's amazement, gave a small
chuckle. "I've always known about the children, Grandma. I expect I shall like them, and I don't think he will be
bringing any more home if he marries me."

Constancy felt herself blushing. Peter, who had been
looking decidedly uncomfortable, saw the blush and began
to laugh. "I can't for the life of me see why I should," he

said. And looking from his face to Elspeth's, Constancy discovered that, after all, she knew very little about this child she had reared as her own from babyhood, and that the girl a woman might know was never the same person a man who interested her might know.

When Elspeth and Peter were married six months later, Constancy was left alone in the big house. For the first time in her life she was obliged to live alone. She felt useless, miserable. She wandered aimlessly about the empty rooms, thinking ironically that she would be grateful even for Tabitha's company now. The house grew hateful to her; reading palled upon her. She spent more and more of her time in the kitchen talking with Eliza. Matt, on his next visit, regarded her solitary state with high disfavor and suggested that she write to Deborah and ask her to return to the islands.

"She could teach in your school, Mother, and it would probably be a favor to her. She is devoted to you—remember how hard she took it when you shipped her back to her grandmother?"

Constancy considered the matter and agreed to ask Deborah. "But I never thought," she commented almost petulantly, "that I'd have to beg somebody to come and be the prop of my old age. It's humiliating. What I want is Faith, but I won't ask her—not with some of the cats alive who dug their claws into her when she left Luke Owens. She's had enough to put up with in her life without facing all that again."

She despatched the letter and awaited Deborah's response with more anxiety than she cared to admit. The surface of her mind was in these months diverted by matters of state. Kamehameha V died at the close of 1872, the last of the Kamehamehas. For the first time a king was elected, and the Hawaiians staged their first important political campaign and discovered the joys of street-corner oratory, the rivalry of candidates, the pleasant excitement of this added excuse for parades, *hulas*, and *luaus*. Lunalilo and Kalakaua vied for the crown, both of them prominent among the *alii*. Lunalilo promised to restore the constitution of '52. He was strongly pro-American, Kalakaua was more inclined to side with Kamehameha V; he distrusted the early constitution and merely suggested revision of the constitution of '64. Lunalilo caught the popular fancy and had the support of the American element. When he was the victor and set about appointing Americans and especially American missionaries members of his cabinet, the missionary element enjoyed once more the long-lost awareness that they were indeed directing God's kingdom on earth.

When Deborah's letter arrived in June of '73, however, the new king was already stricken with the disease that was to bring his reign to a close within a year of his accession to the throne and place him in the gray stone sepulcher in the front yard of Kawaiahao church where everyone traveling down King Street may read the terse inscription, "Lunalilo, Ka Moi."

Constancy, before opening the envelope addressed to herself in Deborah's round writing, stiffened her spine and set her mouth against refusal. The refusal was not forthcoming, but the acceptance was not entirely simple. Deborah was marrying a young teacher in a New Haven academy. She had talked the matter over with him, and they had decided that they would both come. Deborah was sure that Grandma would love Arthur. She added in a postscript that they would come with Matt on his next trip, as the voyage would be less expensive that way and Arthur and she would be poor.

Constancy accepted the changed circumstances of Deborah's coming philosophically. She reflected that Matt's ship was due in August and turned her attention to renovating Deborah's old room. Thus far she had employed only women teachers in her school for the simple reason that the daughters of missionaries were always at hand while the sons were drawn toward more remunerative activities.

When Deborah and her husband arrived late in August and Matt stopped over in Honolulu for three weeks, Constancy felt that the house had come to life again. While he did not quite fulfill Deborah's prophecies, she found Arthur generally likable. However, she found herself capable of administering a snub or two when he went so far as to question the propriety of her reading Voltaire and certain of the Idyls of Theocritus which he came upon for the first time in her library. Deborah's choice of a husband merely confirmed the suspicion Constancy had always cherished that this granddaughter was lacking in imagination.

The years unrolled quietly in the '70's. Constancy kept a firm grip on the reins of government in her own house. Deborah rather tactlessly offered to take over the management of the house. Constancy quirked an ironic eyebrow at her granddaughter. "Are the meals satisfactory?" she inquired politely.

"Oh, *yes*, Grandma!"

"Have I overlooked any of Arthur's prejudices in the matter of food?"

"No! It isn't that——"

"Do I impress you as being in my dotage?"

"Oh, Grandma!"

"Then, as long as I am able to get about without

crutches, and as long as my memory functions, suppose we agree that I am capable of running the house."

Deborah burst into tears. "I didn't mean it that way!" she wailed. "You never used to be sarcastic and cross. I just wanted to help and . . . and spare you trouble."

Constancy reached out the hand that she now definitely realized was clawlike and patted Deborah's heaving shoulder. "Don't cry, my dear," she said gently. "I'm probably a cantankerous old woman, but you see, Deborah, it isn't easy for a woman like me to be reminded of the fact that her period of usefulness is coming to an end. When it has come to an end, I trust that I shall have the wits to know it. Then I'll abdicate."

With regularity and efficiency Deborah produced fat, cheerful babies at two-year intervals. After the arrival of the second, she decided to suspend her labors in the school indefinitely. By 1880 she was pregnant with her fourth. She had outdistanced Elspeth, who had two children in the first five years of her marriage and considered her family complete.

Constancy observed with gratification that Elspeth had been right about Peter. Since his second marriage he had become a model husband and father. There were no further adoptions. He was a member of the legislature and something of a figure in politics. Constancy looked forward to visits from Peter and his family with eagerness that verged on excitement. To herself she admitted that life would be more interesting if fate had ordained that Peter and Elspeth instead of Arthur and Deborah share her house.

The '80's arrived. Despite the fact that Constancy made regular appearances at her school, awarding prizes, presiding over public examinations, and on occasion making brief speeches, she felt that she was occupying a place a little apart from life.

In April of 1887 there was held a jubilee celebration of the arrival of the missionary reinforcement of 1837. The celebration lasted for three days. Looking over the crowd of missionaries and their children, Constancy was made aware of her own isolation. She was the sole survivor of the First Company in Hawaii. She mentally listed the arrivals through the '20's and began on the '30's before she found a representative in the crowd. There was Mrs. Emerson; she came in '32. "She looks older than I do," reflected Constancy with a certain grim satisfaction. Mrs. Parker, reading a paper on the ill-fated and wryly amusing expedition to the Marquesas Islands, had come in 1837. There were few enough even of that reinforcement. Most of these earnest souls were the children of those early missionaries—some were grandchildren. She thought of the days of that long, harrowing voyage around the Horn; she remembered Mr. Bingham bolting down the companionway as if Satan were at his heels just because he had seen a young man kiss his wife as if he enjoyed doing it. She pictured again for the first time in half a century the scene at the breakfast table when Mr. Bingham had implied that Mrs. Holman was responsible for the sugar shortage. She remembered some of the matters that had come up for painstaking discussion at the women's meetings in her early years in the islands.

In the midst of her musings she heard her name called. The woman on her left nudged her. "They want you to read your paper," the woman whispered loudly. Constancy looked down at the roll of closely written sheets in her lap, a carefully denatured account of early days, the '20's, for there was no one else who could speak of the '20's from experience. Suddenly a devil possessed Constancy.

Without thinking twice, she tore the neatly written sheets
into eighths, rose to her feet, and, as she mounted the platform, disposed of the scraps of her prepared speech in a
vase.

She stood before the crowd, erect and poised. It cost her
no little effort to stand perfectly erect nowadays, but she
could do so upon occasion. Her heavy black silk dress
fitted her as no other dress in that gathering fitted its
wearer. Her shining white hair lay smoothly over her ears;
the knot at the back of her neck was smaller now, but there
was nothing wispy or thin about Constancy's hair. The
eyebrows which had not whitened were arresting in her
parchment-colored face. Constancy was age, but she was
not tremulous, pitiful age, as she stood before the assembled missionaries and decided to startle them just once
before she died.

She took as the point of her departure the gist of the
preceding papers, the unqualified praises heaped upon the
pioneer missionaries, the general tendency to deify the departed. Dryly she reminded them of the youth of these
pioneer worthies when they left their homes to spread the
Gospel among the heathen; she reminded them that these
men and women were not born saints. Musingly she described the famous but tactfully forgotten Bingham-
Holman feud, and then guilelessly remarked that she had
recounted the episode merely to demonstrate that missionaries no less than other men and women had their moments of childishness. She was aware of uneasiness in her
audience. Sympathy crept into her voice as she spoke of
how miserable the first arrivals made themselves over the
most excruciatingly exquisite points of behavior, and she
described a women's meeting given over entirely to a
heated discussion of whether they should or should not
allow their small children to get down on the floor with

their chicken bones—not because they might consume a good deal of dirt along with the chicken, but because the children derived so much pleasure from this informal method of devouring their food. She spoke of how their notions of duty induced them to neglect their own children in the behalf of native children, and checked off a dozen deaths that had occurred among the children of missionaries in the early years. She ended with a sincere tribute to the selflessness, the absolute sincerity, and the great fortitude of the fellow laborers of her youth, and remarked as an afterthought: "You are spared the necessity of including my contribution in the book you are planning to make of these collected papers, since it exists only in my head; my reminiscences need not become a part of your history."

Constancy stepped from the platform and walked out of the meeting, not entirely unaware of the glances that followed her. She knew that she had brought into the light of day certain items of missionary history which it was generally agreed were best forgotten or at least ignored. The Bingham-Holman controversy was still a sore point after sixty-five, sixty-six, years with the doctor dust these sixty-odd years, and his widow dead five years. As she stepped into her carriage, Constancy chuckled wickedly, thinking that there was no one in that gathering who would dare to call her to account for her indiscretion. Her mood changed: after all, they might just excuse it on the ground that she was in her dotage and no longer responsible. They could scarcely understand that her gesture meant to her much what sticking out his tongue at a severe teacher means to a small boy.

THE END

THE world receded from Constancy; a fog enveloped her
—a fog that blunted the edge of sound and blurred the
outline and color of sight; voices were thin and far away.
Cracked, elderly voices shouted at her that there had been
a revolution and that Kalakaua was a profligate; it seemed
to her only a day or two later that the same elderly voices
were telling her that the queen was a prisoner in the palace
and that it was certain that America would annex the
islands. And Constancy knew from the way her fingers
beat a rat-tat-tat on the arms of her big chair that she was
impatient with the voices and with what the voices tried
to force upon her attention.

Children, a confusing number of children, came brushing against the curtain of fog that obscured the world.
Now there was one who peered through, who swept back
the obstruction and looked into her face with Sammie's
smile, but his eyes were dark; and in a girl's face, a girl
with yellow hair and a golden brown skin, she was startled
to find Sammie's eyes. Another girl with smooth dark hair
and eyes like Elspeth's sat at her feet and read to her from
the Bible but argued gently against reading from Montaigne when Constancy plucked that name from out the
dark chaos of her mind. This girl, like all the others, called
her Grandma.

Dimly Constancy recalled a white-haired woman with
deep lines in her face who knelt beside her chair and called

her Mother. But that was a long time ago . . . when she had been only ninety-one or -two. She had no daughter who looked like that. But in one of the moments of lucidity that came upon her sometimes in the night, she started up in bed with the cry, "That was Faith! Of course it was Faith . . . and she told me there was a letter she found when she found her husband with a bullet through his head, and that she burned it and never said a word to a soul because it was a confession of murder. But I couldn't believe that it was Faith because Faith was young and full of mischief. Where is she gone? Faith! Faith!" Imperatively Constancy's voice rang out through the sleeping house, and there was a quick patter of feet in the hall and the pale, thin woman whom she now recognized as Deborah came running and said, "Sh! Grandma! You'll wake the children." And when Constancy, her face wrinkling with distress, pleaded, "Call Faith. . . . I must tell her I know her now," Deborah patted the shrunken old arm in its long, white cotton sleeve very kindly and said pityingly, "Don't you remember, dear, that Faith died just a little while after she came here? Why, Grandma, it's been five years now." Constancy sighed tremulously and said, "Yes, yes, child. My memory plays tricks on me nowadays. Go back to bed." But after Deborah had gone out and shut the door behind her, tears gathered in Constancy's eyes and fell on the pillow. "Another of my children that I have failed," she thought miserably.

A half-grown boy with blue eyes and arrogant, sensitive features came sometimes to her room and read aloud to her from scraps of paper in a voice so muffled she could not hear a quarter of what he read, but she knew from the rise and fall of his voice that it was not prose he had written on the odd little scraps of paper. She thought,

"This boy is the poet Sammie was to be—but whose child is he?" And she leaned forward and laid her hand, shrunken now to a bird's claw, on his shoulder and whispered, "Child—you have blood of mine in your veins . . . haven't you?" Immediately she regretted having broken her private vow never to ask questions, for the boy laid his face against her knees and cried, and said in a voice that struck through the paralysis of her emotions to her heart, "Gran! Don't you even *know* me? When I love you better than anybody!"

Sorry and ashamed, she patted his dark hair and murmured compassionately, "There, there, child. You mustn't mind me. I'm proud of you. Don't feel so, my dear. It's fine and comforting to have somebody say he loves you better than anyone else—even if you are an old woman with everything dead but a little slice of your brain."

He raised his head and said earnestly, "Think, Gran. I'm your great-grandson. My mother was named for you, and when she and my father were drowned when I was just little, Grandma brought me here to live with you." And Constancy, because she knew he was distressed, said comfortingly, "Yes, dear, I remember now."

There was one night that stood out in her mind because, when she woke to fearful noise and confusion and a red glare in the sky, she was sure that she was dead and in the hell she had stopped believing in. That was just for a moment. Then the tall, pale woman came hurrying in with a light and shouted at her that it was just fireworks because it was the New Year of 1900.

Constancy jerked her head up from the pillow. "1900!" she screeched, sentience suddenly invading her, "I'm almost a hundred years old! Why have I had to live so long?" Why . . . if Sammie had lived . . . he'd have just passed his seventy-ninth birthday!"

Deborah bent and kissed the wrinkled cheek. "Hush, Grandma! You mustn't talk like that. What would we do without you?"

Constancy said nothing. She was thinking bewilderedly of a seventy-nine-year-old Sammie. She couldn't imagine Sammie as anything but a little boy. If there were a heaven, would Sammie greet her as the little boy she remembered, or would he be an old man with a beard and a bald head . . . and how would he know her when she was a useless old wretch? Dry, tearless sobs shook her body after Deborah left her alone.

One day in April Constancy awoke with her mind clear. When Deborah came in with her breakfast tray, Constancy asked her abruptly, "Is your father alive?" Deborah shook her head. "No, dear, he went with the consumption . . . six . . . seven years ago. We told you, but you confused him with his father and kept saying he'd been dead forty years."

"Poor boy," Constancy murmured, and then said, with a vigor that made Deborah jump, "but he was a perfect lunatic on the subject of religion!"

Deborah looked distressed. "Why, Grandma, anybody'd think you weren't a missionary to hear you talk! And they hold you up as an example of everything a God-fearing woman ought to be."

Constancy laughed shortly. A sudden recollection of a small locked book disturbed her. She eyed Deborah doubtfully and then shook her head. "Deborah . . . send that nice boy to me . . . Hal!" She brought out the name triumphantly. It seemed so easy for her to remember names today.

When the boy came in, she motioned him to the chest

at the foot of her bed and explained what she wanted of him. He brought forth the discolored little volume with its locked clasp.

"There's a thinner book beside it, Gran," he called. "Do you want that, too?"

Silly's journal, thought Constancy. "Yes . . . both." She pondered the matter of their disposal for a moment. "Now . . . you shove my chair into the library. First, though, give me the books."

He managed to push the big rocker through the door of the downstairs bedroom Constancy had occupied since she had become too feeble to manage the stairs, across the hall, and into the library. He stood before her, smiling. "Now what?"

Constancy smiled back. "Build a fire in the grate," she said.

Hal whistled his surprise. She guessed his thoughts. "I don't imagine it's cold," she said patiently. "I want to burn these two journals, and it's got to be done while I have my wits about me." She paused and then added dryly. "You know, it's not every day in the week that I have 'em."

He went out of the room and in a few minutes came back with kindling and newspaper. "There you are!" And he stood back to survey the bright blaze he had coaxed into being.

Constancy handed him the books. "Lay them on the fire."

He did so a little reluctantly and then sat down to watch them burn.

As she gazed into the dwindling flame, Constancy thought, "Now they'll never know what a hypocrite I was. Jonathan! They'll never know how fooled you were. I owed you that, my dear. . . ."

The clarity that had visited her blurred. She was at peace; no thought disturbed her serenity. Yesterday, to-day, and tomorrow merged. Her eyes beheld a neutrality of color. Where was she? Was she still caught in life?

A faint sound caught her attention. She saw a boy, not quite a man, walk over to a fireplace and lay his arm on the mantelpiece. She saw him smile; it was Sammie's smile. A comforting warmth flooded her being. She heard him say, "You must have dark secrets in your past . . . but somehow I always suspected it."

Mischief rose in her heart, gayety that she had not known in years. "Darling," she said, and she recognized the voice of her youth, "I always suspected that you knew . . . from the time you so stubbornly refused to learn the Lord's Prayer. Goodness! Your father got in an awful stew about that! Now . . . it seems to me that it secretly pleased me to have you behave as you did, and yet I was afraid, too. I was convinced, you know, that it was an in-stance of the sins of the mother cropping out in the child. How people can torture themselves!"

She rose to her feet and stretched out her hand to the boy. Her eye fell on her hand, and she laughed a merry little laugh. "It's young again! And to think I was afraid I'd be old to you and you might not recognize me!" Her voice was blithe. "I was afraid," she said, making a droll face, "that you might have a long white beard . . . why, I even pictured you bald! Wasn't that ridiculous? I thought I wanted you to be little and sweet . . . the way you were at four . . . but you're fine this way. Darling, isn't it nice that God isn't the villain I pictured Him?" She took a step nearer him.

Hal had stood amazed. At her movement he was gal-vanized into action. He leaped forward to support her. He had not seen her stand for years. She looked into his face, smiling, but meeting his eye, the smile faded. Fear distorted her features. "Your eyes! They're blue!" she whispered, and then desolation rang in her cry, "I'm alive . . . I'm *alive!*"

The boy shrank before the mortal hurt in her voice, but he had presence of mind enough to catch her when she swayed, and in the instant that he supported her weight in his arms, he was somehow relieved to see the bleak despair in her eyes give way to the expressionless glaze of death.

THE END

Honolulu. August 2, 1933.